# PRAISE FOR *ANALEE, IN REAL LIFE*

A New York Public Library Best Book for Teens 2018

"Milanes has created authentic characters with family
issues that reflect the world we live in. . . . Refreshing."
**—NEW YORK TIMES**

"Janelle Milanes has a rare gift for capturing
the tenuous thread of friendships. Heartfelt and smart,
you will root for and fall in love with *Analee, in Real Life*."
**—LILLIAM RIVERA, AUTHOR OF *THE EDUCATION OF MARGOT SANCHEZ***

"Funny and affecting, well-balanced, and simply fun."
**—KIRKUS REVIEWS**

"An entertaining novel for all teen collections."
**—SCHOOL LIBRARY JOURNAL**

"Genuine and humorous."
**—BOOKLIST**

Also by Janelle Milanes

# THE VICTORIA IN MY HEAD

# Analee, IN Real Life

## JANELLE MILANES

**SIMON PULSE**

New York  London  Toronto  Sydney  New Delhi

SIMON PULSE

An imprint of Simon & Schuster Children's Publishing Division

1230 Avenue of the Americas, New York, New York 10020

First Simon Pulse paperback edition September 2019

Text copyright © 2018 by Janelle Milanes

Cover photograph copyright © 2019 by Miguel Sobreira/Arcangel

Also available in a Simon Pulse hardcover edition.

For information about special discounts for bulk purchases, please contact Simon & Schuster Special Sales at 1-866-506-1949 or business@simonandschuster.com.

The Simon & Schuster Speakers Bureau can bring authors to your live event. For more information or to book an event contact the Simon & Schuster Speakers Bureau at 1-866-248-3049 or visit our website at www.simonspeakers.com.

Cover designed by Jess LaGreca

Interior designed by Nina Simoneaux and Jess LaGreca

The text of this book was set in Adobe Caslon Pro.

Manufactured in the United States of America

2 4 6 8 10 9 7 5 3 1

The Library of Congress has cataloged the hardcover edition as follows:

Names: Milanes, Janelle, author.

Title: Analee, in real life / Janelle Milanes.

Description: First Simon Pulse hardcover edition. | New York : Simon Pulse, 2018. | Summary: Anxious, awkward Analee Echevarria only feels confident playing her favorite online game, but with a potential real-world romance and her father's remarriage looming, she begins to rediscover herself.

Identifiers: LCCN 2017050735 | ISBN 9781534410299 (hardcover) | ISBN 9781534410312 (eBook)

Subjects: | CYAC: Self-confidence—Fiction. | Role-playing—Fiction. | Virtual reality—Fiction. | Remarriage—Fiction. | High schools—Fiction. | Schools—Fiction. | Dating (Social customs)—Fiction. | Hispanic Americans—Fiction.

Classification: LCC PZ7.1.M556 An 2018 | DDC [Fic]—dc23

LC record available at https://lccn.loc.gov/2017050735

ISBN 9781534410305 (paperback)

TO MY VICTORIA, IN REAL LIFE

# Analee,
## IN
# Real Life

# CHAPTER ONE

THE NIGHT IS QUIET AND STILL, WITH ONLY THE *soft sounds of our feet padding along the grass. Xolkar and I hasten toward the rickety old barn in the distance. A growl interrupts the stillness as a creature—half ghost, half skeleton—descends upon us, swiping his long, bony fingers in our direction.*

I have it, *I tell Xolkar, quickly ducking out of harm's way. The creature, not all that bright, wallops the air periodically until I'm up again. I plunge my sword into his rib cage. The ghost-skeleton-thing vanishes quickly in a puff of smoke, inflicting little damage on me. I am a skilled night elf hunter and Xolkar's protector on this quest. His only job is to guard the ampule, which is our key to victory.*

The worgen's coming up, *Xolkar warns as we enter the barn.*

Don't worry, *I tell him with an assuredness that comes easy to me in this world.* We got this.

*The barn is dimly lit, and piles of animal bones are strewed across the floor. The worgen doesn't wait long, announcing himself with a mighty roar and appearing, large and looming, in front of us. I'm the size of his leg, but I'm ready, weapons clenched, fixed in my battle stance. I fear nothing, for I am—*

"Analee?" my dad's girlfriend, Harlow, calls through my bedroom door. "Dinner's ready!"

In the six months we've lived together, she still hasn't learned to pronounce my name right. It sounds wrong coming out of her mouth, too nasally. It makes me think of apple pie and cornfields and other things I'm not.

"I'll be down in a minute!" I call back.

I blame my dad, mostly. He's the one who decided I should be given my great-grandmother's name despite the fact that no one at my school would be able to pronounce it the Spanish way. Imagine having to sound it out for every single new teacher (ah-nah-LEE, by the way) every single school year, when inevitably your classmates will resort to calling you "anally" anyway. That'll give you a snapshot of my problems.

*I am not Analee. I am Kiri the night elf. And I fear nothing—not monsters, not goblins, not people.*

I feel Harlow hesitate by the door before she says, "Your dad says right now. Sorry."

*The worgen takes this opportunity to deliver blow upon blow. Each weakens me, seeps the life out of me until I collapse in a heap on the ground.*

"Crap," I mutter. And I'm dead. The ghost of Kiri floats to the nearest graveyard.

*What happened?* Xolkar, who in real life is known as Harris, asks over the computer. We'll have to start the whole quest over.

*Harlow,* I type. My hands slide off the keyboard.

Dinner is fancy tonight. There are candles involved, and Harlow is using her hand-painted china set. For once, her eight-year-old daughter, Avery, is not allowed to use her phone at the table. Dad stops me when I try to turn on the TV, even though I always watch it during dinner.

"No TV," he says.

"What?" I ask. "Like, forever?" I hate eating without TV, because I'm way too aware of my chewing volume, and Harlow feels the need to fill the silence by asking me embarrassing questions about my love life, or lack thereof.

"Just for tonight," Dad replies.

Harlow is a raw-food fanatic. Tonight she has made us sprouted lentils with tomato and cashew cheese. She acts like this is satisfying, but once I caught her in the kitchen plowing into a bag of peanut butter cups. It was one of the rare moments when I witnessed Harlow being human.

"The table looks beautiful, Raf," Harlow says to Dad, taking a seat next to him. I assume that by "beautiful" she's referring to the fact that Dad put out the place mats.

"Thank you, *mi cielo*." Dad takes Harlow's hand and kisses the skin between her fingers. Gross. They're even more lovey-dovey than usual. Once, I overheard Harlow on the phone with her friend, and she said my dad spoke to her in Spanish whenever they had sex. I tasted vomit in my mouth for two straight days after that tidbit.

Without the TV on, you can hear all the ugly sounds of people eating. Every cough, every scrape of utensils against plates, every clink of ice cubes.

"Well," I say. "This is new."

"What?" Dad asks. He's trying to eat and hold Harlow's hand at the same time, which seems highly impractical to me.

3

"This whole . . ." I motion around the table with my fork. "Arrangement."

"I think it's nice to eat like this," Harlow says. "Like a family."

"Don't get me wrong; it's very wholesome and all. I'm just wondering why."

I wait for Harlow to tell me that she read about it in one of the family life blogs she follows. They all have cutesy alliterative names, like *The Garrison Gang* or *The Cooper Crew*. And the families are *super*-white, like Harlow is, with skin the color of cottage cheese.

She doesn't mention a blog, though. She looks at Dad, and Dad lets go of her hand. That's when I get the feeling that something horrible is about to happen, more horrible than a worgen trying to eat my face off.

"You want to tell them?" Harlow murmurs.

Dad smiles. "You can do it."

"Are you sure?"

Okay, this isn't cute anymore.

"Mom, just tell us!" Avery explodes.

Harlow looks at the two of us with her fixed placid smile.

"Girls," she says, "your dad and I . . . we're getting married."

Avery shrieks. Dad beams. I take a bite of lentils.

Somehow, on the outside, I manage to maintain my composure. The inner me is screaming, throwing paintings off the walls, shattering hand-painted china. Dad and Harlow have known each other for a total of eleven months. ELEVEN MONTHS. Their relationship is barely the equivalent of a human toddler.

It's absurd. It's too fast. It's . . . wrong. Dad and Harlow don't go

4

together. She belongs with the type of guy who wears a man bun and is self-employed and visits ashrams to rediscover himself. Not Rafael Echevarria, insurance salesman.

It doesn't matter. There's no way this wedding is going to happen. Since Mom died, Dad has plunged headfirst into this relationship without thinking things through. It goes against his risk-averse nature as an insurance salesman. Enter Harlow, and every one of his rules for sane living has gone out the window.

I am fully confident that this fling with Harlow is an existential crisis and one day soon his brain will start to work again. They'll have a long engagement until Dad comes to his senses. Or until Harlow meets her true kumbaya-chanting soul mate.

See, I like Harlow enough as a person. I just don't want her in my life anymore.

"How many people are you inviting?" Avery asks. "Can I invite Isla?"

"It won't be a big wedding," Harlow says. "Maybe fifty people or so?"

"Fifty?" I repeat. The panic bubbles in my belly. "Did you say 'fifty'? Or 'fifteen'?"

"Are you wearing a white dress?" Avery asks. "Do Analee and I get matching dresses? Are we in the bridal party?"

Harlow wraps her toned arms around Avery and kisses the top of her head. "You two *are* the bridal party."

"Fifty or fifteen?" I ask again.

"How about a congratulations?" Dad lowers his chin and gives me the stare. He uses it when I'm in panic mode and I forget to behave like a normal person. Which is a lot of the time.

"Congratulations," I echo with what little feeling I can muster. "And when will this joyous occasion take place?"

"Three months," Harlow says, beaming.

Seriously, fuck my life.

Harlow gets up to give me a kiss too, but my brain is too busy to let the rest of my body respond. I hate the thought of Dad and Harlow's impending marriage, but the wedding itself is doomed to be a nightmare.

The ceremony will be all eyes on me walking down the aisle. I'm picturing myself wobbling in high heels in front of Harlow's perfect friends, and then I'm picturing myself falling in high heels in front of Harlow's perfect friends.

There's also the reception, where I'll have to dance. I don't know how to dance at all, especially when it comes to my arms. I don't know whether I should lift them up or keep them at my sides, but isn't it too stiff if I keep them near my sides? Why do weddings and dancing go hand in hand? Why do you have to jerk your body around in rhythm to demonstrate happiness? Also, I won't have anyone to dance with, so I'll just be Harlow's pathetic ugly stepdaughter who sits alone in a corner while the bride and groom feed each other vegan, gluten-free cake.

"Analee, I do have a small favor to ask of you," Harlow says, back at her seat.

I say nothing. I'm not sure what is about to come out of her mouth, but I know that doing a favor for Harlow won't amount to anything good.

"I would be really happy if you would be my maid of honor."

Dad's purposely staring down at his plate because he knows, *he knows*, this is too much to ask. This is Harlow's idea, and he went along with it because he'll do whatever she wants. That's how desperate he is for the stupid piece of paper that will tell him he legally has her.

"I, um . . ." I can't think of a polite way to let her down. It's hard to say no to Harlow when she's looking at you with those big eyes that are not quite blue and not quite green. Avery has a matching set, but I have my mom's eyes, shiny and black.

"It would really mean a lot," Harlow says. "I was hoping maybe you could write something for the occasion. Your writing is so beautiful and honest—"

"Can I think about it?" I interrupt. I need to buy time so that I can figure out a reason to say no.

"Of course," she says. She scoops a pile of mushy lentils onto her fork and feeds Dad like he's a baby bird. He opens his mouth and takes a bite, barely hiding a grimace. This is the curse that Dad has passed on to me. The inability to say no to people, especially to people like Harlow who always expect a yes.

# CHAPTER TWO

MY WRITING JOURNAL WAS NEVER MEANT FOR anyone's eyes but my own. Harlow found it a few months ago when she was dusting my room, and she made a huge fuss over it. She came across some particularly lovestruck entries, and when she asked who they were about, I lied and told her Justin Bieber. She accepted this without question, thereby proving she knows nothing about me.

I like writing more than talking because I can unleash Analee onto the page without feeling worried or awkward. Reading my work out loud would defeat the whole purpose. I don't think Harlow quite gets it, but she loves the idea of me reading my work to all her friends so she can show them what a generous and beloved stepmom she'll be.

> **Harris:** when is the wedding?
>
> **Me:** Three months.
>
> **Harris:** hmm.
>
> **Me:** I need to think of a way to back out. Maybe I can get myself sick before the wedding.
>
> **Harris:** you can't miss your dad's wedding.

**Me:** I can lick some raw chicken and get salmonella. Or eat some shrimp from Seaport Grill. They have mice, but they pay off the health department to stay open.

**Harris:** i have a better idea.

**Me:** What?

**Harris:** you can go to the wedding.

**Me:** Or I can make fake vomit! There are a bunch of recipes online.

**Harris:** or you can go to the wedding.

**Me:** Harris, stop being reasonable and come up with some actual suggestions!

**Harris:** what if you had someone up there with you? for moral support?

**Me:** Like who?

**Harris:** like, i don't know. someone you talk to every day, someone who just helped you defeat the nightmare creature in legion.

**Me:** You don't actually want to come to this shit show.

**Harris:** weddings suck, but they involve a lot of eating, which i'm really good at.

**Me:** I'm not sure I can bring a guest.

**Harris:** no biggie. just throwing it out there.

**Me:** Don't you think that would be weird? Going to a wedding together?

**Harris:** we can always meet before that. the wedding doesn't have to be THE BIG MEET.

## Analee's Top Five Embarrassing Facts about
## Her and Her Best Friend, Harris

1. We've never met in person.
2. We've never talked to each other beyond
   messaging on the computer.
3. Neither of us knows what the other one looks like.
4. Most of what I've written in my journal
   is about him, because . . .
5. I'm hopelessly in love with him.

It sounds stupid, but even though he's never met me in person, Harris knows me better than anyone else in the world. He knows all of my weird social phobias, like how I can't use a public restroom unless it's completely empty, and how I always eat lunch in the library by myself ever since the Incident with my ex–best friend, Lily.

Recently he's been asking when we can meet. He offered to come to me, even though he lives in Seattle and it's almost a six-hour flight to Florida. I change the subject every time he brings it up. It's not that I don't want to meet him. I've imagined the way it could go, thousands of times. How we could meet at sunset on the pier, and he would run toward me and pick me up like I weighed nothing more than a paper bag. He would be handsome, maybe not as perfect as Xolkar, but dark and striking.

I know that real life doesn't live up to the fantasy. It would be way too much pressure, knowing that Harris paid hundreds of dollars and traveled across the country just to see me. It's asking for disappointment, really.

**Me:** Maybe. I don't know.

**Harris:** just think about it, ok?

**Me:** Ok.

**Harris:** but for real this time.

**Me:** Ok.

# CHAPTER THREE

SOMETIMES I THINK MY LIFE CAN'T GET ANY WORSE. My mom is gone. My dad is remarrying a lifestyle guru. My future stepsister is a pint-size pain in the ass. My only friend is someone I've never met in real life.

Then I find out that today we get our lab partners in biology. And we have to slice open a bullfrog. It's a good lesson, I suppose. A reminder that things can always get worse, even when you think you've hit bottom.

First of all, I don't understand why these barbaric practices are still being allowed in high school science classes. A diagram of the frog's anatomy would more than suffice. Or maybe they could make some kind of plastic frog replica with fake body parts. I just don't get why everyone's okay with the massacre of poor, defense- less animals for a lab experiment that nobody will remember in five years.

Secondly, I hate working with people. I'm not a people person, to say the least. I'm always so concerned with what to say to them that my brain goes blank, and I feel like I'm hovering outside my body, watching this weird, mute freak who looks like me but has lost any semblance of personality, and everyone else is also watching the freak, and then I'm back in the freak's body, feeling all these eyeballs fixed on me, and I panic even more.

Mr. Hubbard, our science teacher, has taught at our school for forty-eight years. He's so old that his classroom still has a chalkboard. Every other teacher uses a computerized whiteboard, but Mr. Hubbard refuses to get with the times. While I appreciate his unabashed retro-ness, it's sad to see an old man with wrinkled, yellow chalk-stained fingers.

A bunch of assholes at our school have placed bets on when Mr. Hubbard will die. Everyone started getting in on it when he had to get his hip replaced at the end of last year. It's so gross. I bet the kids betting on him would be the same ones crying the hardest at his funeral, trying to show everyone how much they cared. That's one of the many reasons I hate everyone at this school.

I always get to class as early as possible, so that I can journal before the lesson starts. Writing is my happy time. I can let myself daydream about Harris, which takes a lot of mental fortitude, considering I don't know what he looks like. I know the basic facts that he's brought up casually in our conversations, and which I've not-so-casually burned into my brain: brown hair, brown eyes, medium build. He works out a lot, because he used to be thirty pounds overweight. He told me he's really self-conscious about his stretch marks, and I wanted to tell him that I would find them beautiful, because they're a part of him, and I love everything about him.

Except, he can't ever know that. Harris is the only person on the planet who understands me, and what we have is too important for me to screw up. And I *would* screw it up. If I met him in person,

I would get all tongue-tied and stupid. So I have to do the sappy thing and express my unrequited love in a journal he'll never read.

The class starts to fill up quickly after I've written a few lines. The science classroom is set up with two-person tables, and I'm the only one who's sitting at a table alone. Lily is sitting up front with Chloe. Chloe is part of Colton's crowd, but she and Lily became close after Lily and I split apart. To add salt to the wound, Chloe is infinitely cooler than I am. I'm short and round; she's long and thin. I spend my summers working at the local Dairy Queen; she and her family stay at a villa in Tuscany. I have zero friends at this school; she has dozens. I am a nerd; Chloe is a goddess. I could go on.

The worst part of it all? Chloe's actually a nice person. She can't even be one of those stereotypical mean girls you bash without guilt, and it makes me hate her more. Why would Lily ever be my friend again when she can have Chloe? It's like she has upgraded from microwave hot dogs to prime rib.

I flip to the next page in my journal with unnecessary force, almost ripping off the bottom corner. Instead of writing about Harris, I draw a picture of Lily getting hit by a bus. She is an assortment of limbs scattered on the page. Her hair, glossy brown waves with gold highlights, is flying through the air along with her detached head.

I can be an angry person. Sometimes.

I scribble over it until the page is a giant blob of black ink. Lily is saved, the image of her destruction permanently erased, because I miss her as much as I hate her. Ever since she chose Colton over our eleven-year friendship.

Mr. Hubbard claps his bony hands together to get us quiet.

I huddle over my journal, wishing it would suck me into its pages.

I try to think of Harris, but my mental picture is too blurry and I can't concentrate when I know Mr. Hubbard is going to pair us up with lab partners, and mine could be Lily.

Since the dawn of time Mr. Hubbard has assigned the lab partners in his class, because he doesn't trust us to choose our own. I'd rather he choose. Otherwise, in a class of twenty-five, everyone else would partner up, and I'd be the odd one out. I'd have to go to Mr. Hubbard, and he'd ask one of the pairs to let me into their group, which they would, reluctantly, because a teacher told them to, and the whole class would have their suspicions confirmed: that I, Analee, am in fact a socially defective loser.

As if reading my mind, Seb Matias raises his hand. Seb is Chloe's ex-boyfriend, and he's high on our school's popularity chain, even higher than Colton.

"Can we choose our own partners for this lab?" he asks.

Mr. Hubbard squints at Seb through chunky eyeglasses. His frown lines look like small mountain ridges between his eyebrows. "No."

Sometimes I do love Mr. Hubbard, because I don't think Seb has ever heard the word "no" in his life.

Seb mutters something under his breath, and Matt McKinley, who's sitting next to him, barks out a laugh. Matt is considered popular, although not as popular as Seb or Colton. Our high school's social hierarchy is a strange thing, because I'm not sure anyone even truly likes Matt. He's not a bully with a heart of gold, just a genuinely crappy, mean person. Matt is popular only because people don't want to be his target.

He was the first person to call me Anally, years ago. He came up with it in front of Seb, and even though Seb didn't repeat the nickname, he looked at me and laughed, which was almost as bad.

"Settle down, please," Mr. Hubbard says, rapping his knuckles on his desk and sending himself into a coughing fit. I lean forward, watching him cover his mouth with his chalky fingers, hoping no one wins the death bet today, because honestly, Mr. Hubbard doesn't look like he has much time left.

He pulls himself together, and I swear, Matt looks disappointed.

"Please wait until I read the list of partners before you take your packet," Mr. Hubbard says. In his thin, labored tone, he starts to read from a crumpled sheet of paper.

Partnering with Lily could be either horrible or wonderful. I haven't quite decided yet. Maybe it would be the defibrillator that our friendship needs. She'd be forced to talk to me, and I'd get the chance to finally explain what happened that night.

Or . . . I could be assigned to Matt McKinley, and I'd have to transfer schools.

Mr. Hubbard's eyes scan each of us in turn, then stop at Matt. "Mathew, you're paired with . . ."

I hold my breath and stare down at my shoes, studying the torn rubber sole lining my toes. If I don't look at Mr. Hubbard, maybe he'll forget I'm here.

"Chloe."

My head shoots back up. Matt gives Seb a shrug, while Chloe forces a smile that looks like someone clipped the corners of her mouth up.

"Analee," Mr. Hubbard says. I immediately freak out at the sound of my name, which he says correctly, but it gives me very little comfort at the moment. "You'll be with Seb."

I convinced myself it would be Lily. Something like disappointment sloshes around in my stomach. I slouch down in my seat, peeking at Seb's reaction, and he doesn't even try to conceal his despair. He rolls his eyes and plants his head on the table with a thud.

Well, whatever. He's not high on the list of people I want as my partner either. It's just humiliating, you know? What does he do besides bounce a soccer ball off his thick skull and lift heavy objects every day for an hour? Like that makes him better than me? I'm a freaking night elf, *Seb*.

Mr. Hubbard quickly pairs up the rest of the students. Lily is part of a trio with two of the smartest girls in the class. She gives them each a giant, face-contorting grin because they're not me.

In all, everyone seems reasonably happy about their matches. Everyone except Seb, of course. And, understandably, Chloe.

I'm relegated to picking up a lab packet for me and Seb, because he makes no move to get up from his desk. Unbelievable. The soccer jock can't peel his ass from the chair. I have to drag myself over to him while he sits there, pretending I don't exist.

Inside, my blood is a barely contained tsunami of rage. Outside, I am still quiet, polite Analee.

"Um," I say to Seb, in a truly brilliant opener. His head is tipped back, his eyes focused on the ceiling. I look up too, but there's nothing, except some water-stained tiles in need of replacing. "Should we get started?"

It's my worst habit, to phrase things in the form of a question like I'm asking permission.

He's still staring. I wonder if he's having an absence seizure, the kind without the convulsions. There was a kid in my fifth-grade class with epilepsy, and his seizures weren't dramatic. He would space out for a few seconds, and then he was fine. Seb seems to be blinking normally, though, and I'm not sure about blinking during seizures. I look around for help, but everyone else has started talking or reading.

Finally Seb gives a drawn-out sigh and looks at me. "All right. Let's get this over with."

My sentiments exactly. As soon as I slap the lab packets in front of him, he gets up and says, "There's an empty table over there."

I'm not sure why we're switching tables, until I look at where he's pointing, at Matt and Chloe in the back of the room. I nod and swallow my disagreement. It doesn't seem like the most conducive working environment, sitting by Seb's ex-girlfriend and the boy who won't let my middle school nickname die.

I don't want to argue with Seb, though, so I grab the packets and follow him to the back corner of the classroom.

He's talking to Matt and Chloe already, which I knew was going to happen. I sit and open my packet, trying my best to tune out their conversation. If Seb isn't going to work with me, I'll work by myself. I do things better alone, anyway.

The beginning of the packet is mostly reading about the lab procedures and short-answer questions. Nothing I can't handle. I'm about two pages in when Matt takes note of me and says loudly, "Hey, man. I think Anally started without you."

He does that a lot, the whole talk-about-me-like-I'm-not-there thing. I should be used to it by now, but every time he does it, my body temperature rises like it usually does when I stop being invisible. I keep my eyes on the print, losing the meaning of the English language and observing the group through my peripheral vision.

Seb gives me a cursory glance, then turns back to Matt and Chloe. "Whatever. I'm over this class, you know? Who cares?"

"*I* care," Chloe says. "I have to get my science grade up if I want to get into Brown." She turns to Matt. "Do you want to work over there?" she asks, motioning to the opposite side of the room. "I can't concentrate."

Matt carefully avoids Seb's eyes. "Yeah. Okay."

They leave a broken Seb in their wake, a different version of Seb, now slightly pinker in color. Seb is a bit of an ass, but I almost feel sorry for him. I'm not sure why he and Chloe broke up, but I know that Chloe is the only girl in the history of time who's ever dumped Seb.

"Are you okay?" I ask cautiously, and he rips his gaze away from Chloe to look at me. He blinks, like he momentarily forgot who I was.

"Why wouldn't I be?"

"Just . . ." I don't know what to say now. This is why I don't start conversations with people. I can't talk to Seb about his breakup like we're buddies. What was I expecting, for him to cry on my shoulder? "I don't know. Never mind."

He gives me a strange look, and I feel the urge to crawl under my desk. I get undone easily. Sometimes I feel like I was born missing something that everyone else has, because the ability to be normal always seems so far out of my reach.

Seb leans back in his chair and places the open lab packet on top of his face. He feels no obligation to talk to me, or even show any sign that he's awake. I turn to my own packet and continue reading, and we don't talk for the remainder of the period.

## Analee's Rules for Getting through Classes
## with Minimal Teacher Attention

1. Sit behind someone tall so that they
block the teacher's view of you.
2. Keep your pencil moving so that you always
look busy. (Note—doodling is okay if done with
an expression of intense concentration.)
3. Nod occasionally so that it seems
like you're invested in the conversation.
4. Do not make eye contact.
5. Wear your hair down so that it hides your face.

# CHAPTER FOUR

A LYCRA-CLAD HARLOW IS IN THE MIDDLE OF yoga practice when I get home. She's downward-dogging on her mat, eyes closed, a smile on her face. This is a fairly frequent occurrence since she turned her yoga practice into a brand. She became a certified instructor years ago and two years ago launched a successful YouTube channel called *Hatha with Harlow*.

"That you, An?" she asks, shifting forward into a plank.

"Yep." I drop my backpack by the front door.

"Want to join me?"

Harlow is dying to turn me on to yoga, but I've already told her I'm wound too tight for it. I'm also lacking in the yoga physique. It seems like every yogi I see looks like Harlow, all slender and long-limbed. I would feel way too stubby in comparison.

"I'm okay," I say. "Where's Avery?"

Harlow pushes herself into a terrifying backbend. I'm worried that one day she'll snap in half. "She's at Megan's today."

Avery has inherited not only Harlow's skinny body and colorful eyes, but also her insane flexibility. Harlow has featured Avery in a few yoga videos to promote mother-daughter bonding, and Waspy moms go crazy for them. She asked me to be part of the series, and I refused without hesitation. I'd feel like a fraud, and I could predict all the comments that would be posted: *Who's that chubby Latina? She's doing it wrong. Are you related? She doesn't look anything like you.*

My real mom died of ovarian cancer two and a half years ago. I have her untamable mane of dark hair, curvy body, and wide nose. Those features somehow looked better on her. On me the proportions look slightly off, like I was put together by an amateur in Photoshop.

Harlow is in corpse pose now, which means "Do Not Disturb." Her legs and arms are splayed across the mat, and her chest rises in sync with her slow breathing. Harlow can stay like this for an hour, totally content to listen to herself breathe, while I can't shut my brain off for longer than a few seconds.

I head upstairs, my body brimming with excitement. Opening my laptop, tapping the keyboard with my fingertips, knowing Harris and I will be connected in a few minutes . . . this is the happiest part of my day. Actually, since the whole thing with Lily, it's the *only* happy part of my day.

Harris and I "met" when he recruited me to join his guild. They needed a warrior, and when I'm Kiri, I am a total kick-ass warrior. We fought side by side every night as Xolkar and Kiri. Then the fighting became talking, and we slowly became Harris and Analee. Now we don't go a night without talking to each other.

**Me:** Gross day today.

**Harris:** what happened?

I tell him about the frogs, and Mr. Hubbard's brush with death, and how Matt and Seb still find their toilet humor to be the height of comedy.

**Me:** I'm just sick of being called Anally. Like, how old are we that toilet humor is still a thing?

**Harris:** if it makes you feel better, people call me harry all the time.

**Me:** How would that make me feel better? You think Harry is comparable to Anally?

**Harris:** harry is a horrible name.

**Me:** Are you kidding? EVERYONE named Harry is cool. You've got Harry Potter, Harry Styles, Harry Truman. . . . I'm sorry, you cannot compare Harry to Anus.

**Harris:** um. how did harry truman make the cool list?

**Me:** He was a president.

**Harris:** . . . who dropped the atomic bomb on hiroshima.

**Me:** That was him?

**Harris:** yup.

**Me:** I thought it was Nixon.

**Harris:** nixon was watergate. wow, an. the american public school system has failed you.

**Me:** Fine, so Harry Truman was a dick. But my point is, we'll never have a President Anally.

**Harris:** for the record, i think analee is a beautiful name. the fact that you won't ever be president probably has more to do with you not knowing basic american history.

**Me:** Didn't stop Trump.

**Harris:** don't remind me.

**Me:** you really think analee is a beautiful name?

**Harris:** yes

**Harris:** that's why it fits you

**Me:** You have no idea what I look like

**Harris:** i don't care what you look like

**Harris:** i already know you're beautiful

I smile in spite of myself. This is why I love Harris. It's why I have an entire book of writing dedicated to him, because he is a real-life druid who can somehow make my crappy days not matter.

# CHAPTER FIVE

THE NEXT BIO CLASS IS MORE OF THE SAME. SEB
sleeps with the lab packet on his face while I read quietly to myself
and do all the prep work. I don't mind the quiet, but the problem
is that I'm kind of depending on Seb when it comes to the whole
gruesome, slicing-open-a-dead-frog part. I hate being dependent on
other people. Other people tend to suck.

**Harris:** tell him to get his shit together.

**Me:** Yeah, okay, Harris.

**Harris:** why not?

**Me:** You know I can't do that.

**Harris:** why don't you talk to your teacher, then?

**Me:** You want me to tattle on Seb? That'll do wonders for my social life.

**Harris:** what's the big deal with this guy?

**Me:** He's good at kicking a soccer ball, so everyone's in love with him.

**Harris:** and you?

**Me:** Please.

**Harris:** so then. talk to him.

**Me:** I'm bad at that.

The next day, though, we're supposed to actually get started with the frog, and Seb is still sleeping under the packet.

"Um. Seb?" I try.

He doesn't answer. His body is perfectly still except for his muscled chest expanding with breath. I can make out the shape of his pecs through his shirt, and I instantly feel guilty for not working out with Harlow the other day.

"Seb," I repeat.

He grunts without lifting the packet off his face.

"Shouldn't we . . . um . . . do this?" I ask.

"No." His voice is muffled against the pages.

"Okay . . ." I look around the room, and everyone else is working in harmony, as though to show me that I'm the real problem, not Seb. It pains me to continue this conversation, but the thought of slicing Kermit's corpse alone makes me feel a little dizzy and short of breath. Or maybe that's the smell of formaldehyde wafting from its body.

I snap on a pair of plastic gloves and look down at the frog. It's a vivid green, a color way too bright for something so dead. Its legs are splayed out, poised, as though they're about to propel it through water. I think about how this frog should be gliding around in a creek or flitting through some tall grass, and instead it's lying helplessly on a dissection tray, smelly, preserved in its inaction.

It's so effing sad that I want to burst into tears right here.

Sometimes, when I feel too Analee, I try to be Kiri in real life. I think about what she would do if she had the scalpel in her hands, if she were paired with an uncooperative lab partner. But it never works. Kiri wouldn't, couldn't, exist in a world with people like Matt McKinley and Chloe and Colton.

And if she did, Seb wouldn't ignore her.

I can do this alone. I can. According to the lab packet, the first thing we're supposed to do is cut the frog's mouth, stick a finger inside, and pull on its tongue. I look at Kermit's delicate little mouth, imagining how it flopped open in confusion before he was yanked out of the wild and killed.

I shudder and turn away. "Seb."

Seb gives no indication that he can hear me, but I'm angry now, at him and at the fact that Kermit died in vain because Seb has no appreciation for a life outside his own.

I yank the packet off Seb's face before I can stop to think about it. I surprise myself.

"Aah." He throws a hand in front of his eyes. "Bright."

"I need your help with this."

He groans.

"Please?" I add. So stupid. So unlike Kiri. I'm literally begging him to do the bare minimum of what's expected.

Seb lowers his hand, widens his brown eyes to adjust to the classroom's fluorescent lights. "Yeah . . . I'm not into the whole science thing."

"And you think I am?"

"Well, yeah."

A lot of people assume that because I'm quiet, I must be some misunderstood genius. Really, it's just easy to not say something stupid when you barely say anything at all. My grades are painfully mediocre considering that, with my lack of a social life, I have all the time in the world to study.

"Well, you're wrong," I say to Seb, but I look down at Kermit. Making eye contact with people is exhausting for me. Knowing when to blink, when to glance away, leaving my face and its numerous flaws open to examination.

"Fine." Seb pulls the plastic gloves over his long fingers and reads the lab packet out loud. "Place the frog on its dorsal side and cut the corners of the mouth."

I make a move to gently turn the frog over, but Seb grabs it from the tray and pretends to throw it at Dalia Breneman behind us. He goes from sullen to flirty in a matter of seconds.

"Seb!" Dalia shrieks, lunging across the table to slap him with her notebook. "You asshole!"

Everyone turns to look at us, which is exactly what Seb and Dalia both want. Dalia because she wants it known that the hottest guy in our school has deigned to flirt with her. Seb because Dalia is mildly pretty and he wants to make Chloe jealous.

Chloe, meanwhile, looks thoroughly unshaken. She rubs her button nose with the top of her sleeve and bends over to examine her frog.

Seb's smile shrinks. Our frog hangs limply from his fingers.

I take it from him and lay it faceup on the tray while Seb looks at Chloe.

"I can do it," I offer, and my brain scolds me. I'm being one of those ass-kissers I despise, those girls who cater to Seb's every wish. A people-pleaser like my dad. I shouldn't feel sorry for Seb because his ex-girlfriend has moved on.

"It's fine," Seb mutters. I can see him willing himself not to notice Chloe. He grabs the scissors at the edge of the table and snips the edges of Kermit's mouth, quickly and carelessly. Then he tosses the scissors back onto the table and looks at me, waiting.

I realize he expects me to read him the directions. I clear the fuzz from my throat and read. "Locate the tongue. Is it attached to the front or back of the mouth?"

Seb doesn't hesitate to reach his finger inside the mouth and pull on the stretchy, lime-green tongue. "Front."

He can touch a dead frog like it's no big deal because normal people, like Seb, don't make up crazy backstories about their lab experiments, or imagine a frog torn away from his wife and tadpole babies.

"Locate the maxillary teeth on the upper jaw," I read, and he does. I label the teeth on the diagram in our packet. "The vomerine teeth are in the upper jaw."

He opens the frog's mouth wider, pausing briefly to show me the teeth so that I can mark them on the diagram.

I read, he finds, I write down our results. It makes sense for our roles to be defined this way. Seb is a man of action, while I'm someone who thinks and interprets. Also, I'm still grossed out by this entire procedure. It's messed up for all of us to pretend that a room full of amphibian corpses is business-as-usual.

Around the room, partners talk, laugh, engage. Seb and I work in silence, talking only when we have to, and only about the lab instructions. I'm relieved not to have to make conversation, and at the same time I feel guilty that I don't try. Like there's something wrong with me for preferring the silence.

Once, when Harlow was beginning her whole-foods diet, she gave all our processed food to a homeless shelter and left Lily and me dehydrated kale chips for snacking.

I wouldn't have eaten them at all if Lily hadn't tried them first. She popped one into her mouth, and the leaf crackled between her teeth.

"Well?" I asked. I had picked one up and couldn't bring myself to eat it yet.

"They're actually really good."

"Shut up."

"I'm serious," she said, and took another handful. Bits of kale flecked her lips, and she didn't even care. "You want?"

"Hell no," I said. "I don't see why we all have to suffer for Harlow's latest diet trend."

Lily rolled her eyes, still crunching away. "I'd hardly call it suffering, An."

"A life without Doritos is not a life worth living."

"She's trying to be healthy."

"She's trying to take away my joy."

This brought on another eye roll. Lily had a habit of defending Harlow, which irked me, but I wasn't sure why. Maybe because Lily used to love Mom, and it felt like a betrayal for her to eat Harlow's kale chips and not do me the courtesy of pretending to hate them.

I offered Lily the chip still in my hand, and she snatched it up.

"You're not even gonna try one?" she asked.

"No." I felt needlessly stubborn, but it was the principle of the thing. I was not going to support Harlow's extremism, and I was certainly not going to give up my good old-fashioned unhealthy fried chips to make her happy.

Lily shook her head and brought the Tupperware container of kale chips up to my room while my stomach growled in disappointment. We sat on the rug, the Tupperware sitting between us, and compared the popular guys in our school to old boy-band archetypes. This was all before Lily dated one of them.

"Matt McKinley," she said.

"The ugly one."

"Oh, come on. There are no ugly ones."

"Yes, there are," I maintained. "Every boy band has that ugly member who made it into the band only because he could sing the high notes or whatever."

It was horrible of me to say, but Matt McKinley is a horrible person, so I didn't feel guilty. It felt good to laugh at him behind my closed bedroom door, because he laughs at everyone else out in the open.

"What about Seb?" she asked.

"Easy." I pretended to get swoony. "The heartthrob."

Seb and Chloe had just begun dating at that point. I remember because it was like the tabloids had come alive in the sophomore class. The two most beautiful people in our little world had finally gotten together, and the student body salivated over their coupled existence. Seb and Chloe even had their own set of shippers, a group of freshman girls who awarded them the unfortunate nickname of "Chleb."

No girls were deluded enough to think they could take Seb away from Chloe, but they enjoyed trying. For them it was enough to get one of Seb's smiles, because a Seb smile is different from an ordinary-person smile. "Cheeky," Lily had described it once, and I couldn't find a more fitting word.

"What about Colton?" Lily asked then, and only when I thought about it later did it dawn on me how she had offered his name so shyly.

Colton has a tattoo inching out of his shirtsleeve. He'd had only one girlfriend that I knew of, a college girl named Mia who wore gauge earrings and used to make out with him in the school parking lot.

"Colton is the bad boy," I decided. Even then I had him pegged, but I didn't realize the truth of it.

And even then Lily came to his defense. "But he's sensitive. I think."

"Oh, please," I fired back, rolling my eyes. "He's just good at pretending he is. And getting idiots to fall for it."

She licked the salt from her lips, quiet for a moment. Then, in a smaller voice, "He said he liked my art project."

"What?" I stared at her. "I didn't know Colton was in your art class."

"I didn't think it was worth mentioning," she said.

"You have art with Colton *and* he complimented your project?"

"So?"

"So, I've never seen him talk to a plebeian before."

"It's not a big deal," she said, but something told me it was, or she wouldn't have brought it up.

Every time she said his name, a little smile hovered at her lips. I didn't like it. Not just because Colton was an asshole but because it wasn't fair that Lily was able to smile at things and I still couldn't.

There was a weird silence between us, only for a moment, before Lily shook the tub of kale chips and said, "For the love of God, An, I can't eat all of these myself."

I took one, because eating a kale chip was more appealing than continuing our Colton conversation. The chip was crispy, and I could taste garlic and something that was not actual cheese but faintly cheesy.

It was good, and that made me irritable.

"Well?" Lily asked.

I made a face and lied. "Yuck."

# CHAPTER SIX

DAD AND HARLOW HAVE THEIR FIRST WEDDING-related disagreement when Harlow brings up the venue. Dad wants a traditional church wedding, while Harlow wants a small, bohemian beach ceremony. When Harlow suggests that her friend Samsara officiate, Dad's eye starts to twitch.

"*Cariño*," he tries, "I think Samsara might be too much for my parents to handle."

The four of us—Dad, Harlow, me, and Avery, are sprawled among our living room couches. Harlow is sitting cross-legged with her laptop balanced on her knees. On her screen is an overwhelming Pinterest board littered with flowers and mason jars.

"Raf, she's one of my best friends," Harlow says. "Doesn't it make sense for someone we know and love to marry us?"

"My parents have known Father Medina for thirty years."

"I've never met Father Medina. And we're not Catholic."

"I am."

"Oh, really?" Harlow sets her laptop aside. "When was the last time you went to church?"

I can count on one hand the number of times we've been to

church since Mom died. Once for her funeral, maybe one Christmas Mass, but the only Sunday ritual we consistently abide by is sleeping in. My church is my bed.

I have Mom and Dad's wedding photo in my nightstand drawer. It used to sit on our entryway table, before Harlow moved in and added pieces of herself to the house. Mom and Dad got married in a church, and Mom wore a simple off-the-shoulder dress and a fluffy veil.

"Samsara is bald," Dad replies, flicking the top of his full head of hair in contrast.

"So?" Harlow replies.

"Her actual name is Carrie!"

"That's her given name, Raf. You know she legally changed her name last year."

Dad massages the skin around his eyes. "How do you expect anyone to take our marriage seriously when your bald friend Carrie who now calls herself Samsara is performing the ceremony?"

"Raf . . ." Harlow scoots over to him and plants herself on his lap. She talks to him softly, in the dulcet tones she uses for her yoga videos. "We don't have anything to prove. This wedding is for us."

Her voice always has this magical effect on Dad. All the tension melts from his body, and he taps his forehead against hers. They look at each other, nose to nose, and I know without a doubt that they're having a beach ceremony officiated by bald Carrie.

"Okay, ew," I say, and they both laugh. Harlow slides off his lap.

"Girls," she says to me and Avery. "We're going dress shopping this weekend."

If I had any kind of social life whatsoever, I could pretend I'm busy. Dress shopping means less time talking to Harris, and my weekend time with Harris is precious to me.

But I have no social life, and Harlow is well aware that I spend every weekend confined to my room.

"Yay!" Avery cries, pitching her skinny fist into the air.

"Analee?" Harlow looks at me. "You in?"

They gaze at me with almost identical bright-eyed faces, and I don't want to be the dark stepchild who kills the fun.

"I'm there," I say with labored enthusiasm. Harlow shows me and Avery all the wedding dress pictures she's amassed, and each beaded white gown blurs into the next. After twenty minutes I excuse myself and spend the rest of the night fighting dragon spawn with Harris.

I'm in a mood when I walk into the classroom on Friday. Knowing that tomorrow will be without Harris, and an added crappy bonus of dress shopping and girly bonding with Harlow, turns me into a walking storm cloud.

I don't mean to slam my folder down at the table and wake up a sleeping Seb. Or maybe I do.

He jolts, knuckles the sleep from his eyes. I'm beginning to think he's got a slight case of narcolepsy.

"What?" he asks, peering around the room before settling his gaze on my scowling face. "What happened to you?"

"Nothing." I pull on my goggles. There's no way I'm telling Seb anything. He was allowed to be in a crappy mood about Chloe, so I figure I'm allowed my own dark day.

He doesn't push me on my obvious lie, which I'm thankful for. Instead he puts on his own goggles and arms himself with a pair of scissors.

"I'm going in," he announces. Today is the dreaded day we slice through Kermit's stomach and play with his guts. I can't help myself. I turn away.

The only way to stop myself from throwing up is to think ahead to how embarrassing it'll be if I do. Lily will be horrified. Matt will never let me live it down. And Chloe . . . if Chloe has ever thrown up, it probably came out looking like a beautiful abstract painting. They would save the floor tile and hang it up in the Louvre if Chloe were to vomit.

"Analee?" Seb asks.

It's the first time he's ever said my name. And here's the part that pisses me off: he knows how to say it! He can pronounce it better than Harlow, with the last syllable properly accented. Yet he never once corrected Matt on it.

"What," I answer. I cut the word as short as possible.

"What's your deal?"

My deal is that I have no interest in being Seb's partner. My deal is that he never stood up for me in front of his dipshit friend. My deal is that I want to be home, bathed in the soft glowing light of my laptop.

And then there's Kermit. Poor dead Kermit.

"It bums me out," I mutter.

"The frog?"

"Yes."

"Why?"

Only a heartless monster would ask that question. Isn't the "why" of it obvious?

When I turn to look at Seb, he has the frog in his hand. He pries its mouth open with his fingers and squeezes it shut, over and over, open and shut, turning Kermit into a puppet. In a high-pitched squeak, Seb-as-Kermit says, "Save me, Analee, save me!"

"You're an asshole." I don't say it in a cute flirty way like Dalia. I say it because Seb is being an asshole.

Seb, surprisingly, laughs at this. "And you're a tight-ass."

I bite back a response. I'm armed with a variety of furious comebacks, but they jam my throat, unwilling to come out.

Having had the last word, Seb gets back to work. He lowers the frog back down onto the tray and sticks needles into Kermit's limbs to pin him down. I watch him, the way he squints his eyes while he works and presses his lips together in concentration. Looking at him is easier than looking at the frog.

He meets my gaze, and we face off, goggles to goggles. They look ridiculous on me, but somehow he looks like a high-fashion model. Life is not fair. "Here." He slides the scissors across the table to me. "You try."

I slide them right back over to him. "No, thanks. I'll stick to reading the directions."

"Suit yourself." Seb picks up the scissors and aims them right at Kermit's lower belly. He pauses, the blade tips pricking the skin, and he's about to say something, when Chloe's laugh drifts over to us from the back of the room.

It has a paralyzing effect on Seb. He freezes with the scissors split open, and he turns to look at Chloe and Matt giggling in the corner.

Matt is whispering something into her ear, and she's not pushing him away. She's smiling.

Why am I not surprised that Matt is flirting with his friend's ex-girlfriend? Could it be because he has no soul?

Without thinking, I take the scissors from Seb. I begin to cut along the frog's midline like it's made of rubber. There's that annoying ache of pity again, right in the center of my chest, a butter knife poking my rib cage.

"You don't have to—" Seb starts.

"It's fine."

It's not bad if I think of the frog as a combination of body parts. Not Kermit. Sometimes I do it with myself, too. Like when a teacher asks me something in the middle of class and my face heats up and everyone's waiting on my response but I can't speak because my heart is spasming. I think, *You are not Analee. You are a brain and muscles and bones thrown together at random.*

"What the hell is that?" Seb asks when I lift the flaps of the body wall and pin them back. There are dozens of black dots inside the frog, like a mass of poppy seeds.

"Eggs," I realize out loud. Kermit is a she.

So, of course, the body part trick doesn't work anymore, just like it never actually works in real life.

"Sick," Seb breathes. He momentarily forgets about the Chloe-Matt flirtation.

"You know what?" And I momentarily forget I'm talking to Seb. "I'm fucking done. This is gross. We're slicing up a *pregnant frog* and pretending that it's not horrible. Isn't this animal abuse? Are you telling me that there are no—"

I stop. Rants are common for me, but they're usually done over the computer to Harris, or in person to Lily. Seb is staring at me like I've sprouted horns.

"Wow," he says.

"What?"

"That's the most I've ever heard you talk. Ever."

He's probably right. It sounds embarrassing when he says it out loud, though. There is nowhere to look but down at our unfinished dissection packet. I don't want to see the frog eggs or Seb's face.

I mumble, "Whatever." My body feels like it's shut down. I'm embarrassed that I spoke to him like that, that I forgot who he is. He is the type to date perfect girls and laugh at people and make fun of them for being unable to perform a stupid science experiment.

I wait. There's no laughter. There's silence, except for Seb fiddling with the forceps.

"I'll take over," he says finally. "You read."

I feel him still watching me through his goggles while I read the directions out loud.

# CHAPTER SEVEN

I STARTED MAKING LISTS WHEN MOM WAS SICK.
My first one started as a laundry list of things that would help her
during treatment.

1. Make sure she stays hydrated.
2. Bring her flan from La Vibora.
3. Keep my hands clean.
4. Load episodes of *María la del Barrio* onto the iPad.
5. Act like everything is okay, even when it isn't.

Lists keep me grounded. They anchor my spiraling brain, give
me something to focus on when life gets scary. The sicker Mom
got, the more lists I created. And then when she died, I kept the
lists going. They started as a way to help her feel better, but somehow they ended up helping me instead. I have an ever growing list
of all the things I loved about Mom. Right now it's at one hundred
twenty-six items long.

Mom had her annoying habits too, but now that she's gone, I
miss every single one of them. There was the incessant sound of the

nail clipper while she watched her telenovelas. The way she threw open the blinds every Saturday morning and announced it was time to clean my room. I even miss how whenever I gave her attitude, she would tell me the story of my birth in slow, torturous detail. CliffsNotes version: mucus plug, screaming, poop, and a bunch of other gross things.

My regret? That I only half-listened. That I shrieked and covered my ears instead of writing it all down. Because while Dad was there during the labor, he can't stand the sight of blood and has blocked all the details. I assumed that Mom would be around to annoy me with stories for years and years. But now she's not. She died, and the story of me died with her.

"And that's why you're an only child," is how she would end it after I uncovered my ears, every time.

"And that's why I'm never getting pregnant," I would say in response, which never failed to make her laugh.

# CHAPTER EIGHT

HARLOW TAKES US TO A MASSIVE BRIDAL BOUTIQUE located in a desolate strip mall. It's jarring when we step into the powder-pink room with its crystal chandeliers and plush chaise longues. The room feels like it's trying too hard, like it's well aware that it's situated next to a Blimpie. Harlow brought her best friend, Liz, along with us. Liz is unreasonably tan, even for a Floridian, and practically lives in jean shorts year-round. She's described herself as "unapologetically sassy" on her Twitter account and likes to post pictures of beach sunsets and daily margaritas.

Anyway. I'm not super-fond of Liz. I don't think she likes me much either.

A skinny saleswoman in peep-toe heels and a nametag that says "Marianne" comes out to greet us, and a waft of her perfume hits me. I recognize the scent immediately—violet and plum, with a hint of cinnamon. My mom's signature scent.

I have a bottle of it in my nightstand drawer that I take out and inhale at least once a day. Twice if it's a particularly crappy day. I read that the part of the brain that processes smell is directly connected to emotion and memory. Maybe that's the reason I huff

Mom's perfume like it's glue, because it's the closest I can get to remembering her. Sometimes the pictures aren't enough.

But rarely do I smell my mom outside of my room, in the middle of normal life. I wonder if it's a message from her. Or a warning. Whatever it is, it seems especially wrong for me to smell Mom's perfume today, when I have to watch her replacement try on wedding dresses.

"Which one of you is the beautiful bride?" Marianne asks, and Liz practically pushes Harlow into her.

"This one!" Liz crows. "She's getting married in three months!"

Marianne gives Harlow an approving nod. Harlow has that look, that cover-model-of-a-bridal-magazine look, with toned arms that would be showcased perfectly in a strapless dress.

They all talk a little bit about what type of dress Harlow's looking for, throwing out vocabulary I've never heard used to describe clothes, like "sweetheart neckline" and "trumpet fit." I gaze around the store, feeling unfeminine and clueless. Avery has run over to inspect a rack of glittery dresses.

Marianne sweeps Harlow away into a curtained dressing room, and Liz and I wait on the chaise.

"Avery, hon," Liz calls. "See anything you like?"

"Tons," Avery says. She runs over to us, squeezes her tiny body in between me and Liz. "I think Mom should wear something sparkly."

"I totally agree," Liz remarks. I'm not surprised she and Avery are on the same page. Liz has all the stylings of an eight-year-old. Today she's wearing a shirt that says #SQUAD. "What about you, Analee?"

I'm not sure what any of the dress lingo means, so I settle on, "Something simple. Maybe . . . flowy."

If Dad and Harlow are having a beach wedding, it makes sense to wear something that could get whipped around by the wind.

"That could be nice," Liz says, both diplomatically and unconvincingly. She combs her fingers through Avery's hair in an absentminded way, almost as if it were her own. Liz is one of those women who love to touch and hold and pet people like they're animals. I've always been the opposite—I like a three-foot radius of personal space surrounding me at all times. I picture myself covered head to toe in police tape. DO NOT CROSS.

Liz must sense it. She's never tried to stroke my hair the way she strokes Avery's.

I hear the curtain being whisked back, and Marianne comes out first.

"You ready to see the bride?" she asks us. She reminds me of a crowd warmer. It works, because Liz and Avery cheer and clap like a well-behaved audience. I copy Marianne's worn smile as best I can.

Then Harlow appears.

The dress hangs off her thin frame and falls into a cloud at the bottom so that it looks like she's floating on the sky when she walks. It's simple, no glitter to be found, and the white brings out all the colors in her eyes. Harlow gives a small twirl in front of us, and Marianne brings her to a tri-fold mirror, where we can see her perfection at every angle.

And I think I finally get it. I do. I get why Dad wants to marry Harlow so badly. *I* would marry her right now. The woman was made to wear a wedding dress.

"What does everyone think?" Marianne asks.

Harlow opens her mouth, but Liz speaks first. "No. No way."

"No?" Harlow tears her gaze away from her reflection to stare at Liz. She runs her hands up and down the front of the dress.

"It's boring. It does nothing for your body."

"Yeah, Mommy," Avery chimes in. "We want to see you in something sparkly."

Harlow makes a humming sound and turns back to the mirror. She cocks her head, pressing the fabric against her waist. "I don't know," she says softly. "I think it's nice."

"I do too," says Marianne. "It's very elegant."

"Analee?" Harlow's eyes meet mine in the mirror's reflection. "What do you think?"

Jesus. I feel Liz's and Avery's eyes, silently pleading with me. But when I look at Harlow, I can see her walking down the beach in this, I can see the dress shimmering against blue sky and ocean, I can see Dad's face when she's walking toward him.

"I think it's perfect," I say.

"Okay, next!" Liz says, turning back to Harlow and rendering me useless. "Can you at least try one that Avery and I like?"

"Something sparkly," Avery repeats.

Harlow's smile flickers. "Sure, honey. I'll try it."

Liz leads Marianne to some bedazzled monstrosities on the corner rack, and the two of them march Harlow back into the dressing area with heavy dresses slung over their arms.

Avery and I sit together, listening to the sounds of rustling and zipping coming from the room.

"Remember, your mom's getting married, not you," I murmur to her.

"So?"

"So, she should get the dress that she likes."

"That dress was boring."

I shake my head. "You're just copying what Liz said."

"Nuh-uh."

It's hard to imagine that Avery and I will be related in a few months. We don't look alike, and we don't have any mutual interests. We're just an introvert and an extrovert sharing the same house. Even though Avery's half my age, she's constantly judging me. I thought it would be "older sister knows best" when she moved in, but instead I feel her looking down at me for my life choices. *Why don't you ever paint your nails, Analee? Why don't you have a boyfriend yet? Why doesn't Lily come over anymore?*

Liz hurries out of the dressing room. "Girls, wait until you see this one. She looks *gorgeous*."

Harlow comes out a little less proudly this time. Her shoulders are drawn, and her smile is a straight line. In spite of all this, Liz is right—she does look gorgeous. But the dress itself is hideous. It's an oversize tutu with ruffles and jewels plastered all over the front.

Avery lets out a gasp. "Mommy, you look beautiful!"

"Thanks, baby."

"I think this might be the one." Liz fluffs up the skirt, which does not need any additional fluffing, considering Harlow barely fits through a doorway. "Raf is going to flip his shit when he sees you in it."

Liz is a bit of a fangirl when it comes to my dad. She's constantly talking about how hot he is, and she does it in front of me and Avery, which is both inappropriate and disgusting. More than once I've heard Liz refer to Dad as Harlow's "Latin lover," like he speaks with a seductive accent (his English is almost perfect, with the exception of certain words) and knows how to tango (two left feet, and his salsa is barely passable). Harlow had to give her a whole lecture on harmful stereotypes, but Liz just laughed it off and said, "It's a goddamn joke, Har!"

*It's not funny*, I wish I would have said. *You don't know my dad at all.* I still think about it, months later, how I should have said something.

I look at Harlow's pinched smile now, and the ujjayi breaths she's taking in an attempt to stay calm, and I have to say something.

"Isn't it a little too . . ." *Tacky. Ostentatious. Gaudy. Hideous.* "A little too much for a beach wedding?" I finish.

"The bride can never be too much," Liz argues. She's been flinging the label around all day—the bride, the bride, the bride—with the reverence a Catholic would use to refer to the Pope.

"Analee has a point," Harlow says. "As beautiful as this dress is, I don't know that it will go with the theme."

"If you say so." Liz clucks her tongue and releases the tulle skirt from her fingers.

"You can't go wrong either way," Marianne says, and her smile quivers with pure desperation for a sale. She clasps her hands together. "Shall we look at some more?"

I try very hard to conceal my despair.

A few unremarkable dresses later, Harlow is back in her maxi skirt and sandals. She gives Marianne a kiss good-bye and thanks her, saying she'll be in touch soon.

"You'll make a beautiful bride," Marianne gushes. I briefly wonder about her existence outside of this pastel-colored bridal shop. Her face must be exhausted from all the smiling. Does she go home to a dark room? Spend hours scowling and listening to heavy metal? I think I would have to if I worked in a place like this. A small chuckle escapes as I picture it, and Liz shoots me a strange look. Liz constantly looks at me like I'm not of this earth.

We push open the door and step out into the stifling Florida sun. The air is so humid that it clogs my lungs and causes my hair to swell to three times its normal size. As we walk, Avery and Liz engage in a debate over what color Harlow should paint her nails and whether she should wear her hair up or down for the wedding. Harlow hangs back with me. Neither of us says anything to each other. I wonder if it's rude of me not to act more girly right now. I think I'm supposed to squeal and ask lots of questions about flowers and wedding favors, but I don't have it in me. I can't fake excitement about something I'm dreading. I can't stop thinking about whether Mom can see me right now, if I'm betraying her by participating in this circus.

"I'm glad you came, Analee," Harlow says finally. Even though she's talking to me, she looks ahead at Liz and Avery. "Thank you."

It's nice of her to say that. Harlow is nothing if not polite. But still, she wouldn't thank Avery for the same thing. It would just be assumed that Avery would participate in her mom's wedding dress experience, because that's something that a daughter does for her mom.

I am not Harlow's daughter, and the wedding isn't going to change that fact.

"I still like the first dress," I say quickly under my breath. Not that my opinion matters, because clothes are so not my thing. I don't know what's in style, or the difference between a chapel- and cathedral-length veil. But I do know what it's like to be drowned out by louder voices, like Harlow was today.

Harlow is about to answer when Liz whips around to face us and says dramatically, "I need a drink. Can we go somewhere where I can get a mimosa, Har?"

"Sure," Harlow says. "I know a place nearby." She rushes ahead to Liz, leaving me alone to trail behind the group.

# CHAPTER NINE

I HAVE A SPECIAL CUBICLE IN OUR SCHOOL'S library. It's on the second floor, way in the back next to a shelf of obsolete VHS tapes. It's dusty in this corner of the library, but it's private. When we used to do our homework after school together, Lily would sit at the cubicle on the other side of the divider in front of me. We were separated by a sheet of particleboard, and Lily used to throw paper balls over it when she got restless. She called them paper grenades. Around twenty minutes into homework time, Lily would lose all her attention span. Half of the pen scrawls on these cubicles belong to her. She would draw little cartoon robots one day and then an intricate mandala the next.

These days no one sits across from me. Except for today.

I'm bent over my math homework, and I hear the chair opposite mine scrape against the floor. My first thought is Lily. Lily was the only person I ever saw up here. But when I peek underneath the cubicle, I don't see Lily's shoes. I see rust-colored ankle boots that would look like hand-me-downs if I wore them but look appropriately vintage on everyone else.

I recognize those boots, and the pair of slender legs wearing them. They're Chloe's.

I draw in a sharp breath, debating whether I should get up and leave right now. I have my back to the wall, but the stairwell is closer to Chloe's side. If I leave, she'll see me. She'll think it's weird that I got up as soon as she sat down.

Her phone vibrates against the table right before I can go. I feel the table quiver underneath my elbows. Across the cubicle Chloe sighs, but she doesn't turn it off.

It stops for a second. Then it vibrates again. And again. And again.

Chloe gives another sigh, and I hear her pick it up. "Hello?"

I hold my breath. For what, I don't know. I should leave. Now's a good time, when she's distracted.

"I was busy," she says tersely.

My curiosity gets the better of me. She sounds upset.

"I wasn't ignoring you," she goes on. "I just told you, I was busy. . . . Look, I can't really talk right now. . . ."

The voice on the other end of the phone, from what I can make out, definitely belongs to a guy.

Chloe lowers her own voice to just above a whisper. "How many times are we going to have this conversation? I don't . . . I'm in the library, but—hello? Seb?"

I freeze. There's a pause. The sound of a phone smacking onto a table.

I rearrange my notebooks and textbooks into one neat pile. Largest item on the bottom, smallest perched on top. All I have to do is pick the pile up in one swoop and head down the stairs. I'll be like the Flash, and Chloe will never know I was here.

I've made up my mind to do it, when I hear someone thundering up the stairs. I recognize his voice instantly.

"Chloe, just talk to me for a second."

This is truly painful. I duck my head so low, I'm practically eating my notebook. Don't they know I'm on the other side of this cubicle? Am I that invisible?

"Seriously, Seb? You can't just show up everywhere I am and demand that I speak to you."

"I need to know. I can't stop thinking about it."

"I already told you there's nothing going on between me and Matt," Chloe says. "And even if there was, it wouldn't matter. It doesn't . . . change anything."

Why aren't my legs moving? I have both hands on my pile, and my body is pulling me in two different directions. One is safely down the stairs, away from Chloe's private conversation. The other is glued to this wobbly wooden chair, inching closer to the particleboard to better hear the two of them, like I'm some dippy Chleb shipper.

"Please don't cry," she whispers.

Oh. My. God. Seb is crying? Seb emotes?

My first thought is that I have to tell Lily. Then comes my next unpleasant thought: *Lily will never listen to anything I have to say.* And Chloe will probably tell Lily herself, because that's what friends do. The third thought is, *Poor Seb*, but I quickly push that one away. Seb will get no pity from me. So he doesn't have Chloe. So what? Some of us have no one, and we make do.

"I don't understand what you want from me," Seb says.

"That's just it," Chloe replies.

"What?"

"You don't try to understand, Seb. You don't . . . care. About anyone or anything except yourself."

"I care about you."

Chloe snorts. I would have thought snorting was beneath her. Too undignified. "Funny. You didn't show it until we broke up."

"That's not true."

"I really have work to do here. . . ."

"Please." Seb's voice takes on a new, desperate quality that I've never heard from him before. "Tell me what I have to do, and I'll do it."

"Give me time."

"But—"

There's a rustling of papers and the sound of a book slamming shut. "You asked me what to do, and I told you," she says. "I can't talk about this again. Not now."

"Chloe . . ."

"Just stop!" Her voice pierces through the quiet in the library. "Listen to me. I need to be alone for a little while. Please."

She stands up. Any second now she's going to spot me on the other side of the cubicle. I turn my head, keeping low, wearing my curly brown hair over my face like a shield. I hear Chloe descend the stairs, but I don't dare sneak a peek in case she's still watching.

I'll wait thirty seconds. *One Mississippi, two Mississippi, three Miss—*

"Analee?"

I look up slowly, my eyes panning Seb's body, bottom to top, like a camera. Highlighter-colored sneakers, untucked shirttail, broad chest, lips sagging into a frown.

"Hi," I say in a tiny voice.

"What the hell are you doing here?"

I motion to my notebook. "Studying."

"Right," he scoffs. "Studying."

Like somehow I had a premonition that he and Chloe would have a conversation right across from me. He's so infuriating, assuming that my life revolves around his relationship drama.

"It's what libraries are for," I say. I try to sound sassy but instead come across as defensive.

Seb drags Chloe's former chair next to mine, then sinks into it. For a long time he doesn't speak. He drapes his arms across his widespread legs and stares down at the library's linoleum tile floor.

"So . . . ," he says slowly, eyes still trained on the floor, "what did you hear?"

"I . . . um." *Nothing. I heard nothing.* My brain is screaming at me to deny, but lying is not a good look on me. It tends to give me dime-size hives all over my body. Seb looks up at me, his expression pleading, and I start to pity him again.

"I heard everything," I admit.

*Damn me.*

He groans and rolls his head back against the chair. I get a full-on view of his Adam's apple as he swallows.

"I'm not going to tell anyone," I reassure him.

He stays silent.

"And I wasn't *trying* to listen either."

Still nothing. I rarely see Seb like this, lacking his usual swagger and shit-eating grin. Now he seems . . . unstable.

"I'm sorry," I say finally.

He gives me something halfway between a snort and a cough.

Then he looks at me directly. "I don't need you feeling sorry for me. No offense, but that makes me feel, like . . . one hundred times worse."

Any residual pity I felt for Seb drains out of my body. "What is *that* supposed to mean?"

"Nothing."

I cross my arms in front of me and glare at him.

"Oh, come on, Analee. Don't take it personally."

"Hmm. Let me try not to take this very personal thing personally."

"I'm not trying to hurt your feelings. I just . . . don't want your pity."

"*My* pity. Specifically." I feel like I'm being carried by a current of anger. I let it sweep me into its depths, give myself over to it completely. "You know what? Chloe was right. You don't care about anyone but yourself."

He copies my posture, from the crossed arms to the glare. "You don't know anything about me."

"We've been going to the same school since the sixth grade. I know enough. Sebastian Matias, the heartthrob of East Bay, hotshot soccer goal kicker guy. You date unattainable girls like Chloe because the excitement is in the chase. Even though there is a bounty of gorgeous girls at our school who would drop everything at the snap of your fingers, that doesn't affect you because it's too easy. You want to be adored by the masses, but you don't actually want to adore anyone back."

It's only when I get angry that my mouth can override my neuroses. I'm not thinking about what my body is doing, or how my voice sounds, or the prominent frontal vein that appears on my forehead whenever I get worked up.

Seb doesn't speak for a moment. His face is unreadable. In the silence I wonder if I've gone too far. I think about my body, voice, and vein, and start to shrink back into Analee.

"Huh," he says.

I stare down at my notebook and pick at the frayed corner. I feel shy again, but I ask anyway. "What?"

"I can't figure you out."

"Meaning?"

"Meaning . . . you're so quiet in class that I swear to God sometimes I forget you're right next to me. And then you'll have these random outbursts." He pauses. "Why don't you talk like this normally?"

I look up at him. He's not smiling but also not frowning. I don't know if it's better or worse when people point out that I'm shy. It's not like it's a secret, really. But it's something I don't particularly want to draw attention to, like a glob of spinach stuck between my teeth.

"I do talk like this normally," I say. "Just not . . . here."

"Here as in 'this planet'?"

I give him a face. "Here as in school. I mean, I used to talk to Lily, but . . ."

I don't know what Seb knows about the Incident. He and Colton are friends, so I'm sure he's been fed the same story Lily has. The one that paints me as the wicked witch of the East Coast.

"There are other people besides Lily," he says. He doesn't ask what happened between the two of us, which makes me wonder how much he knows.

"Other people suck." *Except Harris*, I think. Harris defies the category of "other people," since I've never met him in flesh and blood. He is non-corporeal, he is in the air, he is something that surrounds me like a force field against the population of East Bay.

"Maybe that's because you don't talk to them," Seb says.

"I don't have to. Listening is enough."

"Oookay. Whatever." He stands up to leave, and I feel an overwhelming sense of loneliness. It makes no sense. I was fine just a few minutes ago. "I'm gonna go find Chloe."

"Why?" I can't help but ask.

He stops. "Why not?"

I start to question whether I misheard the entire conversation between Seb and Chloe, or Seb is suffering from severe short-term memory loss.

"Because she told you she needs to be alone for a while."

"She didn't mean it. She does this all the time."

"Sounded like she meant it," I mutter.

"You don't know her the way I do."

"I know that," I say. "And I know that the stuff between you guys isn't any of my business."

"You're right," Seb agrees. "None of your business." He rocks back and forth on his heels, looking down the stairs and then back at me. "So, what are you saying I should do?"

I go blank. "You're asking for my advice?"

"Yeah. Are you gonna go all shy on me now?"

It's a strange position to be in. People like Seb, who generally have their shit together, don't often ask walking disasters like me for life advice.

"I don't know what you should do," I say.

"Yes, you do." Seb lifts his eyebrows, still standing there, waiting for my words of wisdom.

So I let it out. All of my thoughts on his situation, unfiltered. "I think you should do what she asked. Give her space. Chloe needs to know that you can respect her needs before she gives you another chance."

Seb sticks his hands into his pockets, paces back and forth. "And what about Matt?"

"What about him?"

"He's all over her."

I stare at him. "You realize Matt is a total asshole, right?"

"That's not true."

"I'm fairly certain it is."

"Matt's my friend, okay?"

I'm not sure what it is about Seb, but it takes only a few sentences from him to piss me off. It must be nice for him, never understanding how it feels to be one of Matt's targets, going through life being adored. Seb is so unaware of how good he has it that I want to shake some sense into him.

"If Matt were your friend," I say, "you wouldn't be worrying about him and Chloe. And if Chloe has half a brain, she won't go for someone like Matt."

"It's complicated," Seb says. He turns and starts heading down the stairs.

I don't think it is, but I don't fight him on it. I'm not sure if he'll listen to me or seek Chloe out again, but I don't ask any more. It isn't my business. Who cares about Chleb anyway? Even if they get back together, it's not like theirs is a love for the ages. They'll go off to college, eventually meet other impossibly gorgeous people, and be nothing more than former high school sweethearts who make small talk over cocktail weenies at East Bay's ten-year reunion.

Seb goes halfway down the stairs, stops, and looks up at me. "I'm a striker, by the way."

"What?" I ask.

"You called me a 'soccer goal kicker guy' during your rant. The position is a striker."

I stare at him, openmouthed like our lab frog. Out of everything I said to him, this is his takeaway?

"I don't really like soccer," I manage to say in my defense. It's the nicest way I can phrase my deep contempt for all organized sports, which began in fifth grade after a volleyball and a busted lip.

"And you've been to how many soccer games?" Seb asks.

Zero. Zero is the answer to his question. But I've never eaten live maggots either, and I'm pretty sure I would hate that, too.

I want to say this to Seb, but nothing comes out.

"That's what I thought," he says, in the most annoying and condescending of ways, and as usual my brain can't form a comeback until it's too late.

# CHAPTER TEN

**Me:** What are your thoughts on soccer?

**Harris:** ?

**Me:** As far as sports go.

**Harris:** i have little to no thoughts about soccer.

**Me:** Have you ever been to a soccer game?

**Harris:** nope. and zero desire to go to one. why do you ask?

**Me:** No reason.

**Harris:** doesn't that guy play soccer?

**Me:** Who?

**Harris:** your lap partner?

**Harris:** *lab

**Me:** Sebastian

**Me:** And yeah. He's a striker.

**Harris:** i don't know what that is.

**Me:** It's not important.

Avery bursts through my bedroom door, without knocking, of course. "Food's ready!" she sings.

I keep my eyes on the computer screen. "Okay."

"I'm hungry," she says, bounding over to me. Avery doesn't take normal footsteps. She jumps, like she's part human, part tiny annoying grasshopper.

"I'll be right down."

**Me:** Gotta go. Dinner.

**Harris:** quest later?

**Me:** Hells yes.

"What are you smiling at?" Avery's head pokes up from behind my shoulder, and I slam my laptop shut.

"I wasn't smiling," I say.

"Who were you talking to?"

"A friend."

We stare each other down, and Avery plants her hands on her hips in her sassy pose. She says the pathetic truth without officially saying it: *How could you be talking to a friend when you have no friends?*

"Do you have an online boyfriend?" she asks bluntly.

*"No."*

If Avery knew how desperately I want Harris to be my boyfriend, I would never hear the end of it. Besides, Harris is already more than a boyfriend to me, and Avery's too young to understand something beyond a label.

"I don't believe you," she says. "You're always chatting with someone. I'm not dumb, you know."

"Not dumb, just obnoxious," I reply.

"Does he go to your school? Is he friends with Colton?"

It jars me to hear her throw out the name so casually.

"No," I snap. "He has nothing to do with Colton."

She drops her hands, backs away from me like I've gone wild. "I was just *asking*."

"Well, stop asking," I say. "Just leave me alone."

Avery gives me a dramatic eye roll. I was never allowed to roll my eyes when I was her age. Dad always threatened a spanking. *No me faltes el respeto*, he'd say to me. I always had to be respectful, no matter how pissed off I felt. But Avery does what she wants, like Harlow.

"If you keep acting like this," she says, "you're never gonna get Lily back."

Does she do that on purpose, the whole ripping my heart out and stomping all over it? Or is she accidentally horrible? I can't figure that out yet. Avery's only in third grade, but she has all the makings of a mean girl. She coats her tiny fingernails with glitter, has a new best friend every week, and manages to make me feel terrible on a daily basis.

"Maybe I don't want Lily back," I say. I'm not sure whether I'm lying or telling the truth. Avery always got along better with Lily than with me because Lily had a higher tolerance for all her Avery-ness.

*Be nice, An*, Lily would say right now. She witnessed hundreds of spats between me and Avery and always guilt-tripped me. "You're so lucky to get a sister. I always wanted one."

"You can have her," I would say back to her, often in front of Avery. Lily didn't know how lucky she was to be an only child.

She had me, though. I tried to be the sister she never had, and before everything got so messed up, I thought I succeeded in the role. Then came Colton, then came the Incident at Gabrielle's party, and then it became clear that, unlike with actual sisters, the thread connecting me and Lily was easily severed. Unlike with actual sisters, now there was nothing left holding us together.

"Girls!" Dad's voice thunders up the stairs. "Get down here!"

Avery stops glaring at me long enough to answer, "Coming!" She sweeps past me, slamming her shoulder against my arm on her way out.



I was one of the last to officially find out when Lily and Colton started dating, even though I was supposedly still her best friend at that point.

Lily and I planned to meet in the library at four, at our usual cubicle, to study for our trig test the next day. And by "study" I mean that Lily was supposed to teach me all over again everything we'd learned in class, since the left side of my brain—or whatever side is in charge of math—is totally deficient.

Except Lily wasn't at our cubicle at four. And at four thirty she still hadn't shown up.

By five o'clock I started to panic. I tore through our school's hallways, peeked inside classrooms, and called her cell phone a total of twelve times. My mind started to run away from me. I envisioned Lily crossing the street and getting barreled by a semi. Or falling down the stairs and getting rushed to the hospital. Because in our entire lives Lily had never let me down. She was always where she said she was going to be.

Even though my mind was spitting out horrible worst-case scenarios, what I actually saw still managed to surprise me. I speed-walked to the parking lot to search for Lily's car. I dimly registered Colton and his girlfriend, Mia, making out, the two of them pressed up against his beat-up Chevy.

Something about it made me pause—the millions of tiny contradictions that my brain totaled up, like the blunt-cut bangs and cropped paint-splattered T-shirt. All of these things that led me to the slow realization that Colton was making out not with Mia but with Lily.

But how? When? The last I had heard, Colton had complimented Lily's art, and now they were full-on snogging in a parking lot? Lily and I both lacked in the sexual experience department, but you wouldn't have guessed it from the way she was expertly maneuvering around Colton's mouth. Why wouldn't she have told me about this? Was she really so desperate to remove me from her life altogether? And that's how it happened. All at once, everything I knew about my best friend was wrong.

That was when the thread that connected us started to fray.

# CHAPTER ELEVEN

WHEN SEB ENTERS THE SCIENCE ROOM TODAY, HE greets me by way of a chin nod. It's new to have someone in our school acknowledge me, even in such a tiny way. I look up from my notebook and give him one in return, which is something I've never done in my life and probably will never do again. It doesn't feel natural on me. It's too cool, too casual.

I go back to writing in my notebook, but I've lost my train of thought. On the corner of the page, I draw a tiny filigree pattern in the hopes that I look like I'm writing something very important and not just doodling to avoid talking.

I'm not sure if I should ask Seb what happened with Chloe or avoid conversation altogether. It's hard for me to figure out what topics are on the table when it comes to small talk. I could mention the dip in weather today, or ruminate as to Mr. Hubbard's whereabouts, but both of these options seem forced. I never had this problem with Lily. I don't have it with Harris, either. I usually launch into my latest tirade without thinking.

It doesn't matter anyway, because Seb immediately turns around in his chair to talk to Dalia. I use the word "talk" loosely, because their lips are flapping but no meaningful communication is taking place.

"What did you do to your hair?" he asks, reaching to yank on Dalia's high knotted ponytail.

"Don't mess it up, Seb!" she whines, swatting his hand away.

"You look like Rapunzel."

"They're extensions. Do you like?"

"They're aight."

"Shut up. You love them."

"Are you asking if you look good?"

"I don't have to ask," Dalia says, swishing her hair around and almost whipping her poor lab partner in the face.

Christ almighty, where is Mr. Hubbard? I've never been more eager to start class. Bring on the dead frogs.

I try to tune out their banter as my inked filigree takes over my notebook page, but their flirting is too incessant, like the drip of a leaky faucet.

"You going to Maddie's on Friday?" Seb asks, and I hear the grin in his voice. The grin of someone who knows he'll get what he wants.

"Maybe," Dalia says coyly. "You?"

"That depends."

"On what?"

"What do you think?" He leaves her with that, turning back to our table. Behind us Dalia laughs. The smugness radiates off the two of them.

"Not going to work," I murmur. It slips out unwittingly, before I can think, like breathing.

"Hmm?" Seb cocks his head at me. "Did you say something?"

"Sorry. Talking to myself."

"If you have something to say—"

"I don't."

I concentrate hard on the ink swirls on the page, imagining what it would be like to shrink so small that I could twirl around on the page's surface as if it were my own private dance floor. This notion fails to distract me from Seb, whose dark eyes stay watchful on my every move. I sigh and sweep my notebook aside.

"I said it's not going to work," I whisper.

"What's not going to work?"

"Your master plan to make Chloe jealous. Girls like Chloe aren't threatened by the Dalias of the world."

"Why not?"

"With Dalia . . ." I peek behind me to make sure Dalia isn't listening, but she's engaged in more babble with a boy at an opposite table. "I can smell her desperation. She's cute and flirty, but she screams 'rebound.' Chloe will know you're not serious."

"Well, then, what do I do?"

"First off, maybe don't use people?"

"I'm not using anyone," Seb says. "Did you ever stop to think that I might find Dalia very interesting?"

"Really?" I ask. "What do you like most about her? Personality-wise?"

"I like her . . ." He stops to think, a smile twitching on his lips. "Point taken."

"Why don't you find someone you actually like? Someone besides Chloe?"

Seb's smile fades. "Because there's no one besides Chloe."

Not this again. Yes, I may be more than a little bitter when it comes to Chloe since she has replaced me in the eyes of my former best friend and is superior to me in every way. Even so, it's insane for Seb to think Chloe is the only person who can make him happy.

I peer around the classroom, trying to find the anti-Dalia. Someone with substance. My eyes rest on Devon. Devon has a pixie cut and a perpetually angry expression on her face. She paints her nails a deep red color, almost black, and plays the cello. I don't know too much about her, but she's different, at least. I think East Bay would implode if Seb dated someone like Devon.

When I suggest her to Seb, he crinkles his eyebrows and asks, "Who's Devon?" which is so obnoxious, because she's been in our school since eighth grade.

"Two o'clock," I say.

Seb glances to his right. "Two o'clock is Briana."

"Briana is clearly three o'clock."

"No, *Lucas* is three o'clock."

"Oh my God." I grab the sides of his head and turn his face toward Devon. "That girl. Right there."

"*That's* Devon?"

"Yes."

"You're kidding me, right?"

"No. What's wrong with her?" My defenses flare on behalf of Devon, even though I barely know her and have never actually spoken to her. So she's not a cookie-cutter Barbie doll. Would it kill Seb to go after someone who's less than perfect?

"The girl scares the shit out of me, Analee," he says in a low voice, dipping his head to avoid Devon's gaze.

"I'm sure once you get to know her—"

69

"She has a voodoo doll in her locker."

I bite back a laugh. "She does not."

"It's decapitated."

"What are you even talking about?"

"I've seen it. This is a girl who decided that stabbing a doll with safety pins wasn't violent enough. This is who you've chosen for me."

"I'm not choosing anyone for you," I say. "This isn't an arranged marriage. I'm only suggesting that you talk to her."

"It was made of yarn," Seb goes on. "With buttons for eyes."

"Fine. Forget about Devon."

If I had the ability to make a voodoo doll, I would make one of Colton. I'd make his poser glasses out of wire and use black marker to draw the tattoo on his triceps. I wouldn't physically hurt him—not badly, at least. I'd just give him pubic lice or an incurable penis rash.

I glance over at Lily, who's talking animatedly with her lab group. We make eye contact while she's midsentence, and she breaks it so quickly that I could have very well imagined it. What does she talk about with those people? With Chloe? I wonder if Lily opens up to them the way she used to with me. I was the only person she confided in when her parents separated last year. I was the only one who knew about her embarrassing crush on Conan O'Brien. When she wet her pants onstage in our first-grade Christmas pageant, I was the one who comforted her. I have all of Lily's past and none of her present.

As I'm thinking about the logistics of cursing someone, and about whether a Ken doll and a well-placed safety pin would do the trick, a baby-faced man wearing a flannel shirt and tight khakis walks into the room.

"Hi, guys. I'm Will," the guy says. "Mr. Hubbard is out sick, so I'm subbing today."

"Oh no," Dalia says, pouting her lips. "Is he okay?"

As if she cares. I know for a fact that she bet on Hubbard dying in May.

"I'm sure he'll be fine," Will says. He smiles at Dalia. "What's your name?"

"Dalia. Like the flower, but without the *h*."

"Wow. That's a really pretty name."

"You think? I always hated it."

"You're crazy."

Blech. Is Will seriously reenacting his jailbait fantasies in front of our entire class?

"Anyway," he says. "I guess we should get started."

I worry he'll be one of those cool subs, the type to make us sit in a circle and have "real talk." But then he gets up to wheel a dusty TV in front of us, and my heart swells with hope.

"You're going to watch a video today," he says. "Hubbard wants everyone to take notes."

Some people groan, but I am positively elated. There is nothing better than watching a video in class. The lack of awkward eye contact, the dim lighting, the pressure to speak completely dissolved. Will shuts off the lights, and I can make out only Seb's silhouette by the muted sunshine pouring through the classroom window.

"I thought of someone else," Seb whispers into my ear, his breath warming my skin.

"Who? Selena?"

He shakes his head. "Selena won't work."

"Why not?"

"I'm not her type."

Will starts the DVD, and the TV screen blinks to life. A narrator who sounds half-asleep drones on about the beauty of life while images of insects and flowers and blood cells flicker on the screen.

"You might be," I whisper to Seb. "Why not give her a chance?"

"Trust me on this one."

"But—"

"She likes girls, Analee. And she's been dating Sasha Finley for the past six months."

"Oh," I say. So. Devon and Selena are out. There are alternatives, though. Someone outside of East Bay, maybe a cool alternative girl from the nearby arts school.

"Anyway," Seb continues. "I have someone else in mind. Someone Chloe would never expect."

I keep my eyes on the TV. "Who?"

An amoeba is on-screen now, or at least I think it's an amoeba. I'm only half-listening to the narrator as the blob on TV oozes and morphs into new shapes.

"You."

Seb says this not in a whisper but at full volume.

It's like I could be on one of those prank shows. I imagine the lights blazing on, the class surrounding me, pointing at me, Matt McKinley with his dumb, openmouthed horse laugh. For a few seconds I can't respond. I'm worried Seb is making a joke that I don't understand.

"What are you talking about?" I say through my teeth.

"We should fake date," Seb says. "It's perfect. You're not the type I'd usually go for, and Chloe knows that. Plus, you'd be in on it the whole time."

I shake my head over and over again as he speaks.

"Tell me why not," he says.

Oh, that I could. The reasons why not are innumerable.

"I have a boyfriend," I blurt out. It's all I can think to say. The truth would be too much to explain, not to mention mortifying. I can't be Seb's pretend girlfriend, because everyone at school would suddenly know who I am. Every pair of eyes would watch and dissect my every move.

Plus, "you're not the type I'd usually go for" is the worst sales pitch I've ever heard, because Chloe is the type Seb goes for, and she is beautiful and smart and confident, which means I am none of those things.

"You have a boyfriend?" Seb repeats, and if I weren't already offended, I would be now at his obvious surprise.

"Kind of," I say. "I mean, we're unlabeled at the moment, but . . ."

"So who is this guy? Does he go to our school?"

"No." I rub my fingers over my notebook protectively, like Seb's words might degrade all its contents.

"How did you meet?"

My cheeks grow warm. I'm not good at thinking on my feet, and every second that ticks by will make me sound more and more full of shit.

"He's a friend," I finally say.

"So not an official boyfriend."

"Well, no. I guess not officially."

"Then? This is perfect. You tell him you're dating me, and he'll suddenly be desperate to put a label on things."

The problem is that Seb assumes all guys are like him. I doubt Harris would profess his love to me if he thought Seb and I were dating. He might shrink away, give me my space, recede into the depths of the Internet. Our relationship, whatever type of relationship it is, would disappear like it had never existed in the first place.

"Come on, Analee," Seb says. "I'll do whatever you want. Seriously. Name it."

I shake my head again. "I'm sorry."

I genuinely am. I wish I could be the type of girl who didn't make a big deal out of every single thing. Better yet, the type of girl someone would want to actually date, not pretend date.

"I could help you get Lily back," he says suddenly, and I tighten my grip on my notebook.

"I'm around her all the time, remember? If you're dating me, I could put in a good word for you. You guys could become friends again."

There's an involuntary pull in my chest when he mentions Lily. What would she think about her former best friend dating the most coveted boy in school? It might convince her to give me another chance. It could remind her that I'm worth something, something that Seb can see and that she once did too.

I glance at her now, to find her watching us. Lily hasn't looked at me in four months, but because I'm talking to Seb, she's looking at me now. Even after months without speaking, I know Lily at her core. She's thinking there is no world in which the heartthrob and the social outcast make a go of it. She's telling herself that she's imagining things.

If I were a braver person, I would plant a giant kiss on Seb right now. I would show Lily that everything she thinks she knows is wrong. And Chloe, and Matt, and Dalia, they would all collectively lose their shit. God, it would be satisfying.

I'm not a brave person, though, so instead I scoot approximately one inch closer to Seb.

"I'll think about it," I whisper. My voice is so soft that I can barely hear myself.

He whips around to face me full-on. "You will?"

"I mean, it's an insane idea and I don't think anyone would actually believe it."

Seb gives me a conspiratorial smile, one altogether different from his cheeky one. "They'll believe what we want them to believe."

I feel myself dangerously close to swooning. Not because he's kinda dreamy—although, to be fair, Seb is objectively the dreamy type, in a stereotypically muscular, boyish, boring way. It's the confidence with which he says the words. Like he'll will them into existence simply because he wants to. I wish I knew what it felt like to have that confidence as my default, instead of fear.

# CHAPTER TWELVE

## Analee's Top 5 Reasons to Fake Date Seb Matias

1. Make Harris jealous.
2. Win Lily back.
3. Learn to be a socially competent person.
4. Help him with Chloe.
5. I wouldn't be alone.

## Analee's Top 5 Reasons NOT to Fake Date Seb Matias

1. It might push Harris away.
2. Lily won't care what I do.
3. Social competence is overrated.
4. Seb and Chloe might be better off without each other.
5. I wouldn't be alone.

HARLOW IS IN THE KITCHEN WHEN I GET HOME, speaking animatedly to her laptop while gesticulating with a banana. She stops midphrase when she sees me walk in.

"Analee, hi!" She taps the keyboard to stop recording and jumps to her feet with impressive energy.

"Hi," I say. "Sorry to interrupt your—"

"It's a bride-to-be nutrition series," Harlow says.

Of course it is. Everything Harlow does becomes part of her brand. Her food, her exercise, her upcoming marriage to my father.

"So, how was your day?" she asks, still holding the banana.

"Fine." I don't elaborate. I never do. We both stare at each other. The banana points at me, inappropriately erect. I wish these awkward silences didn't exist between me and Harlow, but it's become a daily ritual. She asks, I answer, and in the deafening silence I make a beeline to my room so that I can spend time with Harris.

But when I start to exit the kitchen, Harlow says, "Wait."

I turn, and she's giving me her giant Harlow eyes. I wonder how many men she's hooked with those eyes, how many times her parents gave their little girl whatever she wanted when she batted those long lashes.

Harlow motions toward the blender. "Do you mind helping me test-drive this recipe?"

Oh, how I *really* don't want to.

"I should probably start my homework," I say, inching away from her. "What about Avery?"

"She's at Olivia's. I swear, the girl has a new best friend every week." She shakes her head in exasperation, but I see the glint of pride in her eyes. Harlow loves the fact that Avery is popular. I wonder what she would have done if Avery had turned out more like me.

Inwardly, for the first time, I bemoan Avery's absence. She's the usual guinea pig for Harlow's kitchen and yoga experiments. I don't tell Harlow that I have a Hershey's bar in the front pocket of my book bag, and that I'm looking forward to eating it all in one sitting as soon as I get to my room.

But before I can make my escape, my stupid stomach gives me away. It doesn't just growl like a normal stomach would. It roars to life. Traitor. Harlow raises her eyebrows at the sound.

"I guess I could use a snack," I admit lamely.

"Great!" She rushes to the freezer and pulls out packs of chopped mango and pineapple, and unidentified purple goop.

"What are you making?" I ask.

"Tropical acai bowl." She thrusts her iPhone into my hand. "Do you mind filming? Hold the camera at an angle, like this—" Harlow positions my hand so that it's hovering over the counter.

She quickly throws all of the ingredients into the blender, adds a splash of almond milk, and then mixes it all together. Periodically she stops to press the ingredients closer to the blades with a spoon. My arm begins to ache from holding the phone so high. After a minute she shuts off the blender and spoons the dark purple mixture into a large bowl. It looks . . . not totally off-putting. Kind of like frozen yogurt.

"Make sure you get a clear view of the toppings," she instructs. I shake out my arm and reposition the camera. Carefully Harlow sprinkles granola, sliced banana, and coconut shavings onto the bowl. It is truly a work of art the way she arranges the toppings into neat, equal thirds. I don't understand people who put so much care into what their food looks like. I mean, Harlow's creation looks beautiful, but it all becomes slop once it's inside you.

"There," Harlow says. She dusts off her hands as if she's worked in the fields all day, then steps back to admire her culinary masterpiece. "Isn't it pretty? And packed with nutrients, too."

"Can I stop filming?" I ask.

"Did you get a shot of the finished bowl? Here, let me." Harlow takes the phone and sweeps it over the bowl in a truly dramatic overhead shot. Ladies and gentlemen, the Martin Scorsese of food vloggers.

The food is beginning to melt by the time she stops filming and brings it over to the kitchen table. She hands me a spoon, then takes one for herself.

"Okay if we share?" she asks.

I hesitate. I have this thing about sharing food. A spoon soaked with someone else's saliva? Mixing with the food I'm about to eat? Shudder. If Dad were here, he'd bug his eyes out at me in his silent warning.

*Oye. No seas extraña.* Which loosely translates to "Don't be a weirdo."

I am constantly trying to be normal for his sake. For everyone's sake. It gets to be exhausting sometimes.

"Sure," I say to Harlow. "We'll split it."

I stick to my side of the bowl to avoid Harlow's spit, dip my spoon into the purple slush, and take a bite. I'm a little disappointed to find that the food tastes as good as it looks. Icy and refreshing with an added crunch from the toppings. My body practically sings, grateful to have a break from the usual garbage I feed it.

"How is it?" Harlow asks.

"Delicious," I answer truthfully.

She grins. "Really?"

"Yes." I'm shoveling the food into my mouth now. I've forgotten my issues with sharing things. I don't care anymore; I just want to inhale this entire bowl.

"So how's school?" Harlow asks, scooping up some coconut shavings with her spoon.

"Fine, I guess."

"How's Lily?"

I give a halfhearted shrug. Harlow doesn't know that my friendship with Lily is on life support. "Also fine."

"Haven't seen her in a while."

Lily would love this bowl. She kept her admiration for Harlow under wraps around me, but I saw her name among the many on Harlow's list of YouTube subscribers.

"She's been busy," I say.

"Still with that boyfriend?"

I nod, tensing.

"Boyfriends are tough," Harlow says. "It's easy to forget about the rest of the world, you know? You're so caught up in the infatuation, the intensity of first love . . ."

"I wouldn't know," I say dully.

"Oh, come on. I'm sure there are plenty of boys at your school interested in a pretty girl like you."

I stare back at her. Either she's blind or all that yoga has bent her brain out of shape. Or she's just a liar.

"No one at school is interested in me," I say. "And I'm not interested in them, either. They're Neanderthals."

"There must be someone—"

"Nope."

Harlow twists her lip, falling silent. I wish we could have a normal conversation, but it's not possible. There's too much she doesn't know about me, stuff that wouldn't fit into her picture-perfect life. How could I possibly explain that the only boy I'm interested in is one I've never met? How could I tell her that Colton has effectively ended my friendship with Lily forever? That I'm incapable of being a normal girl with normal friends and a normal boyfriend?

Unless.

Unless I did become a normal girl with normal friends and a normal boyfriend. Then Dad would stop looking at me like he doesn't know where I went wrong. Harlow would think I was worthy of being her stepdaughter. Avery would stop making me feel three inches tall. All I have to do is say yes to Seb, and everything could change for me.

Harlow clears her throat. "Know of any good Cuban recipes?"

"Not really," I say. "Why?"

"I may take a break from eating raw," Harlow says. "Sometimes I think your dad misses traditional Cuban cooking, you know? Like, things that he ate growing up, and things that your . . . your mom might have cooked."

My stomach drops a few inches at the mention of Mom. I take another bite of purple goop, barely tasting it this time.

"I was thinking Cuban cuisine with a healthy spin," Harlow goes on.

Good God, I should have known. This foray into Cuban culture isn't for my dad. This is for Harlow.

"It tastes pretty good as is," I say lightly. Dad can't cook to save his life, but we used to order from the local Cuban restaurant, La Vibora. Their Cuban bread is Dad's favorite, and one of its primary ingredients is lard. What would Harlow use instead? Applesauce? Cold-pressed extra virgin olive oil?

"Of course it's delicious, but I'm trying to think of how to make it more accessible to the health conscious," Harlow says.

"But then . . . aren't you just turning it into something else?"

"No," she says slowly. "I don't think so."

If I could be fully myself around Harlow, I would tell her straight-up, *Harlow, for the love of God. Please leave the Cuban food alone.*

"What were you thinking of making?" I ask.

"The one your dad always orders, with the shredded beef. Rope of something?"

"Ropa vieja."

"Right! That's it. But I was thinking, instead of using beef, maybe we could try it with portobello mushrooms."

I drop my spoon into the now empty bowl with a clatter. Ropa vieja is supposed to be a beef stew. What Harlow wants to do is not ropa vieja. It's a travesty. It's sliced mushrooms swimming in broth.

"Sounds interesting," I manage. I bring the bowl over to the sink and wash it out, feeling oddly indignant. Harlow can't just go around Harlow-ifying everything in my life to fit her image. My mind flutters back to Mom and what she would think of Harlow's mushroom stew. Or how she would feel about Harlow's influence on my dad ever since he first laid eyes on her at the gym. The way she turned him into a guy who goes hiking and drinks artisanal beer and wears Ray-Bans. When I see old pictures of Dad, I can barely recognize the man wearing a T-shirt and ripped jeans.

Harlow is still sitting at the table. She whips out her laptop and gets to work, barely noticing when I retreat to my room.

# CHAPTER THIRTEEN

### Analee's Rules for Phone Calls

1. Make sure you're in a room where
no one else can hear you.
2. Put the TV on softly in the background
to minimize awkward silences.
3. Write a script if you have to leave a voice mail.
4. Plan the topics you need to discuss.
5. Have an excuse ready in case you need to hang up.

ON SATURDAY OUR HOUSE IS A DEAD ZONE. DAD is swimming laps outside in the pool, Harlow is sealed up in her meditation room, and Avery is off at another random friend's house. It's so not fair that an eight-year-old has a more active social life than I do.

**Me:** Have you ever been in love?

**Harris:** yes. nikki warner. first grade.

**Me:** Harris . . .

**Harris:** analee . . .

**Me:** I want to know!

**Harris:** why?

**Me:** I just do

**Harris:** ok

**Harris:** i thought i was in love, once

Ow. Why does this admission make my heart hurt? I'm not sure why I asked Harris the question, or what answer would have made me happy. Wait, that's a lie. I know what would have made me happy.

Alternate dream scenario:

**Me:** Have you ever been in love?

**Harris:** yes. i'm in love right now. with you.

Even a flat-out no would have been preferable to his actual answer. It kills me to think of Harris with another girl. Even if it was in the past. Even if it wasn't true love and he only thought it was real in the moment. The past is important. It matters.

It was stupid of me to ask. Harris will never love me the way I love him. I'm just a random girl he talks to over the computer. His happiness doesn't revolve around our conversations like mine does. You can't have real love before you meet someone. And I don't want Harris to meet this version of me. I need to be better for him.

**Me:** When? Who was she?

**Harris:** a couple of years ago. her name was isabel

**Harris:** looking back, though, we had nothing in common

**Harris:** i couldn't talk to her the way i talk to you, for example

**Harris:** what about you? have you been in love?

*Only with you.* How sad is it that there's only one boy I've ever loved and I wouldn't recognize him if I passed him on the street?

But if I lie and tell him I've never been in love, what will he think? That I'm pathetic? That I haven't loved anyone because no one has found *me* worth loving?

**Me:** It's complicated.

**Harris:** cop-out answer

**Me:** My question, my rules.

"Analee!" Harlow calls from downstairs. "You have a phone call!"

The panic starts immediately. It's a Pavlovian response to the idea of talking on the phone. My heart twitches against my chest, my palms moisten. I don't do phone calls. Haven't in years. I own a cell, but it's only for emergencies, and half the time it's out of battery.

Who could be calling me? And why? Is it Lily? No, it can't be Lily. Lily knows how much I hate talking on the phone. It's the feeling of being trapped inside a conversation, with no escape and no distractions. No way to tell what the other person is thinking or feeling. Besides, if Lily wanted to get in touch with me, she would do it in person.

"Analee! Did you hear me?" Harlow calls again. I briefly imagine myself climbing out of my bedroom window and making a break for it. A two-story fall wouldn't kill me, would it? What's the worst that could happen? A broken limb? An excuse to miss some school?

I jerk out of my seat and tear down the stairs, grab the phone from Harlow, and cover the mouthpiece.

"Who is it?" I ask her in a panicky whisper.

"Sebastian, I think he said?" She gives me a knowing smile, completely blind to my internal despair. "He sounds cute. Nice deep voice."

I press the phone against my forehead and close my eyes. Sebastian

Matias is calling me. Most girls in East Bay could only dream of such a miracle, but it makes me sick to my stomach.

"Analee? What's wrong?" Harlow asks.

Again, it's too much to explain to her.

"I don't want to talk to him," I say in a low voice.

"Why not? Is there something I should know about this boy?"

"No, it's not him. It's just . . ."

Harlow grabs for the phone. "Should I tell him you're sick?"

"No!" I twist the phone out of her reach. "He'll know I'm faking. It's fine."

Harlow looks thoroughly confused, because why wouldn't she? It confuses me too, the way I agonize over every typical teenage ritual. My brain knows that none of this is a big deal, but it can't convince my body of this fact.

I go back upstairs and lock myself in my room. To minimize the silence humming in my ears, I turn on the TV for background noise. I do a couple of quick breaths the way Harlow does before she talks to my grandparents.

"Hello?" I say into the phone. My voice, thank God, comes out steadily.

"Hey, Analee. It's me."

"Seb?" I know it's Seb, obviously, but I still feel strange talking to him outside of our stuffy bio lab.

"Yeah."

"Um." I pace around my room, picking up objects I've touched a thousand times, rubbing the plastic nose of my stuffed Hello Kitty. "What's up?"

"I wanted to know if you'd thought about it."

I haven't been able to stop thinking about it.

"Yes," I say.

"And?"

"And . . ." I look at my computer screen, where Harris is typing up a response. If I don't do this with Seb, am I denying myself a chance at something real? Am I settling for an undefined cyber relationship when Harris and I could be more?

"I'll do it," I say. I spit the words out quickly before I lose my courage. Already I wish I could grab them and stuff them back into my mouth.

"I knew you'd come around." There's that confidence again. His voice *is* deep, like Harlow mentioned. I never realized it, but there's nothing else to focus on right now.

"If we do this," I say, "I would need your help with something."

"Name it."

"I have to give a toast. At my dad's wedding."

"And?"

"And I need help, like . . . talking in front of people."

*Being normal* is what I mean to say.

"What makes you think I could help with that?" he asks.

"Because," I reply. "You're Seb Matias. You have the high school paparazzi monitoring your every move and giant crowds of people watching you play soccer each week. Clearly people don't faze you."

He laughs over the phone. It's a full-bodied, genuine laugh, and it makes me feel like I've earned something.

"All right," he says. "I'll do it. Are you busy tomorrow?"

"Tomorrow?" I echo.

"Yeah," he says. "We need to start planning our operation."

"Oh, yeah. Right," I say. I didn't expect Seb to want to get started so quickly. He's never this motivated in bio.

"So?" he asks. "You're free?"

"As a bird."

What a stupid thing to say. It's not even the truth. Harris and I were supposed to embark on a new quest tomorrow, in which Kiri and Xolkar step through the forest portal and stop the Night Cavalry from invading the land.

Then something occurs to me. "How did you get this number?"

"School directory," Seb replies. "I thought about asking Lily for your cell, but then I figured that would look suspicious. If we're quote-unquote dating, I should already have your number."

"She probably deleted it anyway," I say without thinking.

Seb is quiet for a beat. I flop onto my bed, stretching my legs and flexing my feet back and forth, back and forth. I start thinking of excuses to hang up. Maybe Harlow needs my help with dinner. Maybe I have homework to do. Or does that make me seem too Mary Sue?

"Can I ask you something?" Seb says finally, and my wandering mind returns to earth.

"Okay."

"What happened between you and Lily?"

"Didn't she tell you?" I ask. I figured that everyone in her new squad would know by now.

"She doesn't really talk about you. Like, ever."

"Oh." It's all I can think to say. I'm not sure what the worse scenario is, Lily bad-mouthing me all over school or dropping me without a second thought. I had assumed the former, but hearing

Seb say it's the latter brings a new, fresh shot of hurt. I'm not worth talking about at all. An eleven-year friendship dissolved without comment.

"People drift apart," I find myself saying. "That's all."

"Yeah, but you two weren't just people. You were like conjoined twins."

"Well, that was before." Before Colton, I mean, but I don't say his name.

Thankfully, Seb doesn't press me on this. "Okay. So, what time should I come over tomorrow?"

"Here?" I say. "You're coming here?"

"Your mom invited me."

"Not my mom," I say quickly. "Dad's girlfriend." I will not call her his fiancée. This wedding isn't happening.

"Okay, whoever she was. She said I should come by and that any friend of Analee's is a friend of hers."

Freaking Harlow.

"I don't know—"

"Analee," he says. "I'm your boyfriend now. It's probably time I meet the family."

Even though it's all pretend, my body overheats at the bizarre turn of events. I have a boyfriend now. At least for a little while, everyone—my family, my former friend—will see me as normal.

"Fine," I say. "Can you come by around noon?"

"I'll be there."

We exchange cell numbers, and I add a tiny heart emoji next to his contact name. If people are going to believe this, I have to sell it.

By the time I hang up the phone, I'm too exhausted to move

from the bed. My heart is still beating rapidly, equal parts panic and excitement. I clutch Hello Kitty against me, thinking that tomorrow is the first step to being normal. In a matter of days I'll go from Analee, the timid, friendless loser, to Analee, girlfriend of Sebastian Matias, the envy of the masses.

# CHAPTER FOURTEEN

I CAN'T DO THIS. IN THE LIGHT OF DAY, IT'S PLAINLY obvious that this is a disaster waiting to happen. A zit has sprung forth from the side of my nostril, as big as a tumor. Seb is going to find me repulsive. I have nothing to wear for our pseudo-date because I haven't bought new clothes since middle school. After spending a full hour in front of my closet (during which Harris constantly messages me asking about our canceled quest), I settle on my everyday jeans that pinch my love handles and a cleanish T-shirt hanging out of my drawer. So sexy. My hair is big, curly, and unmanageable.

What was I thinking with the *Analee, envy of the masses* crap? Being the envy of the masses means being their target, and I have a slew of things wrong with me that they can pick apart. Today I am going to explain to Seb that this will never work.

The benefit of my online relationship with Harris is that I don't have to agonize over my wardrobe choices. It helps that my Kiri avatar has the body of a goddess, slender and long like Harlow's.

**Harris:** yo

**Harris:** where you at?

**Harris:** analee

**Harris:** aaaaaannnnnnaaaalllllllllleeeeeeee

For the first time in maybe forever, I don't respond to him. I want to, but Seb will be here in fifteen minutes and I have to be ready. Besides, I'm still not sure what I should tell Harris.

I go downstairs, and Dad and Harlow are cuddled on one side of the couch. I was hoping they would be elsewhere by the time Seb got here, but it looks like they're nesting.

"Any big plans today?" I ask them.

"For once, no," Harlow says, closing her eyes contentedly and leaning her head on Dad's shoulder.

"So . . . you're going to be here for a while?"

Dad turns around to look at me. "Why?"

"Just wondering. I have a friend coming over."

"*Quien?*" he asks. "Lily?"

"No, not Lily," I say. Hasn't he noticed that Lily hasn't been over for months? I bite the inside of my cheek. Here we go. The big reveal. "My, uh. My boyfriend."

Harlow's eyes blink open. Dad's eyes do that thing where they grow to double their usual size. We're all silent for a few seconds, and it's enough time to make me want to take it back and confess that it's a lie. It's so obviously a lie, isn't it?

Harlow speaks first. "Wow, Analee! That's . . . that's great!"

I nod. I hope my face is smiling right now.

Dad's isn't. He runs his hand over his beard stubble as his eyes shrink back to normal size.

"Aren't you a little young for a boyfriend?" he asks.

"I'm sixteen."

"I had my first boyfriend when I was fourteen," Harlow tells him.

"That's you," he replies. "Analee is . . . different."

Harlow and I both cross our arms and glare at him, equally offended for opposite reasons.

"What do you mean 'different'?" I ask.

"I didn't mean it in a bad way," Dad says. "I mean . . . *¿Quién es este tipo?* What do you know about this guy?"

"His name is Sebastian Matias. I've known him since the sixth grade."

Dad shakes his head and gets up, leaving a big empty space next to Harlow. "I don't like this, Analee. Going out with some strange boy without permission? You should know better."

"Know better than what?" I ask. "You're acting like I just told you I'm a heroin addict or something."

"Raf, having a boyfriend at Analee's age is completely appropriate," Harlow says. "You should be happy that she's socializing. It's a great sign."

"Happy I'm socializing?" I repeat. "Is this something you guys have been discussing?"

"Of course not," Dad snaps.

"Not extensively," says Harlow.

I can't even formulate a response. It's one thing to suspect that your father assumes you're a loser. It's another to find that he's been discussing it with his girlfriend behind your back.

"We just worry about you sometimes," Harlow says. "All that time you spend alone on your computer . . ."

"I'm not alone," I snap. I'm infuriated by the "we" in her statement. Harlow hasn't known me well enough or long enough to worry about my well-being.

"So you and . . . Sebastian," Dad says. "How long have you two been dating without permission?"

"We just started," I say. "And it's really not that serious, Dad."

"Is that supposed to make me feel better? The idea of my daughter casually dating?"

And right at that moment the doorbell rings. Seb has arrived, ready to witness my fucked up family situation.

"Crap. That's him," I say.

Harlow and Dad are both off the couch now, accompanying me to the front door.

"I don't like this," Dad mutters behind me.

"Go easy on her, Raf," Harlow says in her yogi voice. He mutters something unintelligible.

I open the door, and Sebastian Matias is standing on our doorstep. It's jarring, like someone Photoshopped him in there, blocking my usual view of our driveway and the yellow house across the street.

"Hey, sweetheart," he says. His sneakers today are a bright lime green. I'm convinced he has a collection at home, shoes in every ugly color of the rainbow.

With my eyes I try to send him a stern message to never call me "sweetheart" again, but he shrugs it off.

"Hello," I say. I pull the door open wider and motion for him to come in. We don't hug or give each other a peck on the cheek, like a real couple would.

We will never pull this off.

"Hi, Sebastian. So happy to meet you!" Harlow says, pulling him in for a hug. Harlow, unlike me, is a hugger. She is completely at ease in situations like this.

"Nice to meet you too," Seb says. He notices my dad hovering behind her and straightens up. Seb is taller than Dad by a few inches, but Dad is a lot scarier than Seb is. They shake hands roughly.

"Sir," Seb says with a nod.

Dad nods in return.

I stand there, unable to move, unsure of what the rules are. Can Seb and I hang out in my room? Do we stay down here, with Dad and Harlow awkwardly lurking around?

"Analee, why don't you take Seb upstairs?" Harlow says, as if reading my mind. "We'll be down here if you need anything."

"Um, okay," I say. I start for the stairs, wondering whether I should take Seb by the hand, then deciding against it when he follows me.

"*No cierres la puerta,*" Dad tells me sternly, reminding me to leave the door open.

Before I can answer him, Seb jumps into the conversation.

"*Claro que no,*" he replies in beautifully pronounced Spanish. I stop halfway up the stairs. It never occurred to me that Seb would speak Spanish too. Judging from the expression on Dad's face, he's equally surprised.

"Dominican on my dad's side, Puerto Rican on my mom's," Seb says to us before we can ask.

"We'll keep the door open," I reassure Dad.

He nods, then stands there until Harlow pulls him back over to the couch.

As soon as Seb and I enter my room, I realize I forgot to hide

Hello Kitty under the bed. Seb looks around my room, stopping to examine a picture of me and Lily from our weekend in Key West years ago. Then he heads straight for Hello Kitty, picks her up, and tosses her into the air.

"Be careful with her!" I say before I can stop myself.

His lips twitch. "Her?"

"It," I correct myself quickly.

Seb bites his lip midgrin. He sets Hello Kitty back against my pillows, then sits on the corner of my bed. I take a seat at my desk.

"You know," he says, "you'll probably have to come within three feet of me if this relationship is going to work."

"I just . . . I'm having second thoughts about this whole thing."

"You're making it too big a deal."

"It *will* be a big deal," I say. "Do you realize that our school hangs on your every move?"

"So?"

"So they're all going to wonder what you're doing with me. Matt McKinley will have a field day."

"Matt will be too busy with his raging boner for Chloe," Seb says.

A laugh escapes from me, even though picturing Matt with a boner triggers my vomit reflex. Seb smiles a little.

"Sit down," he says. He rubs the space beside him on my comforter.

I shake my head. "I prefer to work from here."

He rolls his eyes, kicks off his sneakers. Seb has been in my room for one minute and already feels more comfortable in it than I do. He goes through life the same way, kicking off his metaphorical shoes and making himself at home no matter where he is.

I pick up my trusty notebook and flip to a new page. "So what's the plan? What's our backstory? We have to get our lies straight if we want to pull this off."

"Hmm." Seb falls back onto my bed. His feet still touch the floor. "You've been in love with me since the moment you laid eyes on me?"

"Try again."

"You came over to my house one day, wearing only a trench coat."

"God, Seb! Be serious."

"Just trying to make it interesting." He shrugs. "Okay. How about . . . we were working on our science project after school. Just the two of us."

"Go on."

"Both of us leaned over to read our report, and our lips were so close, they were practically touching. Then . . ."

I scribble this in my notebook. I can't look at him right now. My face is on fire. "Then what?" I ask without lifting my gaze.

"You pounced."

I look up.

"*I* am not the one who pounced," I say, laughing.

"Fine. I pounced."

"You kissed me," I clarify. I write this in my notebook, *Seb kissed me*, underlining his name three times for emphasis.

"I did," Seb says. "And you liked it."

It is a furnace in here. It's at least ninety degrees right now.

I clear my throat. "When did this happen?"

"Last week?"

"When you were groveling for Chloe's affection in the library? I don't think so."

"Couple of days ago, then."

I jot this down, then close my notebook. "What happens tomor-row?"

"What do you mean?" he asks.

"I mean . . . do you walk me to class? Do we eat lunch together?"

He sits back up. "Maybe. Yeah, probably."

"Well, which one?"

He laughs to himself, some joke I'm not understanding.

"What's so funny?" I ask.

"Nothing." He fixes his face into a neutral expression. "Will you come sit on the damn bed? I'm cootie-free, I promise."

"No."

"Analee. You're going to have to pull the stick out of your ass at some point."

"Ugh, fine." I don't know why I'm being childish. I get up and sit on the opposite side of the bed.

"Hold my hand," he says.

"What? No."

"If you're scared to touch me, no one's going to take this seriously."

It's not that I'm scared of touching him. It's that I don't let anyone touch me.

He does have a point, though, so I let my hand flop onto the bed, palm-up. I feel him looking at me, but I stare at my hand, zeroing in on the lifeline that runs down to my wrist. My entire body, down to that lifeline, feels shaky. I see his hand slide across the comforter, and then his palm is pressing against mine, soft and warm. When he intertwines his fingers with my own, I feel an embarrassing urge to cry. It's been a long time since I held hands with someone, and it feels so nice, even if it's pretend.

"You're freezing," he says. He uses his other hand to rub the back of mine. I don't know how my body is cold when my organs currently feel like hot coals. We sit on my bed, quietly, only the sound of friction from his hand rubbing mine.

"About tomorrow . . . ," Seb says. "People will say what they want to say. Your job is to relax."

"I'm relaxed," I insist.

"You won't even look at me."

So, I do. I worry he's going to laugh at me again, but his face is serious. No cheeky smile in sight.

"What's the name of that guy you like? Your almost-boyfriend?" he asks.

Seb is stroking the inside of my wrist now, and it's causing my memory to lapse. What is he talking about? I can no longer understand the English language. *Focus, focus, focus, Analee. Stop being stupid.*

"Harris," I say, too suddenly.

"Do you love him?"

"Yes." I answer without hesitation, because it's true. No matter how tingly Seb is making me right now, no matter how good he is with his hands, Harris gets me like no one else.

"Tomorrow you pretend I'm Harris. Okay?"

"Okay." And it strikes me that one day maybe Harris will be the one holding my hand and stroking my wrist, and I won't have to pretend that what I'm feeling is real.

# CHAPTER FIFTEEN

I WAS A DUMB SIXTH GRADER WHEN I FIRST SAW
Seb Matias, too dumb to understand that hot guys are not worth
anyone's time—and that being hot doesn't equal being smart, or
kind, or funny.

I walked into homeroom, and there he was, slouched in the back
row. He was skinnier back then, and he had a mouth full of braces
like me, but he was still one of the cutest boys I had ever seen. I
thought for sure he was a model or a celebrity trying to live like a
commoner. Maybe it was some kind of bizarre social experiment,
like a handsome prince had traveled to East Bay, Florida, to wear a
middle schooler's disguise.

He looked up at me when I walked through the door. He smiled,
and even with his metal mouth, my legs turned to jelly. The seat next
to him was empty, which to me seemed miraculous. How had no one
rushed to take it? It was the briefest window of time when Seb was
another new kid in school, before Chloe and the hordes of pretty
girls latched on to him.

"Analee! Over here!" I saw Lily waving at me from the second
row. She hadn't learned how to do her hair yet—that didn't happen

until freshman year of high school. In sixth grade it stayed in a frizzy ponytail most of the time.

I smiled and took the seat beside my best friend, turning my back on Seb.

Matt McKinley ended up taking that seat next to Seb. The Anally nickname came a few minutes later, and I never looked at Seb the same way again. Lily and I became us, while Seb and the others became them.

Mom picked me up from school that day like she did every day. We went to McDonald's and shared a carton of greasy french fries.

"¿*Como te fue?*" She'd ask me, always in Spanish, how my day was. Unlike the typical teenager, I would tell her. Often in full paragraphs. That day I bitched to her about my name.

"'Analee' was your great-grandmother's name," she said. "And your great-grandmother was a badass."

"Okay, well *I* am not a badass," I replied. "So the name doesn't make sense for me."

If I were truly a badass, Matt McKinley wouldn't have chosen to make fun of me. Seb wouldn't have laughed.

Mom waved a french fry at me. "What do you mean you're not a badass? I take offense at that!"

"Why?"

"Because you're my daughter, and you're an extension of me."

"You could have just named me Ana. My life would be much easier."

"You're questioning your name because of one stupid boy?"

"Two," I corrected. "Two stupid boys."

"*Comemierdas*. Do you want me to come after them? Because I'll do it."

Mom cursed like a sailor, but only in Spanish. She was also prone to threats of violence, mostly when someone messed with me. I obviously never took her up on it, but it was comforting to have the option.

"Analee," she said. She nudged the fries in my direction. "Assholes will always find something to pick apart. If not your name, they move on to something else."

"That is so *not* helpful. Aren't you supposed to tell me that it'll get better?"

"If I were a liar, I might."

Today is the day everything changes. I got two hours of uninterrupted sleep last night. I know because I spent most of the night staring at the time and calculating how much sleep I'd get if I drifted off right at that moment. But then that gave me performance anxiety, which made it even harder to fall asleep.

On the way to school, I convince myself that Seb will call the whole thing off. Maybe he stayed up most of the night too, realizing what a mistake this was. But when I get to school, he's waiting by my locker, holding two paper cups.

"Good morning," he says, handing me one.

"Are we really doing this?" I say in response. The East Bay population is already taking note. The mere presence of Seb talking to me by my locker is drawing attention.

"It's not too late to back out," he says.

I see Lily on the other side of the hallway, chatting with Chloe, Colton, and Matt. None of them has spotted us yet.

"I'm not backing out," I say. Famous last words. I sniff at the cup he's handed me. "Is this coffee?"

"It's a nonfat vanilla latte. Chloe's favorite."

"Can I be honest?" I enter my locker combo with one hand, and the door clicks open. "I, um . . . I kind of hate coffee."

"But it's a latte," Seb protests.

"I know, but even milk can't hide the gross coffee flavor."

"Have you even tried it?"

"I don't need to try it."

"You are so . . ." Seb makes a sound somewhere between a sigh and a growl. "Just try it, please."

"I'm telling you, Seb, I don't like it."

"It takes ten tries of a new food before you know if you like it."

I glare at him suspiciously. "Is that true?"

"Yes."

I raise the cup to my lips and take a small sip. It's not horrible. There's the bitter aftertaste of coffee that I hate, but there's also the milky vanilla flavor that isn't totally unpleasant.

"Well?" He grins at me.

"It's drinkable, I guess."

Seb takes my folder and textbook from my hand.

"You don't have to—" I start.

"In case you didn't know, Analee, this is what boyfriends do. And I'm really good at boyfriending."

"I can see that." I shut my locker door and stare down the hallway. It seems impossibly long and crowded right now. I want to crawl into my locker until everyone goes to class. Seb may be good at boyfriend-ing, but he's making me feel totally inadequate at girlfriending. If this whole thing falls apart, the blame will rest squarely on my shoulders.

"Analee? What's wrong?"

"I've temporarily lost all movement in my limbs," I squeak. "Give me a second."

"Huddle." Seb pulls me aside, blocking my view of the hall with his body. If I weren't so freaked out, I would point out that we're not on a soccer field right now. "I'm walking you to homeroom. That's all. Okay?"

Walking. Toddlers do it all the time. I can handle walking.

"Okay." I straighten up. I take another sip of my not-gross-but-not-good latte.

Seb and I walk in step down the hall, closer and closer to *them*. I focus on placing one foot in front of the other. I don't look at anyone.

Slowly, unexpectedly, Seb links his hand with mine.

There's no turning back now. I don't have to look at anyone to realize the enormity of Seb's move. There are literally gasps that echo through the hall. I hear his name repeated in whispers, so fre-quently that they blend together into one long hiss.

*Seb, Seb, Seb, Sssssssssss.*

I let myself look only as we're passing. Tiny, quick glances. Lily's half-open mouth. Colton's unfazed expression. Matt's arm around Chloe's shoulders. Chloe's furrowed eyebrows. When we finally walk by them, I let out my breath. My whole body is trembling, my coffee cup threatening to spill all over the hallway.

"Holy shit," Seb says out of the side of his mouth. "Did you see their faces? Analee?"

Only a few more steps, and we'll be at the classroom. We round the corner, and Seb lets go of my hand when we reach the class's entrance.

"Oh my God," I say.

"I know! This is totally going to work."

"Did you see how they were looking?"

"Uh, yeah. That was the best part."

"I'm not good with that. People looking at me."

"Really?" Clearly, not wanting to be the center of attention is a foreign concept to him. Popular people think that being popular is everyone's goal. I've never had the desire to be one of them—being respected would be enough.

"Really," I say. "It makes me feel like a goldfish."

Even as I speak, I notice the glances thrown in our direction. Some people outright stare, not even bothering to hide it.

"It's happening now," I whisper to Seb.

"Let them look," he says. "That's the point."

It goes against all my natural instincts. For so long, I've done everything in my power to be invisible. Stay quiet, hide away, avoid all other humans. All attention is negative attention.

"We having lunch today?" he asks.

I don't know if I'm up to lunch. Holding his hand in the hallway caused enough of a commotion.

"I can't," I lie. A girl I've never seen before points at me and whispers something to her friend. I force myself to look at Seb. "I have work to do."

"Do you want me to bring you something? I can swipe some pizza from the cafeteria."

"I'm okay," I say. I smile. "You really are good at boyfriending."

"Please. This is the tip of the iceberg." I notice that he's watching the girls next to us. It's so subtle, the way his eyes flit from them to me.

"Is that so?"

"You'll see." And then his gaze is somewhere else entirely. Not on me, not on the girls. "Though, Chloe took it for granted."

I want to ask him what makes Chloe worth all of this. I want to know why they broke up, what made Chloe give up morning lattes and holding hands.

No, wait. Scratch that. I don't care. Seb and I have entered into a mutually beneficial contract. I scratch his metaphorical back, he scratches mine.

"I won't take it for granted," I reassure him. I take another sip of latte for good measure. It's not so bad, actually. I might kinda like it.

"It doesn't matter," he says, handing me my books. "It's not real."

"I know that," I say quickly. I feel slightly bruised by the comment. Why did he feel the need to tell me that? Does he think I'm secretly pining for him like every other girl in school?

The warning bell rings overhead, signaling that we have one minute to get to class. All of the onlookers around us have vanished, including the girls. Seb is somewhere else too. He's drifted off to Chloe-land.

"I'm gonna go in," I say. I gesture toward the classroom with my coffee cup.

"Okay." He still won't look at me. "See you later." Now that the crowd has diminished, we're back to being strangers. Slowly he turns and wanders away in the opposite direction.

His sneakers are orange today. *They're stupid*, I think, annoyed. *Bright and stupid.*

I walk into class alone and take my seat in the back corner, keeping my head low and ignoring the whispers that fill my ears.

### Analee's Top Lunch Spots

1. Second-floor library cubicle
(note: only when eating a sandwich
that can be easily hidden in backpack)
2. Red bench in quad
3. Empty classroom
4. Stairwell C, the third story
5. Backstage in auditorium
(note: only during drama off-seasons)

# CHAPTER SIXTEEN

BEFORE HARLOW MOVED IN, WE WERE STRICTLY A paper plates house, even when Mom was alive. She and Dad hated doing the dishes, so they bought disposable dinnerware sets in bulk from Costco. You would expect two second-generation Cuban immigrants to be more frugal, to understand the value of money, but Mom found throwing entire place settings away to be a satisfying display of American extravagance. She did it with glee every night, stacking the dishes in one hand and squashing them into the garbage can.

"Dishes are done," she would say, swiping her hands against each other and chuckling to herself. I shook my head, because I had been nagging my family to recycle for years. Mom liked to use the skewed logic that buying paper plates saved us from doing dishes, which saved water. And Dad had a crackpot theory that recycling was actually worse for the planet, based solely on what his friend Manny once said at the office. They were two peas in a pod in their complete disregard for science.

The one thing Mom had in common with Harlow was a love

of cooking, and that's where any similarities between the two end. Mom would fry plantains in a big rusty skillet full of oil. Not the organic, unrefined coconut oil that Harlow orders online but an economy-size vat of hydrogenated, artery-clogging vegetable oil (also purchased from Costco). Mom made hearty, meaty Cuban dishes from her grandmother's handwritten recipe book. She didn't care that my favorite dish, picadillo, looked more than a little like dog food and wasn't nearly Instagram-ready.

But, oh my God, her food tasted so good. Once you took a bite, you didn't care that it wasn't pretty, and you didn't care that it was slowly killing you from the inside. The stuff Dad and I order from La Vibora doesn't compare.

I guess I could scrounge around for that recipe book and try to make it myself, but for some reason I don't.


Harlow is not zen when I get home from school. She's fluttering around the house like a deranged bird, slamming drawers and tearing up and down the stairs. A grim-faced Avery comes out of the kitchen with a broom in hand.

"What's with your mom?" I ask.

"Your *abuelo* and *abuela* are coming over for dinner. We just found out."

I should have realized. The only things that get Harlow this riled up are trans fats and impromptu visits from my grandparents.

"Analee, you're home!" Harlow descends the steps two at a time, then lands with a leap at the foot of the stairs. She's cradling a Buddha statuette in her arms.

"Indeed I am."

"Can you wipe down the dining room table?"

"Sure."

"Oh! And take out the bathroom trash?"

"Sure," I say again. I nod at the statuette. "Does Buddha get a chore?"

"Buddha," Harlow says with a sigh, "is going into the attic. Last time your grandparents were here, they told your dad I was an idol worshipper."

This is actually true. They asked Dad if Harlow was an *idólatra*, but I didn't think Harlow caught it. I love my grandparents. They're awesome in a variety of ways. But they are also some hard-core Roman Catholics.

Quickly I run upstairs to let Harris know I won't be able to talk until late tonight. Then I set to work on my chores. The three of us work in different areas of the house, so, thankfully, I don't actually have to talk to either of them. In the kitchen I hear the clatter of pots and pans.

"Analee?" Harlow calls. "Can you come here a sec?"

When I walk in, she has a spread of organic products on the counter and . . . mushroom caps.

"I think I'm going to debut the mushroom ropa vieja tonight," she says. "Want to help? I could use your expertise."

This is a disaster waiting to happen. My grandparents are traditionalists, in food and in life. They do not want their classic Cuban dishes in vegan form.

"I, um . . . I have to do some homework." I want no part in butchering the food of my people.

"Oh, of course!" Harlow says. "I should have assumed. Well,

that's okay." She pushes her bangs off her forehead and starts to slice the mushroom caps.

I almost feel a little sorry for her. Harlow's used to thousands of fawning followers who praise and worship everything she does. She's in for a rude awakening tonight.

To make up for it, I clean out the bathroom cabinet, and then I spend my remaining hour scrambling to finish my math homework, before Dad's car honks outside.

He and my grandparents arrive at the house together, and I can hear them long before I see them, each talking over the other in loud, singsong Spanish. As they're getting to the front door, I notice that Harlow missed a tiny Buddha on the entryway table. I debate whether I should leave it there, but then I swipe it and stick it into my pocket at the last second.

"*Mi niñita!*" Abuela is the one to throw open the door. She runs right for me and peppers my cheeks with kisses. Abuelo comes next, opting for one giant kiss on my forehead.

"Hi, Luis. Hi, Graciela," Harlow says, and my grandparents each give her a kiss as well. Harlow's body, usually soft-limbed, is rigid with tension. When Dad aims to kiss her lips, she offers him a cheek instead.

*Trouble in paradise?* I think. The visits from my grandparents have lessened since Harlow moved in. Before, they often came over uninvited, but Harlow has convinced Dad that boundaries are necessary, that even though Abuelo and Abuela are his parents, they should still give us at least a courtesy call.

I wish that for once *he* would set the boundaries with *her*. Like telling her to stop force-feeding us her latest health diet. Or saying no to converting our spare room into a stark, barren meditation room that only she uses.

When we get to the table, Harlow has made an arugula salad that my grandparents poke at. Abuela compliments it, then discreetly wrinkles her nose at me. I try not to laugh. Abuelo doesn't even try to hide his contempt for raw vegetables.

"Harlow," Abuela says, but through her accent it comes out more like "Hawor-lo." Understanding Abuela's English is a skill acquired only through years of intense focus and practice. "Deed jou cohl Padre Medina?"

"I'm sorry?" Harlow says through her stiff smile. She looks to Dad for help, but he's looking down at his plate, shoveling salad into his mouth to avoid the conversation. I quickly piece together what's happened. Dad hasn't told my grandparents that their traditional church wedding is a no-go.

Abuela repeats the question again, and Harlow squints and nods. I imagine the wheels in her mind spinning overtime to make sense of the warbled English.

"I haven't called Father Medina," Harlow says. Her smile increasingly grows more and more distorted, almost manic. "Raf? Why is your mother asking if I've called Father Medina?"

Dad has finished his salad. There is nothing to save him now.

"I haven't told them about Carrie yet," he says quickly.

"What?"

"Relax! Just play along."

"I'm not going to play along!" Harlow hisses.

"*Cariño*, please."

"I'm not going to lie to your parents, Raf. You need to tell them the truth."

My grandparents, meanwhile, are watching but not understanding this entire exchange. I stand up, rush around to collect the salad plates.

"I'm going to grab the ropa vieja," Harlow says. She gives Dad a pointed look before following me into the kitchen.

It's quieter in here, and Harlow's smile vanishes completely as she ladles the mushroom stew into bowls, then garnishes each one with fresh parsley.

"I'm sorry," she says softly to me, bent over the food. I'm not sure why she's apologizing.

The voices in the dining room grow louder. I can make out some phrases here and there as Dad tries to quiet my grandparents. It's a different scene from when Harlow's parents, Larry and Donna, were last here. They both speak perfect English at a normal human volume, and make only pleasant, surface-skimming observations.

"Rafael, what a lovely tie." "I just adore the new painting you put in the living room, Harlow." "Larry and I went to the cutest Italian restaurant the other day." *Blah, blah, blah-di-blah-blah.*

"They sound angry," Harlow says now. She drums her knuckles on the countertop, takes a step toward the door, and then steps back into the kitchen. "What are they saying?"

I don't have to strain to hear any more. Abuela is saying that their wedding will be a disgrace, that it's a slap in the face to Father Medina. Abuelo is giving Dad some macho bullshit advice about him being the head of the household and making the decisions for Harlow.

"They, um . . . they still think you should go with Father Medina," I say, which is the gist of it anyway. Harlow doesn't need to know that my grandparents think she's a heathen corrupting their impressionable son.

She exhales, nods. "It's an adjustment, I guess."

"Right."

"They just need to accept that this is our wedding, and we're going to do it our way."

Ha. They're never going to accept that. They're never going to accept Harlow and her tiny Buddha statues and vegan food as a replacement for my mother.

I can't accept it either. Part of me feels sorry for Harlow, because Cubans are stubborn as hell, and we're not going to budge. The other part of me, the darkest part, relishes every second of my grandparents' resistance to this strange woman inserting herself into all of our lives.

Of course I can't tell Harlow this. It's going to be something she'll have to figure out on her own.

I nod and smile at her like I agree. Then I watch as she rolls her shoulders back, cradles a bowl of mushroom stew in each hand, and steps back out into the fray.

# CHAPTER SEVENTEEN

**Me:** HARRIS

**Harris:** ANALEE

**Harris:** where have you been?!?!?!?!

**Me:** Sorry. Things have been kind of crazy.

**Harris:** i had to team up with larzaron for the quest. we got totally fucked

**Me:** Larzaron? Really? He's the worst.

**Harris:** i was desperate

**Harris:** why have things been crazy?

**Me:** I was hanging out with Seb yesterday.

**Harris:** your douchebag lab partner?

**Me:** He's not a douchebag, persay

**Me:** Is that how you spell it? Persay?

**Harris:** per se

**Harris:** and since when is he not a douchebag?

**Me:** He's had a rough time since his girlfriend dumped him

**Harris:** still not a license to be a douche

**Me:** Whatever. He's okay.

**Harris:** . . .

**Me:** What?

**Harris:** nothing

Holy crap. Harris is jealous . . . which means the great boyfriend experiment might actually be working. As a friend, I don't want to hurt him. I'm tempted to come clean and admit that this is all a non-sensical plan to fix my life.

That's the selfless-friend part of me. As the girl who's in love with him, I'll continue to let him think what he wants to think, because making him jealous doesn't completely suck. I know it's immature and, okay, somewhat manipulative. An asshole move, actually. But for once it's nice to feel desired, even if it's for the wrong reasons.

There are five raps on my door. It's Dad's signature knock, which Lily once informed me comes from a tune called "Shave and a Haircut." I don't know how or why she knew that, but she did, and those random assorted bits of trivia make me miss her more.

I knock on my desk, twice, in return.

"You busy?" he asks, hovering in the doorway.

"Nope." I minimize my chat window. Dad shuffles in, rubbing the back of his neck.

"Playing your magic game?"

"It's not a 'magic game.' It's a multiplayer online role-playing game. And no, I'm not playing it right now," I say. I wonder if Dad mentions my gaming to Harlow during their conversations about my social ineptitude. "Just talking."

He sits on the edge of my bed, and it dips under his weight. I still have the same twin bed I've had since I was five. There's a crater-size sag in the middle, and the foam is worn, with a large tear down the side. I just can't get rid of it. I have too many memories of Mom squeezing in beside me whenever I was sick with fever or when she read me bedtime stories in Spanish—one of her many futile attempts at making me bilingual.

"Talking to your boyfriend?" he asks.

"Yes," I say, because bringing up Harris will lead to a different line of questioning.

"What's his last name again?"

"Matias."

"Right. Matias. Like the singer?"

"Um. I don't know."

"Juan Matias?" He sings a Spanish melody in his uniquely tone-deaf way. I want to crawl under my desk. What is this? What is he doing? I can't remember the last time Dad was in my room without a specific purpose. He hasn't been one to hang out. Not in recent memory, at least.

"About Sebastian," Dad says. "This whole boyfriend thing . . . I think we should talk. Go over some rules." He shifts around on the bed, but it only makes him sink lower. "*Ay, coño.*"

"Oh my God, Dad. Please don't do what I think you're about to do."

I didn't think the sex talk would ever come from him. Judging from his sweat-dappled forehead, neither did he.

"Sex," he announces, spreading his arms wide. It's not the smoothest of transitions. I let my head fall forward onto my desk with a loud thud. It hurts, but the pain distracts me from this conversation.

"Sex can be a beautiful part of life. When you're married."

"Please stop," I say without raising my head. "Please. I'll do anything."

"Sebastian is going to try to have sex with you, Analee."

"No, he's not, Dad."

"You need to understand. I'm a man. I know how men think."

I lift my head. "That's an overgeneralization."

"So here are the rules," Dad goes on. "Rule number one: you two cannot be alone in the house. That goes for his house too."

"Is there—"

"Rule number two," he barrels on. "No dates on weeknights. You can see him on weekends with permission. And only when your homework is finished. *And* I need to know exactly where you're going and what time you'll be home."

"I hate doing things on weeknights," I say. Weekends, too, for that matter. Spending the day around everyone at school is so exhausting that I go full hermit when I'm home.

"Rule number three," Dad says. "Don't take Harlow's dating advice."

"Wait, what?" I ask.

"Harlow grew up different from how we did. Her parents were *un poco . . . despistados*. They let Harlow date whoever she wanted, whenever she wanted."

"I'm confused. Are you calling your fiancée a tramp?"

"No!" Dad casts an urgent look at the doorway as if Harlow will magically apparate before us. "She just . . . she wouldn't understand."

I'm not sure I understand either. I can't help but think how much better Mom would have been at this. She would have said all the right things, and maybe it would have been uncomfortable, but it would have also been funny, because Mom was funny. Instead I have Dad, who is currently drowning in my pink comforter. Who is practically slut-shaming my future stepmother and can't even say the word "sex" without turning fifty shades of purple.

"What's going to happen when Avery starts dating?" I ask.

"What do you mean?"

"I mean . . . are you going to give her the same talk? The 'true love waits' spiel?"

Dad blanks. "Ehm. That's up to Harlow."

"Is it? You're going to be Avery's stepfather."

He blinks a few times, letting this fact fully register.

"Shouldn't you two have discussed this co-parenting thing before getting engaged?" I ask.

"Analee," Dad says sternly, in a way that lets me know I've struck a nerve. "You're out of bounds."

"I just don't think it's fair for me and Avery to have different sets of rules."

"Avery is eight years old."

"Yeah, but—"

"We'll deal with Avery when the time comes." He gets up, squeezing his hands together. "Any questions about the rules?"

His rules are ridiculous. Even though my relationship with Seb is pure fiction, my indignation is real. How dare he? First, he barely talks to me anymore, acts like I'm a blemish on his and Harlow's happy fairy tale. Then he has the nerve to march into my room and bark orders at me. As if my imaginary sex life is any of his business.

"What about a car?" I ask. "Can I be alone in a car with Seb? The school library? Underneath the bleachers?"

"Not funny, Analee."

"I'm not trying to be funny. You know, a few rules aren't going to stop two hormone-fueled teenagers from having sex if they want to have sex."

Even if I did have a boyfriend, I don't think I'd have sex with him. Or if I did, it wouldn't happen for a very long time. Everything else in my life is complicated enough without adding sex into the mix.

Dad doesn't say anything, and it makes me feel worse. I didn't mean to be bitchy. Or maybe I did. I can't tell, because most of what comes out of my mouth lately seems to bother him. I don't even know if I'm doing it on purpose or if it's a side effect of my existence.

He's quiet for a long time, and I wonder if I pushed him too far. I almost take it all back.

"Now you know the rules," he says finally. "I'll let you get back to your magic game."

When he starts to leave, I get the urge to grab him by the legs like I used to do when I was a little girl. I sort of hate him, but I want him to stay. Even if it means more awkward sex rules.

"Multiplayer online role-playing game," I mumble instead, but he's already out the door.

There were telltale signs that Dad had a girlfriend, things that were obvious to me only in retrospect. The first sign was the frequent gym visits. Besides the occasional morning jog, Dad had never been much for fitness when Mom was alive. His exercise consisted of walking to and from his car to go to work. At home he lived on the couch, before the big move to his bed at nine p.m.

Mom used to love that he was soft in the middle. The three of us had that belly pouch in common—our *pancitas*, as Mom would call them. She liked to give his a good pinch.

But then she died, and he didn't eat very much, and then he joined the gym. Gradually the pouch disappeared, until one day, without my realizing, it had vanished completely.

The other signs happened quickly. Dad got rid of his ripped, twenty-year-old jeans. His T-shirts became pressed button-downs that he tucked into his pants. He wore boat shoes even though he didn't own a boat.

A couple of times a week, there would be some late nights at work. He never spent the night anywhere, but sometimes he would get home at two in the morning. I would wait up for him at first. I was terrified that I would go to sleep and he would get into a car accident or suffer a sudden heart attack. Sometimes I would drift off and have vivid dreams about losing Mom all over again. I saw her the way she looked in the end, the way I don't want to remember her but the image I can't erase. And then, in my dream, something would happen to Dad, too. I was terrified of waking up as an orphan.

I guess in the back of my mind, I somehow knew that Dad would move on, but I thought I would be an adult at that point. Off in college at least, living my own life, far enough away that it wouldn't affect me as much.

We were eating takeout in front of the TV when Dad first mentioned his yoga teacher.

"I didn't know you took yoga," I said. "I thought you would be one of those old men on the stationary bike."

"Excuse you," he said, swiping one of my dumplings with his chopsticks. "I'm only forty-seven."

"Your hair's gone gray."

"I'm what they call a silver fox."

"Ew, Dad. Who in the world has ever called you that?" I asked. The memory grosses me out now that I can picture it being Harlow.

"No one," he said. "And I *was* doing the stationary bike at first. But I kept seeing the yoga class through the window, and it looked so . . . peaceful."

"Isn't it boring? A bunch of breathing and posing?"

"This class isn't," Dad said. "We have a great teacher. You should try it."

But I never did. I had no desire to struggle through warrior pose in a room full of strangers.

That was the first conversation about yoga. As the weeks went on, Dad quoted his "yoga teacher" more and more, while I spent more and more time in an imaginary online world. Maybe that's why I missed the obvious correlation. Increasing number of late nights equaled increasing references to the mysterious yoga teacher.

Somehow Dad and I started eating dinner separately. He was being pulled into Harlow's orbit, and I escaped to my room every chance I got so that I could spend time with Harris and live in Kiri's skin.

I couldn't know at the time that we were turning into different people. It seemed like every day dragged by so slowly. But now, when I look back, everything happened at once, like a giant cataclysmic shift.

# CHAPTER EIGHTEEN

I'D FORGOTTEN HOW *LOUD* THE CAFETERIA IS. Large amounts of people, in general, are loud. Everyone thinks that what they have to say is so important that they talk over whoever else is speaking, in order to make their inane point, right freaking now, because God forbid you take the time to listen to anyone else in the world. It's like what my third-grade teacher used to say, that people have two ears and one mouth for a reason, but no one seems to remember that.

"Jesus, Analee, would it kill you to smile?"

Seb and I took a small table in the back of the room. As soon as we sat down together, the volume grew ten times as loud. Lily, Chloe, and the rest are sitting a few tables away, at approximately a forty-five-degree angle. They have a perfect view of us.

I spread my lips wide, showing top and bottom teeth. "How's this?"

"Like a scary clown." Seb sighs in disappointment, then takes a bite of his burger. One of his bites equals half the burger, which is probably why he ordered two.

I take a bite of my own bacon cheeseburger. I get a sick pleasure out of imagining Harlow's face if she were to watch me. Dairy *and* pork? Shame.

"Are you going to eat that whole thing?" Seb asks.

"Yes." I take another bite, then hesitate before chewing. "Why?"

"I'm just not used to girls who eat. I always had to finish Chloe's food for her."

I resume chewing. "I'm not Chloe."

"I see that."

"Harlow tends to deprive our family when it comes to food. She's a vegan."

"Nothing wrong with that. It's working for her," Seb says. "Your stepmom is super-hot."

"She's not my stepmom yet," I say. "And you're foul." It doesn't surprise me that Seb would find someone like Harlow attractive, but it bothers me all the same. It's so uninspired.

"She seems nice, too."

"She's okay."

"It could be worse, you know. She could be a huge bitch like my stepmom."

"Can you not use that word? It's so incredibly sexist."

"It's not sexist if it's true."

"I just think you should be better than some macho butthead who throws the word 'bitch' around," I reply. "Be less stereotypical, please."

"Butthead?" he asks, stifling a laugh.

I knew he was going to pick up on that as soon as the word left my mouth. Why am I four years old? "That's right."

"Fine. My stepmom's a dick. Better?"

I sigh. "Now you're trying to be an asshole."

"Jesus Christ. You're impossible." He frowns, then catches himself. The smile falls back into place.

"So, what's wrong with your stepmom?" I ask.

"She's a lying piece of garbage."

"Care to elaborate?"

"She basically brainwashed my dad into marrying her. Then she turned him against me and my brother. He's just, like . . . all about her, all the time."

"I'm sorry," I say. I complain about Harlow all the time, but at least she's never done anything truly evil. "That sucks. What about your mom?"

"My mom isn't around."

On this he doesn't elaborate. He leaves it at that, so I do too. Across the cafeteria Lily looks over at us, and my heart lifts in my chest.

"Do you think everyone's buying this?" I ask. "Our relationship?"

Seb nods. "It's driving Chloe crazy. I can tell."

"How?"

"Look at her."

She's talking to Lily, gesturing with her fork before sticking a bite of salad into her mouth. She doesn't look terribly affected by any of this, but most things in life don't seem to affect her.

"She seems pretty zen," I maintain.

"You have to know her. There are definite cracks in the foundation."

If Chloe's metaphorical house has cracks in the foundation, mine is a termite-infested crap heap.

"I have a soccer game on Thursday," Seb says. "You're coming, right?"

"Ugh. Do I have to?"

"Well, you're kind of my girlfriend? And Chloe used to go to every single game."

In other words I have no choice in the matter. I cannot imagine a worse way to spend an afternoon than sitting in the sweltering heat, suffering from lower back pain because of the bleacher seats, and surrounded by the people I most want to escape.

"Chloe is a saint," I mutter. I finish the remains of my cheeseburger, using my finger to collect the bits of stray meat from my plate.

Seb laughs. "Hungry?"

"Not really." I wipe the rest of my plate clean.

"Do you want some of my fries?"

"Yes." I have no room to be demure. Burgers and fries are freaking delicious, a rarity in my life these days.

"Here." He takes a fry and moves it toward my mouth.

"What are you doing?" I ask, pulling away.

He pauses, fry in hand. "I was going to feed you a fry."

"Seriously?"

"Yes? Girls think that's cute."

"Isn't that a little . . . infantilizing?"

"Analee. Eat the fry." And then he practically shoves it into my mouth. "See? Aren't we adorable?"

I glare at him as I chew.

"Smile," he reminds me.

The strangest thing to come from fake dating Seb is that random people will now say hi to me in the hallways. People whom I've never spoken to in my life, and they all say my name correctly. Go figure.

Guys are also starting to look at me. I'm not sure how I feel about that.

Lily used to scold me for assuming that all attention was bad attention, but I can't help myself. When someone's staring at me, I want to run to the nearest mirror and make sure something in my appearance didn't go horribly wrong. Like, maybe I just got my period and it looks like I'm hemorrhaging blood. Or maybe a giant glob of food is stuck between my front teeth. If people are looking at me, it's for a reason, and it's probably a bad reason.

Physically I guess I'm not totally repulsive. Kids don't see me and run away screaming. But there are a million little things that I would fix about myself if I could, and when people look at me for too long, I think they're figuring out what all those little things are. They might be noticing that my nose is slightly too wide for my face or that my *pancita* makes me look eternally five months pregnant. So, I do everything in my power to become Invisible Girl—using my massive hair cape as a shield, shrinking from people's sight, and maintaining a force field of personal space around me at all times.

Fake dating Seb makes me feel like my Invisible Girl disguise is slipping. Even the teachers are treating me differently. They smile at me when I walk into the room, like they know who I am. By my proximity to Seb, I am suddenly someone worth seeing.

I wonder if this is how Lily felt when she started dating Colton. I never did ask her what it was like.

# CHAPTER NINETEEN

HARLOW HEARS ME WHEN I GET HOME, BEFORE I have time to run upstairs and avoid her.

"Analee?" she asks in her apple-pie way.

"It's me," I call back.

"Can you come here for a second?"

*No. Leave me alone, woman.*

"Okay," I say out loud. I try to sound as pleasant as possible.

When I walk into the living room, I shit you not, Harlow is standing on her head. Sometimes I think she saves her most ridiculous yoga poses for my viewing.

"Hi," she says to me, upside down, like this is a totally normal way to speak to someone. I would be a sweaty, red-faced mess if I were her, but she looks angelic. The blood rushing to her cheeks gives her face a delicate blush.

"Hi," I say.

"Can I talk to you for a second?"

"Sure. . . . Like this?"

She lowers her legs and descends into child pose. Then she sits back on her heels and faces me.

"Come," she says, patting her mat. "Sit."

So this is going to be a long talk. I've never had one of these with her, not even when she started dating Dad. Dad kept acting like this was nothing new, completely business-as-usual for this skinny blond woman to pop up in our everyday lives.

I kick off my shoes and toss my backpack onto the floor, then sit across from her on the mat. Even sitting on a yoga mat feels unnatural to me. It feels like my jeans are going to split open.

"Your dad mentioned that he talked to you last night."

"'Talk' is a stretch," I reply. "It was more a declaration of rules."

I don't tell Harlow that talking to her about this would be a violation of rule number three.

"Go easy on the guy," Harlow says, smiling. "He's feeling out of his element here."

I'm not sure what bothers me more: when Harlow talks to me as if she knows my dad better than I do, or the fact that maybe now she does.

"And what about you?" Harlow asks.

"What about me?"

"How are you feeling? About Seb?"

I start to feel uncomfortable—the two of us, sitting face-to-face, Harlow in stretchy lotus pose, me an awkward mess, my jeans pinching my stomach. There is nothing to distract me from this conversation. I itch to get upstairs and in front of my laptop.

"I'm feeling okay," I say carefully.

"I'm glad. Look, I just want you to know . . ." Harlow untangles her legs and fidgets with her tank top. "I'm here if you want to talk about things. Things that might be weird for you and your dad."

"Um. Thanks."

"Have you been to a gynecologist?"

Oh. We're actually doing this. Like, right now.

"No," I say.

"I can bring you to mine. Her name is Jessica, and she's fantastic. Very gentle. We can look at some birth control options."

"Thanks, Harlow, but I don't think—"

"I'm not saying that you and Seb are going to have sex. I just want you to be informed, okay? Sometimes your dad—"

She stops. I'm curious to know what her criticism of Dad will be, but she finishes by repeating, "I just want you to be informed."

"Thanks," I say again. "I'll, um, think about it."

"Okay."

"Okay." I'm never sure when a conversation with Harlow is finished. When it comes to its natural end, she just . . . stares. Like she's waiting for you to remember something.

"I'm gonna go upstairs," I say. It sounds too sudden, and I almost trip on my own feet when I lift myself off the mat. The epitome of grace, I am.

"Good talking to you," Harlow calls after me. I wonder if she truly believes that, if we were both part of the same conversation.

I get to Seb's soccer game early so that I can sit in the top corner of the bleachers. Soccer games at East Bay are usually packed because our school makes it to state every year, making the scene of screaming, cheering fans sitting ass-to-ass on the bleachers an introvert's nightmare. To say that soccer is a big deal at this school would be a severe understatement. The players are treated like gods, and funds are funneled from our arts and academic programs into the sports budget. Last year they cut the school band to give the soccer players new uniforms.

It's all kinds of gross.

In order to combat any potential boredom and avoid talking to anyone who sits around me, I bring my journal, homework, and a copy of the third Harry Potter. Most people who get here early take the first couple of rows of seats anyway. No one wants to be up here, closer to the hellish Florida sun.

Seb and the rest of the team are already jogging around the field to warm up. Twenty boys in slate-blue uniforms, knee socks, and cleats bounce soccer balls on every available body part. There's something ridiculous yet graceful about the way Seb moves. He juggles the ball from foot to foot, then swings and kicks his legs around like a demented Rockette. When he moves to the side to stretch, I see him look up, his eyes searching the stands. I look around me. The bleacher seats are filling up quickly. I think he's looking for Chloe, who used to be a fixture at these things, but she's nowhere to be found. There's that annoying flicker of pity I feel again. It must suck, knowing that you once had a real girlfriend to root for you at every soccer game, and now you have to settle for a fake one.

But when Seb spots me, I can see his face light up, even from my nosebleed seat. He waves. I wave back, then smile and look down at my knees. Minutes later my phone buzzes inside my backpack. It's a text from Seb, now off the field.

Tell me you didn't bring a book to a soccer game.

I write back, Not just a book. I also brought a journal and some homework.

Girlfriends don't bring books to their boyfriends' soccer games.

This one does.

Nerd.

Jock.

I sigh and put the book away. I should probably keep up the pretense of this relationship by paying attention to the first few minutes of the game.

A chubby freshman squeezes into the limited space beside me, almost knocking me over. He doesn't even apologize.

"COME ON, TIGERS!" he hollers dangerously close to my eardrum. For the love of God. None of these people have any concept of self-control. The game hasn't even started yet.

The relief is that no one here particularly cares what I'm doing. People are chatting with friends, eating junk food, and, for the most part, keeping their eyes on the field. It makes me think I can handle this part of being a girlfriend. I can still be Invisible Girl here, hidden among the mob.

As the start of the game gets closer, the fans get louder. People start hooting and clapping and chanting songs in unison. The guy next to me participates in each and every chant with gusto. His volume increases too, more than I ever thought possible.

When the game starts, I'm totally lost. I mean, I'm not an idiot. I know the basics of soccer. Kick the ball into the other team's net, and that's a goal. Yay.

But the ref keeps blowing the whistle for things I don't understand. Sometimes it's a good thing; sometimes it's not. I base my understanding on the crowd reaction and the guy next to me. When chubby guy cheers, something good has happened, so I clap.

Eventually I start understanding. When someone accidentally kicks the opponent instead of the ball, the opponent gets a free kick. The game isn't so horrible to watch when the ball is in play. East Bay's players are pretty impressive in their nimbleness, especially in comparison with how winded I get when I have to go up a flight of stairs. They can run up and down the field multiple times with no problem. And now that I have a "relationship" with Seb, I feel more invested in the game's outcome. I have a connection to one of those uniformed guys out there, which is something I never thought I'd experience. When Seb tries for a goal and misses, the tiniest bit of disappointment sprouts from deep within me.

"OFFSIDE!" chubby guy screams. He positions his hands around his mouth to make a megaphone, then clucks his tongue and shakes his head. I'm not sure what just happened, but I guess I'm supposed to be annoyed too, so I throw my hands up into the air in solidarity.

The other team scores first. The sprout of disappointment inside me starts to bloom.

"Dammit!" I blurt out.

"FUCK YOU!" chubby guy shouts to no one in particular.

The crowd around us murmurs and boos their discontent.

"Is this yours?" chubby guy asks, holding my book in his hand. It must have slid off my lap at some point.

"Yeah," I say. "Thanks."

He nods, and we both turn our attention back to the game. Seb has the ball now, and he really is kind of mesmerizing to watch. He is the personification of action verbs, all darting and lunging and spinning.

"He's fucking amazing, right?" chubby guy asks me.

"He's my boyfriend," I find myself saying, with actual pride in my voice. Like Seb's supernatural athletic ability has anything to do with me.

Chubby guy turns to gape at me. "You're dating Matias?"

Why the hell did I choose to bring this up? I could have just said, *Yes, he's amazing*, and ended the whole conversation.

"Yeah. We're . . . together." Do people in my generation even say that? It sounds so Marcia Brady when I say it out loud. But the guy doesn't seem to notice.

"Oh my God. You're so lucky."

"I guess so. I mean, thanks."

"Sorry," he says. "I didn't mean it like that. It's just that he's mind-blowingly hot, and I realize that might be inappropriate to say to his girlfriend, but it's not like I have a chance in hell with him, so what difference does it make, right?"

I laugh. "I see your point."

There's something endearing about the way this guy spits out his every thought. It's a trait that has always boggled my mind, because I overthink everything before speaking, analyzing what I'm about to say from every possible point of view before ultimately deciding to keep my mouth shut.

"I'm Elliott," the guy says. "Spelled with two *t*s."

"Analee," I reply. I wait for him to repeat it incorrectly.

"Analee, right!" he says instead. He smacks his palm against his forehead. "Duh, Elliott. I knew that. There's been talk about you."

"Talk?" My stomach pinches. I don't want to be the topic of anyone's conversation. It's never a good thing.

"Yeah, you're the mysterious Analee that Seb's been hanging out with. People didn't know if you guys were official or if you were some rebound. Oh my God, I'm so sorry. I shouldn't have said that."

"It's okay," I say quickly. "I understand. Seb has a lot of admirers."

"Yeah. But talking to you now, you don't seem like a rebound, you know? It's obvious he'd be into you."

This must be what it feels like to be popular. Elliott is totally lying to me right now, trying to get into my good graces. It's not obvious at all that someone like Seb would be into me. He said himself that I wasn't his usual type.

"Okay, I know we just met and everything." Elliott talks like he's on a perpetual sugar high, eyes flitting between me and the field, legs jiggling. "But please tell me what it's like to make out with Sebastian Matias. Does it taste like all your dreams coming true? Does he have minty-fresh breath? Is he light on the tongue, or does it feel like he's swallowing you whole?"

I didn't think this part of the plan through. Of course, as Seb's girlfriend, I should know what it's like to kiss him, but making out with Sebastian Matias is something I only thought about in the brief few seconds of that day in sixth grade. The two of us haven't even talked about the physical stuff yet. Holding hands in public was terrifying enough. Are people going to expect to see it? How much am I willing to do to maintain this charade?

"Kissing Seb . . . ," I start. Elliott stops moving. I wonder again why I engaged in conversation with him, but I'm too far down this path to turn back now. "Kissing Seb is incredible."

Elliott makes a face. "Of course it is. But how?"

"How?"

"And feel free to use detail."

"Um, okay. Well . . . see how he moves on the field?"

"Uh-huh." Elliott's eyes go wide.

"He knows how to work with his body off the field too, if you get what I mean."

What am I even saying? Who is going to believe this?

"You are. So. Lucky," he says again. Apparently Elliott will believe it.

The score is 1–0. Elliott continues to chat as we watch, pausing every so often to scream something at the top of his lungs. I'm not great at talking to people, but Elliott makes it easy. He's one of those people who won't judge you for saying something stupid or awkward, because a lot of what he says is worse.

Elliott tells me that his older brother, now a college freshman, used to play for our soccer team. His name is Neil, and Elliott has been to every single one of his soccer games and every Tigers soccer game thereafter. He explains to me what's going on, pointing out each of East Bay's players and their positions. He's a living soccer dictionary, breaking down vocabulary for me, like a scissor kick and a fifty-fifty ball. I let him talk, for the most part. I'm thankful there are no awkward silences with Elliott.

Then, with a couple of minutes left in the first half, Seb scores. He sends the ball flying past the goalie's open arms and into the corner of the net. Everyone jumps up, including me, and suddenly Elliott's arms are around me and he's squeezing me into a giant bear hug. The two of us jump up and down, and he screams something unintelligible into my ear, and I'm so unreasonably happy that a stupid inflated ball has been kicked into a net.

I seriously don't even recognize myself anymore.

Seb scores again in the second half, and the game ends in East Bay's favor. Elliott explains to me that this is a Very Big Deal, because the team they've been playing against, Hamilton High, is ranked second in the entire state.

"See you next time?" he asks after we walk down the bleachers together.

"Definitely."

The word pops out of my mouth, but I realize I mean it. I want to see the next game. I want to be there for these big sudden moments of happiness. Also, Elliott's over-the-top reactions are just as entertaining as the game.

When he leaves, I linger around the exit to the boys' locker room, where Seb texted me to meet him. There's a throng of people already outside, including a handful of made-up girls in high-heeled boots and tight jeans. They talk in a small, close huddle, and a few of them shoot evil-eyed stares in my direction. Of course. They're here for Seb.

I look down at my hoodie and sneakers as if maybe I had a Cinderella-like transformation in the past five seconds. I didn't know girls dressed up for soccer games. The bleachers are already uncomfortable enough. I don't want to torture my feet, too.

The girls don't stop looking. A couple of them even laugh, and I'm sure it's meant for me. I'm sure they're thinking, *What is someone like Sebastian Matias doing with that frumpy, ugly weirdo?* Because, if I'm being truly honest with myself, I'm such a downgrade after Chloe. Seb knows it; Lily knows it. Elliott was probably thinking it but was actually able to hold himself back from saying it.

The soccer high I felt moments ago vanishes. The girls' laughter grows, planting roots inside my brain until it's all I can hear. I imagine how terrible it's going to feel when Seb comes out. The hot girls will bombard him and flirt and stroke his arm, and I'll be cut off, forgotten on the sidelines. Worse, Seb might laugh at me too.

My fight-or-flight instinct kicks in. It's consistently doing the most, protecting me from any foreseeable embarrassment. All I know is that I have to leave. Like, right now. I want to go to my room and shut out all the laughter and the stares.

When the locker room door opens and Seb steps out, they flock to him. Worse, he loves it. He tries to play it modest, but his cheeky grin betrays him.

His eyes bounce around to every girl, never once looking beyond them to seek me out. I don't matter to him at all in this moment, not when he's surrounded by his fan club. And I'm not going to wait until I matter. I would be standing out here until the end of time. Before he spots me, I escape. I'm faster than any soccer player on that field. I'm Usain Bolt, except not nearly as cool, and fueled by pure terror. When I'm far enough away, I slow down, waiting for my breath to catch up to my body, taking big gulps of air like it's a meal. I don't know when I became this way. This scared, insecure little girl. Maybe I've been this way all along, but I can't remember.

# CHAPTER TWENTY

OVER DINNER, TALK OF THE WEDDING HAS BEEN replaced with what I call the "All Seb, All the Time" experience. I can't watch TV in peace anymore between eating and fielding everyone's questions. Dad wants to know about the soccer game, from team rankings to play-by-play recaps. He finds my proximity to East Bay's soccer star way more interesting than any other part of my life. I do my best to answer his questions, borrowing some of Elliott's terminology.

"So Seb is pretty good, I take it?" he asks.

"Very good," I assure him. "He's a striker."

"Maybe I'll catch one of his games."

"Please don't."

"Don't embarrass her, Raf," Harlow scolds. "She can't bring her dad to her boyfriend's soccer game."

"No, no, it's cool," Dad says. "I'll wear a cap and go incognito. None of your friends will know it's me."

He still assumes I have friends. That's cute.

Dad was super into soccer a few years ago. He followed some Spanish team whose name I never learned, but they ran around in bright red jerseys. You'd think, in all that time, I would have absorbed *some* knowledge of the game, but I have some type of undiagnosed mental deficiency when it comes to sports.

"Do you really have a boyfriend?" Avery squints at me. "Like, in real life? Not on the computer?"

Great. I can't even get an eight-year-old to believe this.

"Yes," I reply.

"Does he go to your school?"

"Yes."

"What does he look like?"

"Like a person," I snap.

"He's very handsome," Harlow says. My cheeks warm.

"I wanna see," Avery whines. "Don't you have a picture of him?"

"No." She brings up a good point, though. What kind of teenage girl doesn't keep pictures of her boyfriend on her phone? I make a mental note to talk to Seb about this. We'll have to up our selfie game, even though I find selfies super-obnoxious. Not to mention unflattering. Every angle brings out the massive scope of my nose, the roundness of my cheeks, the perpetual sheen on my forehead.

Harlow brings her laptop over to the table.

"You're not Googling him, are you?" I ask.

"I'm just showing Avery what he looks like," Harlow says, her fingers tapping the keyboard. "Look, here's his Instagram."

"This is so wrong," I object, but I'm following Avery and my dad as the three of us cluster around Harlow's laptop.

"Why are *you* looking?" I ask Dad. He shrugs.

Harlow clicks on the first picture. It was taken a couple of hours ago—a postgame shot of Seb in his soccer uniform. His brown curls are pulled back by a headband. (Note: most guys can't get away with this look. Seb is most definitely an exception.) His face is pure joy, smile wide, eyes crinkling. I wish I could find something that makes me as happy as soccer makes Seb.

"That's him?" Avery asks, in a tone that fully says, *How the hell did you pull that off?*

She is so offensive.

"Yes, that's my boyfriend." I like saying the word. "Boyfriend." The rounded consonants, the nasal *oy* sound. I like the feeling I get when I say it, how it lets people know I'm wanted. I already know how fleeting the short period of time will be when I can say it. "My boyfriend." Who knows if I ever will again.

"And who's that?" Avery points at a picture toward the bottom of the screen.

*That* is Chloe. More specifically, Chloe in a bathing suit. Even more specifically, Chloe and her abnormally long legs and *pancita*-free stomach in a bathing suit. She's standing at the ocean's edge, hair billowing in the breeze, eyes gazing pensively at the horizon. She's sweaty, but in that sexy, baby-oiled way. Not how I sweat. When I sweat, I look like a glazed donut.

"She's pretty," Avery comments. Thank you, Avery, for another generous sprinkling of salt onto my emotional wound.

The Chloe picture was taken a month ago. Seb's caption: *Love of my life.* I know I'm Seb's fake girlfriend and all, but it still stings. What will people think when they see Chloe on Seb's page, looking like a *Sports Illustrated* swimsuit cover, and then see plain, dumpy Analee on his arm?

Harlow minimizes the page quickly. She's trying to protect my feelings, which only makes me feel worse. I am someone worth pitying.

"Who was that?" Dad demands. "Another woman?"

"Relax, Dad," I say. "It's an old picture of his ex."

I use my "everything is totally cool, Chloe and her amazing body and the fact that she's Lily's new best friend and Seb's irreplaceable dream girl doesn't bother me at all" voice.

"No big deal. I'm sure he forgot to take that picture down," Harlow says in her "oh my God, that girl is way hotter than you but I'm gonna act casual so you don't have a meltdown" voice.

I hate everyone. No one says what they really mean, including myself.

"Why would he break up with *her*?" Avery asks.

Except Avery. For better or worse, Avery always says what she means.

"It's complicated," I say. Even after eavesdropping on their conversation in the library, I'm still not completely sure what happened to Seb and Chloe. In my view, if it's true love, you don't give up on it. But I never believed that what Seb and Chloe had was true love. It was a relationship of convenience. Two hot people who fell into each other and decided to be hot together.

"She's, like, so pretty, though."

"Avery," Harlow says sharply.

"She's not *that* pretty," Dad says. It's such a blatant lie, a move to restore a shred of my long-gone self-esteem. Chloe is indisputably pretty. She might not be everyone's type, but her face is pure symmetry, and her body was sculpted by the gods.

"Whether or not she is pretty has nothing to do with Analee," says Harlow. "It doesn't devalue all the things that Analee brings to the table."

The words lose all meaning when they come from another indisputably pretty person like Harlow. What does she know about feeling like you have nothing to offer? It's not just how I feel about Chloe. It's about everyone else comparing me to her. It's *knowing* that I bring nothing to the table. People like Harlow will always find it easy to value themselves, because the world values them.

"Can we just . . . talk about something else?" I ask. I drain the contents of my glass like I'm downing vodka.

"We can talk about the wedding!" Harlow says. "We're going to have to shop for bridesmaid dresses soon."

"Can they be pink?" Avery asks.

God. It always bums me out that Avery is such a stereotype.

"Close," says Harlow. "Lavender and sage."

Avery squeals and claps her hands. "Yay!"

"Lavender and sage?" Dad asks. "What about yellow?"

Harlow gives him a horrified stare. "Raf . . ."

"What? Yellow's my favorite color."

Harlow has her laptop open again, and she's pulling up some dresses to show us. Dad continues to argue for yellow, since we live in the Sunshine State, while Harlow waves him off.

"Look, Analee," she says. "This style would be perfect for you."

I look at the model on the screen, draped in heavy purple fabric. The dress is cinched just below her boobs, while the lower half is a free-for-all. I decide not to tell Harlow that this is obviously a maternity dress.

"Sure," I say. "Get it."

Because who cares what I wear to this wedding? There's no point in trying to make myself look better than I do. I will never compete with the Chloes and the Harlows. I will always look "less than." Or in this case, "more than."

When I said this kind of stuff to Mom, she would respond the same way every time: "Paging Analee, pity party of one." And then she'd rub the top of my head and plant a big kiss on my cheek. It might sound insensitive to some, but it worked 90 percent of the time. Mom could always make my problems seem smaller. Laughable, even. But now she's gone, and all of my problems, even the ones that should be small, like bridesmaid dresses, are magnified.

"Well, you'll have to come try it on." Harlow laughs. "We can make a girls' day of it. Get our nails done, go to that new smoothie place on Woodland."

"I don't get an invite to girls' day?" Dad asks. He does this fake cutesy pout that almost makes me dry heave. Dad is so obsessed with Harlow. It's like he can't be alone for a second anymore.

"No boys allowed," Harlow says. "Oh and, Analee, make sure you talk to Seb!"

"About what?"

"About going as your date."

"Whoa, whoa, whoa." I raise both hands in the air. "That's . . . He's . . . We're not . . ."

The three of them stare at me, possibly because I've lost all ability to form a coherent sentence. It's not so unusual, what Harlow's suggesting. Seb is my boyfriend, after all, and shouldn't I be thrilled to bring my boyfriend to this disaster of a wedding? It occurs to me that Seb and I never talked about how long we'd keep up our farce. Will we still be together by the wedding? Are we doomed to stay a couple until Chloe and Lily see the light? Or will we fail and eventually peter out after realizing none of it ever meant anything?

It might be nice to have someone along for the wedding. Someone who will save me from the small talk and the dancing and the watching my father marry a woman who is not my mother.

"I'll ask him," I say to Harlow.

Seb might agree to it. He might understand. I think back to our conversation in the cafeteria about his stepmom. The hint of anger simmering underneath the cheeky smile. Anger that might come close to a fraction of mine. Seb hides his well, but I feel like mine is exposed at all times, toxic and black, repulsing everyone around me.

I love lattes now. I hate that I love lattes now, but it is what it is. Seb is at my locker every day like a faithful dog, but even better than a dog, because Seb comes with lattes.

"Got your fix," he says, handing me my cup.

"Mmm, come to mama," I say to the drink. Caffeine is a hell of a drug. I take a long, milky sip.

"Remember when you claimed you didn't like coffee?" Seb asks as I open my locker.

"Nope." I slide my textbook out, which he immediately takes from me. "I don't think that ever happened."

"It's almost like you shouldn't form an opinion before you try something."

I'm too busy savoring my latte to respond. It's gotten easier to talk to Seb. I can't pinpoint when it happened, but I'm not as careful with what I do or don't say. It's harder when the two of us are plunked into the East Bay fishbowl. Even now, when students are hurrying to get to class, I'm keenly aware of how many people stop to look at us. I'm only slightly better at pretending that I don't notice. It's progress for me, getting here. We did it little by little. Seb hands me my morning latte and walks me to my first class, and then later we eat lunch together, just the two of us. I can handle this routine. I'm almost starting to enjoy it.

When the lunch bell rings, Seb is stationed once again at my locker. We head into the cafeteria together and load our trays with chicken nuggets and stale french fries. The perk of dating Seb Matias is that no matter how crowded the cafeteria gets, our table is left open. It's unofficially reserved.

Seb pulls out the chair for me. He's laying the gentleman routine on thick, probably because Chloe is looking in our general direction, though not specifically at us.

"M'lady," he says.

"Thank you, m'lord."

I'm thinking that this fake dating thing isn't so bad. Seb isn't so bad either. I can handle talking to someone one-on-one. It's like talking to Lily, or Harris.

Then Seb ruins it by saying, "We should probably sit with the group at some point."

"The group?" I repeat. My heart seizes in my chest.

"Yeah, I mean . . . that's the goal, right? You get in with Lily, I get in with Chloe?"

That's 100 percent the goal. The problem is, I was just starting to feel comfortable with Seb. Adding other people to the mix could be potentially disastrous, like a chem experiment gone horribly wrong.

"I need more time," I say.

"Why?"

"I just do."

"Has anyone ever told you that you make things way more complicated than they need to be?"

"Oh, okay. Nothing complicated about hanging out with your ex-girlfriend, my ex–best friend, the guy who's trying to bang your ex—"

"All right," Seb says. "I get it. Maybe it is a little fucked up."

"A little?"

"They're still my friends, though."

I don't say anything. I dip my chicken nugget into some ketchup and bite into it. Why is Seb so desperate to call these people his friends? Matt McKinley? Waste of oxygen. Colton? Douchebag. And Chloe? She said she wanted space, and Seb is giving her that space.

"You still have pictures of Chloe on your Instagram," I say. "Did you know that?"

"You're checking out my Instagram?" Seb asks. He looks very self-satisfied right now. I ignore it.

"There was a picture you took of her at the beach."

"Oh," Seb says. He dips a nugget into my ketchup. Without asking. "That was a huge pain in the ass. I had to take seventeen pictures that day before I found one that would satisfy her."

"Hold on," I say. "What?"

"What?"

"You took seventeen pictures of her?"

"That's a rough estimate."

"That's insane," I say.

Seb shrugs. "Every date with Chloe was a photo shoot. She had to approve of every picture I took of her, plus pick the filter and retouch it."

"What about the 'love of my life' caption? Was that her too?"

"No," Seb says. He looks down at his food, focusing much too intently on rearranging his fries. "That was me."

What is it about Chloe? Besides the obvious—that she's smart and pretty and outgoing. Maybe I'm overthinking it. There's no magic Chloe essence that makes her so much better than me. It's a bunch of little ingredients that I lack.

"Do you want me to take the picture down?" he asks.

It doesn't look great for me, as the new girlfriend, to compete with it. And it's wholly inappropriate for Seb to call someone else the love of his life when he's supposed to be dating me. Still, I don't want to make him take it down. It just doesn't feel right.

"It's okay. Keep it."

"You bring up a good point, though," Seb says. He's eaten, like, half my ketchup now. "We need to take some pictures together. What are you doing this weekend?"

I have zero excuses at the ready. And the truth—that Harris and I are going to help an orc widow in the Redlands avenge her husband's death—is much too sad.

"Nothing," I say.

"Let's go to the beach."

I groan. I can't help it.

"Here we go," Seb says, rubbing his hands together. "What's wrong with the beach?"

"Beaches are so overrated. It's one of those ideas that's great in theory but awful in practice. You have to pack all kinds of crap with you—beach chairs, towels, umbrellas, food, water. You sit there for hours, baking in the sun, getting sweaty and sticky, washing yourself off with salt water that dries out your skin. Then you get sand all over the car when you leave. And then you continue to find sand everywhere for a week after."

I don't mean to rant and rave like a lunatic, but my hatred of beaches runs deep. Seb should be looking at me like I've sprouted horns, but instead he laughs and shakes his head.

"You are ridiculous," he says. "And we're going to the beach on Saturday."

"I'm not getting into the water," I say.

"I didn't say you have to get into the water."

"I'm just letting you know."

"Can't you swim?"

"We live in Florida," I say. "Of course I can swim."

"Then what's the problem?"

"Bathing suits."

"I'm not even going to ask," Seb says, fishing out the remains of my ketchup with a french fry.

There's so much wrong with bathing suits. The lack of boob support, the amount of shaving required, the way they put your entire body on display, everything hanging out for the world to see. No, thank you. I'll spare Seb this rant, though.

"Harlow and my dad invited you to their wedding," I say. It's my turn to look down at my french fries. "I know it's super-lame. You totally don't have to go. I can make up an excuse. I don't even know if we'll still technically be a couple by that time."

"I love weddings," Seb says.

I look up. "You do?"

"Yeah. I know that's, like, uncool of me to say or whatever, but

I honestly do. I love watching the bride walk down the aisle. I love dancing to 'Shout.' I love wearing oversize glasses in photo booth pictures."

"Wow," I say.

"Judge me all you want."

"No, no judgment. Does that mean you'll come with me?"

"Sure, why not?"

"But what if you're with Chloe by the time the wedding rolls around?"

"You and I could still go together," Seb says. "As friends."

The word is like a trigger on my heart. It has been so long since anyone has called me a friend. Harris, sure, but it's not the same as having a friend in front of you, breathing and talking and moving. Seb is my friend. When our fake relationship goes to shambles, maybe all won't be lost.

"Did your dad and stepmom have a wedding?" I ask, and Seb's eyes cloud over.

"No," he says. "They married at the courthouse. I wasn't even there."

"I don't know how I'm going to handle Dad and Harlow's wedding," I admit.

"Is Harlow really that bad?"

"Yes," I say, half-joking, half not. "No. I don't know. She's just . . . she's not my mom."

Seb nods like he understands. "When did your parents get divorced?"

I knew this was coming. I always dread this moment in a conversation. The big reveal. When I have to say the words out loud and then get the "I'm sorry" and the awkward silence and that *look*. That look that makes me feel like a puppy at the pound.

"They didn't," I say. "My mom died two and a half years ago."

"Fuuuuuck," Seb says.

I laugh. I don't know why. It's a totally inappropriate thing to do after telling someone your mom died.

"How?" he asks.

"Ovarian cancer."

"Fuck," he says again. "God. That really sucks, Analee."

"Believe me, I know."

He wipes his hands on a napkin, still chewing his food. Neither of us speaks for a few seconds. I usually hate these types of silences. I feel the need to talk to fill the empty space, but I can never think of anything to say. Then I worry I'm a horrible conversationalist, and that added stress prevents me from coming up with any talking points whatsoever.

It doesn't feel uncomfortable now, though. Seb, still eating as always, looks deep in thought.

Finally he says, "No wonder you're so pissed off all the time."

I burst out laughing. "One of many reasons."

"Is that a picture of her? On your phone?" he asks.

"Oh." I can't hide my surprise that he noticed something of mine. Most of Seb's attention span is devoted to himself, then Chloe, then the rest of the student body. "Yeah. It is."

"Can I see?" he asks.

I pull out my phone to show him, thinking he'll give it a cursory glance. Instead he takes it and studies the picture intently, running his finger over the cracked screen.

It's the last picture I took of Mom before she was diagnosed. She, Lily, and I had gone to the mall that day, and we had eaten all the samples in the food court and gorged ourselves on Cinnabons. At some point Lily began talking to a store mannequin. We were hopped up on sugar, and Mom laughed so hard that she cried, and that's when I took the picture.

"You look just like her," he comments.

"You think?" I've been told this before, but I like hearing it. Looking like Mom, even a second-rate version of her, is the one thing I truly love about my appearance.

"Like, exactly," Seb says. "You have the same smile. I mean, the rare times you actually show your smile."

He studies the picture a little longer as I shift around next to him.

"What was she like?" he asks.

I'm not sure what to say. It's been so long since someone brought her up. Dad never talks about her, and Harlow carefully avoids the subject. Avery is barely aware that another woman ever existed in Harlow's place, that Dad and I had a life before they came into it.

"She was . . . ," I start to say, but I'm not sure how to finish the sentence. She was my *mom*. How do you put that connection into words? She was everything. My whole world. The person who made me. It's like someone asking you to sum up your entire existence in a snapshot.

"She was funny," I settle for saying, but it doesn't even cover a fraction of what she was.

"Yeah?"

"Not funny like a comedian. She was goofy. She liked to make people laugh, even if they were laughing at her."

That's where Mom and I differ. I'm terrified of people laughing at me. She welcomed it. As long as everyone else was happy, she was happy.

He smiles, and I have the urge to keep talking.

"And her favorite holiday was April Fools' Day," I say. "She liked regular holidays too, but she went all out for April Fools'. She was a legend."

"Sugar in the salt shakers, that kind of thing?" Seb asks.

I wave the question away. "Amateur hour. It would be a full day of torture. She'd serve caramel onions that were disguised as apples, attach party poppers to the doors, cover my entire room in sticky notes . . ."

As I'm retelling it to Seb, it's like something inside me is uncorked. All the stuff I miss about Mom, all the stuff I want to remember and so I keep it locked tight, is spilling out of me before I can stop it. I can't remember talking this much, for this long, to anybody recently.

"You're lucky," he says when I pause to breathe.

I scoff at this. "Not the word I'd use."

"You had an awesome mom."

"Had," I repeat. The past tense hurts, every time.

"Some people don't even get that."

"I think that makes it easier," I say. "You don't know what you're missing."

"Believe me, you know what you're missing," Seb says. It occurs to me that for all his complaining about his stepmom, he's never mentioned his real mom. I think about bringing it up, but his face closes shut, and I can tell it's the end of that. People think they know Seb, but maybe they know only one version of him. Maybe something inside of him matches what's inside of me. The only difference is, I give in to it completely, and he pretends it doesn't exist.

# CHAPTER TWENTY-ONE

**Harris:** you're blowing me off to go to the beach?

**Harris:** who is this, really?

**Me:** I don't want to go

**Harris:** so don't

**Me:** I have to

**Harris:** why?

**Harris:** beaches suck. get ready for a sunburn and sand in unforeseen places

**Me:** Ugh, i know

**Harris:** you going with the fam?

I pause, fingers draped over the keyboard.

**Me:** No, just a friend

**Harris:** ? did you and lily make up?

**Me:** Not yet

**Me:** Working on it

**Harris:** i guess i'll have to entertain myself while you're gone

**Harris:** even though the internet is no fun without you

**Me:** Uh-huh . . .

**Harris:** no, really

**Harris:** talking to you is the best part of my day

My insides turn to butter. I don't want to leave this conversation and spend the day getting itchy and sweaty. I want to sit in my air-conditioned room and soak up every single one of Harris's words.

**Me:** Mine too

**Me:** Tonight we're delivering the hell out of that trinket, though

**Harris:** promise?

**Me:** I swear on the spirit of orc husband

**Harris:** RIP, orc husband. you are forever in our hearts

I shave every spare inch of my body in preparation for beach day. It's a lot of work, contorting myself into Harlow-like poses so that I can reach the backs of my thighs and around my knees. I start to feel dizzy and light-headed in the process, and I wonder if it's possible to suffer from heat stroke in the shower.

The funny thing is, I don't even believe in shaving. I think all women should agree to go full Chewbacca, grow out all hair everywhere. Unfortunately, the rest of the world doesn't agree with me. And I'm not going Chewbacca by myself.

So, I spend an hour scraping a razor all over my skin. Then I put on the only bathing suit I own, a retro one-piece that makes me feel like Marilyn Monroe. It minimizes my stomach pouch and makes my boobs look fantastic. Not that I care what Seb thinks of my breasts. I'm just saying.

On top of my vintage suit, I throw on jeans and a tank top. Seb already texted me that he's a few minutes away from my house. When I get downstairs, I see Avery decked out in a tiny hot-pink bikini, platform sandals, and sunglasses. I stop in my tracks.

"Where are you going?" I ask her.

"With you."

"Uh . . . what? No, you're not."

"Yes, I am."

"No, you're not."

Dad calls my name from the kitchen. "Analee!"

"To be continued," I warn Avery. She crosses her arms in front of her as I stomp into the kitchen, where Dad and Harlow are drinking coffee at the table. No, scratch that. Dad is drinking coffee. Harlow is drinking what she has previously informed me is called Teeccino, an herbal coffee alternative. Because she's Harlow.

"Why is Avery in a bathing suit?" I ask them point-blank.

"Harlow and I are meeting with the caterer today," Dad says. "You have to take your sister to the beach with you."

I hate it when Dad calls Avery my sister. I know we're supposed to be some beautiful blended family, but Avery and I are not related. We don't share any of the same genes or personality traits. We're glorified roommates at most.

"Can't you guys take her with you to the caterer?" I ask. My voice creeps into a whine. "Or, I don't know, drop her off at a friend's house? She has like a million of them."

Dad and Harlow glance at each other.

"No," he says. "You have to take her."

"But—"

"I packed some lunches for you guys!" Harlow cuts in. She gets up and thrusts a tote bag into my hands. "Chickpea salad sandwiches and trail mix. As a thank-you for taking care of Avery."

I stand there, the tote bag dangling from my fingers. Why do I feel like I've been bamboozled? This is obviously a poorly thought-out plan on Dad's part to prevent Seb and me from going the whole day unchaperoned.

Before I can protest, I hear Seb's car pull into our driveway. He honks, two short taps on the horn.

"He's not coming to the door?" Dad asks. *"Pero es un mal educado?"*

"It's fine," I say. "I told him I'd meet him outside."

Then Avery trots in wearing her ridiculous shoes. She can barely walk in them. "He's here!"

Harlow instructs me to reapply Avery's sunscreen when we get there and to make sure she doesn't go out too far in the water. Dad tells me, in Spanish, that I'm in charge of Avery and I need to keep my eyes on her at all times. Like I *asked* to do this job today. At least Harlow has the courtesy to thank me. Dad's treating me like I'm Avery's on-call nanny.

"Have fun, girls," he says to us as we leave the kitchen. "Do some sisterly bonding!"

I don't respond. I gather the bags together, weighing myself down with towels and sunblock and chickpea sandwiches like a pack mule, while Avery walks beside me empty-handed.

"Bye, Mom. Bye, Dad!" Avery blows them each a kiss over her shoulder. Within a week of moving into our house, she took to calling my father "Dad." Each time I hear the word popping out of her little cherry-colored mouth, it makes my skin crawl. She uses it excessively. "Morning, Dad." "Pass the okra, Dad."

I know I'm being petty. I should be more generous, more . . . big sister-y. Avery's father, some guy Harlow met back in college, abandoned Harlow when she was pregnant, so it's nice that Avery can now plant her flag on a new father figure. But still, I feel a pervasive sense of ownership toward my dad.

When Avery and I step outside, Seb is sitting in the front seat of his car with one arm stretched carelessly over the steering wheel. I stomp ahead of Avery and yank open the door to the passenger seat.

"We have to take Avery with us," I tell him.

Seb pulls off his sunglasses, looks at me. "Who?"

"Harlow's daughter."

And then Avery pokes her head under my arm to talk to Seb. "Hi! Are you Analee's boyfriend?"

I push her out of the way. "You ride in the back. And don't ask questions."

"Ow!" She rubs her arm where I touched her. "That really hurt!"

"Please. I barely touched you." I toss my bags into the back and plop into the passenger seat. Avery frowns when I shut the door on her.

"Sorry in advance," I say to Seb.

Before he can answer, Avery opens the car door and slides into the backseat. She massages her arm with one hand and glares at me.

"It was the other arm," I remind her. She's full of shit, just as I suspected.

Seb cranes his head to look at Avery. "Hi, little girl."

"I'm not little," she informs him. "I'm eight."

"My mistake." He raises an eyebrow at me, and I close my eyes and shake my head to let him know that I have no part in this.

"Buckle up, little girl," he says to Avery. I stifle a smile as she now aims her glare at him. Finally. A sane person who doesn't treat Avery like a spoiled little princess. For the first time in a while, I feel like someone is on my side.

The last time I went to the beach was right before Mom was diagnosed. I don't remember this fact until I sink my feet into the sand and hear the seagulls flying overhead and smell the salty ocean. Combined, all of these sensations jolt the memory from the recesses of my brain.

I call this phenomenon Painful Sensory Memory Bomb.

I remember it all. Mom whipping out a comically oversize hat, complete with a chin strap, and wearing it like it was a completely normal thing to do.

Dad and I looked at each other and completely lost it.

"What?" she asked, and her confused expression combined with the ridiculous hat only made us laugh harder.

She rolled her eyes at us and pulled out her book. I can't remember what she was reading that day. Probably something by Stephen King. Mom was obsessed with him, always calling him her book boyfriend.

"Where," I asked, in between gasps for air, "did you get that?"

"Get what?" Mom asked as though a person could be unaware of a spaceship parked on top of her head.

"Did you see her carrying it?" Dad asked me. He squeezed his eyes, still damp from laughter.

"No," I said. "It just . . . magically appeared. Like a gift from God."

Mom reached up to touch the hat's wide straw brim. "Wait. Are you talking about my sun hat?"

"Sun hat!" Dad repeated, and for some reason it became the funniest thing either of us had ever heard.

Mom got all huffy and said, *"No se porque te ríes*, Ms. Green Panty Hose."

She was grasping at straws, referencing the kiwi-colored tights that I got in eighth grade. They made me look like Elphaba from *Wicked*.

"And you?" Mom turned to Dad. "One word: muttonchops."

Her attempts to deflect the insults were unsuccessful—we didn't shut up about her sun hat for the rest of the day. But that's how our family displayed affection: unrelenting mockery. Now I have a new family and we gingerly walk on eggshells around one another.

I don't know what Dad did with Mom's sun hat. If we still have it, I don't want to see. It has forever lost the potential to be funny. There are so many things that suck about death, but one of the worst is how it contaminates whatever it touches. Everything that was once funny about a person becomes sad. And I'm not sure it will ever be funny again. It just sucks that something that made Dad and me laugh so hard that day will now only cause us pain.

Then I think, *What happens when Dad dies?* I'll be the only person in the entire world who knows the significance of the sun hat, the sole keeper of its memory.

"Here." Seb plants a beach umbrella into the sand and twists. I shut my memory down, return to the present. It's jarringly bright out here, barely a cloud to shield us from the brutal sun. Avery runs ahead of us without hesitation, kicking off her platform shoes. Then she splashes around the water's edge. I lay out the beach towels while Seb strips off his T-shirt with zero inhibitions.

And . . . wow. Seb has muscles. Not the big, hulky steroid-type muscles but the ones that look like chiseled marble. I look away, hoping he didn't notice my wandering eyes. I lie back against my towel, pulling out my copy of *Harry Potter and the Goblet of Fire*. I'm currently rereading the series for the eighth time.

"Where's your bathing suit?" A shadow falls across my page. I look up to find Seb staring down at me.

"Under this." I pull on my shirt strap.

"And you're keeping your clothes on because . . ."

"I don't know. There's a chill."

"It's ninety-two degrees."

"Thanks, Al Roker."

"Do you want to go into the water?"

"I told you," I say. "I don't do that. Salty, sticky, et cetera?"

"Suit yourself." He turns and walks away.

"Keep an eye on Avery," I call after him.

He waves a hand in my direction, then throws himself face-first into the crashing waves, splashing Avery in the process. She shrieks and jumps back.

Not wanting to get drenched in salt water is a perfectly valid desire when spending a day at the beach. It's not like I came to have a good time. I mean, Seb and I might take a few pictures indicating that yes, we are having a good time. But it doesn't have to be the truth.

Being here, around Seb's toned body and Avery's tiny one, doesn't leave me wanting to expose my less-than-ideal girth. It's not like I hate *everything* I'm working with. My calves have a nice shape, my boobs are full, my waist is fairly defined. People won't notice the good things, though. They'll pick up on everything that's wrong with me instead. Avery will be blunt as usual, saying something horribly offensive that she doesn't realize is horribly offensive. Seb will overhear, and he'll probably agree even though he won't comment. Not to mention all of Seb's followers who will tear me apart if they see a full-body shot of me in a swimsuit.

No. Better to leave the clothes on.

"Analee!" Seb's voice carries over the tide. I look, and he's grinning, waving his arms wildly. I can't help but laugh. He looks like a little boy. Avery's next to him, finally immersed in the water. She dunks her head in every time a wave hits, then comes up laughing and coughing up seawater. I don't know that I've ever seen Avery look her age more than she does now. I've always just thought of her as a mini Harlow without the zen.

"Come in!" Seb hollers before getting a mouthful of water.

I shake my head at him and return to Harry Potter. Harry has snuck into the prefect's bathroom, and he's trying to figure out the golden egg before the second task of the Triwizard Tournament. I don't care. I can't focus. I hear Seb and Avery laughing and splashing around. A couple of feet away two sisters are digging a hole with plastic shovels. I lay the open book over my face and close my eyes. All the noise fades into the background, and I start to relax.

Until it starts to rain.

I jolt, let the book fall beside me, then blink. How is it raining? I'm under an umbrella, and the sun is still blazing.

Then I look up to see Seb, standing over me, dripping water right onto my face.

"Quit it," I say, using my arm to shield myself.

"I can *see* you sweating. Come on. Get into the water with us."

"I'm not sweating. I was perfectly dry until you came over."

Except I am sweating. Profusely.

"You're saying I made you wet?" Seb asks. He snickers.

"Oh my God. Please go away."

"Sorry. I couldn't let that one slide."

"You could have. . . . You *should* have."

"Seb!" Avery screams from the water. "Look at this one!"

"We're chasing waves," he tells me.

"Thrilling."

"More thrilling than sitting here, fully clothed, reading a boring book."

"It's not boring," I inform him. "It's Harry Potter."

"Ah," he says. "You're one of those."

"One of those . . . ?"

"Those weird Harry Potter nerds."

"Weird Harry—excu-excuse me?" I sputter. I grab a fistful of sand and throw it at him, but he ducks right in time to crouch beside me laughing. I, on the other hand, am not laughing. This is so not a laughing matter.

"First of all," I say, "it's weird *not* to like Harry Potter. Harry Potter is a central part of mainstream culture at this point."

"I've never read it." He has the audacity to state this fact proudly.

"I feel sorry for you. You should be deeply ashamed of your ignorance."

He shrugs. "I don't know. Stories about magic and wizards and stuff don't interest me."

"Oh really? What about stories about love and friendship? And heroism? And honor in the face of impossible circumstances?"

"Eh," he says, and I feel an all-consuming rage boiling within me. Seb looks at my face and starts to laugh. "It is so easy to piss you off."

I sit up. "This is a serious problem. You *have* to read Harry Potter. I can't fake date someone who hasn't."

"No, thanks."

"Seb. I have a copy I can loan you."

"Hmm." He takes one of my curls and twirls it between his wet fingers. "And if I read it, what are you going to do for me?"

I slap his hand away. "Ew. Are you bribing me for sexual favors?"

"Analee." He looks annoyed. "I'm not an asshole. And I definitely don't need to bribe women into having sex with me. God."

"Fine. So what do I have to do?"

"Ah, ah, ah." He wags a finger at me. "You're going to have to trust me on this one. I'll read the first book of Harry Potter if you do something for me in return."

"And I can't know what it is?"

"Nope."

"Then no way. That's not fair."

"Have it your way." He cups a handful of sand and lets it run through his fingers. "I don't have to read the book."

The thing is, it's such a travesty to go through life without having read Harry Potter. How can you ever be truly fulfilled as a person?

I let out a puff of air, thinking on this.

"You can trust me, you know," Seb says. He gives me a sideways glance, and I turn my head to meet his gaze. God. When did his face go from something I wanted to hit to something I wanted to stare at for hours on end?

I look into his eyes, soft and dark and searching. The funny thing is, I *might* be starting to trust him. A little.

"All right," I say. "I'll do it."

"Shake on it?"

I offer him my hand, and he grips it in a firm shake.

"Don't make me regret this," I add. His only response is to lean forward and yank the book right out of my hands. It's typical Seb. So entitled.

"Hey!" I protest, sitting up.

"Come into the water with me. Just five minutes."

"No."

"Come on, Analee."

"No."

"You're hopeless." He tosses the book back at me. "I'm going to hang out with the fun sister."

So much for Seb being on my side.

"She's not my sister!" I call as he hurries back into the water. Of course he kicks up sand all over my towel as he leaves. I try to tune out the sound of his and Avery's laughter. Let them have their stupid fun. I have a book to get back to.

I press my hand against my forehead and peer out at them. I envy the way they can fully let go, laugh without worrying about how it affects anyone around them. And I am totally freaking sweating my ass off. I want to sink into the ocean and suck up its water like a sponge.

I force myself to stare at my book. I didn't bring sunglasses, so I have to squint while I'm reading. Another reason I hate the beach. It's too bright. I like being indoors, where I can control the temperature and lighting.

"Analee!" Avery flops onto the towel beside me, her skin wet and cold. Apparently it's her turn to bother me.

"What." I stare at my book even though the words have lost all meaning. I'm too uncomfortable to focus.

"Seb wants me to convince you to come in."

"Go tell him you were unsuccessful."

"He said it's my mission. I'm Secret Agent Pink, and he's Secret Agent Striker."

"And you just revealed your secret identity to me, so I'd call this mission a fail."

"Ugh." Avery squeezes out her hair. "You're always like this."

"What are you talking about? Like what?"

"You're always so . . . like . . . mean."

"I am not *mean*. Not always, at least."

"You never smile."

"I smile . . ." I say this entirely unconvincingly. While frowning.

"You're always on the computer, sitting in the dark."

"Not today," I reply. "Today I'm at the beach."

"Yeah, and you're not even wearing your bathing suit."

I go silent. I think of how silly Mom looked in her sun hat and what I must look like, fully dressed in the epic Florida heat. As annoying as she is, maybe Avery has a point. Maybe I need to escape from the shadows once in a while.

I mentally calculate how long it'll take me to shed my clothes and hide myself in the water. I think I could make it in fifteen seconds. Too little time for anyone to really see me.

"Fine," I say, rising. I leave a big sweaty imprint on my towel. "I'll go in."

"Really?" Avery's eyes widen in disbelief.

"Yes."

"Yay!" She claps her hands and shoots Seb a thumbs-up. He raises a fist in triumph. I'm surprised either of them care whether I join them or not. But it feels kind of good that they do. Like I matter, even a little bit.

I quickly unzip my jeans and slip them off, then pull my shirt over my head and toss it to the ground.

"Whoa," Avery says, staring at me. My heart sinks. I know she'll say something about the way my thighs jiggled or how the bathing suit clings to my belly.

"You have big boobs," she says instead, which is still such an Avery observation, but I can't get too upset about it. She could have said a number of worse things.

"You need to get a filter," I tell her.

"What does that mean?"

"It means keep your mouth shut once in a while."

"Whatever. Race you to the water!"

We take off, and I hear Avery screech behind me. The two of us make it to the water at roughly the same time. I collapse into it, closing my eyes and letting myself fall under. When I come up, Seb is treading water beside me.

"Yesssss, Analee!" he says, raising his hand to high-five me. I reluctantly oblige.

"I did it," Avery says proudly. "I got her to come in."

"Nice work, Agent Pink." Seb offers her a high five too, and she slaps his hand with glee.

"Look, here's a big one!" she says, pointing at a wave rolling toward us.

"Let's do it." Seb grabs each of us by the hand, and we face off against the incoming wave.

"Go!" Avery shouts.

The three of us dive in, the water rushing into my ears, my legs kicking and splashing against the current. When I come up for air, I'm choking on salt water, but I feel . . . okay. I forgot how light the ocean makes me feel. How gigantic it is compared to everything else in my life. How it connects everyone and everything. Even me, Seb, and Avery. For now, at least, until they start to annoy me again.

We stay in the water for an hour, lunging into waves and floating on our backs. Avery has limitless energy. Seb and I hang back while she continues chasing waves.

"We have to take some pictures," Seb reminds me. My head is tipped back, eyes closed. I'm counting the sunspots I see through my eyelids.

"Oh yeah," I say. I can't believe I forgot our primary purpose for being here.

"Come on." He takes my hand and leads me to the shore. I stand up, forgetting I'm nearly naked, until Seb pauses to stare at me. His eyes run up and down the length of my body, with some definite lingering going on in the chest area. He doesn't look away, like I would.

I suddenly don't know where to put my hands. I try to cross them in front of me, but it leaves my belly exposed. Then I move them down, but the position is awkward and unnatural.

"I like your bathing suit," he says.

"Um. Thanks."

We continue walking. He must not have noticed the way my thighs bulge out of it. Or he did notice but he's trying to cover it up by focusing on the suit. Suddenly I hate this stupid bathing suit. It's not something Marilyn Monroe would wear. It's total grandma fashion, minus the floral print and the bathing cap. I think back to the insanely gorgeous picture of Chloe wearing a string bikini like a pageant model. What the hell am I doing? Seriously. There's no way I can allow Seb's eight hundred seventy-six followers to see me in a frumpy grandma suit.

Seb and I make it back to our spot, and he immediately takes out his phone.

"I look like crap," I mutter, putting a hand in front of my face.

"Analee?"

"What?"

"Shut up."

I laugh. "I do! I look like my *abuela*."

He throws an arm around me and sticks his other arm, the one with the phone, in front of us to snap the picture.

"Hey!" I yank the phone from his hand. "Delete it, Seb. Seriously."

"Nope." He takes it back. He has those stupidly fast athlete reflexes.

"Please." I'm getting panicky now. I start to shiver from the water cooling my skin, and I rub my hands up and down my arms to keep warm.

Seb holds the phone directly in my eyesight. "Look. This is a great picture of you. Stop being ridiculous."

The picture is slightly tilted, but Seb was able to get both of us in it. He's smiling broadly and I'm midlaugh, looking up at him. I can barely recognize myself, the way my nose crinkles up and my eyes get all squinty when I'm laughing.

This is what happy looks like on me. It's been a while since I've seen it.

"I guess it's an okay picture," I concede. "But what if someone posts a bitchy comment?"

"They won't."

"But what if they do?"

"I'll delete it."

"But other people will see it."

"And?"

How am I supposed to answer that? Seb has no insecurities when it comes to his looks, so if someone were to target him, nothing they wrote would affect him. People can hurt you only if you're scared that what they say is the truth. Seb believes the best of himself. The problem is, I can only believe the worst is true when it comes to me.

He notices me shivering, and he grabs an extra towel to wrap around me. Through the towel, he gives my arm a squeeze. I begin to warm up.

"People can be mean," I say. Harris would agree with me. The mean ones are everywhere, even when we quest. People who insult you, people who ooze hate and anger into the world until it blocks all the good stuff.

"Not all of them," Seb says. I can't figure out if he's overly optimistic or privileged.

"A lot of them."

"I disagree," he says. "The mean ones are just the loudest."

I look at the picture again. I want to be this version of me—laughing and happy and not the sad girl Avery sees sitting alone in her bedroom. Maybe it's a choice sometimes. I have to consciously let this happy Analee out for air. Maybe sad and scared go hand in hand, and the more I hide in the shadows, the less of a chance I have to be this smiling girl in the picture.

"So?" Seb asks, his finger hovering over the phone. "To post or not to post?"

But I can't do it. Because posting the photo has the potential for disaster, and I've made a conscious attempt to live my life disaster-free.

"I can't," I say. "I'm sorry."

I've disappointed him. Worse, I actually care. And if I care this much about what Seb thinks of me, how will I feel when I'm exposed, body and all, to most of East Bay?

"Don't be sorry," he says. "But, for the record, you look hot in that bathing suit."

"I do not," I reply.

"Swear to God."

I'm sure he's only saying it so that I'll let him post the picture. Still, something like electricity buzzes under my skin.

# CHAPTER TWENTY-TWO

### Analee's Rules for Using the Bathroom at School

1. Go during first period, when it's most
likely to be empty.
2. Use the bathroom on the second floor.
3. Corner stall, always.
4. Hold your business until there's no one around.
5. Three layers of toilet paper on the seat.

I FOLLOW EACH AND EVERY ONE OF MY BATHROOM rules the Monday after beach weekend. I flush my layers of toilet paper, unlatch the door, and exit the stall. I stare at my mirrored reflection. The girl staring back at me has sun-kissed cheeks and glowing skin, free of breakouts. I don't know if East Bay's local beaches have magical skin-healing properties, but I look . . . not awful. My reflection smiles at me.

Just as I turn on the sink to wash my hands, Lily walks in.

My smile vanishes. It makes no sense, her being here right now.

She has English Lit first period, on the other side of the building. And she never uses the bathroom in the morning. Lily is strictly an afternoon bathroom user.

The two of us haven't stood within six feet of each other since the Incident.

She doesn't say a word when she sees me. She walks right up to the adjacent sink and leans forward, pulling a tube of lip gloss from her pocket. I try not to stare as she puckers her lips and slathers them in pink goo.

It's just that, in spite of what happened between us, I can't help missing her. It kills me that I have no idea what's going on in her life. Not just the massive, Colton-type stuff but the little things. What TV shows is she watching these days? Did she notice that Mrs. Ludinsky's new haircut resembles a mullet?

I turn off the faucet and grab a paper towel to dry my hands. I'm about to slip out of the bathroom, when Lily speaks.

"Are you really dating Seb?" she asks. She slips the lip gloss back into her pocket and looks at me, waiting.

I freeze, holding the wad of paper towel in my hand. This situation is too much for my brain to compute right now. Lily. Next to me. Talking to me.

God, how can I lie to Lily? She knows me better than anyone else. But I *have* to lie. I'm doing it for Seb, and I'm doing it to show Lily that I'm not the person she thought I was.

"Yes," I say. I don't look directly at her. I look at the Lily in the mirror.

She makes a humming sound that I can't interpret.

I should just leave, but I can't move. I'm hoping that, magically, everything will return to normal between us. That we'll be able to talk without it feeling like a test.

Lily brushes past me while I stand there like a moronic statue, wishing for something that will never happen. Dammit. *I* wanted to be the one who leaves first. She pauses at the door, then turns back to me, fingers still on the handle.

"Be careful, okay?" she says.

"Hmm?" *Throw the goddamn paper towel away, Analee. Move. Leave. What is wrong with you?*

"With Seb, I mean."

"Okay," I answer, half-dazed, but she's already out the door. I don't even think to ask her why.

I used to believe that the trouble with Lily began with Colton. Now, when I look back, I see that the crack in our friendship formed much earlier. It deepened when Mom got sick, after every missed chemo session, when Lily accepted Harlow as part of our lives, when she chose finding happiness with everyone who wasn't me. Yes, by the time Colton appeared, our friendship had a deep chasm running straight through its center. It was only after Colton that I bothered to notice.

I couldn't tell Lily after I had seen her and Colton making out in the parking lot. I tried to, nearly a thousand times. But then I would chicken out. I'm not sure what was stopping me. Lily and I had always been fans of the TMI, no-holds-barred conversations: everything from the color of period discharge to the mechanics of sex. Now, though . . . everything felt different.

Time passed, and every day I would promise myself that I'd ask her tomorrow. Then tomorrow became the day after that, and the day after that, until I had a wake of missed opportunities under my belt.

After a week people at school started talking, noting the starry-eyed glances that Lily and Colton gave each other and the not-at-all subtle hand grazing between the two of them in the hallways. I decided to wait. Why should I be the one to bring it up?

The problem is that the longer I waited, the more furious I became. Best friends didn't do this. They didn't make out with tattooed boys in public places and just fail to mention it.

Exactly nine days after the face sucking, on an ordinary Friday at lunch, all the anger contained inside me finally boiled over.

I was watching Lily, the way she took tiny bird bites out of her sandwich, the way she hummed as she chewed, like our lives were as normal as they'd ever been, and I snapped.

"I saw you, you know," I spat out.

"What?"

"Last week. I saw you. In the parking lot."

Based on my tone, anyone eavesdropping might have assumed that Lily had done something truly awful. I sounded like a player in a real-life game of Clue. *Lily Nadarajah, in the parking lot, with her lips.*

Lily put down her sandwich. She was acting calm, but by the way she kept blinking, I could tell she was the slightest bit freaked. Well, good. I wanted her freaked, like I'd been freaked when I'd seen her.

I won't lie. Part of me took pleasure in the fact that I could finally unleash all the anger and resentment that I'd been feeling. Not just at Lily but at everyone. I was so tired of Lily being happy when I could never be. If I had to sink, I wanted to grab her by the ankles and pull her down with me.

"Saw me doing what?" she asked.

"Really?" I asked. "You're really going to play dumb right now?"

Her blinking intensified. "I was going to tell you."

"When? Before it spread around the entire school? Because if that's the case, you're too late."

"It hasn't—"

"It has. Sarah was talking about it in homeroom today."

I wanted her to come up with some mind-blowing defense. Some reason that she had to keep it a secret, like blackmail or extortion. *Something.* But she just sat there, blinking, and I let my anger spew out of me. I was so tired of keeping things inside, letting them rot and fester, and I just wanted to empty myself out.

"I mean, God, Lily. I thought we were friends."

"Hey." Her eyebrows bunched together. "We *are* friends."

"Friends talk to each other."

"We talk every day! All the time!"

"What good is that when you keep this giant secret from me?"

"I wanted to tell you."

I shook my head. "If you wanted to, you would have. It's pretty simple."

"Okay, you know what?" Lily sat up straighter, and the blinking stopped. She was starting to get angry too. I could always tell with her. "This, right here, is why I didn't tell you."

"What are you talking about?"

"If I told you, I knew you'd be all weird and angry about it!"

"I'm only 'weird and angry' because you hid it from me!" That was a lie. I was angry that she kept things from me, of course, but I was also pissed off that it had happened. It felt like a betrayal of sorts. Lily and I always kept to the wings, commenting on all the assholes in the spotlight. Now Lily was inching into the light, while I would be stuck in the dark. Alone.

"Can't you just be happy for me? Please?" she asked.

"Happy that you swapped spit with Colton? Like that's some major life accomplishment?"

"Stop it. That's not what it was."

"He used to do it with Mia all the time. Remember? You said Mia was pathetic and that she should get a hobby."

What Lily said: "Because I was *jealous* of her. I like Colton, Analee. I like him and his friends. I like being around other people once in a while and laughing and not feeling shitty all the time."

What I heard: *I don't like you anymore.*

Naturally, I didn't take this well.

"I'm *so sorry* that I've been such a burden on you," I said. "I didn't realize my mom's death would put a damper on your social life."

Lily's head snapped up at the mention of Mom. "That's *not* what I meant."

Her voice was low, raw. I realized that it was the first time I'd mentioned Mom to her since the day of the funeral.

"I just . . ." She gave a shaky sigh, cleared her throat. When she spoke again, her voice sounded like her voice. Whatever emotion it had contained had melted away. "I just wish you would try to give things a chance. That's all. And I'd really like it if my friend and my boyfriend could get along."

That day, I hated the sound of the word. "Boyfriend." The harsh consonants, the whiny *oy* sound. I wanted to put Lily on mute.

"You guys are . . . official?" I asked.

"Yes," Lily said. She dipped her head and gave a bashful smile, looking full-on like a rosy-cheeked princess.

I should have wanted to see my best friend happy, but it only made me feel more pain. Maybe I was a selfish person at heart. If I couldn't be happy, I didn't want anyone else to be.

"I'll give him a chance," I said. Not because I meant it but because I was scared that things with Lily would truly be over if I told her what I really thought.

"That's all I ask."

"But I still think his tattoo is stupid."

I thought she would agree with me, or laugh, but she didn't respond at all.


Harlow bought me condoms. They're in a cardboard box on my nightstand with a note attached that says,

*Just in case. Be safe.*

*-H*

It's mortifying.

What if Dad had come into my room and found them? Not that he ever really comes in here anyway. Lately he's wanted nothing to do with me or my living space. But still, it was a risky move.

Each condom is wrapped in blue tinfoil. I open one, out of curiosity. The condom is more slippery than I expected. I roll it down over my middle and index fingers, then display it like a sock puppet. I think about whether Lily and Colton use one if they have sex. Is she on birth control? Is she being safe? They must be having sex at this point. They're practically dry humping in public, so one can only assume that all bets are off in the privacy of a bedroom.

I wonder how often Chloe and Seb used to do it. I don't like to think about it for some reason, but my brain has masochistic tendencies. It flips through images of Chloe in a matching lace bra and panties set and Seb's shirtless body, which I can now picture in torturously perfect detail, thanks to our beach outing. I picture them in a sweaty synchronized dance, and it makes my stomach turn.

I'm not sure I'll ever be okay enough to be naked in front of someone. Why does everyone act like sex is no big deal? You have to (a) find someone willing to sleep with you, (b) have the confidence to disrobe in front of them, and (c) know how to move and when. It feels like at some point everyone got a manual to life, and I lost my copy.

Also, who is going to want to have sex with me? Maybe in the future, when I'm around thirty . . . if, by some miracle, I have managed to cure myself of all my physical and emotional flaws.

"Analee?"

Oh God, no. Dad's heavy footsteps thud up the stairs, and I realize that I still have my fingers in a condom. I slap it off and fling it across the room, then stuff the box of them under my pillow.

When Dad walks in, I'm flopped belly-down on the bed, feeling my heart pound against the comforter.

"Yo," I say. To my father. For no apparent reason.

"What's wrong?" he asks immediately.

"Nothing. What do you mean? Why do you ask?"

"You're all red."

"That's just . . . I'm warm," I say. "It's warm in here."

In moments like these it's super-clear that I could never be a CIA operative or a spy or any job that requires a modicum of cool. Plus, Dad and Harlow like to keep the thermostat at a crisp sixty-seven degrees.

"Harlow's speaking at a wellness panel tonight," he says. "And Avery's at Leia's house. So we're on our own for dinner."

"Could we order something really unhealthy?" I ask. "Like, fried and slathered in grease? And eat on the couch in front of the TV?"

My dad glances behind him as if Harlow will sneak attack us for the mere thought. Then he looks down at his stomach, at his missing pouch. I can almost see the tug-of-war happening in his brain.

"Come on, Dad," I say. "Live a little."

He sticks his hands into his back pockets and sighs. "Okay."

"Really?" I sit up.

"Yeah. Let's do it."

"Can we order from Wings Express?"

"Sure," he says. He tosses one last look behind him. Is it normal to be this terrified of your fiancée?

Forty-five minutes later we're sprawled on the couch with TV trays in front of us. The TV trays almost didn't make it through Hurricane Harlow, but Dad managed to convince her that one of us might use it if we're home alone. Harlow spurted something about being present during meals and eating mindfully, and Dad made a lot of agreeable grunts, but in the end the TV trays stayed. A rare victory for Team Normal.

"She means well," Dad says suddenly in between mouthfuls of fried chicken.

"Who?" I ask. But I know who.

"Harlow. With the vegan dinners and all. It makes her feel good."

It's as if he's reading my mind. I stare at the TV. "It doesn't make *me* feel good."

"Come on, that's not true. You've lost a lot of weight since Harlow's been making us dinner."

I pause, a greasy chicken wing wedged between my fingers.

"Not that you needed to," Dad says quickly. It leaves me cold. "I'm just saying, you look healthier. And this garbage? It can kill you if you eat it long enough."

"We used to order from Wings Express all the time," I argue. "We survived."

"We didn't know better."

He's including Mom in that "we," and it makes me furious. As if we were a family of idiots until Harlow came along to enlighten us. As if Harlow could ever be superior to Mom in any way, shape, or form.

With my teeth I tear a chunk of flesh from my chicken wing. I chomp down on it, avoiding Dad's eyes and willing myself not to cry. Thank God the TV is on, because Dad and I don't speak for a long time.

"You finished?" he asks me after a few minutes. There's one chicken wing remaining. It looks cold, and the barbecue sauce on it has formed a crust. I grab it and eat it anyway, just to spite him.

"Now I am," I say with my mouth full.

He throws the trash into the take-out bag and dumps it outside, then comes back in, asking where Harlow keeps the air freshener.

"Why?" I ask.

"It smells like grease in here."

"So?"

"So, I don't like it."

"You? Or Harlow?" I'm tired of tiptoeing around her. The fact that my father, a grown man, has to hide all evidence of a fried chicken dinner puts me over the edge.

"Both of us," he says.

"The smell never bothered you before."

"Well, now it does," he replies. His voice grows tight.

I know I'm being difficult, but why can't he see how much Harlow has changed him? He's become a completely different person, whereas she has remained her annoying self. I march over to the kitchen, grab her chemical-free sage-scented air freshener, and slam it on the table in front of him.

"*Oye*," he says.

I don't answer.

"I could do without the attitude."

"I don't have an attitude," I say with as much attitude as I can muster. Then I sweep by him and head back to my room.

"Don't walk away from me when I'm talking to you," he calls out behind me. Every time he's said it to me in the past, I've listened. There was always an implicit "or else" in those words.

This time I don't care. I used to think my dad was larger than life, my personal Goliath. Now I see him for what he really is—powerless.

"Analee!" he says more loudly.

I shut my bedroom door in response. Moments later I hear the spritz of the air freshener.

# CHAPTER TWENTY-THREE

SEB FINISHES THE FIRST HARRY POTTER IN A WEEK. When he calls me early Sunday morning and asks to borrow the second one, I almost burst with pride.

"I can't wait till you get to the third," I gush. "It's my favorite. Well, either the third or the sixth. It depends on my mood. Ugh, I'm so jealous of you right now!"

"Okay, calm down, you nerd. Are you free today?"

"Yes." I answer without hesitation. To my surprise I want to see him. And talk to him about how wonderful Harry Potter is.

"Good," he says, "because I'm cashing in on my favor."

All my positive emotions sour. I was hoping he'd forget about our deal. He says he'll pick me up at eleven.

"What do I wear?" I ask, throwing open my closet doors. I can barely dress myself as it is, let alone when I have no idea where we're going.

"Your usual jeans are fine," he says. "Don't worry."

And then he hangs up, leaving me to worry.

—

We pull up in front of the public library. I look around, convinced that Seb made a wrong turn. I have the second Harry Potter on my lap, so I'm not sure what he needs to check out of the library. Unless this is school-related . . . but I've never known Seb to do anything school-related on a weekend. Does he want me to tutor him? Does he realize my grades are average at best? Maybe he's picking something up for someone and this is just a stop on our way to some other mysterious undisclosed location.

"Good God," he says. "You're stressing me out."

"I haven't even said anything!" I protest.

"You don't have to. Your eyes say it all."

"My eyes say nothing."

"You look like a caged animal."

That is surprisingly close to how I feel, but I blink a few times to relax my eyeballs. "So . . . why are we here? What's this favor?"

"You," he says, leaning over me to pop open the passenger-side door, "are hosting a Harry Potter read-aloud this morning."

"I'm what?" I grip the sides of my seat like a gust of wind could knock me over. All the moisture in my mouth dries up.

"The library was looking for volunteers to read stories to kids in the neighborhood."

I say nothing. I shake my head as hard as I can until my vision blurs.

"They're *kids*, Analee," Seb says.

"I hate kids."

"You have a kid sister."

"Yeah, and she sucks." My breathing comes out in rapid bursts of air. I'm not doing this. I will stick to this seat like a chewed piece of gum, and Seb will have to physically pull me out of this car to change that.

"Come on," he says. "You'll feel much better about making a toast at your dad's wedding when you have experience talking in front of people."

"Why is *this* your favor? How does this benefit you in any way?" I ask.

"It doesn't. I just want to help you."

I would be oddly touched, but there's no room for any other emotion inside me besides complete and utter terror.

"Will you at least come inside?" he says.

"No."

"Really? You're going to let down a group of little kids who want to hear a story?"

"The world is a cruel place, Seb. They'll have to learn that lesson eventually."

He shakes his head. "You're being selfish."

"You're being pushy," I reply. "I don't like talking in front of people, and if I have to, I want to be prepared for it. You can't spring this on me and expect me to go through with it."

He sighs and turns off the ignition. "You wouldn't have done this if I had given you a *year* to prepare."

That's undoubtedly true, but I don't admit it. I grind my teeth together and stare at the library's entrance. A mom pushes through the doors, holding hands with a little girl. The girl is younger than Avery, with a round face and a lightning scar painted on her forehead. I relax my grip on the seat.

"How about this?" Seb says. "I'll read with you."

"You read all of it," I counter.

"You're just going to sit there?"

"Yes."

"But you'll go inside?"

"If you read it all, I'll go in," I say, against my better judgment.

Without another word Seb gets out of the car and shuts the door. He walks toward the library, shoulders tight, eyes straight ahead. I know he's annoyed that I'm not like his other friends who can talk in front of a crowd without sweaty palms and trembling bodies and sick stomachs. Well, I'm annoyed too. I hate that what comes so easily to everyone else is insurmountable to me.

When I walk inside the library, there's a small group of kids seated on a rainbow-striped rug. A lot of them look around Avery's age. Some are much too young for the series; some look big and gangly like they're on the cusp of being too cool to hang out for library story time.

Seb settles into a fluffy armchair in front of the kids. He sits like he owns the room—legs out in front of him, arms draped casually over his knees.

"You guys ready for a story or what?" he asks.

"Yeah!" they cheer. The girl with the painted lightning scar claps her hands in delight, and I can't help but smile at her.

"Do you guys like . . . Harry Potter?"

The kids go nuts in response. It looks like the front row of a Taylor Swift concert. And Seb is a natural at this. He's doing a way better job than I could have.

But when he cracks open the book and starts reading . . . it's not the best. He doesn't change his vocal inflections at all when he's reading as different characters. He rushes through certain moments when he should be pausing to let the story sink in.

When he gets through chapter one, a kid with curly brown hair and glasses raises his hand to ask a question.

"What house would you be in?" the boy asks.

Seb scrunches his eyebrows. "House?"

"Yeah, like Gryffindor, Ravenclaw, Hufflepuff, or Slytherin?"

This is a question I've asked myself many times. I've taken numerous online quizzes and mulled over my inherent personality traits. Seb thinks about it for exactly half a second.

"Ravenclaw," he answers. "Coolest name."

I shake my head vigorously. What is he thinking? You can't choose a house like that. The house chooses you. Seb catches me, and his eyes crinkle in the corners.

"Do you disagree, An?" he asks. Every child-size head in the room whips around to look at me. I freeze.

"Guys," Seb goes on, "Analee is a Harry Potter *expert*. Do you want to meet her?"

I'm shaking my head again, this time on purpose. He can't do this to me. He wouldn't.

The kids cheer again. At this point I believe they'd cheer anything Seb has to say. *Hey, kids, want to try crack cocaine? Yeah! Want to form a cult that worships Bahamut and brings about the apocalypse? Yeah!*

Seb waves me over, his smile widening. The kids are squirming. Lightning girl is looking at me with wide brown eyes. Damn it all.

I walk through the circle and stand stiffly next to Seb's chair.

The glint in his eyes reveals the obvious: this is all a ruse. Seb is purposely doing a terrible job. He's making a mockery of the Harry Potter series, and he knew it would annoy me enough to want to fix it.

"Say hi to Analee," Seb says to the kids.

"Hi, Analee!" they all shout at me. Literally shout. It's unnerving to have your name screamed in unison from the mouths of babes. They do say it correctly, to their credit.

Seb nudges me in the back.

"Oh, um, hi," I blurt out. If they notice my discomfort, they don't show it. One is blatantly picking his nose, and another is playing with her shoelace.

"Kids, I'm going to let Analee read the next chapter because she's a waaaay better reader than I am," Seb says. He leans down to talk to the girl with the faux lightning scar. "Can I sit next to you while Analee reads?"

She nods shyly.

"Wait, Seb!" I grip his sleeve, but he gently unravels my fingers.

"You'll be fine," he whispers. "I promise."

He guides me into the chair, then places the book on my lap. And suddenly I'm alone up here, with ten pairs of eyeballs locked on to me and a group of parents in the background surveying the scene. Am I supposed to say something to these kids? Ask questions? Make conversation?

I watch Seb squeeze into a small spot near lightning girl. He looks like a giant as he attempts to fold his long legs underneath him. It hits me now, what a nice thing he's trying to do for me, even though I want to run right out of here, past the large Dr. Seuss display and the gray-haired librarian at her desk, to freedom. Away from all the kids. Away from everyone.

Seb shoots me a thumbs-up, and I make my decision. I can do this. I'm just going to read, that's all. It's something I've been able to do since I was three years old. I don't have to work the kids into a spiritual frenzy like he did.

"Chapter two," I start. My voice comes out normal even though my mouth is bone-dry. Lightning girl perks up, scooting closer to my feet.

I continue reading. In chapter two Harry is living a miserable life with the Dursleys, and there are hints of magical happenings here and there. If I focus on the words, I can forget about the wiggly rug rats in front of me. I give Uncle Vernon a low, growling voice, and it earns me some scattered giggles. When I look up from the book, I meet Seb's eyes. He gives me a wide, dimpled smile, and I feel myself start to relax. This isn't so bad. The kids are just as captivated by my reading as they were when Seb was talking to them.

I keep going. I pause at the important moments so the kids have time to digest the story. At one point the nose-picker raises his hand.

"Why are they so mean to Harry?" he asks.

"That's a great question," I reply. "Does anyone have a guess? Why are the Dursleys so mean to Harry?"

Lightning girl's hand shoots up. "They don't like magic!"

She beams when I nod in agreement. "I think you're right. The Dursleys don't want to live in a world where motorcycles fly and wizards cast spells."

"But why?" the nose-picker asks.

"Maybe they're scared," another boy suggests.

"They might be," I agree. "Maybe they're used to life the way it is and they don't want things to change."

The kids all start coming up with a host of other reasons why the Dursleys don't like magic. One girl compares it to when her sister could do a handstand and she couldn't.

"Oh, so you think the Dursleys are jealous?" I ask. I hadn't considered that angle. It's kind of amazing what kids will come up with when you actually listen to them.

A few of the others agree. A less perceptive child insists that we're all wrong, that the Dursleys are just mean bad guys. Throughout the conversation Seb stays quiet, his eyes bouncing from me to them.

"Do you think mean people are mean for no reason?" I ask them. I think of Matt McKinley, my own living prototype for a storybook villain. I wonder if he was born with a cruel streak or if it developed over time.

"They might be sad," a girl says. "People can be mean when they're sad."

This raises a whole other topic for discussion. I've lost track of how long we've been talking when I notice the gray-haired librarian making her way toward us.

"I'm very sorry, everyone, but we're out of time for today," she says, and she's met with a chorus of groans from the kids.

To my surprise, I'm feeling the same way. I got through story time. I spoke in front of people. Mini-people, but people nonetheless. And, once I got past the sweating and difficulty breathing, I even managed to enjoy it. Who doesn't want to talk about Harry Potter for an hour? I watch the kids run to their parents. A couple of them wrap their spindly arms around my waist in a quick hug, and I melt a little bit.

"So . . . ," Seb says as a frazzled dad pulls the last remaining child away from us. "Am I imagining things, or did you actually enjoy public speaking today?"

I try to glare at him, but I can't stop smiling. Stupid traitorous face. "Yeah, yeah."

"It was very Gryffindor of you to conquer your fears like that."

"Excuse me," I say, bristling, "but I am a proud Hufflepuff through and through. And, while we're on the subject, you are so *not* a Ravenclaw."

"I could be a Ravenclaw."

"I don't think so."

"Why couldn't I be a Ravenclaw?"

Before I can give him the dozen reasons I have at the ready, I feel a tap on my shoulder.

"Hi . . . Analee?" the librarian asks. "I just wanted to tell you what a great job you did with the kids."

"Really?" is my instinctual response. I don't know why I'm questioning her. What would motivate a sweet old librarian to approach me solely for the purpose of lying?

"Oh yes," she replies. "They just adored you. We would love to have you back sometime."

"You're in luck—she's free most Sundays," Seb cuts in.

The librarian claps her hands together. "Terrific! We'll pencil you in for Sundays."

Whoa. Wait. This is all happening too fast. I will my mouth to move, but it hangs open like it's missing a screw.

"Sure," I finally manage. "Sundays are fine."

As she leaves, the voice in my brain asks me what the hell I'm doing. My Sundays are for being Kiri and slaying worgens and talking to Harris.

Seb squeezes my arm with one hand and pushes the library doors open with the other. "Hey. Should I be insulted that the librarian didn't ask me back?"

"Did I just sign up to read at the library every weekend?" I counter. I'm still a little stunned at what's transpired today.

"You did. Because you're a Gryffindor."

"Oh my God, I'm not a Gryffindor."

"You're a Gryffindor."

Walking out of the library, in the middle of a conversation about the Sorting Hat, I almost grab my phone to call Mom. I want to tell her what I did today. The urge to talk to her, the moments when I forget she's gone . . . they always happens like this, in the middle of normal life when I least expect them. I think of my grief as a masked intruder, stealing any small moment of happiness.

"What's with the face?" Seb asks.

"Just thinking."

"About?"

"My mom." I decide to say it. Let the words hang there. Wait for Seb's discomfort.

But his face doesn't slam shut, like Dad's would, and he doesn't change the subject, like Lily.

"Was she a Harry Potter nerd like you?" he teases.

"The biggest," I say.

"What house?"

"Oh, Gryffindor," I say. "Without a doubt. She was fearless."

"Like mother like daughter."

"Oh my God, you are so bad at sorting people."

He laughs and opens the car door to let me in.

I fully believe that Seb is wrong. I'm definitely more Hufflepuff than anything else. But today, for me, took guts. And I pulled through. I'm not recklessly brave like a Gryffindor would be. I don't jump into situations or try to be a hero. Still, maybe somewhere in me, amidst all my Hufflepuff nature, is a quieter Gryffindor courage that's sitting there, waiting to be unleashed.

# CHAPTER TWENTY-FOUR

ON THE DAY OF MOM'S FUNERAL, I WASN'T ABOVE wondering what to wear. You would think that something as frivolous as fashion wouldn't matter so much after your mom died. You would think a person would be above it all, busy thinking existential thoughts and searching for spiritual fulfillment. The thing is, though, that you can't think about the giant, tragic, life-changing stuff. It's too much for a human brain to process all at once. So you obsess over the details. You give them meaning.

I stood in front of my closet for an hour. I considered Mom's favorite dress of mine, sunset-colored with a scalloped skirt. She once said it made her think of mangoes. But then I thought, *Shouldn't I wear black? I'm in mourning.* But Mom hated black. The inside of her closet looked like a bag of Skittles.

Except, it occurred to me, Mom wouldn't care what color dress I wore today or any of the days after. Mom was no longer here.

*Back to clothes, look at the clothes.* I couldn't jump to the bigger things. Skirt? Pants? I called Lily, but she didn't answer. I settled for the mango dress with a black jacket. It clashed terribly.

The drive to the funeral home was bright and too quiet with just me and Dad in the car. We both had forgotten how to talk to each other without Mom. I sat in the backseat, because the front seat was hers. Even after she died, I was always making space for her. It was like I expected her to stroll back into our lives, as if the past months had been just a cruel joke.

He put on the radio, the oldies station, and they were playing the song about Pasadena from that band that sounded like the Beach Boys but they weren't the Beach Boys. The song was aggressively happy. About an old woman who drove too fast. Who cared? Now whenever I heard it, I would think about Mom's funeral, and this pleasant song that had no effect on most people would be devastating to me.

Details I remember about the drive to the funeral: a man selling churros on the sidewalk. A squashed bird in the middle of the road. A cloud shaped like a snail.

It was a closed casket funeral. I insisted on that, because Mom would never want people to see what she looked like at the end of her treatment. She wasn't herself then, anyway. She was gone long before that, the life leaking out of her like air from a punctured balloon.

My grandparents smothered me in hugs and kisses. My dad stood stiffly in the back of the room, as far away from the casket as he could get. People talked to him and he talked back, but his face was wiped clean of all emotion.

And then there was Lily. She walked in with her parents, wearing the perfect funeral outfit: a black pencil skirt and a dark purple blouse. Her parents nudged her toward me before they went to talk to my dad.

For the first time ever, I didn't know what to say to her. We hugged, which felt wrong. Neither of us were big huggers.

"I have the homework for you," she said. "All the teachers said there's no rush. And to email them if you need extra time."

"Thanks."

I suddenly wasn't sure what else to say to her. I was used to having issues with small talk, but I had never had them with my best friend.

"I'm sorry," she finally said, stiffly. She teetered in her heels. "About all of this."

By "this" I assumed she meant the most horrible thing that had ever happened to me. Sorry wasn't nearly enough. But then, what could anyone say that would be?

"Thanks," I said again.

She breathed out, sounding relieved, like she could cross something off her list. Provide the barest possible comfort to best friend? Check.

When the service started, I sat in the front with my dad. I tried desperately not to imagine what Mom looked like inside that casket. I thought about her before the cancer, how she laughed with her mouth wide open and wore Dad's T-shirts tied in a knot against her hip. How she opened a giant bag of tortilla chips to share with me and Lily and asked us for the latest school gossip. Lily was happy to oblige. She talked with Mom in a way I never could with her mom. Like you would talk to a friend, not a mother.

I cried. It was the first and only time I ever cried in public. Big fat whopping tears that ran down my face and neck. People got up and told stories about Mom. I had so many stories, but I didn't move. Maybe I should have. I should have done it for Mom, but I wasn't strong enough. Dad didn't go up either. He sat there, stone-faced, but I saw the tears lining his eyes. He was a silent crier, like me. We hated to show ourselves to other people. If I had the ability to cry on the inside, until my whole body filled with salty tears, I would do it.

I tore my eyes away from Uncle Jorge, who was speaking. I searched around the room until I found her. Far away from me, in the back corner, Lily was crying harder than anyone else.

# CHAPTER TWENTY-FIVE

MATT MCKINLEY PLOPS HIMSELF DOWN AT OUR lunch table while Seb and I are splitting a piece of chocolate cake and I'm ranting about Harlow. Matt comes out of nowhere, like a bout of food poisoning, and instantly I tense up. He has the effect of making me crave the sweet release of death when he's anywhere within ten feet of me.

"What's up, bro?" he asks Seb, taking the seat in between us even though no one asked him to sit down. "Why don't we ever see your ass anymore?"

"Been busy," Seb answers. He pokes at the cake without looking at either one of us.

"Your girl's got you quarantined or something?" Matt laughs.

"Nah, man," Seb says.

I'm sitting right fucking here. Even when I'm Seb's girlfriend, I'm still less than human in Matt McKinley's eyes. I'm not even worth acknowledging.

I wish I could say something to him, call him out, but I'm afraid of what he would say back. He has his choice of everything wrong with me, and I know he would pluck the one thing I'm most insecure about to display to the world. People like Matt have a gift for cruelty. Even Seb knows it, which explains his uncharacteristic silence.

"So how's it going with you lovebirds?" Matt asks. He breaks off a chunk of cake with his fingers, also without asking. And I'm officially done eating it.

"Fine," Seb says.

"You sure?" Matt finally looks at me, and his eyes twinkle with something like mischief, only more evil. My heart sinks. He knows. Matt somehow knows we're faking it. It's all over his face.

"Yeah, dude," Seb replies. "What's the problem?"

"Some would see you two as . . . tame."

"Meaning?" Seb clenches his jaw.

"Meaning G-rated. Meaning full of shit."

"Who cares? We don't need to prove anything to anyone."

"Just saying." Matt takes another piece of cake and pushes his chair back to stand. "See you later."

As soon as he's out of earshot, Seb slams his fist onto the table. "That's it. We have to make out."

"Whoa, whoa, whoa." A confusing rush of emotions takes hold of me. Fear and annoyance and maybe, *maybe*, the smallest hint of excitement. But the fear and annoyance are way stronger.

"Did you hear what he said?" Seb asks.

"I did," I say slowly.

"He's calling us out."

"Remind me why you're friends with that guy again?"

"Analee . . ."

"I'm serious! He's such a mega-douche. You see that, right? You have to see it."

Seb sighs. "He can be. I guess."

"He can be?" I repeat. "It's his natural essence. He just *is*."

"You don't know him. He's going through a lot."

"I hate that excuse," I say. "Plenty of people are going through a lot, and they still manage to act like civil human beings."

"Regardless, we don't need him spreading the rumor that we're faking this."

"So, what do you suggest?"

"We have to act like a couple. We have to do more than hold hands in the hallway."

"You're right, but—"

He suddenly jolts forward, springing toward my face.

"Seb! Hold on!" Instinctually I duck away, almost falling out of my chair. Seb freezes, still leaning over the table.

"What's wrong?"

"You can't just attack me like that!"

"I was going to kiss you!"

"Really? Because it looked like you were about to choke me."

He flops back into his seat. "Sorry."

"It's okay," I reply. "But oh my God, the intensity in your eyes . . . that was legit terrifying."

"Sorry," he says again, laughing. He rubs his fingers through a patch of curly brown hair.

"I'm just not sure I'm good with our first kiss being in the middle of the school cafeteria," I say. "And I'm not really good with spontaneity in general."

"I get it. Too much too soon."

Entirely too much for someone like me, but I don't know how to explain that to him.

"So, what's the plan?" he asks. "Do you want to set up some practice runs?"

I make a face. "Like we're playing soccer?"

"Analee, soccer is a metaphor for life. Don't you get that yet?"

"Silly me. I thought it was an excuse to run around in knee socks and kick a ball into a net."

"Oh my God." He puts his head in his hands. "Why am I quote-unquote dating you? They're soccer socks, Analee. Knee socks are for Catholic schoolgirls."

"Same thing."

"Ignoring you now."

"Good."

"So where do we practice?" he asks. "Your place? After school?"

"Can't," I say. I quickly explain my dad's antiquated rules for dating his daughter.

"Your dad doesn't trust me?" Seb asks, looking wounded. He puts his hand over his heart.

"Considering you tried to put the moves on me in the cafeteria, can you blame him?"

"So somewhere that's not public, but our houses are out," Seb murmurs. He snaps his fingers. "I got it."

"What? Where?"

"I'll pick you up on Friday night. Make sure Avery has a playdate."

# CHAPTER TWENTY-SIX

I BARELY REMEMBER MY FIRST AND ONLY KISS, aka the Incident. Only bits and pieces come to mind. I remember my head pulsing in time to a monotonous base line. The stale stench of beer on Colton's breath. I remember lying down, stiff and unmoving, his tongue poking through my lips, his hand running up and down my rib cage.

"You are so beautifully sad," he whispered into my ear.

I hated that he said that. Colton said crap like that all the time, and everyone thought he was so deep and sensitive. He wasn't. He observed us all like a detached anthropologist of emotions, all the while feeling nothing himself. Lily couldn't see it because she feels everything, all the time.

After a while Colton got tired of kissing someone who wasn't kissing him back. He slipped out of the room, presumably to find Lily. I wanted to go find Lily too, but my legs were uncooperative. In my drunken state the most I could do was turn over and fall asleep.

# CHAPTER TWENTY-SEVEN

ON FRIDAY NIGHT SEB PULLS INTO THE ENTRANCE of Midtown Cinema, and I'm sitting next to him, sucking on my fifth spearmint Altoid. I feel jittery. I'm going to kiss Seb Matias today. Not that I like him in that way, but inside, sixth-grade Analee is thrilled with this development. The most handsome boy in school is going to lock lips with me in a darkened theater as romantic movie music swells in the background.

Seb nabs a parking spot by the theater's entrance. I pop another Altoid. It's just kissing. Lips on lips. Seb's lips. Seb's tongue.

Jesus Christ. I can't do this.

"You okay?" he asks as we get out of the car.

"Peachy," I reply.

Midtown Cinema used to be a cool indie theater. They ran midnight showings of cult classics and foreign films, and their lobby had a bunch of old Hollywood memorabilia on display. At some point last year the theater changed ownership. Now it plays tired superhero sequels along with every other theater in the East Bay area. It's what living here does to all people and places—whatever is different will be squashed and molded until it looks identical to everything else.

"What are we watching?" I ask Seb as we wait in line.

"*Gregor the Lion: Journey to Africa.*" In sync we scoot up as the line moves forward.

"You're kidding."

"Nope."

"Why are we watching a kid's movie?"

"Because we're not here to actually *watch* a movie," Seb says. "We have work to do."

Sixth-grade Analee shrivels and dies at his words. Kissing me is in no way pleasurable. It's not fun, or enticing, or even tolerable. It's work. Like taking a final.

Seb pays for my movie ticket when we get to the window.

I pull out my wallet. "I can—"

"Nope."

"But—"

"Shh."

I roll my eyes and stick the wallet back into my purse. Seb makes zero sense. He makes kissing me seem like this laborious effort, but then he acts all boyfriendy. It must be leftover instincts from the days of Chleb.

My mind shoots back to Chloe again. She's a dancer, which means she knows how to do all kinds of things with her body. Plus, she's always wearing this yummy pink-tinted lip balm that makes her lips look extra inviting. Kissing Chloe must feel like eating strawberry shortcake. Except this strawberry shortcake knows how to move her mouth the perfect way and has a perfect model body and says the perfect thing at the perfect time, and you know what, fuck strawberry shortcake. I'm a girl who always preferred a hearty steak over dessert.

"You want some popcorn?" Seb asks as we walk into the lobby.

I look longingly at the golden kernels overflowing from the popcorn machine. I inhale the butter-soaked air.

"I can't," I say.

"Why not?" He frowns. "Don't tell me you're on a diet."

"No," I say, "although I probably should be."

"Oh, stop it. I like your body."

I momentarily forget how to breathe. Guys like Seb don't look at girls like me, not in that way. I don't look like the girls on the covers of magazines. I don't have a thigh gap or even a thigh slit. I'm just . . . I'm a lot. On my thighs, on my ass, everywhere else. Too much, some might say.

"You like Chloe's body," I correct.

"I can't like both? Buy yourself some popcorn." He pulls a twenty from his pocket and hands it to me.

"Okay, ew. You're not, like . . . my sugar daddy." I push his hand away. "I have money. And I don't want any popcorn because we're going to . . . you know." I pucker my lips into a smooch.

He stares blankly at me. "So?"

"I just think we'll get kernels stuck in our teeth and popcorn bits in our mouths and it's not going to be a pleasant experience."

He keeps staring at me like I'm this otherworldly freak, when all I'm *trying* to do is be a considerate person.

"Okay, then," he says finally. "Let's go inside."

"You're acting like I'm unreasonable."

"You *are* unreasonable."

The ticket-taker raises an eyebrow at us when we show her our tickets.

"Enjoy your movie," she says. She doesn't conceal the amusement in her voice.

Seb and I sit in the corner, in the very last row of the theater. We're ten minutes into the movie, and a CGI lion cub is frolicking across the screen. The room is practically empty except for a handful of exasperated parents and squirming kids in the first few rows.

I assume Seb will be making the first move, but he sits there with his eyes on the screen. Is there something I'm supposed to be doing right now? Am I too stiff? I'm sitting on the edge of my chair, my hands folded tightly on my lap.

"Seb," I whisper.

"Hmm?"

"When do we start?"

Even in the darkness I see him close his eyes and shake his head. "You really need to chill out."

"I just want to get it over with."

"Gee, thanks."

"Come on. You're not looking forward to it either."

"Fine." He pivots his body so that he's facing me. I turn to face him. He puts his hand on my shoulder. I don't know what to do with mine, so I settle for lightly resting it on his knee, then think better of it and drop it onto my lap. The movie light flickers, and I'm dimly aware that on-screen Gregor the Lion is crying behind bars at the Central Florida Zoo. I hate animal movies. They are so manipulative.

"Stop looking at me like that," Seb whispers.

"Like what?"

"Like I'm a dentist about to give you a root canal."

"That's my resting face," I whisper back.

"I can't kiss that."

I stretch my mouth open and closed, blink my eyes a few times, then puff out my lips.

"What the hell are you doing?" he asks.

"Facial exercises."

"You're stalling."

"So are you," I say.

"No . . ." But I can hear a tinge of uncertainty even in his whisper.

"What if we start with a small kiss?" I say. "Like a one-second kiss. On the cheek."

"Oh my God. That's how I kiss my grandmother."

"It'll be a level-one kiss."

"You're such a nerd. Fine." He leans over and kisses my cheek-bone. The kiss is soft and quick. And surprisingly easy, maybe because all I had to do was sit here.

"Level two," I say. My palms begin to sweat. "Pop kiss on the mouth."

"Okay," he replies. We lean into each other, and before I can think about which direction to tilt my head or whether I'm supposed to open or close my eyes, his lips meet mine for the briefest second, before we pull away.

"Nailed it," he says. "What's level three?"

Nailed it? Ugh. Why do I get nervous around idiots like this?

"A longer kiss," I say.

"Tongue or no tongue?"

"No tongue."

"Is tongue level four?"

"Yes," I reply.

"You are so weird." And then, before I can prepare myself, he cups my chin and brushes his lips against mine, so softly, it tickles, then parts his lips slightly to kiss me.

Okay, so he knows what he's doing.

I follow his lead, parting my lips too, alternating smaller kisses with longer, deeper ones.

You think you have your pride, you know? But I would neglect everything—family, friends, maybe even Harris—to kiss Seb until my lips were too chapped to do it anymore. Kissing Seb is *fun*. And he's so good at it that I forget to wonder if I am. What does it matter, anyway? The whole thing is a sham.

We move on to level four without stopping. Seb makes the move, of course, and it feels completely different from the Incident with Colton. My senses are sharpened today. I feel the rhythm of Seb's breathing, his fingertips brushing my skin, the faint stubble on his chin. Usually I hate being touched, but I'm surprised to find that I'm enjoying it. The concept of time eludes me. Have we been at it for seconds or minutes? Is the movie almost over? Did our kissing break the space-time continuum?

We don't stop until a harried-looking father with a screaming baby in his arms makes his way up the aisle. On the movie screen Gregor has stowed away on a cruise ship.

Seb and I sit back in our chairs. I'm breathing too hard, feeling physically exhausted from our make-out session.

"You're a good kisser," he says.

"Stop."

"What?"

"You don't have to say that."

"I know I don't have to," he says, sounding exasperated.

"And this movie is so dumb," I say. "How the hell did Gregor get on a cruise ship?"

"The little girl put him in a suit and a top hat."

I'm baffled. "What?"

"Yeah. He stood on his hind legs."

"Oh my God. I know this movie is for kids, but the complete disregard for quality, or pure common sense, is insulting."

"Analee," he says.

"What?"

And then he kisses me again. And I know he's not doing it because he's overwhelmed by his all-consuming passion for me. He's doing it to shut me up. I just can't bring myself to care at the moment.

# CHAPTER TWENTY-EIGHT

**Harris:** i still don't understand why you saw the movie in the first place. obviously you're not the target audience.

**Me:** Okay, I know, but let's talk about the fact that Gregor was at a Parisian cafe eating a baguette

**Me:** A baguette, Harris!

**Me:** A hostess let a LION sit at a table. A waiter then took that lion's order.

**Harris:** again, i ask: why did you see this movie?

**Me:** I told you, I had to go with Avery

I hate lying to Harris, but I still don't feel comfortable telling him anything Seb-related. Besides, all that kissing meant nothing. It was all in preparation for the day I'll kiss Harris, someone I can actually stand. We won't need to have levels or watch silly kids' movies. Our kiss will be under the most perfect, romantic circumstances.

**Me:** Anyway. What did youuu do last night?

**Harris:** went into gorizon's lair

**Me:** Wow, really? Who helped you with that?

**Harris:** this shape-shifter named celestina

**Harris:** she was pretty awesome

**Me:** Never heard of her

**Harris:** we might want to invite her into our guild

**Me:** Do we really need another shape-shifter, though? We already have Gordon.

**Harris:** gordon is twelve, Analee. and he's banned from using the internet for a month

**Harris:** why don't we do a quest with celestina tonight? you can see what you think

**Me:** Maybe

**Harris:** you okay?

**Me:** Totally

Who is Celestina, and why has she entered our lives? Why is Harris questing with another girl? It's partly my fault. I've been neglecting him and our quests. He has every right to enlist other people for help.

It's just . . . Celestina? Couldn't Harris have teamed up with a fat troll or an orc or a goblin? Celestina sounds so beautiful and mystical. I imagine a towering, golden-haired beauty casting spells and taking off into the night sky as an exotic bird. Suddenly even Kiri doesn't seem like enough. Kiri is a hunter with no magical powers or shape-shifting skills.

My phone buzzes from the floor. It's a text from Seb.

What are you up to?

Nothing, I type. I don't care how pathetic I sound. Seb already realizes I'm pathetic.

Am I allowed to come over? Stepmonster is around and I need to escape.

Dad isn't home, but Harlow is. Technically we are abiding by Dad's rules. Although if I decided to go against the rules and have sex with Seb right here in my childhood bedroom, Harlow would probably cheer us on while pelting us with condoms.

Yes, I text back. I'm surprised I don't make up an excuse to get out of it, but the idea of Seb coming over doesn't bother me. More than that, I want to see him. I want to kiss him again. Not because I have feelings for him. I know way too much about Seb now to think of him in a romantic way.

**Me:** Sorry, I think I hear my dad calling me. Ttyl

**Harris:** ttyl

Seb remains, undeniably, a soccer-obsessed doofus who is still, like, 10 percent asshole. But he's a doofus that happens to be God's gift to kissing.

When I answer the door, I expect a level three at least. But he stays fixed on my doorstep.

"Hey," he says.

"Hi," I reply. I move to the side so that he can come in. Not even a level-one kiss on the cheek.

"Thanks for letting me come over."

"No problem," I say. We stand there without moving. It hits me that Seb might still consider kissing me a job, and he doesn't want to perform on his off-hours. We had our practice session, and the rest is reserved for show.

Why did I assume he wanted to kiss me again like I wanted to kiss him? Seb has made out with some of the most beautiful girls in school. He's used to this. He was probably bored and had nothing better to do than see me today. It's not romantic. It's practical.

"Seb!" Harlow comes up behind us. She's wearing her barely-there leggings, which basically amount to a second layer of skin, and a crop top. It's embarrassing. Her look screams high school cheerleader at practice, not future mother figure. "I didn't know you were coming over today!"

"Sorry," Seb says quickly. "I thought Analee—"

"No, this is actually perfect," Harlow says. "I could really use both of you guys."

"Sure," Seb says. I bulge my eyes out at him in silent warning.

"Great. Follow me!" She turns and goes toward the living room. I smack Seb in the head.

"Ow. What the hell?" he says.

"Lesson number one," I whisper. "Never agree to a favor for Harlow."

"You make everything such a big deal," he whispers back. "I'm sure it's fine." He follows Harlow, which leaves me no choice but to reluctantly follow him.

In the living room Harlow has the couches pushed against the walls and two yoga mats on the floor. Seb shoots me a confused eyebrow raise, and it is impossible for me to hide my smirk.

"I'm trying to work on my partner yoga series," Harlow says. "I was going to have Avery help, but her miniature size might be a problem."

"I'm down," Seb says. He kicks off his blue sneakers and steps onto the mat without needing to be asked.

"Great!" Harlow presses her palms together. "Analee?"

"I don't think so," I reply.

"Oh, come on, Analee," Seb says. "Don't be so you."

I glare at him.

"Partner yoga has a lot of benefits, Analee," Harlow says. "You might find it brings you two closer together."

"I think we're close enough."

"Personally," Seb says, "I've found you to be a little distant lately." He is *such* a dick.

"Please?" Harlow asks. She's using the same tricks on me that she uses on Dad. The soothing yogi voice, the doe eyes.

I sigh and slip out of my sandals. What other choice do I have? The apple doesn't fall far from the spineless tree.

Harlow uses her phone to play a background track. The living room is filled with the sounds of crashing waves, twittering birds, and the low drones of what I'm guessing is a didgeridoo, based on the World Music class I took last year. It all seems so artificial. Like we're pretending we're not stretching in our living room deep in the Florida suburbs.

"Let's get started," Harlow says in this ridiculous breathy voice. Why do all yoga teachers talk like they took a bunch of Vicodin? I catch Seb's eye, trying not to laugh, but he's watching Harlow with a serious expression. Harlow instructs (gently, of course) me and Seb to sit back-to-back.

"Now what?" I ask.

"We're simply going to breathe," Harlow replies.

"Aren't we doing that already?"

"Analee, try to focus on the way your breath moves instead of what's to come. Just be here now, in this moment."

Great. One minute into the class, and I'm already doing it wrong.

We breathe in and out through our noses. I feel Seb's back expand every time he inhales, and soon we're breathing and moving together. Our bodies are so close that I can't feel where mine ends and his begins. I lose track of time the way I did yesterday in the theater.

Harlow has us hold hands and twist our upper bodies. I feel my tension, holed up in my shoulders and upper back, begin to melt. Then she has the two of us face each other, feet touching.

One of us stretches forward, the other pulls back. When it's Seb's turn to stretch forward, his face clenches and turns red.

"Holy crap, that hurts," he mutters.

"Oh my God," I say. "Am I more flexible than you?"

"I have tight hamstrings."

"In other words, I'm more flexible than you!" I announce gleefully. "I win!"

"It's not a competition," Harlow reminds us, but even she cannot rob me of this triumph.

The best part of yoga practice is the end, when we lie flat on our backs in corpse pose. Harlow has us following our breath through our bodies, and it's one of the few moments in my life when I feel momentarily carefree. I'm not thinking about the stupid didgeridoo playing in the background, or that I'm lying down next to the most wanted boy in school, or that Dad and Harlow's wedding is around the corner. All I'm thinking about is breathing.

"Namaste," Harlow says to close the practice. She gives me and Seb a deep bow, and Seb bows back in return.

"Namaste," he says.

They both look at me, and I give them the slightest lean forward. That's the most they'll get from me. I'm definitely not saying "namaste." Give me a freaking break.

"That was so awesome!" Seb says. He raises his hand to give Harlow a high five. "I feel like that guy in the Fantastic Four, the stretchy one?"

"Mr. Fantastic," I cut in. I have a feeling Seb has never read a comic book in his life.

"I'm so glad you liked it," Harlow says, eyes shining. "You two looked great. I might have to get you on video."

"Yes!" Seb says as emphatically as I say, "No."

"Just think about it," Harlow says.

"How did you get into all this?" Seb asks, gesturing toward the mats.

"What?" Harlow rolls up the mats, and Seb and I help her pull the couches back into their usual position. "Yoga?"

"Yeah. Did you always want to do it?"

"Definitely not," Harlow laughs. "I wanted to be a lawyer."

"Really?" It shoots out of my mouth before I can help it. Usually I try to show as little interest in Harlow as possible, but I could never imagine her trading in her tie-dyed leggings for a pantsuit.

"Yup. I lasted a whole year at Columbia before I could admit that I hated it."

I had no idea that Harlow went to law school. I knew she got pregnant in college, but I assumed she dropped out of school to take care of Avery.

"How did you go to school and manage with Avery?" I ask.

"It was hard," she says. "I lived with my parents. They helped out with Avery while I was in school, and then I'd take care of Avery and stay up all night studying."

"So when did yoga enter into it?" Seb asks.

"My friend was teaching a class in Manhattan, and she made me promise I'd go. Truth be told, I thought I'd hate it. I didn't have the time, I had work to do, I had a million excuses not to try it. But then I went. And when I entered into child's pose for the first time, I burst into tears in front of the entire class."

Involuntarily I throw a hand over my mouth. I know how embarrassing it is to lose your shit in front of a bunch of strangers, but I didn't think embarrassing moments happened to people like Harlow.

Harlow shrugs. "It wasn't fun, but I needed to have that moment. It made me realize that I wanted to change my life."

"So you moved here?" I asked.

"Yes," she says. "I worked as a waitress and got my yoga certification. Then I became a yoga teacher."

"And then you met my dad," I say.

It's so bizarre the way a chance event can change your entire life. If Harlow had never taken her friend's yoga class, she and Dad would never have met. Or if Dad had joined a different gym. Or if Mom had gone to the doctor earlier and caught the cancer in time. Dad would still have his pouch and his old ripped jeans, and Harlow would be blissfully unaware of his absence in her life.

"What's going on here?" Avery asks accusingly. She appears in the doorway, both hands on her bony hips.

"Hey, little girl," Seb says.

Avery softens, drops her hands. Seb somehow possesses the unique power of lowering her brat factor by just a smidgen. "Oh. Hi, Seb."

"Come here, ladybug," Harlow says. She goes over to Avery and pulls her into an embrace, peppering tiny kisses all over her cheeks.

"Moooom, stop!" Avery whines, struggling to free herself.

I look away. I'm feeling too many things at the moment, and feeling too much always makes me uncomfortable. I feel sympathy for Harlow, which I hate, because it's hard to dislike someone while simultaneously feeling bad for them. I feel sympathy for Avery, who grew up with a busy mom and an absent father. But more than anything, I feel sympathy for myself. No, worse than sympathy. I'm downright pitying myself. I don't have a mom who will hug and kiss me like Harlow does with Avery. Not anymore. This is an immutable fact, and that reality hits me with the force of a wrecking ball to the chest.

"You ready to go to Lainey's?" Harlow asks Avery.

"Yes," Avery replies. "I've been waiting *forever*."

"Well, thank you so much for your patience," Harlow says. She laughs, gives Avery one more kiss on the cheek, and then grabs her keys. "Let's roll."

"Um, Harlow?" I ask.

She turns around. "Yes?"

"Seb and I aren't . . . um . . . allowed . . ."

I feel younger than Avery right now. Why am I even being this Goody Two-shoes? Any teenage girl would kill to have the house all to herself and her, for all intents and purposes, boyfriend.

Harlow checks her cell phone. "It's okay. Your dad won't be home till later, and I'll only be half an hour."

"I can go," Seb says, throwing his hand toward the door.

"No," Harlow and I say in unison.

"That's silly," Harlow continues. "You don't have to cut your visit short because of me."

"You sure?" Seb asks, and I think he's talking to Harlow, but his eyes are watching me.

"Yes," I say.

And then Harlow sweeps Avery out of the room and we hear the car backing out of the driveway, and it's just the two of us, alone, in a quiet empty house.

Thank you very much, Harlow, for making Seb and me all stretchy and limber and then leaving us by ourselves, because all I want to do is jump on top of him. Again, I have to make it clear: I don't have feelings for Seb. It's just that I've never had a boyfriend, so I'm pretty much a live grenade of sexual frustration.

"What should we do?" Seb asks.

If I were not Analee, this is when I would walk right up to him and kiss him. No hesitation. And then he could pick me up like I'm as light as a feather, and I'd wrap my legs around his waist and we'd tumble to the floor in a flurry of passion.

"We could watch TV," I suggest.

Okay. Alternate fantasy. Seb could now say, *I have a better idea.* Then he could come over and kiss me and pick me up, and I'd wrap my legs around his waist and we'd tumble to the floor, etc.

Instead he says, "Sure," and throws himself onto our couch. I sit a safe distance away from him. We spend the rest of the afternoon watching TV and not kissing.

# CHAPTER TWENTY-NINE

"WHAT DOES IT MEAN IF A GUY IS ACTING DISTANT?"
I ask Elliott during Seb's soccer game on Monday.

It's been three days since Seb and I kissed in a movie theater. Two days since we sat next to each other on the couch and didn't touch each other.

I must be the worst kisser in the history of time. Seb lied to make me feel better about it. That's the only explanation for why he has now seemingly rejected me.

"Seb is acting distant?" Elliott asks.

"Less affectionate," I specify. I steal a glance around the bleachers. It seems like the entire student body is at the game today, including Chloe and Lily in the first row.

"Has he been sick?" Elliott asks.

"No."

"Tired? Stressed?"

"Maybe? I don't know." It occurs to me that I *could* just ask Seb how he's been feeling. In fact, I didn't even ask him what was going on with his stepmom on Saturday. I was such a hornball that I lost all ability to act like a human being.

"I'm sure it's not you. There are dozens of reasons why Seb might be out of sorts. I would just talk to him about it." Then he stands up and screams, "GET IT, TIGERS. GET IT!"

We're up by two so far, but the other team steals the ball. Elliott curses and sits back down.

"Will you calm yourself?" I ask him. "There are three minutes left in the game."

Sometimes Elliott can be so rational and levelheaded, but then he'll watch a soccer game and turn into this veiny red monster. I call it "the Elliott Effect."

"You know that soccer is very anxiety-inducing for me, Analee," he replies.

"Isn't it supposed to be fun?"

But then the other team scores a goal, and I rise to my feet along with Elliott to boo and shout. I become a mini-monster. If the Tigers win this game, our school makes it to state. If they lose, the entire season is over.

I still can't believe I care about this stuff.

"We have this," I tell Elliott with certainty. Out on the field Seb is nervous. If I didn't know him the way I do now, I wouldn't be able to tell. He's shaking his arms out and pacing back and forth. It makes me jittery, watching him.

Elliott grabs my hand, and a reverential silence falls over the bleachers. It reminds me of the few times I went to church when I was younger, and the priest would deliver his sermon. Only, here soccer is God and the boys on the field are doing his holy work. Elliott and I wait out the clock. The other team has possession of the ball. The striker kicks the ball and it goes flying across the field. . . . There is a collective gasp as everyone holds their breaths . . . and our goalie blocks the shot. The buzzer sounds, and we all jump up and cheer.

"Yas, yas, yas!" Elliott repeats in my ear over and over. "Playoffs, bitches!"

Moments later, as the stands begin emptying out, my phone buzzes with a text from Seb: Woohoo!

Yay! I text back.

We're going to Bruno's Pizza to celebrate. You're coming.

"Crap," I say out loud.

Elliott tries to peer at my phone. "What?"

"Seb wants me to go with them to Bruno's."

"With the soccer team?" He clutches his chest. "Oh my God."

"Oh my God" is right. I feel comfortable enough hanging out with Seb, alone, but we've never tried it in front of all his popular, athletic, ridiculously good-looking teammates. I already feel my tongue retreating into my throat.

"Wait," I say to Elliott as something occurs to me. "You should come."

"Shut up."

"Seriously. I don't know the soccer guys very well, and—"

"No, really, Analee. Stop talking. I'm there."

I still hate the thought of going, but having Elliott by my side feels like draping a security blanket over myself. A very loud, very excitable security blanket.

By the time we get to Bruno's, it's packed full of people pressed against windows and spilling outside into the parking lot. Everyone is smiling and laughing and talking at screaming volume. I shrink against Elliott. My instinct is to turn around and go home. I can already see what's to come: I'm going to have to squeeze against strangers, deal with stares and small talk, swallow down my self-hate all night. I'm mentally exhausted by the thought of all this.

"Hey, there's your boy!" Elliott points to the back, where Seb is seated at the head of a long table like he's Henry VIII. Leaning next to the table, talking to him, is Chloe.

Now I really have to go.

I step backward, almost fall over Elliott.

He catches me by the shoulders. "Whoa. You okay? I know. He makes my knees weak too."

"No. It's just—"

My heart won't slow down; my palms won't quit producing sweat.

"Come on. Let's go over to him," Elliott says.

Seb is still deeply engaged in conversation with Chloe, and their cozy interaction is driving me crazier than I'd like. If Seb and Chloe get back together at this very moment, how will I survive the embarrassment? Why did I even come here? My presence makes no difference to Seb now that he's getting the attention he craves from Chloe. Did he forget that he invited me here?

I'm frozen, stuck between my exit and Seb, when Elliott makes my mind up for me.

He cups his hands over his mouth and hollers, "SEEEHB!" and his voice travels clear through the pizzeria and across the planet to Indonesia.

Seb stops midsentence. He sees us and waves. Dumbly I wave back. I can't bring myself to push through the crowd, so I'm relieved when he gets up from his chair and starts walking over. We're still playing the game tonight. Maybe I won't be humiliated.

"He's even more gorgeous up close," Elliott whispers to me as Seb approaches. "I don't know how you function."

Before I can open my mouth to say hi, Seb swoops me into his arms and shoves his tongue into my mouth. I'm not exaggerating. It slides right on in there. Elliott makes a whooping sound, and I try to reciprocate the kiss, but all of a sudden my mouth fails me. I know. This is what I claimed I wanted, isn't it? Another make-out session with Seb?

But not like this. This doesn't feel like it did in the movie theater. It feels rushed, and forced, and . . . wrong. It feels the way it did with Colton.

I pull away from Seb, frowning, but he doesn't notice. His eyes are on Chloe, and Chloe's eyes, along with everyone else's, are fixed immovably on me.

"Come on, guys. Sit down with us." Seb pulls me by the hand, and Elliott follows. He doesn't need to push through the crowd. The crowd parts for him, and he walks by in a parade of back slaps and congratulations. I keep my head bent, avoiding the inquisitive stares and focusing on matching Seb's footsteps and slapping something I hope resembles a smile onto my face.

"Here, Analee. Take my seat," he says, pulling out his chair for me.

"Oh, no. That's okay."

"I insist."

I see what he's doing. Seb wants to prove himself the ever-devoted boyfriend. I plop down in the seat, surrounded by fourteen soccer players whom I've never met. This is my nightmare. Around me everyone is already engaged in easy conversation. Lily and Chloe are talking, Elliott is interrogating Seb on his soccer training, and the rest of the team interacts like family members at the dinner table. I am most definitely the odd one out.

Somewhere along the way I missed a lesson on how to strike up and maintain a conversation with another human being. My brain rattles through a variety of conversation starters. I could talk to one of Seb's teammates. *Congratulations*, I could say. *You played great.* But then he would say, *Thank you*, and it would be up to me to say something next. Other people are able to spit out talking points without hesitation, but my mind empties out and I forget how to form words, let alone sentences.

One of the players next to me, Bo, gets up to talk to a pretty girl who's been eyeing him from the other end of the pizzeria. I expect Seb to take the available seat, but I get a strong whiff of coconut shampoo and turn to find Chloe now sitting beside me, smiling. It's a little bit like having Angelina Jolie suddenly join me for dinner. Chloe has that A-list appeal that mesmerizes you. Seb has it too, which is why they were such a breathtaking couple, and why I feel unworthy as her successor. I've never been this close to her before, close enough to see the light sprinkle of freckles on her nose and the long, dark lashes framing her honey-brown eyes.

"Hey, Analee," she says as if we've been friends for years.

"Hey." I try to smile, but it's hard to smile when you feel miserably inadequate.

"Seb's told me a lot about you."

"Has he?" Oh my God, what the hell is Seb telling Chloe about me?

She laughs, as if reading my thoughts. "Don't worry. It's nothing bad!"

"Oh, okay."

"You looked so freaked out."

I give an awkward laugh that's half a sigh of relief. "You never know."

"I think you've been really good for Seb, actually," Chloe says. She presses her finger against Bo's glass of soda and traces a smile into the condensation.

"Really?" I ask. It feels strange to talk about Seb as if he had nothing to do with Chloe in the recent past.

"Really," she says. "He seems more . . . focused lately."

If she only knew that the one thing Seb is focused on is winning her back.

"Well, he's been . . . great," I say. I decide to do Seb a favor and talk him up a bit. It'll at least give me something to say. "He's so thoughtful and, um . . . sweet."

Chloe wipes her fingers on her jeans and smiles at me again. "He can be."

"Chloe!" One of the soccer players, Jason, leans over the table and slaps her hand. "I miss you, boo!"

"Aw, I miss you too, Jay!" Chloe grins. "How's Tara?"

"She's good, she's good."

"Tell her I said hi, okay?"

She talks to a couple of other guys from the team the same way. Unintentionally flirtatious, oozing charm and sex appeal. I sit there like a lump. I can't compete with her, and I honestly don't want to. All I want to do is sit and watch the girl who can do everything I can't.

"Analee, don't let these guys give you any trouble," she says, giving the guys a wink. She's the type of girl who can make a wink look sexy, not cheesy. I fall in the latter camp, which is why I would never even attempt one.

While they go on talking, I excuse myself, pretending to go to the bathroom. Instead I get up and pull Seb away from Elliott and a few of the other soccer guys.

"I think I'm going to take off," I say.

"What? Already?" Seb asks. "We didn't even get to hang out."

"It's just . . . it's weird to sit there and talk to Chloe."

"Is she bothering you?"

"No, she's actually being really nice." Annoyingly nice. It would be easier to deal with Chloe if she were a massive bitch. I think I'd prefer it.

"Did she say anything about me?" Seb asks. Hope flickers across his features.

"She said you seemed more focused."

"Focused," he repeats. Ironically, he can barely focus on my words. His eyes constantly shift to Chloe.

"Anyway," I say. "I'm going to go."

"I can drive you home," Seb offers, but he's not even looking at me, and I can tell he's boyfriending again, going through the motions of being a good boyfriend without any actual feeling behind them. Besides, I don't want to pull him away from his teammates and fans. He should soak up the glory while I retreat into my cave. I can go home and quest with Harris or something.

"It's okay," I tell him.

"You sure?"

"Yeah."

When I say good-bye to Elliott, he pouts. "Analee, no! You can't leave yet!"

"My dad's expecting me," I lie.

"Boo. Well, text me that you got home okay."

I promise him I will, and then I creep along the wall, outside of the crowd, until I reach the exit doors. I step out, and even though the humid Florida air hits me like a brick wall, I finally feel like I can breathe again.


Dad, Harlow, and Avery are sitting on the couch watching a movie when I get home. It's rare that the three of them are doing the same thing at the same time in the same place. I pause in the doorway, watching them. They look like a family. Avery is sitting in between them, her head resting on Harlow's shoulder. Dad has his arm stretched behind the couch. He pauses the movie when I walk in.

"Hey, how was the game?" he asks. Harlow and Avery both lean over to look at me. I feel uncomfortable, like I've intruded on a private moment.

"Good," I reply. I glance up the stairs at my closed bedroom door. "We won."

"Congrats!" Harlow says.

Avery leans her head over to look behind me. "Where's Seb?"

"Oh, he's . . ." *Making the moves on his ex-girlfriend.* "Celebrating with the team."

"Do you want to come watch the movie with us?" Harlow asks. "We just started."

I start to say no—the word is my default—when Avery sits up and

230

says, "Come on, Analee. Watch with us! And don't even think about going on your computer."

"Aww, you hear that?" Dad asks. "Your little sister wants to watch a movie with you!"

Usually his family-pushing makes me ill, but tonight it's a nice change of pace to be wanted after sitting at a table where no one knew my name.

"I'm changing into my pj's first," I concede, and Avery lets out a cheer.

When I get to my room, I don't touch my computer. If I open that laptop, I'll be sucked inside all night. I throw on a T-shirt and my worn plaid shorts, then head downstairs to find that the movie's been paused for me.

"Come on, *mija*," Dad says, patting the spot on the couch next to him.

I sit on one side of him, with Avery on the other. He throws his remaining free arm around my shoulder and gives me a light squeeze. It's one of the few times he's touched me since Mom died. The only other time I can remember vividly is at Mom's wake, while I stared down at a glossy wood casket and tried hard not to think about her body lying inside. Dad came up behind me and fixed his strong hands on my shoulders, like he could sense I was moments away from collapsing. That semi-hug, a rare moment of affection from him, meant everything to me. Mom was gone, but someone still had my back.

And then Dad grew sadder and sadder, and we each cocooned ourselves in our separate sorrows. Dad, like me, pulls away when he's hurt. It didn't matter when Mom was alive, because she had more than enough affection for both of us.

I let myself relax under the weight of Dad's arm now. Things still aren't the way they're supposed to be—I will never view the four of us, disparate and thrown together in desperation—as family. I've come to terms with the fact that when Mom left us, so did any hope of having a true family. We were ropa vieja once, and now we're mushroom stew. It's a poor substitute for the real thing.

Avery bursts out laughing at something in the movie. I realize I haven't even been paying attention. She looks up at me and Dad, as if trying to verify that the movie is actually funny. It occurs to me that, maybe for Avery, she's getting the family that she's wanted. What feels forced and unnatural for me might be real for her.

I smile back at her.

# CHAPTER THIRTY

IN THE AFTERMATH OF LILY'S AND MY BROKEN
friendship, I spent days piecing together the series of events that led
to the Incident. How I found myself at Gabrielle's party that night,
why I decided to get drunk in her kitchen, and what Colton told Lily
after everything went down. Here are what I've determined are the
factors that led to our permanent destruction:

## 1. Pressure

The week before Gabrielle's party, Lily slept over my house. We
were in that dreamy, half-awake state when you've decided to turn
the lights off and there's a movie playing softly in the background.

Out of nowhere Lily said, "I think I want to go to the Sweetheart
Dance." Immediately I sat up in bed.

"Ew, why?" is what popped out of my mouth.

She paused, and when she spoke again, annoyance sharpened the
edges of her voice. "Because I've never been to a dance before. It
might be fun."

"Lily, it won't be fun. I'll tell you exactly what it'll be. Someone's
iPhone will blast awful Top 40 music on Mr. Morrison's speakers.

It'll be so loud that your eardrums will explode. Meanwhile, a bunch of idiots will be dry humping each other on the dance floor while guys smuggle beer bottles in their crotches."

"Or," Lily says, "I might have a romantic slow dance with my boyfriend like a normal person."

It stung, hearing her say that. Mostly the term "normal person" did it. Up until that point, Lily and me bashing stupid crap like high school dances had been *our* normal.

"Well, I'm not wasting my time," I said.

"I didn't ask you to," she replied.

## 2. Mom

October sixteenth is the most miserable day of the year. It's the day Mom died, and it happened to be the day of Gabrielle's party two years afterward. Lily convinced me to go with her and Colton. She said it would make me feel better, that it might get my mind off the anniversary of Mom's death. As if anything could ever distract me from the fact that Mom's gone. The closest I can get to forgetting is when I quest with Harris, because when I quest, I can make myself an entirely different person. Kiri's mom didn't die of ovarian cancer. Kiri doesn't have to deal with awkward high school parties.

If I had to be Analee on October sixteenth, I wanted to make myself as different as possible. I guess I wanted to prove to Lily that I could be just as normal as she was.

## 3. Alcohol

Right away I regretted going to the party. Lily wore this cute patterned minidress and lined her eyes with heavy kohl liner. I had opted for jeans, as usual. I didn't know people got dressed up to go to a friend's house. Lily insisted I looked fine, but "fine" sounded a lot like "shitty."

Ten minutes into the party, I was sitting on one end of Gabrielle's couch, and Lily and Colton were making out on the other end. I remember seeing Chloe and Seb pressed up against the wall, his hands cupping her ass. Everyone was making out or talking or playing beer pong on Gabrielle's table.

So I wandered into the kitchen, where Gabrielle and a friend were tossing back shots of Jäger.

"You want one, Annalise?" she asked. I realized she was talking to me, even though her eyes kept bouncing around the room.

"Okay," I said, because there was nothing else for me to do there. I didn't bother to correct Gabrielle on my name. She was close enough.

I downed the Jäger in one bitter gulp, and it threw me into a coughing fit. It tasted like black licorice and cough syrup.

Gabrielle and her friend giggled.

"Want another?" she asked, clicking her fingernails against the green bottle.

I really didn't. I also didn't want to be there in the first place, but if I left, it would only prove Lily right.

"Okay," I said, sliding the shot glass over to her.

## 4. Inexperience

Once there was a young, foolish girl who had never tasted alcohol before and thought it would be wise to take four shots of Jäger in the span of five minutes. Even Gabrielle, who was struggling to stand, told me to slow down.

"I don't feel anything yet," I said between the third and fourth shots. "When do I feel something?"

I expected the booze to hit me all at once, but it snuck up on me. Walking into Gabrielle's living room felt like balancing on a tightrope. I couldn't find Lily. I bumped into a massive armchair on my way to the bathroom. When I sat on the toilet, I calmly observed the way the room tilted back and forth like in a fun house.

The only good thing about getting drunk was that I didn't think about Mom. I thought about how to walk in a straight line, how to find Gabrielle's room, how good it would feel to close my eyes, just until everything stopped tilting.

## 5. Colton

I think I must have fallen asleep, but I'm not sure how long I was out. When I opened my eyes, I saw a figure sitting on the edge of the bed, facing me. It sounds terrifying, but I was too exhausted to feel scared.

"Who is it?" I mumbled, my cheek still pressed against Gabrielle's down pillow.

"It's me." I recognized his voice. Husky, like he had a perpetually sore throat.

"Where's Lily?" I tried to sit up and couldn't. Oh my God, my head. Had someone pounded on it with a mallet while I'd been sleeping? I felt like a human Whac-A-Mole.

"Out there," he said. My eyes adjusted a bit to the darkness, and I could make out Colton's arm waving toward the door. He smelled like he had bathed in sour beer. It leached out of his pores, contaminated his breath.

"Analee," he said. I didn't answer. I felt his hand massaging the top of my head, and all I remember was thinking, *Is this normal?* And then thinking, *I don't even know what normal is. That's why I'm here.*

He crouched down in front of my face, wobbling unsteadily and gripping my shoulder for balance. That's when it all went down.

Soon after the Incident at Gabrielle's party, Lily stopped speaking to me. She didn't ask me what happened; she didn't yell at me; she didn't do a thing except forget our entire friendship. I'm not sure what Colton told her. Sometimes I'm not even sure it really happened. Maybe alcohol gives me a unique hallucinatory side effect. Or maybe I'm remembering things wrong, and I'm the one who kissed Colton first.

But that doesn't seem likely. I've never felt the slightest attraction to Colton. His moody, tortured artist shtick, while attractive to most hot-blooded teenage girls, leaves me cold. It's so manufactured. Colton can listen to the Cure as much as he wants, but he's still a rich, white trust fund kid. From what I remember of our kiss, it wasn't exactly something I'd been yearning for. It was like Seb's kiss at the pizzeria—one-sided, aggressive, violating.

When I see Seb at my locker the next morning, holding out my latte, I'm reminded of our kiss, and I suddenly want to throw the latte in his face.

"No, thank you," I say coldly.

He crooks an eyebrow at me. "Why not?"

"Because I'm not in the mood for a latte. You didn't even ask me if I wanted one."

"You always want one."

"Maybe I want a different flavor," I say. "You could ask me some-time. Maybe I want to try caramel or hazelnut or lemon or something."

"I don't think they serve lemon lattes," he says, barely trying to hide a smile.

"That was just an example."

"Okay," he says. He yanks his arm back. "I apologize. Next time I'll ask you what flavor you want."

I don't know why I'm mad at him, but I am. And when he looks at me like that, like I'm trying to be funny, it makes it worse.

"I'll drink it today since you bought it already," I mumble, taking it from his hand.

"How generous of you."

I take a long, slow sip, then say, "I'm not Chloe, you know."

"I'm aware."

"Just because she loved vanilla lattes doesn't mean I have to."

"So this is about Chloe?" he asks, sipping his own coffee.

"I don't know. Maybe."

"Well, I obviously did something to piss you off. Or Chloe did. I'm still not sure how to translate your answer."

I open my locker, let my gaze rest on the stack of books inside. I don't want to look at Seb when I say this.

"Last night," I say. "At Bruno's. I didn't like the way you kissed me."

He doesn't say anything for a few seconds. Then, "What do you mean?"

"I can't explain it," I reply. "I just felt . . . used."

My eyes blur with tears. I close them, will them to dry up. I know Seb will make fun of me for being weird and prudish about a stupid kiss.

"Hey." He rests his hand between my shoulder blades. "I'm sorry, Analee. I thought you'd be okay with the kiss, but that's my bad. I should have asked you first."

"It's stupid." Once I'm sure my eyes are dry, I turn back to him.

"No, it's not."

"We made an agreement to use each other. I can't feel mad when you actually go through with it."

"You're allowed to feel however you want," Seb says. He takes my books under his arm and shuts my locker. "Look, next time I'll ask you. Or, if you want, we don't have to kiss at all."

"I'm not saying that," I reply hurriedly.

He stops and looks at me. "So, what are you saying?"

"Look, I know this is a business transaction of sorts, but I don't want it to feel like one when I'm being kissed. I know it's torture for you—"

"Torture?" Seb says. "Why do you think that?"

"Because it's obvious!" I throw my hand up, forgetting I'm holding the latte, and a few drops splash out of the cup.

"Analee," he says. "Get your head out of your ass."

"Excuse me?"

"I happen to *like* kissing you."

"Liar."

"There you go again." He shakes his head. "If I didn't mean it, I wouldn't say it. Besides, I figured *you* didn't want to kiss *me*."

The idea of any girl not wanting to kiss Seb Matias is so absurd that I burst out laughing. "Why?"

"Maybe because you acted like I had the plague when I was over at your house?"

I stand there, openmouthed. "You didn't touch me after yoga!"

"Neither did you!"

We stare at each other, and this time I don't look away. The student body continues to move around us. Someone nudges my shoulder as they walk past, but I barely register the movement. I'm breathing far too heavily for someone who's standing still, but Seb's chest rises and falls in sync with mine. It's like partner yoga all over again. All I can think about is what Seb said. Is it possible he was telling the truth? Did he want me to kiss him like I wanted him to kiss me? Above us the bell rings, and I'm snapped out of whatever it was that just happened. We have one minute to get to class.

"Come on." Seb manages to grab my hand despite balancing my books and his coffee in the other.

He hands me my books when we're outside the classroom, then hesitates. "See you at lunch?"

I nod. Then, before I can overthink it, I rise onto my tiptoes and kiss him, quickly, on the lips.

# CHAPTER THIRTY-ONE

HARLOW'S LATEST DIY WEDDING PROJECT IS A
trial run of table centerpieces. Roses, hydrangeas, orchids, wild-
flowers, and baby's breath are all stuffed into reusable glass contain-
ers. Harlow will diligently paint over mason jars and wine bottles,
but God forbid she put flowers in a vase, or use any item the way it
was originally intended.

"Don't you think you're getting a little carried away?" Dad asks
when Harlow starts arranging flowers at the kitchen table. Discarded stems and leaves litter its surface.

"Not at all," she replies smoothly. Her hair is knotted into a
crooked, messy bun. She looks more than a little demented with
a pair of scissors in her hand. "Do you prefer the mason jars or the
wine bottles?"

Dad steps back, tilting his head and twisting his lips. "I'm not sure."

"What about you, Analee?" Harlow asks.

The truth is, I really don't care. I actively hate anything having
to do with this wedding, including every reminder that I will have to
speak in front of fifty people.

"The wine bottles?" I throw out. This seems to please her.

"You're working yourself too hard, *querida*," Dad says, massaging the back of Harlow's neck.

"This wedding is right around the corner, Raf," Harlow says. "Did you talk to your parents yet?"

"About what?"

"About the venue?"

Dad pauses to play with a rose petal, which means no.

Harlow groans. "Raf, the longer you wait, the worse it'll be."

"It's a difficult conversation."

"And a necessary one, don't you think?"

"You don't know my parents," Dad says. "They have to be eased into these things."

Harlow continues to snip away at her flowers. "Your parents escaped a Communist regime when they were teenagers. I think they can handle a beach wedding."

Dad widens his eyes at me in a silent plea for help. I shrug. He can dig himself out of this one. My grandparents will never consider a marriage valid unless it takes place within the stained glass windows of a church.

"Do you want me there?" Harlow asks. The scissors dangle from her fingertips as she eyes my dad. "When you talk to them? Maybe we should do it together."

"I don't think that's a good idea," Dad says. He takes a step backward.

"Oh," Harlow replies. She resumes working on the centerpieces with renewed intensity. *Snip-snip, snip-snip.*

"They might take the news better if it comes from me," Dad says. "That way they can't blame you."

"I'm sure they'll find a way," Harlow mutters.

*Snip. Snip. Snip.*

Whoa. This might be the first time in history that Harlow has ever muttered a passive-aggressive comment under her breath. Usually she's all about releasing emotions in a gentle, constructive way. Even Dad looks taken aback.

They both go silent, and I feel obligated to say something, even though I have nothing to contribute to this particular conversation.

"Do you need help with that?" I ask Harlow, pointing to the quickly dwindling centerpiece.

She stops snipping and puts the scissors down. "No, thank you, Analee. I think I'm finished for the night."

Then she goes upstairs and leaves me and Dad alone in the kitchen. Dad sticks his hands into his pockets, surveying the discarded plant remains, before heaving a long sigh and grabbing a trash bag from under the sink.

"I don't know why we can't stick some flowers into a vase and be done with it," he says as he swipes the plant bits into the bag.

Those were my thoughts exactly, but I'm surprised to hear them come out of his mouth. He never criticizes Harlow's choices in front of me.

"I guess she wants it to be unique," I reply, though why I'm coming to Harlow's defense, I have no idea.

He doesn't say anything in response. I listen to the rustle of the bag and the slap of his shoes against the kitchen tiles.

Then he says quietly, "It was a lot simpler when your mom and I got married."

I almost stop breathing. Dad hasn't brought Mom up so casually since Harlow entered our lives. I'm not sure whether I should ask questions or if my interruption will scare him away from the topic.

"You got married in a church, had the reception at your parents' house, *y ya*," Dad says. "That was it."

I don't speak. I grab a few leaves Dad missed and toss them into the trash.

"Do you know what your grandparents are going to say when I tell them we're getting married on the beach?" Dad asks me.

I can predict that it will involve a lot of Spanish curse words. Abuela will clutch her rosary, and Abuelo will rant about how everyone's going to hell.

"*Padre perdónalos, no saben lo hacen!*" I cry in Abuela's raspy, high-pitched timbre.

Dad laughs. It's nice to make him laugh like that, in a way that Harlow and Avery wouldn't exactly understand. It's like he and I still share something that's only ours.

"That's good," he says. "Can you do Abuelo?"

Abuelo speaks in a kind of singsong bark. I mimic him in a flurry of curse words, shaking my fist toward the sky. I feel like a desperate clown, but it works. Dad is cracking up, almost wheezing with laughter. I try to keep up my Abuelo impression but end up losing momentum.

Dad sits down next to me at the table while he collects himself. I forgot that hanging out with my dad could actually be nice, when he's not worshipping at Harlow's altar or being a fascist about my dating life.

He takes a deep breath, chuckling periodically. "Thank you. I needed that."

"Glad to be of service."

"You're funny, you know that?"

"I'm not funny."

"You are. You were a clown when you were younger. You had this comedy routine where you pretended to juggle tangerines and then hit yourself in the face."

"Sounds very sophisticated," I remark as Dad studies me. It makes me self-conscious. "What?" I ask.

"Nothing. You just . . . you seem happier lately."

I give a halfhearted shrug. Since Mom died, I've accepted the fact that happiness is futile. Maybe I'm happier, but I'm not sure I can ever be *happy*.

"Is it because of Seb?" Dad asks.

"Daaaad," I say. "No."

"That's such a crazy assumption to make about your boyfriend?" he asks.

I can't help but smile slightly at the word. Sometimes sixth-grade Analee takes over, and the thought of Seb as my boyfriend—even when it's a complete lie—gives me tweeny feelings.

"You're still following the rules, right?" Dad asks. His face grows serious. It's like he momentarily forgot that he is supposed to be wearing the Dad mask.

"Yup."

He nods. "I like Seb. He's a good kid."

"He is."

"But he's still a teenage boy. And teenage boys will always make stupid decisions."

"Most of them," I say. "But that doesn't mean I will."

Just as Seb hands me my latte the next day, there's an announcement over the intercom for all students to report to the gym.

The two of us head over together as I quickly try to down my latte. It's salted caramel today and it's tasty, but sickeningly sweet if I drink it too fast.

"What do you think this is about?" I ask Seb. We follow the mass of students cramming through the gym's double doors.

He squeezes past a small redheaded freshman girl, who practically swoons at his touch. "Maybe a surprise assembly to congratulate the soccer team?"

"Oh my God."

"What?"

"You're so full of yourself."

He pinches my waist, and I hate the sound that unwillingly comes out of my mouth. This vapid squeal.

"They've done it before," he says. "The cheerleaders hand out flowers, and the band plays 'Eye of the Tiger.'"

"Of course they do."

But when the gym floor clears up and everyone takes a seat on the bleachers, there are no band members, no cheerleaders. Only our principal, Mr. Ortiz, standing somberly in the middle of the floor, spinning the microphone around in his fingers.

"Analee! Seb!" Elliott calls out from the bleachers on the left. "There's room here!"

It's a free-for-all in here, but most people sit where you would expect. Chloe, Matt, Lily, and Colton are sitting on the opposite side of the bleachers. Seb and I awkwardly climb over the people in the first few rows to reach Elliott.

"So, what do you think is going on?" Elliott asks after we plop down beside him.

"I think we're obviously all here to worship at the altar of Seb," I say, which elicits another pinch from Seb. I slap his hand away.

When I look more closely at Mr. Ortiz, though, I can tell there's something wrong. Mr. Ortiz is one of those rare principals who's beloved by the student body. He's always smiling, and he knows every single person's name in this school. Even mine. I heard that he studies our school's yearbook once a week so that he can say a personalized hello to anyone he passes in the hallway.

But today Mr. Ortiz is not smiling. He stands there, waiting for the noise to die down, and after a trickle of seniors walk into the gym and sit down, it finally does. He clears his throat, and the microphone shrieks with feedback.

"I'm afraid I have some sad news today," he says. There's no faster way to get students' attention. A hush falls over the gym. Some people lean forward eagerly, as if they're watching a movie.

Mr. Ortiz clears his throat again. I've never seen him so uncomfortable. "As some of you may have heard, one of East Bay's most beloved teachers, William Hubbard, passed away yesterday."

I stop listening. The microphone feedback happens in my brain—this loud, screeching sound that makes me clamp my hands over my ears like I can drown it out.

For most of my high school life, Mr. Hubbard looked close to death. I imagined him permanently old, living another twenty years as his frail, hunched self. You see people a certain way, and they become fixed like that. I didn't imagine Mr. Hubbard as William Hubbard, as someone who had been young once, vibrant and full of color before deteriorating into what we saw in the classroom.

Mr. Ortiz goes on, his voice clear but shaky. He talks in clichés. Everyone talks in clichés after a death. I heard all the clichés after Mom's. Time heals all wounds. She's in a better place. At least she's not in pain anymore. All those words, just a group of sounds rearranged to give all this horrible crap some kind of deeper meaning.

"I'd like to invite anyone who wants to share something about Mr. Hubbard to the stage," Mr. Ortiz says, even though there is no stage, just a hardwood floor with a picture of our school's mascot, a poorly drawn cartoon tiger. "A funny story, a nice memory . . ."

I have none of those things about Mr. Hubbard. His death can't take away the fact that he was a tired old grump and a boring teacher and now he's lying on a cold metal table like one of his frogs.

Dalia raises her hand, and Mr. Ortiz looks relieved. "Yes, Dalia. Come on up."

She makes her way down the bleachers, wiping an invisible tear from the corner of her eye. Dalia placed her bet on Mr. Hubbard dying in May.

She lifts the microphone to her glossy lips. "Mr. Hubbard was the best teacher I ever had—"

The feedback loop begins in my head again, louder this time, drowning out her empty words, drowning out my own thoughts. I feel my breakfast creeping its way back up my esophagus. I know with certainty that if I don't leave right this second, I am going to vomit all over the bleacher section.

"I have to go," I mumble, standing up and scooting by Seb's

knees, catching a stranger's shoulder here and there so that I don't tumble over.

"Are you okay?" I hear him whisper behind me. I think it's him, at least. It might be Elliott, but I'm too far now, making my way down the rows. My feet hit the gym floor, and I speed-walk through a few students standing near the doorway.

Nobody stops me. My legs carry me down the long corridor, past classrooms, lockers, the cafeteria, and finally, outside. The sun whites out my vision, and I have to close my eyes for a few seconds to adjust. The sun is always brightest on the saddest days. On the day of my mom's funeral, it was a sticky ninety-six degrees. A bright, cloudless day, like a massive *Fuck you* from nature itself.

I sit down on the grass with my knees up and lodge my head between them. I start to cry. And even though there's no one out here, I'm so freaking embarrassed with myself. I barely knew Mr. Hubbard. I wasn't even all that fond of him. Yet here I am, snot-faced and shaking over the fact that he's not here anymore. Someone who hobbled around and wrote with chalk and ate tuna sandwiches at his desk just . . . stopped existing. Who is he leaving behind? Did he have friends? A family? Or did he have only us, a bunch of students who placed bets on when he would finally kick the bucket?

A pair of cyan sneakers enters my line of vision. I know who it is, but I look up anyway, acutely aware that I'm a sniveling mess, into Seb's concerned face. He followed me here. For some reason, it makes me cry even harder.

He sits down next to me on the grass without saying anything. I wish I could shut my tears off like a faucet, but they're still coming, rolling down my cheeks and dangling past my jawline. I know what

I look like when I cry. It's not cute. But I'm too sad to worry about what I look like, and in some messed up way, that's almost a relief.

Seb lets me cry it out for a few minutes. He doesn't fidget or try to make me feel better. Instead he says, "I didn't take the bet."

Between sniffles I say, "I know."

"I'm sorry."

"You're sorry you didn't take the bet?" I reach into my jeans pocket, hoping that some tissues will magically appear, but I come up with nothing. I have no choice but to let the snot flow freely. I bet when Chloe cries, her nose leaks liquid diamonds.

"No," Seb says, flexing his feet inside his sneakers. "I'm sorry you're upset. I didn't know you and Hubbard were close."

I shake my head, blubbering, "We weren't."

"Oh. Then . . . ?"

"I just feel like I'm surrounded by it," I say. "Death and darkness and sadness. All the time."

Seb doesn't say anything. What can he say? He hasn't experienced loss like I have. The closest he's come to it is getting dumped by Chloe. Otherwise Seb is living in a world of unicorns and rainbows, beloved by everyone, unafraid of whatever life throws at him.

"What can I do?" he finally asks. He scrunches the bottom of his shirt in his hand and uses it to wipe away my tears and snot. It's so unexpectedly sweet (and disgusting) that it has the opposite effect of what he intended. A new current of tears rushes out of me.

"I'm sorry," I cry, covering my face with my hands. He takes them both in his and gives me a face that clearly says, *Don't be stupid*. But I *am* sorry. I feel like I'm infecting him with my sadness.

"Analee," he says softly. He rubs a thumb over my cheek and then slowly, carefully kisses the corner of my eye, right where a new tear is forming.

I look up at him with blurred, tear-coated vision. I want him to kiss me again. I want more of it, because kissing him is one of the ways I can forget about all of this. Kissing him is like stepping into a beam of light.

As if he's reading my mind, Seb kisses me again, this time on the other side of my eye. I don't use words. I circle my arms around his waist and pull him toward me, and there's no resistance on his part. I feel my urgency mirrored in his movements—the way his hands run across my back, the way his hips press into mine. We kiss. We kiss so hard that it drowns out my thoughts, and Seb lowers me onto the grass, and I know I'm a mixture of tears and sweat but it all feels so . . . *good*. And I can't remember the last time I felt good. I don't want to stop feeling it. We roll around in the grass, kissing and baking in the sun. I don't care that after this I'll look like hot garbage. Or that I'll get grass stains on my favorite pair of jeans.

I think I understand Lily now. Is this how it felt with Colton in the parking lot? Kissing so long that you almost stop breathing? Not caring who might see you? If Seb and I were real, I would do this for hours and hours every single day. I see it now. The way being with someone is a drug that makes you forget about everyone else in your life.

Seb's fingers dip under the edges of my shirt, brushing against my skin, and I shiver. It scares me, how easily I could see myself giving in. How I'm thinking about the condoms stashed in my closet and how, yeah, maybe Seb and I are a ruse, but if kissing him feels like this, what would sex feel like?

All of a sudden a stampede of footsteps seems to shake the foundation of the school. I unwrap myself from Seb, and we sit up. His hair is sticking up in a hundred different directions, and I don't want to know what mine looks like. The assembly has ended, and whatever went on out here with me and Seb is effectively over. I'm not sure what to say to him now. *Thank you? That was fun?* A few students start to make their way outside, talking in that excessively loud way that people talk, laughing like Mr. Hubbard's memorial assembly didn't just happen.

Seb is the one to break the silence.

"So, what level was that?" he asks, flicking a blade of grass off my shirtsleeve.

"I think we beat the game," I reply.

# CHAPTER THIRTY-TWO

## Analee's Top School Make-Out Spots

1. Inside Seb's car
2. Baseball dugout
3. Behind the music building
4. Projection room
5. Upstairs utility closet

IN A STRANGE TWIST OF FATE, SCHOOL HAS NOW become my release. Ever since we kissed after assembly, Seb and I make out any possible moment we can. In empty classrooms before school starts, between classes, after school before his soccer practices. I still don't feel comfortable making out in the hallway where everyone is bound to see. I know that's kind of the point of our relationship, but I'm not there yet. Maybe not ever.

So what are the two of us doing, exactly? If this isn't all for show, why bother to keep it up at all? These are the questions I want to ask when Seb slides on top of me in the backseat of his car. But then he'll kiss the spot right where my earlobe meets my neck, and

I'm rendered useless. I never thought of myself as the type to get like this with a boy. I remember rolling my eyes when Lily and Colton dove face-first into each other's throats. But now, more than questing with Harris, or stressing over where to eat during lunch, or wondering whether Lily hates me or not, all my energies are poured into making out with Seb.

I think he's enjoying it too. I mean, he has to be, right? Why else would he be doing it? But then really, is it such a badge of honor when a boy enjoys making out with you? Teenage boys are supposed to be testosterone-driven sex maniacs, so I assume they would make out with anyone. Sometimes, though, in those moments when we pause to catch our breath, he'll look at me like he's deep in thought, or he'll tuck a strand of my hair behind my ear. I used to see him do that stuff with Chloe in the early days of their relationship. I rolled my eyes then too. Now it all makes me turn goofy.

"I don't remember the first time we met," Seb says after a particularly sweaty session in the utility closet. I adjust my shirt to cover my stomach pouch. The shirt is riding higher and higher with each consecutive make-out, along with Seb's hands inching up past my waist and toward my chest. We haven't moved past kissing, but even as that has gotten more intense, it has seemed like less than enough.

"I do," I reply. I'm breathing hard as Seb curls his fingers around my belt loop.

"And?" he asks.

"First day of sixth grade."

"Right." He kisses me from my neck to my collarbone. "Did I talk to you?"

"No." I think back on that day, and how strange life is, that the cute boy in the back row is now kissing me in a closet.

"Did you . . . like me?"

"I thought you were cute," I admit. "For, like, five minutes."

"You don't think I'm cute now?"

"I mean . . . you're good-looking enough, I guess."

"Good-looking enough," he repeats. "Wow. I'm overwhelmed by your praise." We're back to making out now. His hands roam down my waist, slide into my back pockets.

Yes, I decide. I might, at some point in the foreseeable future, have sex with Sebastian Matias. I don't care if this isn't real. Life is short, and whatever this is feels amazing, and I want to experience more amazingness.

"So what changed?" he asks between kisses.

"Hmm?" I can't focus on this conversation right now. His hands are moving everywhere, up my shirt now and underneath my bra strap. My heart jitters at the thought of what might happen next.

"You said I was cute for, like, five minutes," he murmurs. "What happened in those five minutes?"

His fingers fiddle with my bra hooks. I want to reach around and do it for him, then strip him naked and have sex with him right on top of this mop bucket.

I am so gross. I need to get a grip.

"What?" I ask.

"What happened in those five minutes?" he repeats.

"You opened your mouth," I end up saying, and his hands stop moving.

It *so* doesn't come out the way I meant it to. It's the truth, but I wanted to relay a joking, unaffected tone. Instead it comes out the way I really felt that day. Bitter. Pissed.

Seb pulls away. A hurt expression crosses his face. "Ouch?"

"I didn't mean it like that. You just . . . you weren't very nice to me."

"What did I do?" he asks, and he looks so horrified that I regret bringing it up in the first place.

"Just forget it." I stand on the tips of my toes to kiss him again, but he shakes his head.

"I don't want to forget it."

And just like that, our happy make-out bubble is popped. I groan and sit down on the mop bucket. This definitely wasn't part of my sex-fueled fantasy scenario. And the longer I spend in this closet without kissing Seb, the more it sinks into my head, how unhygienic this spot is. Seb leans against a shelf of dusty cleaning products, waiting for my answer.

I tell him everything. With my head down and my hands in my lap, I explain how he laughed when Matt McKinley made me feel like dirt.

"But I didn't say anything," he protests.

"No, you didn't. That's almost worse."

I give him other examples. It's not just about me and a stupid nickname. It goes beyond that. Seb holds an infinite amount of power at our school, but he chooses to stand idly by while the powerless are bullied and mocked.

He takes it all in without speaking. Once in a while he paces the short length of the closet, but then he resumes his post by the cleaning supplies. When I finish talking, I look up at him.

"This is what you think of me?" he asks quietly.

"I don't know," I say. But the answer is yes. Seb doesn't go out of his way to make other people miserable like Matt does, but he doesn't exactly put others above himself either.

He squats down beside me. His fingers, steepled together, rest on his chin. There's muffled commotion out in the hallway as students start getting ready for class. I shouldn't have said anything. I didn't think my opinion would have such an impact on Seb. My mind inadvertently flashes back to the conversation between him and Chloe that day in the library. What was it she said? Something about Seb not caring about anyone but himself.

"I hate that I made you feel like that," he says finally.

I will forever regret bringing this up. It's so embarrassing to reveal that I've been holding on to a four-year-old slight, one that is now throwing Seb into a crisis.

"It's not just you," I reply. "It's everyone, really."

"Do other people see me like that? Like some spineless asshole?"

"Come on," I say. "You know most people worship the ground you walk on."

"Right," he says dully.

I wonder if that's part of the problem. Seb is so used to the constant adoration that he's terrified something will one day take it all away. I can't exactly relate. The good thing about not having anything is that you don't worry about losing anything.

I stand up and wipe off my jeans. Seb stays low to the ground, staring intently at the concrete floor.

"Seb?"

"Yeah?"

"It's okay. It was years ago." I figure this is something a rational

257

human being would say. Someone not like me. I extend my hand, and he takes it, hoists himself up. Before I can open the closet door, just a crack to see if the coast is clear, Seb pulls me toward him to kiss me again. This kiss is different. This one feels new. It's weird to have spent a number of hours kissing Seb and get one that surprises me.

"I'm sorry," he whispers, and I can barely remember why I was angry with him for so long.

# CHAPTER THIRTY-THREE

THIS IS WHAT I HAVE WRITTEN FOR HARLOW AND my dad's wedding toast:

*Good evening, everyone.*

I already hate it. Does any sixteen-year-old actually say "good evening"? It reminds me of an old butler or a restaurant hostess. Besides, I haven't exactly been feeling the love between Dad and Harlow lately. As the wedding prep heightens, the tension between them thickens. Our house is festooned with fabric samples, candles, and, inexplicably, ivory-colored metal birdcages. The birdcages are empty, and I have to wonder, will birds inhabit them at any point? Is Harlow planning to release white doves at the ceremony? I don't ask these types of questions.

Meanwhile Harlow posts chirpy online videos about DIY weddings and then quietly sulks at Dad during dinner. Since the controversy about Carrie and the beach ceremony, my grandparents refuse to attend the wedding because they consider it a slap in the face of Jesus or something. So then Dad suggested to Harlow that they make a quick trip to the rectory, to which Harlow bristled and said,

"Absolutely not!" Part of me thinks my grandparents aren't resistant to a nontraditional wedding. They're resistant to my dad marrying a nontraditional woman.

Mom didn't care about the things Harlow cares about. She and Dad had a totally average church wedding followed by an uneventful reception at her parents' house. She didn't cultivate boho chic looks or meditate or follow a raw, plant-based diet. She *did* wear her comfiest pair of jeans almost every day and salsa dance while she vacuumed the house and eat fried sweet plantains with her dinner. She always said that as long as she had her family, nothing else mattered. I miss the way she didn't care. I wonder if her easygoing attitude, now gone from my life, is the reason I suddenly care way too much about *everything*.

*It feels good to be Kiri again. I run along Azeron Lake, my silky lavender hair flying out behind me, my crossbow strapped against my back. Azeron is a gorgeous pool of sparkling silver water. A light mist hangs over its surface, and mossy rocks line its shore. I wait by the north side of the lake, where I instructed him to meet me. Moments later I hear the sound of footsteps squishing against the grass, and he bursts through the forest and bounds over to me.*

Bernard? *I ask the squat gnome when he appears beside me.* That's the name you go by?

Bernard is a wise name, *he says.*

What happened to you? *I ask.* You've only been doing this for five minutes, and your health is already low.

Dude, I know. This fucking thing started attacking me! I didn't know how to fight back, so I just ran away.

*I retrieve a healing potion I have inside my backpack.* Was it a worgen?

No, *he says.* It was like this . . . crazy mutant pig monster.

Pig monster? *I apply the potion, and Bernard returns to full health.* Wait . . . are you talking about a boar? Like one of those ordinary boars that roam around?

Trust me, Analee. There was nothing ordinary about this boar.

Kiri, *I say.* My name is Kiri.

Seb has no idea what he's doing. You don't call people by their real names here. It takes you out of it.

Now my cell is ringing, and I know it's him.

"What?" I answer.

"So tell me how I kill things."

"Did you click on the boar?"

"No. I just pressed random keys in the hopes that something would work."

"Great plan. Weird how it didn't work out for you."

It's strange to be Seb's all-knowing spirit guide right now. Usually it's Seb teaching me the ways of the real world, but today he has stepped into *my* world. Over the phone I explain how to strike an opponent in the game. But before I can finish, he's charging into the forest.

"Let's doooo it!" he hollers, his voice attacking my poor unsuspecting eardrums. It's so typical of Seb. Diving into something without a clue of what he's doing. Harris meticulously plans every mission after analyzing our set of skills, surrounding environment, and available inventory.

*Bernard immediately stumbles upon a boar grazing along the edge of the forest. The boar turns on him, preparing to strike. Bernard isn't fast enough. He hesitates, and the boar springs into action and rams into him repeatedly as Bernard cowers, wounded.*

*Quickly I load my crossbow. Pull the string back. Aim. Shoot. The boar dies instantly, exploding into thin air. Bernard stands there, swaying slightly, in the same spot where he was wounded.*

"Wow," Seb says to me over the phone. "That was badass."

I feel a surge of pride, which is ridiculous because I've never done anything truly badass in my entire life. Fighting a boar online doesn't take courage. It takes a few well-timed taps on a keyboard.

"You'll get used to it," I say. "Your reflexes will improve in time . . . Striker."

"You did *not* just go there."

"I mean . . . nationally ranked soccer star can't kill a level-one boar?"

"I almost had him! You jumped in before I could deal some damage."

"Fine," I say. "Next time I'll let you handle it—aka leave you to die."

"Very nice, An. Hey, do people have sex in this game?"

"Not possible."

"Does that mean you've tried?"

"No!"

I've thought about it, though. Not about having virtual sex. I think that would make me feel more pathetic than I already do. But sometimes I think about what sex would be like if I looked like Kiri. If Harris looked like Xolkar, and our beautiful toned bodies had beautiful toned sex together.

It would probably, I realize with a sickening feeling, look a lot like the perfect sex that Chloe and Seb used to have.

There's a figure who suddenly appears beside me and Seb on-screen. It flickers. Then, as quickly as it appeared, it vanishes. My heart plunges to my feet.

"What was that?" Seb asks over the phone.

Was it who I thought it was? It could have been another random user. There is a limited variety of characters, so it's easy to find one that looks like someone else.

"Was that a glitch?" he goes on.

"No," I reply, because I know it wasn't a random user or a glitch. It was Harris. I've been spending less and less time with him online since delving deeper into the Seb charade. Tonight I made up a crap excuse for why I couldn't quest with him, and now he's caught me killing boars with someone else. Why do I feel like I've been caught in a tawdry affair?

"Hello?" I realize that Seb's been talking while I've been deep inside my own twisted head.

"Sorry," I say. "It's . . . That guy was Harris."

On-screen Bernard and Kiri are frozen in place.

"Harris?" Seb repeats. "Who's—"

There's an abrupt pause. I can picture the realization dawning on Seb. He gets this face when things click into place, where one eyebrow lifts slightly higher than the other, and the corners of his lips tug downward.

"Your almost-boyfriend," he pieces together.

"Yes."

"You've never met him in person."

It's a uniquely embarrassing moment, when your fake boyfriend realizes that you have another fake boyfriend.

"That doesn't matter," I say. My voice has a bite to it. "Harris knows me better than anyone else."

Although, he doesn't know what's going on between me and Seb, which is pretty much the biggest thing happening in my life right now, besides Dad and Harlow's upcoming nuptials. How well does Harris know me now, really? Would he think I'm capable of making out in a broom closet? Or would that scare him off?

"You never talk about him anymore," Seb points out.

"I think about him."

"When?"

"All the time."

"When you're with me?"

No. When I'm with Seb, I'm thinking about Seb. But I'm not going to tell him that.

"All the time," I repeat. "Don't you think about Chloe when you're with me?"

Not a word. Not a freaking word from him. His silence is like a shiv, relentlessly piercing my chest, rendering me breathless. I'm pissed off, and I don't know why. Of course he's thinking about Chloe. He *should* be. She's a major reason why we're doing this whole thing.

"Anyway," I glide on. It's kind of remarkable how unaffected my voice sounds. "What am I supposed to do now?"

"You do nothing," Seb says. "Your almost-boyfriend caught you gaming with another guy. He's obviously jealous, based on his disappearing act."

"I don't want him to be jealous."

"Analee, you are such an amateur. When a guy gets jealous, that's exactly when he makes his move."

"Harris doesn't make moves. And I don't like playing these games."

Seb gives a dark laugh. "What do you think it is we're doing here?"

He's right, is the depressing thing. The two of us? We're a game. Pretend. Make-believe. Is that all life is? A series of games? Let's say Seb is right and Harris makes a move. Am I reduced to a prize won through some macho pissing contest?

And the Seb thing. I know we're not real, but I wanted to believe there was some shred of authenticity behind it all. I don't expect Seb to profess his love to me, but it'd be nice if he didn't hate spending time with me. Even if he thought of me as a friend . . . I could be friends with Seb. I could be acquaintances with Seb. Really, I just want to be anything but a means to an end.

# CHAPTER THIRTY-FOUR

DAD AND HARLOW ARE ARGUING WHEN I GET home from school on Monday. The tense, passive-aggressive silence that's been simmering for weeks has reached a full-on boil. I know that it's normal for couples to fight, but this isn't normal for Dad and Harlow. Especially Harlow. When she gets mad, she usually shuts herself up in her meditation room and comes out an hour later smiling and sleepy-eyed. She *never* raises her voice.

Except for right now. She's raising it louder than Dad's, and Dad has this booming tenor that can fill up the whole house.

I sneak past the kitchen, where they're facing off against each other. I've mastered going up the stairs silently, like a true Invisible Girl would. I know how the second-to-last step creaks in the middle, and how you have to place one foot on each side of the first few steps so they don't cave in. Sure enough, Dad and Harlow haven't noticed that I'm here. Their unhinged yelling continues, and I lock myself in the bedroom to block out the noise.

The problem? I can't go online. I haven't talked to Harris since I shot a boar for another man. The second problem is that if I'm not online, there's no other way for me to contact him. I can't see him in person, and we've never exchanged phone numbers. If not for the Internet connection, Harris does not exist.

I should just do it. Log in. The worst that can happen is that Harris will ignore me.

Ugh, but that actually *would* feel like the worst possible thing. I'm already Invisible Girl in real life. I can't handle being that to Harris, too.

I flop down onto my bed with dramatic gusto. My gaze wanders around my room, from my open, disheveled closet to the half-eaten breakfast bar on my nightstand. Then back to my closet.

My closet is open, and I'm sure I closed it this morning. Some of my shoes are scattered around, and while I'm generally a messy person, I can usually recognize my type of mess, and this is not mine. My first thought is Avery. Maybe she was ransacking my closet to try on my clothes. That's something little sisters do, right? Even when their big sisters are, like, five times their size? And have the fashion sense of a ranch hand?

Amidst the many piles of shoes, I see a definite empty space where something was moved.

I sit up.

The condoms.

Shit.

Shit, shit, shit, shit, shit.

And now I am 200 percent certain that I am the cause of Dad and Harlow's epic showdown in the kitchen. I run to my bedroom door and open it a crack so that I can hear what they're saying.

Harlow is midsentence, something about sharing a life together.

"She's *my* daughter!" Dad's voice rings out so clearly, I don't have to strain. "The rules are my call!"

Harlow's voice rises to match his volume. "So that's it? I get zero input on Analee?"

"You don't get input on her sex life. She shouldn't even have one!"

My dad and future stepmom are discussing my sex life. It makes me want to curl up into a little ball and die right here, right on this spot on my carpet with the mysterious brown stain that I suspect and hope is chocolate.

Harlow starts arguing that if I were going to have sex, she wanted me to be safe, and Dad barks back, "She's not allowed to have sex! That's not how we raised her!"

I physically jolt at that word—"we." The acknowledgment of Mom.

From Harlow's pause I can tell that it takes her by surprise too. "I just think," she says, and her tone is noticeably softer, "that Cristina would have wanted—"

"It doesn't matter what you think!" he shouts, and the world seems to stop. I have never, ever heard Dad talk to Harlow like that. For so long, it seems like our lives have revolved around what she thinks.

Then, more quietly, he adds, "You didn't know her." And his voice breaks in this way that makes me want to cry. Harlow gets quiet too, and there's an unbearable silence that is almost worse than the shouting.

The thing is, Dad doesn't talk about Mom. Not to anyone, really, and especially not to Harlow. I get it. I do. Dad and I are both the type to keep our feelings locked up tight. The bad thing is that the feelings don't disappear. They grow and mutate until they have to escape sometime.

I hear the front door close and Dad's car start up. I get the pang of fear like when I was little.

Where is he going? Is he leaving forever? Am I going to be abandoned by both parents now? I went to exactly three sessions with a psychologist after Mom died. I remember that the psychologist's name was Wendy, and she would wait for me to talk, even if I had nothing to say and there were long gaps of awkward silence. She had a beauty mark in the middle of her chin and fluffy brown hair.

I didn't get a chance to tell Wendy about my fears. I could have, I guess, but I didn't want to come right out and say them. I worried that Wendy would judge me, because I would see her writing things in a little leather-bound notebook. I didn't like it. Why should I be all transparent when Wendy wouldn't tell me what she truly thought about me?

I should have kept seeing Wendy, because clearly I have not adjusted to life yet. I told Dad that I was fine after those initial sessions, and he didn't push me. I think he wanted to believe I was okay.

The house is so quiet, I wonder if Harlow went with Dad. I wouldn't be surprised if they said fuck it all and just eloped. I creep down the stairs to listen. Nothing. Not a sound. My stomach gives a premature growl. Honestly, I think there's something wrong with my metabolism. I ate a bag of chips not thirty minutes ago. I edge down the stairs one by one, then pause at the kitchen doorway.

Harlow is sitting with her back to me, as still as a statue.

I don't know what to do here. Option A: ask her if she's okay, give her an awkward pat on the shoulder, make excuses for my father.

Option B: get back upstairs before she knows I'm here. Of course I go for Option B. But as I turn to leave, my stomach emits the loudest gurgle. It sounds like someone's drowning in there.

Harlow's head whips around. Her eyes are pink and bleary.

"Oh, I—I didn't know you were home," she says. She turns around and tries to wipe her face discreetly. Silently I curse out my stomach. I feel like I'm imposing on a private moment. I know that I hate when people see me cry. I can't imagine how someone as image-conscious as Harlow must feel.

"Sorry," I say. "I was hungry, and I didn't . . . I thought you had left."

"I'm hungry too," Harlow says, getting up suddenly. I wonder if she has a magical acai bowl that cures sadness. She doesn't head for the refrigerator, though. She swipes her keys up from the table and spins them around her finger.

"Come on," she says to me, and I really wish I could stay behind and have the house to myself, but I follow her command.

She pulls up in front of a McDonald's. It's not just any McDonald's, which would be shocking enough for Harlow. It's the McDonald's I always went to with Mom.

I don't believe in an afterlife, but if I did, this would be Mom banging me over the head with a sign. It's too much of a coincidence for Harlow, the picture of health, to suddenly crave what she once referred to as "Satan's excrement."

Harlow shuts off the ignition and stares at the glittering golden arches. I can see her mind furiously at work, running through a long list of McDonald's crimes against humanity: low employee wages, slaughterhouses, economic imperialism, the infamous pink sludge.

"I'm not having meat," she says. I can't tell if she's talking to me or to herself.

"Okay," I say.

We step out into the parking lot, and Harlow pushes the glass doors open with a newfound resolve. When she gets to the counter, she orders two large fries and sodas. They hand us the tray of food, and Harlow dips her head down to *inhale the smell*. I don't even recognize her anymore.

"Um, Harlow?" I try as we head to the nearest booth.

"Mmm-hmm?" She takes another whiff of french fries.

"Since when do you eat this stuff?"

"It's poison, I know. Full of preservatives and high fructose corn syrup and God knows what else."

With that said, she folds an entire large fry into her mouth and chomps down on it, closing her eyes for a brief moment.

"So why—" I start to ask, and she says simply, "I just had to have fried food today."

I nod. "Understandable. I feel that way pretty much every day."

Harlow sighs, and we eat quietly for a moment. I feel like Wendy, trying to be okay with the silence and waiting for Harlow to fill it.

It works. She takes a gulp of soda and says, "I guess you heard your dad and me arguing before."

"A little," I lie.

"Enough to know what we were fighting about?"

Oh God, she's going to make me say it, isn't she?

"Sex," I say to my fries.

"Kind of," Harlow replies. "I mean, yes, your dad was definitely upset that I got involved in your sex life. But it was more than that. The two of us are very, very stubborn people."

She leans back against the vinyl booth. "Maybe I was wrong to interfere. But here's the thing, Analee . . . I do care about you."

I keep filling my mouth up with more and more fries. If I don't eat, I'll cry. I'm not sure why this is the case, but I can feel the tears burning behind my eyes.

"I think your dad is scared," Harlow continues. "He wants to do right by your mom. And sometimes that fear can make him . . ."

"A tight-ass?" I supply.

She laughs. "Your words, not mine. And look, I didn't know your mom. Your dad doesn't like to talk about her much, because it hurts him when he does. But I can't help thinking that she would want you to have someone to talk to about all this stuff."

The fucked up thing is that, as different as Mom was from Harlow, I could see them getting along. I think Mom would get a kick out of Harlow's ridiculous recipes. Mom was always down to try anything. There's no way she'd permanently give up her tostones and pastelitos, but she might try going raw for, like . . . a day. She would possibly consider adding acai bowls to her morning routine. Mom had the unique talent of being traditional and embracing the unusual all at once.

"I think my mom would have liked you," I tell Harlow. I'm not sure what makes me say it. Maybe it's that I've never seen Harlow look so unsure.

"Really?" she asks. She smiles.

"Yeah," I reply. "This version of you, I mean. The Harlow that eats french fries once in a while."

"Only once in a while," she stresses, pointing a fry at me.

"Are you and my dad going to be okay?" I ask her. I'm not sure what answer I'm looking for.

Harlow touches the soda straw to her lips, smiling slightly. "Yes. We'll be fine. I think we've both been . . . not ourselves lately."

"I'm sorry my grandparents have been so . . ." I trail off, but Harlow seems to understand my meaning. She nods.

"We're all a little . . . you know. I can be just as stubborn as they are. Maybe more so."

"True," I acknowledge before I can bite my tongue. She laughs.

"They also loved your mom. And miss her. And I'm sure this wedding stirs up a lot of emotion," she adds. There's no self-pity in her voice. "I have to try to remember that."

I never thought about how hard it must be for Harlow to live in Mom's shadow. This will be her first wedding, but it's Dad's second. It must be a strange feeling. Harlow always seems so perfect, with heaps of self-confidence to spare, but it can't be easy to live up to someone's memory. Especially when Mom fit so seamlessly into Dad's family.

"So," she says, fishing a fry from the bottom of her carton, "how are things with the boy?"

I should lie. My mouth is primed to spit out the word "fine." Conversation over. Instead I blurt out, "Confusing."

Whyyyy? Why am I inviting questions about my fake relationship?

Harlow, of course, latches on to this. "Confusing how?"

"Well," I start. *Stop talking. Close your mouth.* "I'm not sure Seb is all that into me."

There I go again. Practically begging to be interrogated. Since when do I spill my thoughts so openly? To Harlow, of all people? She's just so sad right now, with her chewed soda straw and salty fingers. It's making me careless.

"Can I tell you what I see?" Harlow asks.

I shrug.

"I see a guy who chooses to spend his free Saturday doing yoga in your living room."

"He was extra bored that day," I reply.

"And takes your little sister along to the beach."

"It would have been rude not to," I mumble.

"And stares at you when you're not looking."

"Probably taking inventory of what's wrong with me."

"No," Harlow says. "It's definitely a good stare. Like the kind your dad gave me when he started taking my yoga class."

I shudder. "Okay, Harlow. TMI."

She laughs again. "Want me to demonstrate?"

"I really don't," I say, but I can't help the tiny half smile curling on my lips.

"I'm Seb," she says, rolling her shoulders back. She looks down at the table, then slides her gaze up to my face, her mouth stretching into a goofy grin.

"Oh my God, he does *not* look at me like that!" I say, and laugh. I will never be the recipient of a look like that. That one's reserved for the Chloes and Harlows.

"I witnessed it firsthand," she maintains.

I don't believe her, but it's nice to think about. I mean, I hope one day a guy actually does look at me like that. I just don't see it happening, is all.

I wonder how Dad would look at Harlow right now if he saw her. I've never liked her more than I do in this moment, open and honest, licking the salt from the corners of her lips, her wispy hair sticking up like someone rubbed a balloon on her head.

"What?" she asks when she catches me staring. She raises her hand to smooth down her hair.

"You should leave it," I say.

"You're kidding."

"Why not? Be messy. No one will see it except me anyway. None of your online followers would ever set foot in a McDonald's."

Harlow considers this, lowers her hand. "That's a good point."

"Even if they did," I reason, "they might like it, seeing you look less than perfect."

"Oh, they see that all the time," Harlow says.

"Really? I never have. Everything you do is perfect. *You're* pretty much perfect." I've never been so comfortable telling Harlow what I think. Maybe seeing her at her lowest has given me a newfound burst of courage.

"Analee, I'm nowhere near perfect."

I roll my eyes. Here comes the part where she tries to be relatable. Like she's not a tall, leggy, blond goddess deigning us mere mortals her presence.

"I'm serious," Harlow presses. "I have a long list of insecurities just like everyone else."

"Such as?"

"Such as . . . well, where do I start? I wish my hair were thicker, like yours. I wish I weren't so skinny. I wish my boobs were bigger. I wish I didn't have man hands."

At the last one I burst out laughing.

"I'm serious!" Harlow says, but she's laughing too. "Look at them!"

She dangles both hands in front of me, and if I'm being brutally honest, they are a *tad* oversize compared to the rest of Harlow's tiny form.

"The point is," Harlow says, lowering her hands, "that I don't dwell on the flaws. I even try to love them, on a good day."

"I don't see myself loving all this"—I gesture down at myself—"anytime soon."

"I'm not saying it's easy. I work at it every day."

I thought being Harlow meant loving yourself effortlessly. She's undoubtedly beautiful, but it's like my rose-colored glasses have been shattered and I can see her clearly for the first time. She isn't perfect. I've just been blind to her flaws and hyper-focused on my own. My mind wanders to Chloe, another goddess in the making. I remember what Seb mentioned about her trying to achieve the ideal, carefully cultivated image to post online. I wonder what her list of insecurities would be. Nothing comes to mind, but then again I never would have expected Harlow to take issue with her own appearance.

"Can I give you a piece of advice?" Harlow asks.

"Okay . . ."

"Life is not about perfection. It's about acceptance."

What a very yogi thing to say. I try not to roll my eyes again, because I know she's trying to help. It's just that, to me, some things are easier to accept than others.

"It's ironic," Harlow goes on, "but the more you accept yourself and stop caring about what other people see, the more those people will see how amazing you are."

"That *sounds* nice, but how do I actually do it? I mean, how do I stop caring?" The questions pop out before I can stop myself. I hate giving Harlow the satisfaction of knowing that her words are having an impact on me, but I have a dark, twisted need to know her secrets.

"It's a process," she admits. "I'm still learning. Positive thinking helps. I also stopped forcing my body into what it *should* look like, because it shouldn't look like anything other than what it is. And most important . . ." She pauses to slurp up the remains of her soda, then says simply, "When I'm not feeling confident, I fake it."

I'm baffled by this. Harlow is always preaching self-love to her followers. Is it nothing more than a ruse?

"Doesn't that mean you're just . . . lying?" I ask.

"I don't think so," Harlow reasons. "The more you fake it, the easier it is to believe it. It's not technically a lie if you believe it, right?"

Oh my God, what is happening to me? Is Harlow actually making sense? Could her power-of-positive-thinking shtick actually work?

"Ready to go?" she asks. She piles all of our crumpled napkins onto her tray because Harlow is nothing if not clean.

I nod, and she dumps our trash out, then walks in step with me out to the parking lot. We're both carrying ourselves more lightly, despite consuming all that sugar and fried food.

"Harlow?" I say when the car is in sight.

"Yes?"

"I like your mushroom stew," I say. "But, with all due respect, I don't think you should call it ropa vieja. It's just not right."

She looks at me in surprise. "Is it bad that I did?"

"It's not a punishable offense or anything," I reply. "I would just call it what it is, though. Mushroom stew. Don't try to Cubanize it."

I have never spoken to Harlow like this. I wonder if she'll snap, the way she did with Dad today. She doesn't say anything as she unlocks the car doors and we slip inside.

The car is so hot that my skin prickles. We sit there for a minute, and Harlow doesn't start the car.

"I was trying to relate," she says, and her voice goes up as if she's asking a question. She stares at a spot on the windshield. "It gets complicated, being the non-Cuban."

Harlow and I were finally getting to a somewhat good place, and then I had to open my mouth. Since when am I the guardian of Cuban culture? Who cares if Harlow wants to substitute mushrooms in a stew? I'm a crappy excuse for a Cuban anyway. My Spanish is awful. I don't know proper vocab, only slang words that would get me laughed out of actual Spanish-speaking countries.

"I shouldn't have said anything," I say.

"Of course you should have said something," Harlow says. "I need someone to call me out on this stuff."

"Yeah, but—"

"I promise, Analee. You should always say what you feel."

I feel guilty when I say what I feel. Because who cares about what I have to say? What if people think it's stupid, or pathetic, or unimportant? Harlow seems to care, for some reason. She studies me now, intently, and I wish she would start the car so we could get home.

Finally she inserts her key, the engine turns, and she backs out of her parking spot. I stare at the feathers dangling from her keychain.

"What if we call it Mushroom Surprise?" she asks.

I wrinkle my nose. "Do people *want* to be surprised when they eat?"

"Surprised by the excellence of it."

"What about," I say, "Magical Mushroom Medley?"

"Ooo, I like the alliteration," Harlow says. "Although . . ."

"What? There's an 'although'? It's perfect!"

"'Magical' makes me think of psychedelics." Harlow checks the rearview mirror before switching lanes.

"Okay, so not 'magical,'" I say. "Magnificent?"

"Better. Or marvelous?"

"Harlow's Marvelous Mushroom Medley," I say out loud. I can already see Harlow narrating the recipe video, complete with jaunty stock music and bubbly fonts listing the ingredients.

"Analee," Harlow says, fully serious. "I think we have something here."

# CHAPTER THIRTY-FIVE

DAD AND HARLOW STILL AREN'T SPEAKING TO EACH other. Both are acting like this is a normal way to behave with someone you're marrying in a month. Even weirder? Dad hasn't said one word to me about the condoms. I expected him to march into my room and relay his list of rules all over again, but . . . there's only been crickets.

He's talking to me, at least, which is more effort than he's giving Harlow. But our conversations skim the surface, both of us carefully avoiding anything close to the topic of sex or boyfriends or Trojans of any kind. It's as if the box of condoms mysteriously disappeared from our existence and his memory. Not that Dad and I ever shared deep philosophical discussions in the past. But lately our conversations have been more deficient than usual.

Like this morning, he comes in from a run while I'm eating breakfast and says, "Woo. It's hot out there today." He says it in this *voice*, like he's the dad on one of those gross heartwarming family-friendly shows. And I'm thinking, *Uh, yeah, Dad. We live in freaking Florida. What else is new?* But his fakeness makes me act fake too. So instead I say, "Yeah. Florida, right?" Then he lets out another "woo," grabs a juice from the fridge, and hauls ass out of the kitchen.

I hate small talk enough. It's worse when I have to make it with my own father.

People never just come out and say what they mean. It's exhausting. You have to sift through words upon words of bullshit in order to get to the tiniest morsel of truth. I guess I'm no better. I keep all my truth sealed inside me. Some of it slips out in impromptu rants, usually to Seb, for some reason, or Harris. But for the most part I swallow my thoughts and feelings down to avoid making waves out there. Not even a ripple from me.

Dad does it again the next day, when it's raining.

"Woo. It's really coming down," he says.

And I just snap. Maybe it's because the only time my dad talks to me is when he's delivering a daily weather report.

When he grabs his juice and turns to leave, I hear myself say, "You shouldn't be mad at Harlow."

He pauses. Then, "I'm not."

I hate when he does this. He always acts like everything's fine when it isn't.

"She was trying to help," I go on. I don't add what I'm thinking: *Since you didn't bother.* My dad's preferred method of dealing with things is to not. Just let go and hope everything will work out okay. Maybe yes, Harlow overstepped, but only because he's eternally standing still.

"I'm not mad at her," he says again. He hesitates at the door, like he wants to say something else, but then he leaves without another word.

**Harris:** hey

On the night Harris resumes talking to me, the stars shine a little more brightly. I want to answer him solely in exclamation points and the happiest emojis I can find: rainbows, hands clapping, smiley faces, party favors. Because it's *Harris*. And he's not going to stop talking to me forever even though I had an online thing with a boy who wasn't him.

I don't want to scare him off, though, so I allow myself a lonely exclamation point.

**Me:** Hey!

Do I bring Seb up? Do I apologize? Do I act like Dad and pretend nothing ever happened?

**Me:** So . . . haven't talked to you in a while

Long pause. No answer. I look away from my computer, count to ten, and snap back to the screen. Still nothing. I close my eyes and hum the chorus of a Beatles song. When I open my eyes, he has responded.

**Harris:** you've been busy

There it is. The passive-aggressive morsel of truth.

**Me:** Yeah

I have so much to say to him, but my fingers don't move. I don't know where to begin. Part of me is tempted to tell him everything. Part of me is curious about playing the game and taking Seb's advice. I drum my fingers on the keyboard and wait.

**Harris:** i've missed talking to you

Is it possible for your fingers to melt in relief? Mine do. They practically ooze onto the keys.

**Me:** I've missed talking to you too. Like, a lot.

**Harris:** i'm not gonna lie . . . i was kinda upset when you blew me off to go online with some dude

**Me:** Ugh, I'm so sorry

**Me:** I suck

**Me:** I wasn't even going to go online, but he told me that he was going to try the game, and I guess I got excited to introduce someone new to that world

**Harris:** it's ok. i get it.

**Me:** I'm a turd. A gigantic, epic, post-McDonald's poop

**Harris:** has anyone told you you're kind of obsessed with mcdonald's?

**Me:** We have a love-hate relationship

**Harris:** so

**Harris:** who was that guy?

**Me:** Who?

What a stupid, transparent thing to type. Like we weren't just talking about this.

**Harris:** the guy who couldn't kill a boar

**Me:** He's just this guy from school

**Harris:** the soccer-star lab partner?

**Me:** Yes

**Harris:** so are you guys . . . a thing?

The little Seb on my shoulder keeps plotting away. *Play the game, Analee. Make him jealous. Tell him about making out in the broom closet.*

I mentally flick little Seb away. I'm sick of playing games. I'm sick of hiding how I really feel, all the time, twenty-four hours a day, until I'm numb with exhaustion.

**Me:** We're definitely not a thing

**Me:** Just friends

**Me:** If that

There is no possible explanation for why I feel as guilty as I do right now. Seb and I *aren't* a thing. We can barely handle this show-mance, let alone an actual, committed, know-someone-better-than-you-know-yourself relationship.

**Harris:** good

**Me:** Good?

**Harris:** yes

**Me:** Why is that good?

This, I know, is the moment I've been waiting for. All those mushy letters to Harris in my journal, filled with longing and vulnerability, have built to this. My heart feels like it could burst through my chest. This could very well happen. The boy I love might love me back.

**Harris:** it's good because

**Harris:** i don't know

**Me:** Okay . . .

**Harris:** it just bothers me to think about you dating this guy

**Me:** Why?

Oh God. Another unbearable pause. I stand up. My body feels like it's hopped up on caffeine and sugar, like I've downed twenty nonfat vanilla lattes. But I shouldn't think about nonfat vanilla lattes, because nonfat vanilla lattes make me think of Seb. I imagine him faithfully waiting by my locker every morning, holding one out to me, wearing his absurdly bright shoes.

**Harris:** it's obvious, isn't it?

**Harris:** i like you, Analee

**Harris:** i've liked you for a while

**Harris:** you had to have known

**Harris:** hello?

**Harris:** Analee?

Now my body won't move, no matter how much I will it. Why. Am. I. So. Dysfunctional? This, right here, is what I wanted! It's happening! This is the elusive happiness that everyone else seems to have, right here on this LCD screen, and all I have to do is take it. I sit back down. I take a few ujjayi breaths, as demonstrated by Harlow during yoga instruction. Finally I'm able to lay my fingers over the keys and type a response.

**Me:** Sorry

**Me:** I'm here

**Harris:** you're weirded out, aren't you

**Me:** No! Not at all

**Harris:** i know you don't feel the same way about me

**Harris:** honestly, i'm used to that

**Harris:** the girls i've liked in the past don't usually go for guys who spend all their free time gaming

**Me:** Harris

**Me:** I do feel the same way

**Harris:** wait. what?

**Harris:** are you messing with me?

**Me:** I swear I'm not

**Harris:** holy shit

**Me:** I echo that sentiment

**Harris:** so . . . what now?

That's the big question, isn't it? What now? My thoughts return to Seb. Do we end whatever it is we've been doing? Do Harris and I end up together in virtual bliss? I didn't think this far ahead. Honestly? I never expected my showmance with Seb to actually work. I didn't fully consider that, at some point, we could each get something we want. This is a good thing, what's happening with me and Harris. I should be bouncing-off-the-walls excited, but my feelings are all swirled together and I can't tell any of them apart.

I'm relieved when my bedroom door swings open and Avery marches in.

"It's called knocking," I tell her. I try to sound cross, but I'm happy for an excuse not to think about the tangled mess of Harris and Seb.

"Whatever." She throws herself onto my bed, burying her face in my comforter.

**Me:** I g2g

**Harris:** you're kidding, right?

**Me:** I'm sorry!

**Me:** Family stuff

**Me:** I promise we'll talk about this later

**Harris:** ok

I don't know how to say good-bye to him now that we're in this new, weird stage of our relationship. Do I send him a heart emoji?

It doesn't seem right. My relationship with Harris has thus far consisted of slaying monsters and calling each other "dude."

**Me:** Bye, H

**Harris:** bye, analee

I turn to deal with my latest problem, the one unmoving in my bed. I walk over to Avery and give her a poke on the shoulder.

"Ow," she whines into the comforter.

"What's your deal?"

"Nothing."

"Avery," I say, "I'm not in the mood for your dramatics. I have enough drama in my life right now."

"I'm not being dramatic."

"Right. Because barging into my room and throwing yourself onto my bed is totally normal behavior."

"It is."

Ugh. I always forget that little kids don't understand sarcasm.

"Is everything okay?" I ask.

She raises her shoulders.

"Do you want to talk about it?"

More shoulders. This is new. I've never known Avery to turn shy.

"It'd be a lot easier to talk to you if I could see your face," I say.

She lifts her head up slightly, then rolls over onto her back and immediately covers her face with her hands.

"For Christ's sake—" I start as I pull her hands away. Then she looks up at me with teary eyes, bluish-green, just like Harlow's. I soften. Even at Avery's young age, I've never seen her cry. I've seen her roll her eyes, yell, and throw tantrums, but never cry.

"What's wrong?" I ask. "And don't shrug at me again."

She stares up at my ceiling and rubs her nose. "Are Mom and Dad still getting married?"

"Yes," I say.

"How do you know?"

"I just know."

"But they're mad at each other."

I am so *not* equipped to handle this. How do you talk to an eight-year-old about this crap? Isn't this the kind of thing guidance counselors are for? I'm not sure what the appropriate thing to say is. I could make something up and reassure her that Dad and Harlow are totally fine, even though our dinners are spent in careful silence and shifty glances. You're supposed to lie to kids, aren't you? Isn't that what Santa and the Tooth Fairy have taught us?

It's strange to think that in less than a month I'll technically be considered a big sister. Big sisters are supposed to be cool and wise and a bunch of other adjectives I'm not. I have nothing to offer Avery. I don't know what the hell I'm doing.

I decide to go with the honest approach and hope for the best.

"Yeah," I say. "They're mad at each other."

"But what if they decide not to get married?"

A couple of months ago I would have been thrilled at this development. But somewhere along the line a shift took place. I no longer dread the idea of Dad and Harlow locking it down. I don't want Avery to cry, and I don't want Dad to go back to who he was right after Mom died. I want everyone to be . . . happy. I mean, I don't think I'll be happy either way. I can't figure out what the hell will make *me* happy.

"They're going to get married," I tell Avery with a surprising amount of certainty.

"They're *fighting*."

"Here's the thing," I say. I sit next to her on the bed. "People who love each other a lot are going to fight once in a while."

She stares back at me.

"I know it sounds weird, but it's true. It's a good thing to fight sometimes. That means you're really comfortable with a person and you can tell them what you think and feel."

As I speak, it occurs to me that I've never, ever fought with Harris. Sure, we've had different opinions. We've argued over the best way to complete a quest. But for the most part Harris and I live in a fantasy world, where the only fights to be held are with monsters instead of people. How much do I actually know about him?

I know that he hates brussels sprouts, that his favorite movie is *Eternal Sunshine of the Spotless Mind*, that his first and only kiss took place at an ice-skating party in the sixth grade. I know that the girl ignored him the next day and the rest of the year and then transferred schools in seventh grade. What I know about Harris is a collection of anecdotes, scraps of conversation. I've never heard his voice, or felt his lips, or even seen what he looks like.

"Do you and Seb fight?" Avery asks.

"We have," I say. "I didn't like him very much at first."

"Why not?"

"Well . . ." I lie down next to her on the bed. I have a lot to say about this. "I thought he was conceited, lazy, selfish, rude, shallow, vapid . . ."

Avery lets out a giggle. "I think he's nice."

"Of course you do. No girl is immune to his brainwashing tactics, even the young ones like you."

"But you *like* him now, right?"

"I guess," I say. And I say it very reluctantly. I feel like I'm betraying my former self when I say it, because I can still see the Seb from sixth grade. I can picture the open mouth full of braces, laughing at me, whispering about me with Matt McKinley. There once existed a version of Seb who treated me like I was nothing, and I can't forget about that. I'm not sure I can ever forgive him for having been that Seb. Even if he happens to be really good at making out.

"You should tell him you like him," Avery urges. She flips onto her side to face me. "Don't be like Mom and Dad."

"He knows I like him," I insist.

"He might not. You always walk around like this." Avery wiggles around in the bed with her hands on her hips and scrunches her eyebrows together. She looks like Oscar the Grouch.

"You are such a brat," I say, but she's too busy laughing at herself to hear me. When she finally calms down, she lets out a self-satisfied sigh and rolls onto her back again.

We both stare up at the ceiling.

"Do I really look angry all the time?" I ask. I immediately hate myself for asking a third grader this question. Especially one like Avery, who has the sensitivity of a toaster.

"Yeah. You do. You should look at Seb like this instead. . . . Look, Analee. . . . Are you looking, Analee?"

I turn my head. She is, of course, being ridiculous. Big fluttery eyes and her hand over her heart.

"You finished?" I ask her.

She bats her eyes for a few more seconds, then drops her hand to her side. "Yes."

"Great."

She sticks her tongue out at me, then asks, "Can I sleep in here tonight?"

"What?" I sit up. "No."

"Please?"

"Aren't you too old for this?"

"It would just be for tonight," she says. "I promise. I'll sleep on the floor if you want! You don't even have to share your bed."

"Why do you want to sleep in here?"

"I don't know."

"Not happening. Sorry."

"Come *on*."

"Avery, my sleep is precious. I like to sleep in the middle of the bed with my body sprawled out, and I toss and turn a lot during the night. Plus, you snore."

"Fiiiine," she says. She drags herself off my bed and shuffles toward the door, head down, shoulders drawn. I *know* she's being dramatic, and yet . . .

"Avery," I say.

She pauses.

"Only for tonight," I warn.

"Yay!" She sprints out of the room, only to return seconds later, armed with a pillow, blanket, and a pink teddy bear.

I have no idea when I turned so soft.

# CHAPTER THIRTY-SIX

USUALLY I HATE TALKING TO ANYONE ON THE phone, but every day after Mom's funeral I waited for Lily to call me. The feeling of dread that usually accompanied my ringtone was replaced with hope, then crushing disappointment when I checked the caller ID and it was only Abuela or a telemarketer.

For days I waited, and for days she didn't call.

I gave her the benefit of the doubt. Maybe she was busy with school. She sent emails, mostly homework assignments, tidbits of school gossip, a perfunctory closing line like *Let me know if you need anything else!* The exclamation point felt painful, like a stinger through the chest.

The anger stirred inside me, but I couldn't release it. Not at Lily. She was one of the few people left in my life, and I couldn't afford to lose anyone else.

When I got back to school, I thought I wanted people to treat me like they usually did. That is, I thought I wanted to be ignored, unseen, left alone. But when I was, I was disappointed. It was one of the first times that being alone felt lonely.

Lily and I sat together at lunch, and everything was normal, which was by default wrong. Because life shouldn't be normal after your mom dies.

"Okay," she said. "Let's see what else you missed. . . . Dalia and Liam possibly hooked up at Sierra's party, even though Liam just asked Sierra out the day before."

What I'd missed. Like I had just come back from vacation.

I didn't care. I *so* didn't care. Lily knew me well enough to tell, but she kept going anyway.

"Oh, and I started bingeing this show that I overheard Lena talking about. I think you'd really like it . . ."

I let her talk while I took in everything happening around me. I felt unfocused, like I was trying to make out the scenery through a heavy fog.

*Mom is gone, Mom is gone, Mom is gone.*

I looked at Lily, who was deliberately not looking at me, who was still talking like nothing significant—beyond Dalia and Liam and this new TV show she was watching—had happened in our lives. I squeezed my plastic fork so hard, I thought it would break in half.

For the first time ever, I wanted to shake my best friend. I wanted to scream at her for moving too fast, jumping from one topic of conversation to another without standing still long enough to acknowledge how horrible everything was. For making me feel stuck while she could move forward.

In the middle of talking, she gave someone across the room a tiny wave.

"Who are you waving at?" I interrupted.

Lily lowered her hand, the smile fading from her lips. "Chloe."

"Since when are you friends with Chloe?" It sounded accusatory.

Maybe it was. I was having trouble breathing, walking, talking, and Lily was waving to people we used to observe from a distance.

"We're not exactly *friends*. We were partners on an English project last week. I like her a lot, though."

I frowned.

"Anyway," Lily went on, "you really should check out that show. There's another one I started watching last night, but—"

Lily dove headfirst into normalcy, while I became more determined to avoid it.

"Can you stop?" I asked finally when she paused to take a breath.

"Stop what?"

I wasn't sure how to answer, because I wasn't sure what I was asking. Stop talking? Stop living your life?

"I just don't want to hear about a TV show right now," I muttered.

Lily sank into her seat. "Sorry."

"You don't have to apologize."

"Sorry," she said again. "I mean . . ."

I'd made it weird between us, and it still wasn't right. It didn't feel right for things to be normal, either. Where did that leave us? I wanted to tell Lily that I missed Mom, and that I didn't know how to act with people anymore, and I wanted to ask her if she was still sad too or if the tears I'd seen during the funeral had been a fluke.

Instead we ate the rest of our lunch in silence. I thought about how much happier Lily would be to sit at a table with Chloe instead of me.

# CHAPTER THIRTY-SEVEN

SEB ISN'T AT SCHOOL TODAY. HE TEXTED ME THIS morning that he had a fever and almost fainted when he got out of bed. He said he'll miss me, which, whatever. I think he was joking.

When I walk to my locker, everything is suddenly bare. It's like when you remove a piece of furniture from your house and the entire room looks empty and wrong. I realize that I've accidentally gotten used to Seb waiting for me here. He's my trusty old sofa.

I don't have him as a protective shield when I walk to homeroom either. Before Seb and I started this whole thing, I didn't exactly need one, because no one looked at me. But now I'm *seen*. That's the only way I can describe it. It's like "dating" Seb has allowed me to take up space in the world. People smile at me. In a crowded hallway they scoot over to let me walk by. One small freshman girl with glasses even waves to me.

It's weirding me out. The power of Seb exceeds his presence. It's like he has imbued me with it.

In the cafeteria I'm planning to stockpile some food and escape to one of my secluded pre-Seb lunch spots, but Elliott comes up behind me and tugs at my hair.

"Where's your other half?" he asks.

For a quick second I think of Lily, who for years was known as my other half. Then I realize who he means.

"Out sick," I say.

"Ooo." Elliott waggles his eyebrows. "You gonna go over to his house after school and play nurse?"

"Ew, no, you perv." I pause. "Wait, am I supposed to? Is that a girlfriendy thing to do?"

"Nah." Elliott stacks three slices of pizza on his tray. I grab two. We move down the line. "Normally I avoid sick people. *However*, Seb Matias is the exception. I would take him covered in boils and sores."

"I should probably do something," I say. "Something nurturing. I've never been the nurturing type."

"Sponge bath?"

"Elliott!"

"Just wanted to make you blush."

"Silly Elliott. I'm not white enough to blush." But my skin feels warm and tingly at the thought of giving Seb a sponge bath. Seb's toned arms . . . Seb's toned legs . . . Seriously, there is something wrong with me.

"Bring him some chicken soup," Elliott says, and I snap back to the din of the cafeteria. We pile more food onto our trays, and somehow I find myself walking with Elliott to a nearby table. Elliott motions for me to sit down, and all my plans for a secluded lunch away from society fly out the window.

"Analee, this is my friend Jared," he says, nodding his head toward a boy with chin-length black hair.

I say hi, and Jared goes, "I've heard a lot about you. The school won't shut up about Sebalee."

I almost fall out of my chair. "Seb and I have a couple nickname?"

"Duh," Elliott says. "The shipper wars are in full effect."

Aaaand cue the anxiety.

"Don't worry. I think you're winning," Jared says to me.

"Not possible," I reply. Seb and Chloe fit together seamlessly, each one so perfectly skinny and attractive. They are the couple in those stock photos that come with a picture frame.

"It's true," Elliott assures me. "Everyone thinks you're, like, authentic."

"Isn't that just a nice way of saying I look like crap?"

"It's a compliment," he says, punching me on the shoulder.

"Oh!" Jared dabs at his lips with a napkin. "Did you guys hear about Lily and Colton?"

I jolt.

"Um, no," says Elliott.

I look around the cafeteria and notice that neither Lily nor Colton is anywhere to be found.

"She dumped him," Jared says.

"No!" Elliott cries.

I stay silent. I'm not sure I believe it. Lily has worshipped at the altar of Colton for so long that if anyone were getting dumped, it'd be her.

Jared and Elliott dissect the news from every angle, hypothesizing what went wrong and when. I sit there and try to decipher my feelings, or lack thereof. I thought I would be ecstatic if this day ever arrived. Instead I feel . . . well, I can't exactly tell what I feel.

I always thought that on the long-awaited day when Lily and Colton broke up, Lily and I would finally resume our friendship. I guess it was a stupid assumption to make. The day is here, and I haven't gotten anything from Lily. Not a text, not an email, not even a smile to show me that everything between us will go back to normal.

"Analee? What's wrong?" Elliott pauses in the middle of his new theory that Lily is dating an older man who goes to the nearby university.

"Nothing," I say, but a lot about this is wrong. It's wrong that someone I used to share everything with has gone through a monumental life event and I had to hear about it through the East Bay grapevine.

I get up, leave my tray on the table, and apologize to Jared and Elliott, who look totally confused. I don't want to listen to any of this anymore. If Lily wants to permanently cut me out of her life, I can do the same to her.


When I ring the doorbell at Seb's house, a petite woman with a pierced lip answers the door. She doesn't say hi, just looks me up and down in a way that makes me feel idiotic. I don't say anything either. I stand there with my stupid plastic bag of chicken soup and stare at her.

"Who are you?" she finally demands.

This is the scariest woman I've ever met in my entire life.

"Um . . . is this Seb's house?" I ask.

She rolls her eyes. "He's upstairs."

It almost sounds like an invitation, but she doesn't budge to let me in.

The bag is starting to cut the circulation from my fingers. I switch it to my other hand. "Can I . . . um . . . see him?"

"You a friend of his?" she asks.

"Yes. Um. Girlfriend." Has anyone in life ever uttered the word "um" this many times in the span of a minute?

She smiles. Not in a nice way. "You're not his girlfriend."

Whenever I think about which superpower I would want most, teleportation is the one that springs to mind. Like right now, under this woman's sneering gaze, I want to disappear in a burst of molecules that can rearrange themselves on an entirely different continent.

"I am," I say in my most assertive voice, but she looks thoroughly unmoved. This woman can smell weakness. She is a jungle cat; I am a gerbil.

She moves over slightly, still holding the door. I guess this is my invitation. I slip past her, plastic bag still dangling from my fingertips, and hurry upstairs out of her sight.

There are three bedrooms upstairs and only one closed door. Due to my excellent deduction skills, I surmise that Seb is behind the closed door. I hesitate. Will he be happy to see me? Is this a stupid idea? What if he's sleeping? I wouldn't want anyone to see me when I'm sick. Maybe if I had a *real* boyfriend, I would allow it, but definitely not a fake one.

I knock softly.

"Yeah," comes his voice. Something about it soothes my nerves.

I open the door a crack and poke my head in. "Seb?"

He looks pitiful. Pale and tired, with a computer positioned on his lap. When he sees me, his face breaks into a grin.

"Thank God," he says. "I thought you were *her*."

I make sure the door is shut tight, then say in a whisper, "Seb, she is a *nightmare*. Is she always that mean?"

"She's actually been better than usual today. No screaming."

"I will never complain about Harlow again." I hover by the door, still wondering if I should be here. Being sick is so private. I haven't been around anyone sick since Mom, and to see someone like Seb, who should be running around on a soccer field, bedridden and lethargic . . . it makes my stomach drop. It makes me think about things I'm determined not to think about.

"Get over here," Seb says, patting the spot next to him on the bed.

I creep closer. "Are you going to infect me?"

"I might," Seb says. "But you're gonna want to see this."

I get into the sickbed and lie stiffly beside him, and he shows me his computer screen.

"Shut up," I say. "You got to level five?"

"Analee, I have killed. So. Many. Boars."

I press my hand to my chest. "I could not be prouder. But you know there are other ways to level up, right?"

"Yeah, but I'm not ready for questing."

"Wow." I sink back into the pillow. "So Seb Matias is a chickenshit."

"Did you not hear about all the boars I killed?"

"So much to learn, young Bernard."

"Good thing I got a skilled teacher," he says, setting the laptop aside. He puts his arms around me and pulls me into his chest.

"You better not be contagious," I groan, but I let him do it. Let me get sick. Who cares? I lay my head on his ridiculously hard pec and breathe in his scent. It's slightly stale today, but still deliciously Seb.

300

And then I remember Harris.

Is Harris my boyfriend now? Am I cheating on him? I should definitely not be in Seb's arms, or in his bed. It feels so nice, though, with the rise and fall of his chest, and his hand stroking my arm up and down, up and down, in a way that makes me excited and sleepy at the same time.

But what are we *doing*? Seb and I are not a couple! This is all kinds of ridiculous.

I clear my throat. "Seb?"

"Hmm?"

"You were right about Harris."

"What do you mean?"

"I mean, I think we're . . ." This should not be difficult to say. This was one of our goals all along. "I think we're dating now?"

His hand stops moving. I feel his body tense against me. Or maybe it's me. Maybe I'm the one who tensed up, and that's what he's responding to. Whatever it is, the air has shifted. And Seb isn't talking, and now I'm not talking either, and everything is awkward.

"Oh," he says finally. "That's . . . great. That's great, right?"

"I mean . . . yeah. Yeah, it's great. It's not official yet, I guess. He just said he liked me, and I said I liked him."

"That's great," he says again. "I'm happy for you. This is what you wanted."

"It is, yeah. It *is* what I wanted."

What is wrong with me? Why am I talking like this? I've lost all ability to form an original sentence.

"Well, in that case we should probably stop pretending," Seb says.

I lift my head from his chest. "What?"

"If you have an actual boyfriend now, you're not going to need a fake one." He removes his arm from my shoulders, and I suddenly feel lonelier than I have in a while.

"But what about Chloe?" I ask. "You want her back, don't you?"

He doesn't say a word. Does that mean he changed his mind? *Stop it*, I tell myself sternly. I shouldn't care if he changed his mind. Chleb, no Chleb, it makes no difference in my life.

"Yes," he says finally.

Oof. My heart feels sore. Which goes to show how idiotic I've been this whole time. Never get invested in people. They will all let you down.

"So we'll stay together until you get her back," I say.

"Analee—"

"It's fine. Harris will understand."

"I don't think your boyfriend is going to be cool with you dating another guy, unless you have some polyamorous arrangement that I don't know about."

"He doesn't have to know," I say.

Seb casts a doubt-filled stare in my direction.

"It's not a big deal," I go on. "You and I are just pretending anyway."

"Why would you risk your new relationship to help me?" he asks.

I shrug and roll onto my side, my back to Seb. I feel the prickling sensation behind my eyes that comes right before the waterworks. It's a rational question. If I'm finally getting what I've wanted with Harris, why am I almost crying at the thought of losing Seb?

"Hey." His hand cups my shoulder.

*Don't say anything. Not a freaking word. Be cool.*

"I just know you're not going to talk to me anymore," I whine.

Oh my God. Way to say the worst possible thing in the worst possible way.

"What? What do you mean?"

"If we end this," I say, "you're not going to talk to me anymore. Everything's going to go back to the way it was before."

I can't do it again, I realize. I can't deal with another person leaving me. I'm starting a collection of people who have vanished from my life—Mom, Lily, even my dad. When Mom left, she took a giant piece of him with her. He's here physically, but he's not the same. I see my life stretching ahead of me. I see me walking alone on a dark, empty path, leaving a series of phantoms and broken relationships in my wake.

"Bullshit, Analee."

"I'm serious."

"So am I. Do you really think I hang out with you only to win Chloe back?"

I shrug again. "I don't know."

"You think that little of yourself?"

I turn around to face him. "I *don't* think little of myself."

But I do. How could I not? It's what all of my past experience has taught me, that I wasn't enough for the people in my life.

Seb stares me down like that, face-to-face. It's impossible to turn away and, worse, impossible to lie.

"Fine," I say. "Maybe I'm lacking in the self-confidence department, but . . ."

"But what?"

"But look at Lily!"

"What about Lily?"

"She cut me out of her life completely," I say. "Like I was nothing."

He rests his head on his hand. "Are you going to tell me what happened between you two?"

"I don't know."

"Have you ever told anyone?"

"No." Maybe it's time I did. Seb doesn't push, but he keeps staring at me, waiting. I don't know where to start, so I tell him everything. From the chemo sessions to the funeral to the night of the Incident. How Lily and I never got any closure, no final conversation to tie our friendship up in a neat little bow.

After I explain it all to him, he stays quiet.

"As you can see," I continue, "Lily doesn't care if I live or die."

"Oh, please. I don't think that's true."

"No? Then what's stopping her from talking to me again?"

"Have *you* tried talking to *her*?" he asks.

"No."

"Why not?"

"Because. She obviously made her choice."

"But she might not know the full story," Seb points out.

"She knows *me*. Or I thought she did. If our friendship were worth anything, she would at least talk to me."

"I agree that she should," Seb says. "But people aren't perfect."

"Or," I posit, "she decided I'm dead weight and has forever cut me out."

"Wrong." He pokes me on the nose.

"Uh, you can't just dismiss what I'm saying—"

"I just did."

When I think back on my friendship with Lily, some blurry

details sharpen into focus. Lately I was the one doing the majority of the judging. Lily remained fairly quiet. There would be a half-hearted laugh, or a forced murmur of agreement. It seems so obvious now. She wanted to be a part of it all, all the stupid high school shit that I assumed the two of us were above. She wanted the boyfriend and the pretty friends. She wanted to be known. Even if it came at my expense.

Except now she has broken up with Colton, and I don't know what that says about her. I'm not sure what any of it means.

When I bring this up to Seb, he says, "Lily finally dumped him?"

"What do you mean 'finally'?"

"You know as well as I do that Colton's a dick."

"If he's such a dick, then why are you friends with him?" I counter.

"I'm not. We know the same people and sometimes share the same lunch table, so the school has decided we're friends."

"Well, you haven't done much to dispel that notion."

"It's not like I can choose a new group of friends."

I burst out laughing, right in his face. "It's exactly like that! Take your pick. Everyone in school would sell their soul to be friends with Seb Matias."

"Not you," Seb says quietly.

"Huh?"

"You wanted nothing to do with me for years. People like you aren't interested in being friends with me."

"People like me," I repeat. I don't know what he means. Freaks? Loners? "Please define."

"You know," Seb says. "You're smart. You think about things, you analyze. You have strong opinions about unicorn lattes."

305

"Don't get me started on fucking unicorn—"

"You're an interesting person. You don't care how many goals I score during soccer season or any of the other stuff people drool over."

I kind of grumble under my breath, because Seb is being nice to me and I don't know how to respond to compliments.

"And, Analee?" He dips his head so that his eyes meet mine. "No one who knows you would ever think you're dead weight."

At his words, something comes over me, because before I know it, I'm kissing a sick Seb in his bed. It's so dumb. Here I am, catching all of his germs, ignoring the fact that I almost maybe technically have a boyfriend. *Just one more time*, I think. *Before Harris and I make it official. This is only a good-bye kiss.*

# CHAPTER THIRTY-EIGHT

EVER SINCE ROLLING AROUND WITH SEB IN HIS sickbed, I haven't been able to go online. I can't face Harris, even when I don't have to actually see his face. So instead of hunting monsters or defining my new relationship, I pour all of my energy into writing a toast for Dad and Harlow, the soon-to-be-married couple who have yet to speak to each other since the Great Condom Catastrophe. Although, earlier tonight Dad did ask Harlow during dinner if she wanted a water refill. It was a huge leap of progress in their relationship.

Right now my toast is exactly thirty-seven seconds long. It's also horrible, but I don't care if it's horrible. I care about getting through it without any of the following happening: stuttering, fainting, shaking, crying, and anything else that would generally cause humiliation.

I'm crouched over my writing notebook with a red pen in hand. If I crossed out every cliché in this speech, I would be left with five seconds of material. I take out only the obvious ones, like when I wish them a lifetime of joy and happiness or when I call Dad the man of Harlow's dreams. I'm trying to figure out the next line, when all of a sudden Avery's high-pitched voice blares through my closed bedroom door.

"MOM! DAD! ANAAAALLLEEEEE!"

Without thinking, I toss the pen aside and barrel down the hall. Dad and Harlow are halfway up the stairs, and the three of us storm into Avery's room like the National Guard. She's standing in front of her desk, frozen, staring at a spot next to her computer. Relief washes over me. From the way she was screaming, I expected to walk in on some grisly crime scene.

"*Pero qué pasó?*" Dad asks. When he's freaked out, his instinct is to go with his first language.

Her eyes not leaving the desk, Avery points at something near her computer. "Bug."

"You've got to be kidding me," I blurt out. Even Harlow shakes her head.

Avery turns to us with teary eyes. "No! It came from my head! I was scratching, and—"

"Shit," Harlow and Dad say in unison. They glance at each other, and I see Dad's mouth twitch into an almost-smile.

"What's the big deal?" I ask. "So a bug landed on Avery's head."

Dad and Harlow walk over to the desk to inspect the creature. I stay behind. Only Avery would allow a bug to bring everyone's life to a screeching halt.

After a second Harlow takes a shaky breath and turns to us.

"It's a louse," she declares. Dad curses in Spanish and, in one quick swooping motion, slams his hand on top of the bug.

"Wait," I say. "You're telling me that Avery has lice?"

Avery bursts into tears. Harlow nods at me and then rushes over to her, strokes her hair, and murmurs softly.

Of fucking course. This is the problem with having so many goddamn friends like Avery does. One of them is bound to give you lice.

And now my head itches. I don't know if it's the hypochondriac effect, but there is an unbearable itch behind my right ear.

"Okay," Harlow says. "We need a lice comb and that medicated lice treatment. Raf?"

"On it," Dad says, jingling the keys in his pocket.

"Don't get the comb that zaps them," Harlow instructs. "It's a waste of money. Breaks in five seconds. . . . Analee?"

"Yeah?" I'm furiously scratching the nape of my neck.

"Let me check your hair."

I will say this for Harlow—she is a boss when it comes to lice. She picks at my hair with her bare fingers as I stand there, nervous and itchy and completely grossed out. Is this what I was missing out on as an only child? Someone to infect me with parasites? Because if so, I'll pass.

Harlow clucks her tongue. "Two combs, Raf. And four bottles of treatment."

"What!" I screech. Maybe I misjudged Avery, because all I want to do at the moment is burst into tears. Unfortunately, I don't have the excuse of being a third-grade drama queen.

"Sorry, An," Harlow says as Dad rushes off to buy the supplies.

"I can't have lice, Harlow," I say. "I wash my hair every night!"

"They actually like clean hair. It's easier to cling on to. And regular shampoo doesn't kill them. It's kind of fascinating, actually, how they've developed an immunity in order to survive—"

"All I hear is that I have mutant bugs living in my hair," I interrupt as Avery's wailing grows louder. "Avery, will you please quit it with the waterworks!"

Instead her wailing grows more intense. I wonder if I've overstepped my bounds as stepsister. I expect Harlow to scold me or give me a dirty look for snapping at her precious little girl.

Surprisingly, though, she doesn't. She presses a finger to her temple and says, "Really, Avery, this is not a fatal diagnosis. They're not going to *kill* you."

"They'll just feed off your blood," I mutter under my breath so that only Harlow can hear. She widens her eyes at me in warning, but her lips turn up at the corners.


Revolting fact of the day: killing lice is an aphrodisiac to Dad and Harlow. Avery and I sit side by side on kitchen chairs with clean towels draped over our shoulders. Dad combs out my lice; Harlow, Avery's. It's a painstakingly slow process. After pouring smelly goop over your head, someone has to comb through your hair one small section at a time, using a special metal fine-toothed comb.

As this is going on, Harlow and Dad are bragging about how many lice they get per section.

"*Coño!*" Dad exclaims, inspecting his comb. "I have six here."

"You do not," Harlow laughs.

"*Mira.*" Dad pauses to show her. It's like they're immune to how horrifying this is in every possible way. "In your face."

"It's not a competition, Raf."

"Not anymore," Dad says. "What was your record, again? Three?"

"I'm not finished yet," Harlow retorts.

"Ow!" Avery yelps as Harlow scrapes the side of her head with the lice comb.

"Oops. Sorry, ladybug."

I got so used to the tension, I forgot how gross Dad and Harlow can be when they flirt with each other. They think they're so slick about it too, like I'm as stupid as Avery. Take their code for sex. It's disgustingly transparent. Preface: my dad is not a film connoisseur. His favorite movie of all time is *Super Troopers*, followed closely by *Robin Hood: Men in Tights*. So when he asks Harlow, out of nowhere in the middle of dinner, "*Citizen Kane* tonight?" with a not-so-sly wink, I'm not under the impression that he actually intends to watch a 1940s black-and-white film about a newspaper magnate.

"Seven!" Harlow says now triumphantly.

Dad makes a *Hmph* sound. "Girl, you lie."

"Are we supposed to go to school tomorrow?" I ask.

"Of course," says Dad. "Why wouldn't you?"

"Maybe because I'm infested with bugs and my hair smells like Pine-Sol?"

As if I weren't a social pariah already. Oh no. What if the lice got Seb? We were lying together in his bed, our foreheads touching, our scalps dangerously close to each other.

"If Analee gets to miss school, I get to miss school too!" Avery declares.

"No one is missing school," Harlow says. "You heard what your dad said."

And just like that, any leftover tension between them thaws. Dad has never really called the shots in our dysfunctional household. He makes the rules for me, and Harlow makes the rules for

Avery. We are together and completely separate all at once.

"Whoa, look at this big guy!" Harlow says suddenly. I shudder.

Dad whistles. "That's a fat one! Girls, you have to see this."

"I'll pass," I mutter.

"I can't believe that in one week I get to marry the second-best lice killer on the East Coast," Dad says as he drags the comb across my scalp. *I* can't believe he's trying to make this a romantic experience.

"Can you both please keep in mind that these things have been living on our heads?" I ask.

Harlow chuckles. "Speaking of, Raf. . . . I've been thinking a lot about the wedding . . ."

My thoughts fly. Is Harlow bailing on the wedding? She wouldn't dump my dad in front of me and Avery, right? She's supposed to be this sensitive, empathetic yogi.

And, okay, if you put a gun to my head and asked me what I really thought of Harlow, I would say that maybe she's not as bad as I once assumed. I still think her meditation room is a dumb waste of space. And her continuous obsession with the latest nutrition fad makes me want to pull my lice-ravaged hair out. But, despite the long list of things that annoy me about Harlow, she's a decent person, I think. With the exception of buying me condoms, she seems to make Dad happy. I've learned from experience that Happy Dad is a much better alternative to Depressed Dad, who doesn't come out of his room and is so busy wallowing in his own sadness that he can't notice yours.

Harlow continues, "If you really want Father Medina to perform the ceremony, I'm okay with it."

Dad stops combing. "You're kidding."

"I'm not. But only if it's what *you* want."

"I've thought about the wedding too," Dad says with a sigh. I look at Avery in my peripheral vision. Did they suddenly forget we're still in the room, or . . . ?

"I want bald Carrie to officiate," he decides.

"Raf . . ."

"No, really. I'm not just trying to do what you want. I'm not trying to go against my parents. I like Carrie fine. She's a nice person. She knows the two of us. And, to be honest, I think Father Medina is going a little senile."

"But your parents . . ."

"They have to learn that you and I make the decisions. It's about what we want, not what they want."

"Raf," Harlow says again, but this time her voice is gooey and soft. "I love you."

"I love you too."

They both stop combing as Avery and I sit here. I hear their lice combs clink together when they embrace. It's really pretty gross. Meanwhile, I keep imagining the multitude of bugs running rampant across my scalp.

"So we still have to go to school tomorrow?" Avery asks.

"Yes," Dad and Harlow say in unison.

They get back to work on our hair. I can practically feel the smiles radiating off them.

"*Citizen Kane* tonight?" Harlow murmurs to Dad.

# CHAPTER THIRTY-NINE

AS DAD AND HARLOW'S WEDDING DATE APPROACHES, I've been having more and more dreams about Mom. The worst kinds of dreams, because they're vividly realistic yet just the slightest bit off. Sometimes you know you're dreaming, and other times you're positive that this is your life, even when nothing about it makes sense.

I wake up at two in the morning with a tear-soaked pillow and a runny nose. Mom was here, in this house. All of our traditional old furniture replaced the boho-style decor, all of Harlow's Buddhas were gone, the meditation room was back to being a guest bedroom accented by Mom's woven floral throw pillows.

She was helping me get dressed for the wedding. In my dream I didn't question the absurdity of Dad and Harlow getting married while Mom was still in the picture. I accepted this strange dream reality as Mom zipped me up in a hideous orange ball gown.

"I still don't have my toast written," I told her. There was a vague sense of panic about this, but I was still able to function, whereas in real life I would go into cardiac arrest.

"Make it up as you go, *mija*," Mom said. It was really her voice. Lower than Harlow's, slightly husky but warm. It was the voice that lived on through her outgoing voice mail greeting that I called every day for a year after she died.

In this dream Dad and Harlow weren't getting married at the beach or the church. The wedding was being held in the back room of East Bay's most elegant McDonald's. I don't know how I got there, but I did, and the place was packed with wedding guests, all of them strangers. I looked for a place to write my toast, but I couldn't find a pen and paper. One of the guests told me to check in front, but as I was going to, the ceremony began.

None of this was normal, but I didn't realize anything was wrong until Dad walked down the aisle.

*That doesn't make sense*, the voice from real life interrupted. *Why is he getting married? Where is Mom? I just talked to her. She zipped me into my dress.*

The rules of dreamland started to crumble.

"Mom?" I whispered. All around me guests laughed and talked in the middle of the ceremony. I scanned the crowd for Mom's curly dark hair. I thought I spotted it in the first rows, but no. The hair was too coiffed to be hers.

"Mom!" I called, but nobody heard me. The din of the wedding grew louder, and I had to shout to compensate. I called for her, over and over. I didn't know where she'd disappeared to.

"Excuse me," I said, trying to get the attention of a woman in front of me. She was engaged in conversation with a man beside her. He looked a little like Seb—tan and chiseled. Both of them ignored me.

"Excuse me!" I said again. "Have you seen my mom?"

"Who?" the woman asked lazily.

Fragments of real life cracked through the facade. I got the feeling that I wasn't going to find my mom again. Something was seriously wrong. I pushed my way through the guests, up front to Dad, so that I could survey the room. I screamed for her as the wedding music kicked in. Nobody cared that she wasn't there. Only me.

And then I woke up. I remembered all over again that she was dead.

I'm too unmoored to fall back asleep. I can't handle another dream about Mom. People don't die only once. They leave a wake of smaller deaths behind them. Every dream, every memory bomb, every moment of happiness. It seems as though, ever since she died, I have to lose her every night.

In the darkness I stumble over to my desk and open my laptop. The light emitted by the screen is harsh, but I need it to be. I want to be jolted back into real life. It's better than the alternative, which is lying alone in bed, crying in the dark.

I know, without a doubt, that I'll find Harris online. If there's one thing I can count on, it's the fact that Harris is always online.

Sure enough, as soon as I log on, he messages me.

**Harris:** you're here!

**Me:** I'm here!

**Harris:** what happened? you disappeared again

What happened is that I'm socially inept. I love Harris, but I don't know in what way. Am I *in* love with him? Can I be in love with someone I've never actually seen or felt? Can I be in love with someone when another guy gives me goose bumps and a bunch of other inappropriate bodily responses?

I still don't know.

What I do know is that I don't want to vanish from Harris's life

316

without a trace. I don't want to make anyone feel the way I did in my dream. And, at the very least, I want a friend.

> **Me:** Well, let's see. I found out I had lice, I still have a shitty incomplete toast for Dad and Harlow, and I just had a dream about my mom
>
> **Harris:** wow
>
> **Harris:** now i feel selfish
>
> **Harris:** i just thought you had changed your mind about me and didn't know how to tell me

*It's actually way worse than that, Harris.* How do I tell him that my mind hasn't been made up ever since Seb entered the picture?

> **Me:** I think we need to meet
>
> **Me:** Just to talk about all this in person
>
> **Harris:** yes
>
> **Harris:** let's meet
>
> **Harris:** when?
>
> **Me:** I'm not sure yet
>
> **Me:** But I think before we make any decisions about us, we have to talk it over
>
> **Harris:** sure
>
> **Harris:** whatever you want
>
> **Me:** Until then . . .
>
> **Me:** Can we quest? You be Xolkar, I'll be Kiri?
>
> **Harris:** you know you never need to ask

And in mere minutes I'm way too busy fighting off fire-breathing demons to worry about the personal ones showing up in my dreams.

# CHAPTER FORTY

WHEN MOM WENT THROUGH CHEMO, I WAS AT every appointment. We'd sit in a curtained-off section of a large beige room. I brought my backpack, which was stuffed with my iPad, my homework, and treats for Mom.

"How's Lilypad?" Mom asked one day when I was particularly annoyed at Lily. It was the second time I'd invited her to come with me to chemo, and the second time she'd made up a totally transparent excuse as to why she couldn't.

"She's busy," I said. "She has an art project due."

Lily had lied to me, and in a twisted domino effect, I lied to Mom to protect her feelings. Still, I couldn't keep the frown off my face.

"Go easy on her," Mom said. I couldn't believe it. The woman with cancer was telling me to go easy on *Lily.*

"Why should I?" I slumped down in the straight-backed chair next to Mom's recliner.

"Because I think this is hard for her."

"Hard for her," I repeated with a snort. "Meanwhile our lives are fantastic."

"*Nena* . . . I know it sucks for you, too. But you're stronger than she is."

"I'm not, actually. This whole thing sucks."

It wasn't true, either. I wasn't stronger than Lily. Throughout our entire friendship, she was always better at talking to people and acting like a functional human being.

"It does suck," Mom said. "But you're here, right? You're dealing with it."

"I guess," I replied. I had to deal with it, whether I wanted to or not.

"Not 'I guess,'" Mom said. "You are. And all this stuff, it might be too much for Lily. Some people are scared to give in to sadness. Not you."

I knew the type of people she meant. There had been friends of hers, even some family members, who hadn't called her back after her cancer diagnosis. It was like they fell off the face of the earth. And still, Mom wouldn't let it get to her. I didn't think I was that big a person. If it were me in her chair attached to an IV, I would keep a tally of every single soul who'd abandoned me during my time of need. That was the difference between me and Mom. She saw the good in people, and I saw all the ways they would fail you.

"So, *que tienes* in that giant book bag?" Mom asked, tipping her head back. Her eyes fluttered open and closed, like the mere act of talking now exhausted her.

I pulled out the flan and tapped the plastic spoon against her arm.

She managed a smile. Not of the giant, face-transforming variety. A weak imposter. *"Ay, que rico."*

I noticed she barely took a bite before setting it aside.

The week before the wedding is a blur of last-minute dress fittings and seating charts. Harlow and Dad are now working in perfect harmony. Together they sit on the living room floor in front of dozens of gift bags. Dad plops mini water bottles with personalized labels into each bag while Harlow evenly distributes Florida oranges. Seb, Avery, and I have been assigned to dispense the maps, locally made condiments, and sunblock.

"You can't tell me you had nothing better to do with your night," I say to Seb.

"Would you stay home with the stepmonster if you were me?"

"Hell no. I'm still recovering from our last interaction."

Dad and Harlow giggle together as Dad feeds her an orange slice.

"Those are for the guests!" Avery scolds. She goes over to try to smack it out of his hand, but Dad picks her up and throws her over his shoulder.

"You're lucky," Seb says as we watch them. Funny. I'm busy fighting my gag reflex.

"Oh yeah. Truly blessed," I reply. I toss a map into the bag in front of me.

"I mean it. Harlow's really great. Avery adores you."

"She doesn't adore me."

"She adores you."

"She gave me lice."

"Love lice."

I watch as Avery squeals and Harlow plants a kiss on her belly button.

"But I miss my mom," I say quietly, into the bag.

Seb doesn't say anything. He massages my knee, and I let my head fall onto his shoulder. I appreciate that he doesn't pretend to understand what it's like for me. After Mom died, a lot of people would say things to try to make me feel better, like, "I know how sad you are," when in reality they had no fucking clue. An overused three-letter word like "sad" doesn't begin to describe what you go through when you lose your mom.

Losing your mom feels like falling down a deep, dark hole and having no idea how to claw your way out of it. After some time you get the strength to get up and start climbing. You start to feel okay. You laugh at things that are funny, you brush your teeth, you do your homework. Then grief comes back, with no warning, to beat the crap out of you. You make it through the beating. You're scarred and battered and broken, but you limp through your life, knowing that the grief will come back to visit you again. Sometimes in the middle of a nightmare, sometimes in the smallest, most innocent of moments.

So yeah. You could say I feel sad, but that doesn't really do it justice.

In Spanish, Dad asks us how the gift bags are coming, and Seb answers him without missing a beat. Hearing Spanish from Mom and Dad growing up, it was always just whatever. Suddenly, coming out of Seb's mouth, it's undoubtedly the sexiest language ever to have been spoken.

"You okay?" Dad asks me.

I nod, lifting my head from Seb's shoulder. Dad looks at me, then at Seb as if wanting reassurance.

"She's just a little under the weather," Seb lies.

"Why don't you go lie down, sweetie?" Harlow asks me. "Seb can go keep you company."

I look to Dad, thinking of the condoms, then thinking of my father thinking of the condoms, and I expect his face to reflect that. But, surprisingly, he nods in agreement and says, "Get to bed, *anda*. Avery can help with the rest of the bags."

"Really?" I ask him. What kind of voodoo magic is Harlow working?

"Yes," he says, and Harlow gives him an approving nod. "I trust you."

"Do you want me to take your temperature?" Avery asks me, jumping up from the floor. "I have a thermometer!"

"It's okay—" I start to say, but she bolts past me up the stairs.

"Come on," Seb says, taking me by the hand and following her up. "I'll tuck you in."

I trail behind him, rolling my eyes. "All right, everyone. Let's stop acting like I'm an invalid."

I'm walking past my dad and future stepmom, holding my fake boyfriend's hand, and it feels like the most natural thing in the world. It's scary how close to happy I feel right now, because I've learned, over and over again, that happiness can easily be snatched away. This thing with Seb is temporary. My new, jigsaw-puzzle family might not last either.

"You should drink some lemon water!" Harlow calls after us.

"Will do!" I call back. I shake my head at Seb.

"*Y echate* some *Vivaporu!*" Dad yells, which is Cubanspeak for Vick's VapoRub. Cubans consider it a magic elixir that will cure any ailment from a head cold to a fever. Whenever I used to get the sniffles, Mom would make me slather it all over my chest, nose, and throat. The eucalyptus smell haunts me to this day.

Seb throws back the covers when we get to my room.

"You realize I'm not actually sick, right?" I ask, but I get into bed anyway.

"I got you out of wedding duty," he says. "You have to maintain the ruse."

Avery storms into the room with a thermometer and a wet washcloth.

"Here," she says, slapping it over my forehead. It's ice-cold. She attempts to stick the thermometer into my mouth, but I smack it away.

"Thanks, but I'm good," I reply.

"But you might have a fever! Once, when I was little, I was one hundred and four degrees. Mom was *crying*—"

"Hey, Aves," Seb says. "Why don't you go help your mom and dad with the bags? I'll make sure to take Analee's temperature."

Avery squints at him. "You promise?"

"I promise."

"Call me if it's a fever," Avery says. "I'm a really good nurse."

"You're the best." Seb smoothly plucks the thermometer out of Avery's fingers.

The thought of giving this up—this guy who can handle my annoying stepsister, who can fill my house with Spanish, who can somehow make me feel like I'm not completely repulsive—it hurts. Why did I ever agree to this arrangement of dating with an expiration date? Why did Mr. Hubbard throw Seb and me together as lab partners and doom me to this hellish dating purgatory?

"What's happening in there?" Seb asks, tapping me on the head.

"It's a total shitstorm."

He climbs into bed next to me, and my eyes dart toward the open door. I know Rafael Echevarria suddenly fancies himself a cool dad tonight, but catching me and Seb in bed together would be testing his limits. And possibly endangering Seb's life.

"I'm fast," Seb reassures me. "I'll hear him coming up the stairs."

"If he sees you in bed with me, you're dead man walking," I warn.

"I'll take my chances." He wiggles his eyebrows like a total goofball.

And even though I swore that our last kiss would actually be the last kiss, the habit is hard to break. Kissing Seb is comfortable yet still manages to inject me with a shot of adrenaline.

I wonder if kissing Harris would feel the same way.

Harris. Dammit.

I detach myself from Seb, and he blinks.

"What's wrong?"

"I don't know," I say.

"Analee . . ."

"It's the truth!" I say. "I don't know! I don't know what this"—I motion between us—"is. I don't even know what we're trying to do."

"We're trying to get Chloe and Lily back, for one."

"By making out in the privacy of my bedroom, where they can't see us?"

Seb sighs. He has nothing. No answers. Neither do I.

"Is this about Harris?" he asks.

"I don't know."

"Will you stop saying that?"

"Well, I don't!"

"Are you guys official yet?" he asks.

"No."

"Are you going to be?"

I stay quiet, and Seb shifts away from me. It's such a slight movement that I wouldn't have noticed if my entire body weren't tensed up, like it's waiting for an electrical shock.

"We're going to meet," I say. "In person."

He snorts.

"What is *that* about?" I ask.

"What?"

"You know what. That bitchy snort." I press the washcloth to my forehead. Suddenly I need it. I'm overheated and my temples are throbbing.

Seb is silent again, and it's infuriating.

"Would you care?" I ask. "If Harris and I dated?"

I look at him. He stares up at my ceiling. I wait for another mini-eternity.

"Yes," he says finally.

"Why? Why would you care?"

"I don't know."

"God. That *is* annoying."

He laughs. "I was being serious."

It's like I want to tell him something so badly, but I don't understand what it is or how to say it.

"I'm not sure how I feel about Harris," I admit, which is the truth, but it's not exactly what I wanted to tell him.

"Hmm."

"That's it?" I flip onto my side to look at him. "All you have to say is 'hmm'?"

"I'm processing."

What do I even expect him to say? It's not like he's going to declare his love for me right here in my bedroom, while I'm wearing a washcloth and tiny streams of water are pouring down my face. I don't even know if I want a declaration of love. Also, let's be honest. No one could truly love me. I come with way too much baggage.

"I guess you have to figure out what you want," Seb says.

No shit. But I think I might know what I want, at least in this moment. I want a family. I want to walk down the hallways at school and not feel like a stranger. I want Seb Matias and his stupidly bright shoes.

Is this how Lily felt? Is this why she started dating Colton? To feel a connection to something outside of our two-person club? And is it possible for me to understand her but still hate her a tiny bit?

There's a clomping sound on the stairs, and, true to his word, Seb is fast. He springs off the bed and kneels beside it, adjusting my washcloth.

"Mom and Dad want to know how you're feeling." Avery's tiny body appears in the doorframe.

"I'm okay," I tell her.

"And Dad says no funny business."

Okay. There's the Rafael Echevarria I know.

"No funny business," I promise.

"Do you want me to wet the towel again?"

"No, thanks," I say. I already look like a drowned rat.

"Did you take your temperature?"

"Not yet. I will."

"Don't forget," she scolds, then pops back out of the room.

I expect Seb to climb back into bed with me when we hear her descend the stairs, but he lowers himself onto the floor more firmly, resting his hands on his knees.

"Gun to my head?" I say, my gaze lingering on the doorframe. "I would say that Avery's okay. Annoying as hell, but okay. I think she's maturing out of her brat phase, don't you? I don't want to say it's my influence, but it's definitely—"

"I think you should meet Harris," Seb says out of nowhere.

There's the shock I was waiting for. On a surface level his words shouldn't hurt the way they do. He's not saying anything explicitly mean. But the disappointment feels familiar. I feel like I'm back in sixth grade again and I'm watching him laugh at me. It's a thinly veiled rejection. By encouraging me to meet Harris, he's letting me down easy. He might as well have said, *I would never want to date your ugly face, Anally, so Harris is the best you're gonna get.*

"I *am* going to meet Harris," I say, my voice turning cold. "I don't need your permission."

Seb looks taken aback. "I know you don't. . . ."

"Soon I think. The sooner the better."

"Okay. . . ."

"Yeah. Okay."

I want to shove him, hard, against the wall. No, that's not enough. I want to take off one of his ugly neon sneakers and beat him over the head with it.

"Did I say something wrong?" he asks.

"Nope."

"Then why are you looking at me with dagger eyes?"

"I'm not," I say, even though my eyes could probably pierce steel.

I don't have a reason to give Seb dagger eyes, though, so I'm going to deny, deny, deny.

"I'm still going with you to the wedding, right?" he asks.

"If you want. I don't care. Don't do me any favors." I know I'm being a bitch, but I can't stop it. It's bubbling out of me like hot liquid magma.

"What's with you? Of course I want to go with you to the wedding."

"Great. That's settled, then." I slap the washcloth off my head and get up. "I'm going to help with the gift bags. You should probably go back home."

He gets up from the floor, looking so lost that I almost feel sorry for him.

"It's fine," I find myself reassuring him. "I'm just . . . tired."

The longer I stay in this bedroom with Seb, the sicker I actually start to feel.

We walk downstairs silently, and I mentally tick off the names of all the people I hate. Harris, for putting me in this awkward position in the first place. Seb, for having zero interest in me and turning my life into this confusing catastrophe. But most of all myself, for caring about whether Seb likes me or not. I don't understand. A few months ago I couldn't care less what happened to Seb. On-again, off-again with Chloe? Didn't make a difference to me. If he got run over by a bus, I'm sure I would have felt a flicker of sympathy, but that's as far as my emotional attachment went.

Now he's making me *feel* things. It sucks.

When we get to the door, he turns to me. "See you tomorrow?"

I wish I didn't have to. Even looking at him jumbles my brain.

I can't tell whether I want to make out with him or slap him. Both sound equally appealing.

"Yup."

He nods, shuffles his feet. This is the moment when he'd normally kiss me good-bye, but now it's . . . weird. It's like now that Harlow and Dad are free of tension, Seb and I took it over for ourselves.

"Bye," he says. He extends his hand, and I'm slightly horrified. Is he giving me a handshake? But then he grazes my arm instead, halfway between a pat and a squeeze.

"Bye," I say. For a moment I'm tempted to undo the damage, press him against the door and have my way with him. But no. I have to be smart. I have to detach myself now before I get in any deeper.

When he leaves, there's nowhere for me to go. I don't want to talk to Harris right now. I don't want to be around Dad and Harlow's happiness. Instead I go back to bed and turn off the lights in my room. I almost, *almost* consider calling Avery in and inviting her to sleep over again. That's how desperately alone I feel. Instead I curl up into a ball and shut my eyes tight, willing myself to fall asleep as soon as possible so that I can stop thinking.

# CHAPTER FORTY-ONE

"ANALEE!" HARLOW CALLS FROM THE BOTTOM OF the stairs.

A primitive growl escapes me. I will begrudgingly admit that Harlow isn't the worst person in the world. But still, the sound of my name coming out of her mouth will always trigger my deep-seated animalistic rage. I walk over to my door to poke my head out.

"Yes?" I ask, perfectly pleasant.

"I was going through some stuff in the bedroom closet, and I found a box that belonged to your mom. . . ."

*Kaboom.*

The Mom bomb is always unexpected. Even though she's always on my mind, she's also the last person I expect to hear about. I'm used to everyone avoiding her in conversation, shunning the topics of moms and cancer completely. On the rare occasion when someone mentions her, like now, it sends a jolt through my system.

"I didn't look through it," Harlow says, "but I thought maybe you might want to."

Before Harlow and Avery moved in, Dad and I donated a lot of Mom's stuff to charity. Everything else, the stuff we couldn't bear to part with or look at, went into a cardboard box and up to our cramped, musty attic. Dad was in charge of the bedroom closet, but he must have missed this box.

"I'll take care of it," I tell Harlow.

She nods and heads back into the kitchen. When she's gone, I creep into the hallway, a mix of dread and excitement worming its way into my stomach. Finding things of Mom's, things I've never seen or maybe forgotten about, is almost like having a new conversation with her. I want to look inside the mystery box, but I want to savor this moment. Because in this moment there's something new to discover about Mom, and once I look through the box, it might be the end. It might be the last thing of Mom's that I've never seen before.

I go into Mom and Dad's bedroom. I can't quite consider it Harlow and Dad's, although as I walk in, I realize it is. All traces of Mom have disappeared. The room smells like Harlow's essential oils, and Mom's antique headboard has been replaced by a hanging purple tapestry that Harlow bought at a yoga retreat.

I find the box in the back of the closet. I recognize Mom's loopy, uneven handwriting on top of it: *Happy Things*.

I've never seen this box before in my life.

Gingerly I open it, my hands shaking as though I'm doing something illicit, like I'm about to uncover a stash of cocaine. I never know if I'm violating Mom's privacy by going through her old stuff, but I figure she would have gotten rid of anything she didn't want us to see. Besides, she was an open book with us. The queen of over-sharing.

There is no cocaine inside the mystery box, only a mess of envelopes and papers. Photos are scattered on top, one of a young Mom and Dad laughing in a candid moment, one of me in a set of plush

Mickey Mouse ears at Disney World. Pictures of friends and family, of Mom wearing a marinara-sauce-splattered smile when she was young.

Below the pictures I find dozens of open envelopes with Mom's name on them. My breath catches in my throat, but I don't stop to think. I dive in and open the one on top of the pile. It's a letter written to her from Dad. The date scrawled on the top corner tells me he wrote it when she was sick.

> Dear Cris,
>
> Today I was thinking about our first date. We tried to get into La Sardine on a Friday night without a reservation. I had saved for a month to afford the meal, but when we got there, the wait was two hours long. As soon as the host told us, you said "Hell no!" so loudly that every customer stared. I was too busy laughing to be embarrassed. Then I remember you winked at me and said you were going to take me out instead.
>
> We went to the grocery store in our fancy clothes, and you bought ingredients to make peanut butter and jelly sandwiches. I didn't want to tell you how much I hated peanut butter. I would have gladly eaten a pile of dog crap if you served it to me. I was already yours, the moment I saw you, before the date even started.
>
> All my love,
> Raf

Something shatters inside my chest. I set the letter down. It physically hurts to read this, to picture Dad living inside a memory when in reality the love of his life was leaving him forever. I hurt for him. I hurt for Mom when I think about her reading these. I even hurt for Harlow. As much as I complain about her, as much as I resent the way she's made herself at home here, this house pulses with stories and memories of Mom. They haven't gone away with the change in decor. They've been hidden, stuffed into a closet, but they're still here.

I wonder how it made Harlow feel to find this box. She claims she didn't look through it, but she chose to tell me about it instead of telling Dad. Since the day she moved in, I always resented Harlow for encroaching on our space, but it must have been hard for her, too.

I fold the letter up, to be just as I found it, and stuff it back inside the envelope. There are so many other letters in here, filled with memories that Dad has never shared with me. I want to read every single one of them, to soak up all of the stories about Mom that I've never heard, but I don't think I can. They're not mine to take. It's up to Dad to decide whether he wants to share them someday or keep them trapped inside this box.

I dig through more letters, pictures, and some old Mother's Day cards that I gave to Mom over the years. I stop when my fingers scrape against canvas. Underneath the mess, buried at the bottom of the box, is a piece of art.

It's an oil painting of Mom. The colors are bright and over-the-top, her hair streaked with blue and red, her face splotches of vivid hues. It shouldn't work, but it does. A rainbow exploded all over the canvas, and the end result is unmistakably Mom. I don't think anything else has captured her essence so beautifully.

Did Mom hire someone to paint her before she got sick? When

would this have happened? My family doesn't really "do" art. Mom used to buy wall decor on clearance from T.J.Maxx. She was too impatient to wander around an art museum when there were errands to run.

I run my fingertips along the edges of the painting. My eyes drift over Mom's wild hair and chin and shoulders, down to the signature in the bottom right corner.

There it is, in her flawless script: *Lily Nadarajah*. I should have immediately recognized that this painting was hers. The blazing colors, like the canvas was set on fire, the bold strokes.

If Lily painted this, why haven't I seen it? I've seen everything Lily's ever drawn, painted, or sculpted. I flip it over, because I know Lily always dates her paintings on the back. This was done two and a half years ago, during Mom's surgery and fifth round of chemo, when she didn't look like the woman in the painting anymore.

It's so Lily, I realize. It's so Lily to paint Mom the way she was, colorful and happy, instead of what she became at the end.

I think about what Mom said, about how people are too scared to give in to sadness. Looking at this painting now, I don't see just Mom. I see Lily, much more clearly. This painting was Lily's way of preserving Mom the way we knew her. It was Lily's way of helping Mom remember who she was before the cancer tried to wipe it away.

Lily always poured every emotion into her art. I know painting this must have been hard for her, so hard that she couldn't talk to me about it. Why didn't I open my eyes and consider how she was dealing with Mom's death? Mom was right. I could give in to the sadness, but Lily tried to erase it. That doesn't mean she didn't care. When I look at this painting, it's obvious that she did. I just couldn't see the way she cared.

I imagine Lily holed up in her studio, giving herself over to her feelings in the place where she felt safest. I imagine Mom getting the painting and seeing herself outside of the muted hospital colors.

This painting doesn't make everything okay between us. Lily was my friend, and she wasn't there for me the way I needed her to be. But maybe it's not as simple as I thought it was. After all, I was my mom's daughter. Everyone expected me to grieve. I took time off from school, I met with the counselor, I had relatives coming over to clean and cook and hug me even when I resisted them.

But who was there for Lily? Who helped her process what *she* was feeling? Her parents aren't exactly the warm, cuddly type. She didn't have any friends in school besides me. She never asks for help when she needs it, opting instead to paint her cries for help.

It's possible that she felt even more alone than I did, and the thought makes me sick.

I have the uncomfortable thought that maybe it takes two to ruin a friendship. Maybe I never recognized Lily's grief because I was too busy drowning in my own.

## CHAPTER FORTY-TWO

THE MORNING AFTER I FIND HER PAINTING, I RUN into Lily, literally, when I'm walking out of the school bathroom. My face slams into her shoulder, and she almost topples over backward.

"Argh!" I grunt, cupping my hand over my nose. *Oh my God, it hurts. Please don't let it be broken.* I can just imagine giving my wedding toast all bandaged up like I'm Two-Face. I check my hand, and a smear of blood stains my fingers.

"Oh my God," Lily says. "Analee, are you okay?"

I'm so obviously not, but for some reason I nod. "How bad is it?"

"It's, um . . . Let's go to the bathroom."

She steers me by the shoulders while I cover my nose to stop the bleeding. When I face the mirror, I see a multicolored bruise running down the bridge of my nose.

"Holy mother of God," I say. "This is actually worse than what I imagined."

I catch Lily's eye in the mirror. She studies me, her mouth scrunched up. "It's not broken, though?"

"It doesn't matter if it's broken or not. Look at me!"

"Okay, yes. It's bad. But it'll heal. And in the meantime there's always concealer."

"Fuck me," I say, leaning into the mirror. "It's starting to swell."

"Here." Lily grabs a handful of paper towels and runs water over them. She squeezes them out and hands the wad to me.

"Thanks," I mumble. I touch it lightly to my nose, grimacing at the dull throbbing feeling when I touch the bruise. As if I didn't hate my nose enough. Now it's going to double in size and turn every color of the rainbow.

"You always stare at your feet when you walk," she says. "I'm surprised you don't get into more accidents."

"Are you seriously going to lecture me right now?"

"I'm stating an observation."

"What about you?" I shoot back. "You were practically sprinting for the bathroom! Maybe if you didn't travel at the speed of a freight train—and why were you coming in here anyway? You know I use this bathroom in the morning. You're an afternoon user. And you use the one on the first floor."

"Jesus," she says, shaking her head. "I forgot about your rules."

"They're not rules. They're just . . . how things go."

"So I'm not allowed to vary my bathroom schedule without your permission? How much notice would you prefer? Would two weeks do it?"

"Oh, shut up." I inspect my nose again in the mirror. I don't know why. I guess I'm hoping a bunch of wet paper towels will have magical healing powers.

"You should get an ice pack from the nurse."

"Ugh. It looks all squished."

"Do you want me to go with you?"

"And it's turning purple. Great."

"You'll be fine."

"By this weekend?" I ask.

"What's this weekend?"

"Just my dad's wedding," I say. "No big deal."

Lily blanks. "What?"

"Yeah. I have to give a toast. While all this"—I circle my finger around my nose—"is going on."

"Your dad and Harlow are getting married this weekend?"

"There's a good chance."

Her eyes cloud over. "Holy shit. I had no idea."

"Well, why would you?" I reply.

"I don't know. I just . . . I thought I would have heard." She leans against the towel dispenser, staring down at the floor. "How are you feeling about it?"

And the extent of the damage between us hits me in that moment. Now she decides to ask me how I'm feeling. Now, when I needed that question so badly back then.

"Do you honestly care how I'm feeling?" I ask, turning to face her.

"Of course I care," Lily says, but she doesn't meet my eyes. This conversation is hard for her. That's fine. Hard is better than nothing.

"You should try showing it more often." I toss the wad of paper towels into the trash and sweep past her.

"Wait," she calls after me. "I'll come with you."

"Don't bother," I say without turning around.

Honestly. Who the hell does she think she is? She decides to start speaking to me again, and I'm supposed to jump at the opportunity like a faithful dog? I mean, yes, I wanted this. In theory my goal was always to get my best friend back. But seeing her again reminds me how pissed off I still am about everything that happened between us. And all the paintings in the world still won't make up for her absence.

I storm out of the bathroom and use my fury to propel me down the hallway, through the throngs of students gathering around lockers and strolling to class.

Then I remember what my nose looks like. Maybe the old Analee would have gotten away with escaping the attention of others, but this Analee, girlfriend of the school soccer star, doesn't have that luxury.

"Oh my God! What happened, Analee?" asks a complete stranger. She and her friend look at me with overstated concern. It's bizarre to be faced with people who somehow know your name (and, bonus, can say it perfectly) when you've never seen them before in your life. This must be a fraction of what Seb gets on a daily basis.

I skid to a stop beside them. "This?" I say, pointing to my nose. God, what is wrong with me? Like it could possibly be anything else. The girls don't laugh or anything, though. They nod earnestly.

"Did someone hit you?" the friend asks, somewhat eagerly.

"Yeah. Got hit with some brass knuckles," I say. "Turf war earlier this morning."

It's the world's dumbest joke, and they actually *laugh* at it. The type of laugh where they tip their heads back and open their mouths wide so that everyone can see them and be jealous of this hilarious conversation. This is a taste of popularity, I realize. People don't care what comes out of your mouth as long as you're talking to them. I can see how it would be addicting. It's not real, though. I'm not funny.

There's desperation seeping out of their laughs. They're not trying to connect with me, at least not in any genuine way.

"Make sure Seb takes good care of you," the first girl says to me. She turns a slight shade of pink when she says his name.

"Will do," I say. I give them a flick of a wave and continue walking to the nurse. Despite the fact that nothing about our interaction was real, and my nose is killing me, and my first full conversation with Lily since our fight was more of a snipe fest, I can't stop the smile from spreading over my face.

I think bridesmaid dresses are designed to enhance your worst features. I survey myself in my full-length bedroom mirror. This was a mistake. I wanted to see how the dress looked with my new nose, and the answer is . . . not good. The fabric drapes over my stomach pouch, the cut strangles my boobs, and the color clashes with my bruise.

"You look so beautiful!" Avery screeches. I jump. I'm not sure how long she's been standing in the doorway. She usually clomps around like her shoes are made of lead, so I get fair warning before appearances.

"I look like a clown," I reply.

"Your nose isn't *that* bad. It's just plump."

"Oh, perfect. That's one of the worst words you could have used."

The wedding is in two days, and the swelling has gotten worse. When Seb saw me after the accident, he threw his hands over his face like he'd caught a glimpse of Satan himself. Yes, he tried to play it off as a joke, but I knew the truth. And then he gave me a tiny kiss on the tip of my bruised, bulbous nose, which was kinda sweet but only led to continued confusion on my part.

Speaking of confusion . . . My laptop dings, which means I have a message from Harris.

"What's that?" Avery asks. She glares at the computer like it personally offends her.

"A message," I say. I waddle over to the laptop (there is literally no room to walk in this stupid dress) and tap on the touch pad.

"Are you cheating on Seb?" Avery cries suddenly.

I pause, still hunched over my laptop, fingers poised over the keys. "What are you talking about?"

"You still have that online boyfriend?"

"I don't have—"

"You can't do that to Seb, Analee! He loves you so much!"

Avery's greatest strength is also her greatest weakness. She gives her heart away too easily. Look how quickly she adopted my dad as her own. It took only a couple of months before she was tossing around the word "Dad" and buying him a personalized mug on Father's Day. Now she's gotten too attached to Seb. It was bound to happen. Seb is handsome and charming and athletic and every now and then shows himself to be a decent person.

Avery's still young. She'll learn. Under my tutelage, she'll grow more and more jaded.

"I'm not cheating on Seb, Aves. I can have friends who are boys."

"Just promise me you won't break up with Seb."

I pause. Do I have to deliver this cold life lesson now? Should I encourage her fantasy, like when we set out a plate of gluten-free maple almond flour cookies for Santa Claus? I look at her, those blue-green eyes and the trembling chin, and I want to lie to her. But I can't.

"I can't promise you that," I say gently.

"Why not?"

"Because . . . sometimes things change. People leave. They grow apart."

Her eyes get teary. "Is that going to happen to Mom and Dad?"

Dammit. So much for being honest. I'm not entirely heartless, so I say with as much conviction as possible, "No. No way. Dad and your mom are special."

And I suddenly realize who I'm going to write this toast for. I'm going to keep Avery believing in love. For her, love still means forever, and . . . I don't know. Maybe being so naive isn't the worst thing in the world. What's the point of knowing better if it just makes you miserable? Maybe I shouldn't try to make her more like me. Maybe I should try to be more like her.

My laptop dings again.

"I promise I'm not cheating on Seb, okay?" I reassure her.

"You better not be." She sticks her tongue out at me and sashays out of the room. There's the brat I know.

> **Me:** Yo
>
> **Harris:** yo
>
> **Harris:** so 2 days, right? till the red wedding?
>
> **Me:** Seriously? How do you remember the date of my dad's wedding?
>
> **Harris:** i remember everything you tell me
>
> **Me:** Damn, dude. Stop being so thoughtful. You're making me feel inadequate
>
> **Harris:** you're more than adequate
>
> **Me:** blushing

**Harris:** how's the toast going?

**Me:** I think I've reached a turning point. I've been struck by inspiration from the unlikeliest of sources . . .

**Me:** My almost-stepsister

**Harris:** i thought you couldn't stand her

**Me:** Most of the time I can't

I talk to Harris for a couple more minutes and then get to work, flipping through my writing notebook, past lists of rules and rants about Lily and early love letters to Harris that he can never read, filled with longing and sadness. I open my notebook to a fresh page. I try to remember what it felt like before Mom died, before the world became gloomy and hostile. I was never as open and trusting as Avery, but I did believe in things like happiness. I let myself feel it without worrying that it would all go away.

For me this wedding will be all about dodging awkward moments, surviving two minutes of public speaking, and trying not to think about Mom. But for Avery it's a chance to solidify the family she's always wanted. I think it's the same for Harlow, too. For so long it was only her and Avery, ever since she was pregnant at nineteen. I used to think Harlow was this vapid, image-conscious control freak, but when I'm totally honest with myself, she's kind of badass. She wanted to go to law school, and she made it happen as a single mother working multiple jobs. Then, to the disapproval of her parents and everyone else in her life, she quit the corporate world and become a yogi. Harlow has no problem pursuing happiness at full steam. No wonder Dad, the guy who sits and waits, who carefully measures all possible outcomes before making a decision, fell for her so quickly.

I'm not fully sure what this wedding means to Dad. I pause, an ink spot dotting my paper. I know he's gross with Harlow. Their over-the-top PDA is worse than all the horny teenagers at my school combined. I know he's been less mopey since she entered our lives. She has definitely improved his fashion sense. Despite all this, I'm not sure what their relationship is based on. They started as polar opposites, and no matter how much Dad spends on a new wardrobe, I find myself still waiting to be convinced that they have this deep, forever kind of love.

I think about Avery's question. Will Dad and Harlow last? I never questioned it with Mom. Mom and Dad were . . . comfortable. They spoke in streams of Spanish and cleaned the house in their pajamas. They weren't perfect. They had fights, but they fought openly and made up quickly.

*Stop it, Analee. Must not think about Mom.* Especially not when I'm in the middle of writing a toast for Dad and his new wife.

I go back to Avery. I think about what to say to a little girl on what might be the happiest day of her entire life. I continue to write.

# CHAPTER FORTY-THREE

WHEN HARLOW ASKS ME TO DO SOME YOGA WITH
her later, I say yes. I don't know why. Maybe I'm full of pent-up nervous energy and I need some physical release. Maybe I need to clear
my head of boys and the mess that comes with them. Regardless,
Harlow is ecstatic with my change of heart.

She drives me to her teaching studio, which we have all to ourselves. It's the first time I've ever set foot in it. As we walk in, I
imagine it filled with lines of yogis and Dad, clumsily attempting a
balance pose while drooling over his hot blond yoga teacher.

This is the spot where Dad and Harlow fell in love. It's still not
easy to think about.

I used to believe that Dad's feelings for Harlow were a betrayal
of Mom. Of me, even, because Mom and I were a joint package.
Her rejection was mine, too. Now, in the smallest of ways, I understand how you can feel things for two different people. With Seb
I feel connected to and excited about life. Seb is vanilla lattes and
Harry Potter story time and crowded bleachers. It has always been
different with Harris. Harris is late nights and long conversations

and escaping to magical worlds together. I don't know if there's a better or worse in my case. Only different.

The studio is decorated for maximum wellness, with floor-to-ceiling windows on one wall and greenery hung along another. In the front of the room sits a white Buddha statue surrounded by flickering tea candles. Harlow turns on this soft chanting music and places two mats on the floor.

"We'll go through the sequence together slowly, and then start speeding it up, okay?" she says.

I nod, digging my heels into the mat. Regret flutters in my chest. I don't know what possessed me to come here.

We start slowly, as promised. I sink into downward dog, tilting my butt to the ceiling and bearing down with my legs. I have to admit, though I'd never say it out loud to Harlow, that it feels good. I can feel the tension in my muscles loosening. The chanting drills itself into my brain, and if I close my eyes, I can feel my body vibrating in time to its rhythm.

We go from downward dog into a warrior pose. My body sinks into it naturally. I like the feel of this one. I can physically embody Kiri in this pose, pretend I'm drawing my bow and arrow, eyes fixed on my target.

"You're strong," Harlow says, eyeing me from my heels to my outstretched arms. "Keep holding on to the pose. Breathe through it. The shaking is your body's way of powering through."

I follow Harlow's sequence over and over again, losing count of all the warrior poses and chaturangas and half-moons. After twenty minutes my body is crying, but it's still doing everything I ask it to do. *I'm strong*, I think, just like Harlow said. I never used the word to describe myself. It's strange to think of myself not as Kiri but as Analee in this new, positive light.

Finally we settle back into downward dog, then child's pose. I press my forehead into the mat. Yoga is surprisingly exhausting. In the commercials you always see these smiling, sweat-free women holding their poses. Me? I'm still shaking, my body drenched.

When it's time for our cooldown stretch, I copy Harlow's movements. She's able to sit with her legs extended and reach her toes, but I can only get to my calves for now. We hold the stretch for a long time. I run my hands up and down my legs. My muscles are still twitching, totally unused to physical exertion.

What could I make my body do, if I stuck with this yoga thing? Could I press up to a handstand, like Harlow? Get through warrior pose with minimal shaking? Read a wedding toast and live to tell the tale?

I look down at my thighs, and when I'd normally zero in on the cellulite dimpling the edges, right now I feel a flicker of gratitude. These thighs have been touched by Seb Matias, have powered through a yoga session, have literally carried me through life, and all I've ever done is criticize them. I'm a huge jerk to myself. I am my own personal Matt McKinley.

Harlow and I lie on our backs for corpse pose, and I think about how life would be if I could give myself a freaking break, if I could adopt a Kiri warrior attitude throughout my day and maybe practice liking myself a little more.

The chanting trails off, and I hear Harlow take a deep inhale. My eyelids flutter open.

"How do you feel?" she asks, turning over onto her side to look at me. I stare up at the ceiling, at the light from the candles dancing on its surface. I wonder if this is how Dad felt when he came to yoga classes. Stronger. Like he could conquer his grief and find happiness again. Like being scared might be okay because you can push through that fear and come out a better person.

I prop myself up on my elbows and face Harlow.

I can't explain all of this to her, so I say, "I feel pretty good." And she smiles at me like that's enough.

## Analee's Top 5 Physical Features

1. How thick my hair is.
2. My smile.
3. I can fill out a pair of jeans.
4. Boobs!
5. I look like Mom.

# CHAPTER FORTY-FOUR

THE DAY BEFORE THE WEDDING IS STRANGELY calm. Harlow and Dad decided not to have a rehearsal dinner before the event so that they can take care of some last-minute wedding prep. Avery is out, probably catching lice, at her new friend Emily's house.

**Harris:** how's the toast going?

**Me:** Pretty much written. Now I just have to worry about reading it

**Harris:** you'll be great

**Me:** You say that, but I'm pretty sure I won't be. When I have to talk in front of people, I tend to sweat. A lot.

**Me:** Like, I have to wear those antiperspirants for male athletes that Harlow preaches against because they're full of aluminum

**Harris:** sexy

**Me:** So sexy

**Harris:** you've had all that practice at the library, though

**Me:** But those are kids

**Me:** They're too naive to realize I'm a human disaster

**Harris:** what if you looked out onto the crowd and saw a friendly face? would that make you less nervous?

**Me:** I'm not going to look at the crowd. I'd pass out.

**Harris:** okay, i think i'm being too subtle

**Harris:** what if i were there with you?

**Me:** Harris, I'm sure you have a very friendly face, but I've never seen it

**Harris:** you could, though

**Me:** You know the wedding is tomorrow, right? It's not like Seattle is a hop, skip, and a jump away from Nowheresville, Florida

**Harris:** i'm not in Seattle

**Harris:** not at the moment, i mean

**Me:** ?

**Me:** Then where the hell are you?

The doorbell rings downstairs, and I almost fall out of my chair.

It can't be. That would be ridiculous. It is, quite simply, a total coincidence that the doorbell rang right at this exact moment.

It's Avery, back from her friend's house. Or maybe Seb, looking to escape his stepmonster's clutches. I make all kinds of rational excuses, but it doesn't explain why I feel like my blood has been replaced with ice water and my social anxiety gag reflex has been activated.

"Analee!" Harlow calls up. "There's a young man here to see you!"

Oh God. No. This isn't happening. I'm not ready. I lunge for my men's clinical-strength deodorant and reapply it under my shirt.

**Me:** Harris

**Harris:** yes?

**Me:** that's not you

**Harris:** it is, actually

**Harris:** surprise! i'm messaging you from my phone right now

**Harris:** don't freak out

Somehow I manage to yell, "Be right down!" and my voice comes out entirely normal.

**Me:** You're here? Right now?

**Harris:** do you want me to leave?

I have to pull it together. I have no choice. The boy who might be the love of my life is standing in my living room.

**Me:** No.

I start walking. I let my natural instincts take over, because my brain has officially stopped cooperating. One step at a time, out of my room, head low, inching down the stairs, eyes on my feet so that I don't face-plant.

Harris is here. In person. A flesh-and-blood Harris, not a stream of words on a computer screen.

I don't look up until I reach the bottom step.

I take in his appearance, little by little. A mop of brown hair. Medium build but slightly round. An overlap between his two front teeth when he smiles. Which he is. He's seeing me for the first time, and he's smiling.

Shit. I forgot about my nose. I clamp my hand over it, and Harris smiles wider.

"It's kinda cute," he says, his first ever in-person words to me.

His voice is higher than I imagined in my head. Not abnormally high or anything, just not like Seb's lower baritone.

"How are you here?" are my first ever in-person words to him. Blech. I deserve to get hit in the nose again. Who says that?

"Cutting right to the chase, as usual," he says. "Don't worry. I'll explain everything."

I do cut to the chase. I have to remind myself that he knows things like this about me.

"Want to take a walk?" I ask. I have to escape Dad and Harlow, who have become eerily silent in the kitchen. This will be fun to explain later. The social outcast who went from no relationship prospects to two boyfriends at once.

Harris nods, motioning for me to lead the way.

There is nothing to see around my neighborhood except identical Spanish-style houses painted in nondescript shades of beige, pinkish beige, and yellowish beige. I also forgot to take into account how goddamn miserable it is outside. Sweat begins to dot my hairline.

"I'm sorry if this is weird," Harris begins. "Me showing up at your door without warning."

"It's . . ." What can I say? Romantic? Maybe in theory, but out here in the unforgiving sun, with sweat dripping from my pores, the reality says otherwise.

"It's a little weird," I admit. "Just . . . talking to you like this. In person."

It's more than a little weird. It's scary. It's like my security blanket has been ripped away from me.

Harris grimaces. "I thought it might be too much. But Seb gave me your address and told me how much you wanted to meet—"

"Seb? You talked to Seb?" I stop dead in my tracks. Why the hell is Seb talking to Harris? And how could he think I'd be okay with this? Is he trying to call my bluff? He doesn't even know Harris. For all he knows, he gave my home address to some sick Internet predator.

"Well, yeah," Harris says. "We were on a quest, and we got to talking."

This is a lot to take in. I'm trying to focus on Harris, sweaty and real in front of me, but my mind boomerangs back to Seb.

Why is Seb encouraging this? Does he want me to end up with Harris? Is this his way of saying he's effectively finished with this thing we have, whatever it is?

And then I realize that this is Harry Potter at the library all over again. Seb knew I was too scared to meet Harris in person, so he pulled the trigger *for* me.

Fine. If he wants me to be with Harris, I can be with Harris.

"I'm glad you came," I say.

"Analee, you don't have to bullshit me."

He said my name right. He's only ever seen it online, but he said it right.

"I mean it." I laugh. "I just had to get over the initial shock."

"I know. You weren't expecting me to be this devastatingly handsome. Go ahead. Breathe it in."

I laugh and push him away. In that moment it stops feeling weird. It's only Harris. And honestly? Harris is cute.

We circle the block, talking about Seattle. I complain about the humidity in Florida.

"Are you wearing your heavy-duty ultra-strength men's deodorant?" Harris asks, pretending to lean in and take a whiff.

"As a matter of fact, I am."

It would kill me to admit this to most people, but I know Harris won't judge me for it.

He recommends his brand of antiperspirant and says, "As a fellow sweat monster, I know what I'm talking about."

"Sweat monster?" I repeat. "Really? You're a level five at best."

Harris lifts both arms, revealing pools of sweat soaking through his shirt. I expose my own sweat stains in return. It is utterly unromantic.

"Tie," he decides after comparing.

"Um, no? I clearly won. You never could admit defeat."

"I seem to recall you trying to beat the Baroeks seven times in a row before I had to force you to give up."

"That was different. I had those fuckers, but you kept screwing me up."

It boggles my mind that Harris and I met fifteen minutes ago, not fifteen years ago. We walk around my block a few more times. I see Dad's face poking out from behind the curtain in our front window. Just when he started relaxing about Seb, a new mystery boy shows up on his doorstep. The worry must be killing him.

"Where are you staying?" I ask Harris.

From the embarrassed look on his face, I expect him to give me the name of the seedy motel on Franklin Street. Or worse, ask to stay at my house.

"Tampa," he says instead.

"Aren't we vague."

"A hotel in downtown Tampa."

"Which hotel?" I ask.

He scratches his head and stares at a dog barking through a chain-link fence. "Ocean Palms?"

"Ocean Palms?" I push him again. I can't help it. He's been dropping bombs on me all day. "As in the luxury resort with the wraparound pool and spa center?"

"I haven't been to the spa center."

"Damn, Harris." We pass by the dog, who goes ballistic at the sight of us. Harris gives him a whistle. "I didn't know you were loaded."

"My parents do well for themselves," he says. He still doesn't look at me.

"Wait a sec," I say. "How did you get to my house? Did you cab it from the hotel?"

He rolls his head back, closing his eyes for a brief moment. "I may have hired a driver for the weekend."

"Let me get this straight," I say. "Your parents let you fly to Tampa to meet some random girl for the first time. They book you at the only five-star resort near this town, *and* they hire you a personal chauffeur for your visit?"

And then I remember that I may know Harris, but I don't totally *know* Harris.

"I know," he groans. "It's sick. I have money. A lot of it."

"Gross," I say. "What good are you now? All bourgie and preppy . . ."

In truth I'm somewhat flattered that Harris finds me worth all of this. The plane ticket, the hotel, the private car. Unless he's regretting it now.

I look at him, and his eyes finally meet mine. His scrunch up when he smiles. He takes my hand, and we continue walking. I feel pretty confident in the assumption that he's not regretting meeting me.

"I wanted to ask you something," he says, and my stomach flips over. Not in the swoony, lovey-dovey way. In the terrifying, twin-girls-at-the-end-of-a-dark-hallway, clown-in-the-woods way. I'm just getting used to Harris away from the computer screen. The idea of adding another component to our relationship is too much for my body to handle. It's moments away from completely shutting down.

"I was thinking," he says, "if you're open to it, that I could . . . possibly . . . be your date to the wedding tomorrow?"

"My date," I repeat.

"We could go as friends. Or more. Whatever you want."

"It's just . . . It's not going to be fun," I say.

"It will be if you're there."

"I'll be so nervous about the toast, though. And I hate dancing. And Harlow's friend Liz will be there. She buys her clothes off Gwyneth Paltrow's website and pays, like, two hundred dollars for a cotton T-shirt. And—"

"Okay," Harris says, letting go of my hand. "I get it. Clearly you don't want to go with me."

"It's not that," I protest. Even though it is, kind of. It's not something I can explain to him, or to myself. I *should* want him there with me. But when I picture walking down the aisle in my unflattering bridesmaid dress, I imagine Seb's face smiling back at me. Not Harris's.

I hate myself right now for screwing this up. Here in front of me is everything I ever wanted, except somehow I don't want it anymore. Instead I want Seb and his dopey shoes. Obviously it's the wrong choice. If my life were a movie, audiences would be shouting at the screen for me to wise up.

Maybe I'm just not giving Harris a fair chance. Seb and I have been physical for a while now. I'm sure there's a scientific explanation for my attachment to him. Something related to pheromones or dopamine. Maybe I need to try to make that part work with Harris, or I'll regret it forever.

"Harris," I say. I take both of his hands in mine. I step closer to him, tilting my chin up to his face. Yes, I'm doing this. Yes, I feel ready now. I've had enough hours—no, weeks—of practice with Seb to feel like I can kiss a boy. Having your first make-out session with the best-looking, most popular boy in school is like skipping peewee football and heading straight to the Super Bowl.

I lean up on my tiptoes to graze my lips against his. He responds. His movements are tentative. He cups his hand around my waist, then removes it. He slides his tongue near my lips. Then it retreats back into his mouth like a scared turtle. He's gentle, though. And he's not bad at this.

I want so badly for it to feel like it does with Seb, because Harris is obviously a better fit for me. We have practically everything in common, he's cute—but not in an out-of-my-league, scary way— he's sweet . . .

And I feel nothing. My reaction is all head, no heart—brain waves that quickly compare his kissing style to Seb's, calculating the amount of time we've been at it, wondering if Dad and Harlow are worrying about us. Harris brings that out in me. Seb shuts it down.

I pull away to catch my breath. Neither of us says anything, until finally Harris offers me another smile and says, "That was nice."

"It was," I say. *Once more, Analee, with feeling.* "It was really nice."

Harris lets out a laugh, a big squawk that makes me jump. "You are a *terrible* liar."

"I'm not lying! It was nice!"

"You're bullshitting me again. I know you better than you think."

We've circled back to my house. Dad's and Harlow's heads pop back behind the window curtain as it falls into place.

I sigh and lower myself onto the front step. "It's . . . It wasn't bad. . . . I mean, it was good. I just—"

He sits beside me. "Is it all happening too fast?"

I nod slowly. "Maybe? A little?"

"It doesn't have to. I'll take this as fast or slow as you want."

I don't want to go fast *or* slow. I need everything to come to a screeching halt.

"You're still upset about something," he says.

I pull my sweaty hair off my neck and gather it into a knot on top of my head. How am I supposed to do this? I'm not built for this crap. Boys aren't supposed to like me; they're supposed to ignore me. Never in my life did I think I'd have to figure out how to let one down. "I've had a lot on my mind."

"Like what?"

"You don't want to know," I say. An ice cream truck makes its way down the street, bleating out that song. What song is that anyway? Does it have a title? Did it ever serve a purpose beyond working sugar-addicted kids up into a frenzy?

This is the kind of thing I would type to Harris. He loved to waste his time by looking up the answers to my random, meaningless questions. I don't ask these questions now, in person. I sit in silence, watching kids and belabored parents popping out of their houses.

"Maybe I can help you with it," Harris says.

"That's the problem," I reply slowly. "It's not an *it*."

I can feel him looking at me. The heat from outside slowly works its way into my cheeks. "It's a him."

"Ah," is all he says.

I desperately want to switch places with one of the kids out here. Let them have the difficult adult conversation while I eat a chocolate-vanilla swirl covered in rainbow sprinkles.

"The soccer-star lab partner," he says quietly to himself.

I hide my face in my hands. "I'm so sorry, Harris."

"Why are you sorry? You can't help the way you feel."

"I don't know why I like him. I can't stand him most of the time."

I'm scared of how Harris will look at me after this revelation, so I peek at him through my fingers. He's not smiling at me anymore. But his face is earnest, open.

I lower my hands. "He doesn't even feel the same way. I mean, he practically bought your plane ticket to come see me. Why would he do that if he had . . . you know, feelings for me?"

"Does he know you have feelings for him? You're not exactly an open book."

"I'm not sure," I say. "I mean, he *should* know."

"He could be wondering the same thing right now."

I shake my head. "Seb isn't the type to sit around and wonder. If he wanted answers, he would ask me."

"Then why don't you ask *him*?"

"Because," I say. "I'm afraid to know the answer."

"Kiri of Eromar is afraid to talk to a boy?"

"In real life I am the anti-Kiri."

"I don't believe that," Harris says, drumming his fingers against my knee.

"I hate that I'm obsessing over a boy."

"Me too," he says, laughing.

"Oh God. I'm so sorry," I say again. "I shouldn't be talking to you about another guy. That's so insensitive."

"Hey. I may not be gung ho about this Seb thing," Harris replies, "but I'm still your friend. You can talk to me about anything. Like always." He peers at me. "Are you about to cry?"

"Shut up," I say, wiping my face with my sleeve.

"Aww. Kiri." He throws an arm around my shoulder. "You're such a sap."

We both lean in toward each other, our heads clinking together like champagne glasses.

"Ow," I whimper, and he laughs, and I don't know whether I'm laughing or crying, but it feels good, like something inside me is expanding.

A car pulls up to my driveway, and for a second my mind whispers hopefully, *Seb?* But it's Avery who hops out of the passenger side, a frown creasing her face.

"Who are you?" she asks, stopping right in front of Harris.

"Don't be rude," I scold. "This is a friend of mine."

"Just a friend?" Avery looks Harris up and down with a face like she just took a whiff of Harlow's colon-cleansing vegetable juice.

"Just a friend," Harris confirms.

"She has a boyfriend, just so you know," Avery says. "And it's not you."

I see the hurt flash across Harris's face.

"Avery, go inside," I snap.

"Avery," Harris says in a softer tone, "I promise that you have nothing to worry about."

Her eyes dart from me to Harris before dropping to the ground.

"Okay," she relents.

"Nice shirt, by the way," Harris says. "I love Wonder Woman."

"Me too." Avery looks up, matching his smile. She's so easy.

"I've seen the movie twelve times," Harris says.

"*I've* seen the movie twelve *hundred* times."

"Wow," Harris replies. "You must be a super-fan."

"I am," Avery says. She beams with pride.

Behind us the front door opens a crack. Harlow peeks out.

"Hey, ladybug, come inside," she says. "I need your help with something."

"Fiiiine," Avery says, dragging her feet past us and toward the door. Once there, she turns around. "Sorry if I was mean before," she says to us, then quickly shuts the door behind her.

Harris and I look at each other.

"Consider yourself lucky," I tell him. "An apology from Avery is a rare phenomenon."

"Nah, she's cute," Harris says with a flick of his hand.

"She gets attached to people easily," I remark. Sometimes I envy Avery for that. The ability to latch on to someone despite the fear of getting hurt.

361

"I think everyone gets attached," Harris says. "It's part of being human."

"Were you always this wise, or is this a new facet of your personality that I'm just discovering?" I ask.

"Always. You just don't pay close enough attention."

"Really? I feel like all I do is pay attention." I get up from the step and bend down to touch my toes. I can only reach my shins.

Harris rises too, wiping some imaginary lint from his jeans. "So, what the hell do we do now?"

I look longingly at the ice cream truck, then back at him.

"You'll spoil your dinner," he warns.

"Harlow's making raw zucchini pasta tonight."

Harris makes a gagging sound. "Okay, then. Let's get us some ice cream."

"Did I mention I'm glad you came?" I ask him.

"You did now." He smiles at me. "And I'm glad too."

We hold hands as we walk down the street. It's totally friendly and unromantic, but more important, it feels really, really nice.

Seb texts me later that night: Interesting day today?

I respond: Why would you give my address to a complete stranger???

Don't worry. I put him through a rigorous interrogation process before he got anything from me, he texts back. So . . . what'd you think?

He was nice.

Nice? Seriously? That's all you're gonna give me?

He wasn't a hideous Internet troll. He was Harris. But in person.

There's a pause, and then Seb's next response comes in.

What does that mean? Are you guys dating now?

No, I text back. I think we're better as friends.

I stare at my phone. Seb's response to this development might tell me everything I need to know. Do we go for this? Is our relationship real on any level, or was it truly all for show?

Hmm, he writes back.

Argh. He is as elusive as always. I throw down my phone in disgust, and it buzzes right away. Against my better judgment I pick it up.

Am I still your wedding date tomorrow? he asks.

If you want to be.

This time he responds right away. I do. Not gonna lie, I'm excited . . .

Despite the fact that tomorrow is a celebration of my father marrying someone who isn't my mom, I can't help but be a little excited too. Like it might be the start of something real for me and Seb.

# CHAPTER FORTY-FIVE

ON THE MORNING OF DAD AND HARLOW'S WEDDING, I open my eyes to find the sun bursting through my window, and to find . . . my dad. Sitting freakishly still by my bed. I bite my lip to keep a scream from slipping out of my mouth.

"You're awake," he observes calmly.

"What?" I check my cell. It's two minutes past seven. "How long have you been sitting there?"

"Only about a minute."

"Um . . . why?"

"You snore very loudly, did you know that?"

"I did not." I sit up, rubbing the exhaustion out of my face. "Did I miss something? Is there a reason you're watching me sleep?"

"Let's go for a drive."

"Now?"

"Yes."

"On the morning of your wedding?"

"Yes."

This can't be what I think it is. I had plenty of reservations about Dad marrying Harlow, but . . . this isn't right. Not today.

"You're going to be a runaway groom?" I whisper.

Dad rolls his eyes. "*Monga*. Of course not. Go get dressed and meet me by the car."

Because Dad gives no indication of where the hell he's taking me, I put on my standard—jeans, tank top, and flip-flops. The house is quiet. No sounds of Harlow clanging around the kitchen or Avery dancing around the house to her tween pop songs.

The car's engine is already running when I get outside. I open the door and flop into the passenger seat. Dad doesn't say a word to me. He backs out of the driveway, and then the car presses silently onward. Dad is always careful to stay just slightly above the speed limit. Enough to pass by a cop car with the confidence that they won't stop him.

I have a lot of questions, but Dad isn't exactly inviting any conversation. I want to know where we're going. I want to know why he's bringing me along on this mystery detour, hours before his impending wedding. I want to know why he left his fiancée asleep in bed. Is he having second thoughts? Is he in a state of crisis? What do you say to your dad in this situation? I have no wisdom to offer him. I'm barely holding it together as it is. My thoughts bounce from my toast to Seb to an entire future with Harlow and Avery.

Then Dad pulls into the cemetery.

Despite the wide scope of my imagination, I never would have thought he'd bring me here, especially not today. We've been here only once together. I've made separate visits on my own, to sit and talk to Mom and just . . . remember. I have no idea how many times Dad has visited since the funeral. It's not something we talk about.

He parks the car and steps out without saying a word. I watch him for a second through the windshield. He's wearing his pre-Harlow clothing. He does that occasionally, when he's out running errands or cleaning the house. His back is turned to me, stiff and upright, as he gazes over the headstones.

When I get out of the car, he starts walking with urgency. I know I'm supposed to follow him to Mom, so I do.

My hyperactive mind has finally quieted. Visiting Mom is painful. Every time. It's reopening a wound to experience the pain all over again. I wonder why I choose to subject myself to it. Is it obligation? Maybe a little. But it's more than that. I need to hurt sometimes, when I can't pretend to be Kiri or the Invisible Girl. There's a strange relief to leaving yourself open and raw, to letting yourself hurt instead of blocking yourself from it.

Mom is located next to a droopy elm tree. It provides a sliver of shade over her headstone. Usually I sit in the grass, next to that sliver, talking out loud in my best normal voice, pretending we're sharing a carton of french fries. Today I hover over Dad while he kneels in the grass.

It seems like we should have brought flowers or something, or whatever the proper etiquette is on the day when your dad is marrying another woman. Dad and I aren't very good at that stuff. Ironically, Harlow is. She knows instinctively what to do in almost any social situation. She would bring the perfect bouquet of flowers for Mom.

Dad doesn't say anything for a while, and I figure this is it. We'll be here and have a moment of silence for Mom. But then he speaks, still staring at her headstone.

"I love Harlow very much, but your mom . . . ," he says. His voice, usually loud and booming, is so soft that the slight breeze almost overpowers it. "I'll never love anyone else the way I loved her."

I didn't know until now how badly I needed to hear those words. I didn't know how badly I needed Dad to just *mention* her. I think I get it, what he's saying. Once someone close to you dies, you can never love quite as openly and carelessly as you used to.

"Is it okay to feel like that on the day of your wedding?" I ask him.

"I don't know. But it is what it is."

I crouch next to him, the two of us and Mom forming a triad. The original Echevarria family.

"Dad?" I say. "I'm okay with you marrying Harlow."

He looks at me, guilt pulling at his features. "Are you sure?"

"Yes." For the first time, I can say that I'm sure I want this wedding to happen. "I'm glad you won't be alone anymore."

"I wasn't alone," Dad says. "I had you."

"Yeah, but . . ." I hesitate. How do I explain that physically we lived in the same house but emotionally it felt like we'd each moved to a separate corner of the world?

"I know I can be hard to deal with," Dad goes on. "Especially after your mom died. . . . Harlow says that I tend to 'retreat.'"

"You do. But so do I."

"I'm your father, though. I should have—" His voice catches, and he leaves it at that.

"I think," I say slowly, "that we both were doing the best we could."

He nods, staring down at the grass. "You're so much like her. I see it more and more, especially as you get older."

"Really?" I always found more similarities between me and my dad than me and my mom. Mom was better than the two of us. She was on a different playing field.

"It hurt, back then. I would look at you, and I would see only her."

"I'm sorry," I say instinctively.

"No," he says. "I'm glad for that now. Now when I look at you, I can remember her." He taps his hand against his thigh. "Harlow and I talked a lot about death. She liked to quote this Buddhist monk. He said something about how we're not just bodies, we're elements outside of our bodies too. And if we stop looking at people as only made up of their bodies, we don't completely lose them when they die. They're all around us. In their kids, in the earth . . . *bueno*. I'm not explaining it right."

"No, you are," I say. "I get it."

I like this idea. My grandparents like to talk about Mom in heaven, looking down at us, but I could never let myself believe it. What was she made of? Vapor? Was she a floating body in another dimension? Did she look the way she did before or after the cancer ate away at her? Did she have 24/7 access to our daily lives? Was she watching me and Seb in the broom closet? I never thought the concept held up when examined under a microscope.

But I can picture Mom as part of me, as part of the earth, and the air, and the water. I press my palms down into the grass, like I can soak up even more of her.

"We should go," Dad says after a few minutes. "They're going to wake up soon."

"Okay."

He gets up first, then grabs my hand to pull me along. You'd think we would leave the cemetery feeling sluggish and depressed, but I feel completely renewed. I feel ready for today. Seb, the toast, Dad and Harlow exchanging vows. I can handle this.

"I wanted your thoughts on something," Dad says as we walk

back to the car. "Would you be okay if . . . we brought Harlow and Avery here sometime?"

The thought never occurred to me. I've always considered my life to be split into two parts—before Mom died and after. Some people, like Harlow and Avery, have been placed neatly in this "after" box, never to be mixed in with the "before" box. Maybe that's wrong. Maybe I need to stop defining my life by Mom's death. Maybe I should think of my life as a series of connected people and events.

"I just think she should know them," Dad continues.

I picture all of us, together, here. I want Mom to know that we're not abandoning her, that we're taking her with us.

"I think she should too," I say.

There's no time for quiet reflection when we get home. Harlow and Avery are up, breakfast is served, dresses are steamed and ready. Liz comes over to do our makeup. When she sees my nose, she lets out a bloodcurdling scream.

Welp. There goes my self-esteem today.

"I thought it was getting better," I say, poking it with my thumb. It doesn't even hurt anymore.

Liz composes herself, then says, "It's okay. I have tattoo concealer. I'll make it look normal."

Liz gives Avery a touch of mascara and sparkly lip gloss. Then she sits me down on the kitchen chair next to the window and *cackles*. I don't know that I've ever heard someone cackle, outside of a wicked witch in a movie. "I can't wait to get my hands on you."

She opens a giant toolbox filled with eye shadow and foundation and piles of makeup brushes.

"Not too much, okay?" I say. "I don't wear a lot of makeup."

"Don't worry. You're gonna look fab."

And then my face is prodded and brushed, poked and dusted, even sprayed. I follow her instructions, looking up when she wants me to, closing my eyes when she asks.

Harlow comes over, barefaced at the moment but still naturally beautiful.

"Wow . . . Analee," she breathes.

I know she must want to follow that up. It's not a good *wow*. It must be a, *Wow, Analee, you look like garbage.* There have been too many unidentified substances slathered onto my face. I'll have to wash it all off.

When Liz whips out her handheld mirror, the girl who stares back at me is not Analee Echevarria. This is a girl you'd see having lunch with Chloe, taking Instagram pictures in a dimly lit bathroom. I didn't know I could look like this. I don't know that I *like* looking like this, but I guess it's nice to know that I could if I wanted to. Liz is beaming with pride, so I say, "Oh my God. I love it!"

She shrugs, like how could I not? "I knew you could be gorgeous with a little help from Dior."

"Oh, she was gorgeous even without Dior," Harlow says, giving me a wink.

"You should really be wearing some makeup every day," Liz advises me. "Just the essentials—primer, foundation, bronzer, highlighter, brow gel, eyeliner—"

"Liz, you do that to your face on a daily basis?" Harlow cuts in.

"Are you kidding? At minimum!"

This sets Harlow off on the amount of chemicals contained in makeup. She tosses around some scary words like "parabens" and "phthalates," and waxes poetic about the importance of buying organic, cruelty-free brands. I get up from my chair and text Seb.

Well, after ten pounds of makeup on my face, I've finally achieved the elusive goal of looking like Latina Barbie. Hope you're excited.

Seb usually answers my texts right away, but this time there's silence. Huh.

I wait a couple of minutes, then try again. Meet you at the ceremony?

Radio silence.

An hour later, still nothing. Liz, Avery, and I have our bridesmaid dresses on, and we wait, all decked in pastels like a window display of French macaroons, for Harlow in the living room. Dad is already at the venue because he was set on not seeing Harlow until the ceremony.

"Do you need help?" Liz hollers.

"I'm good!" Harlow calls down.

Moments later I hear the bedroom door open. Our heads whip around to face the stairwell. As Harlow descends, Liz instinctively grabs my and Avery's hands.

Harlow looks angelic. She's wearing the first dress she loved that day in the bridal shop, and I can't imagine anything else looking more perfect on her. Pieces of her hair are weaved into small braids, while the rest tumbles down her shoulders in perfect S-shaped waves. Her makeup is light, but the mascara makes her eyes pop, more blue than green today, as if they want to match the ocean.

Liz and Avery let out matching squeals, jumping up and down, telling her how beautiful she looks. There is no mention of the bedazzled dress, because it's a hideous distant memory compared to this one.

Harlow entertains her adoring fans, striking a silly *Vogue*-like pose, then looks at me. "What do you think, Analee? I need your brutally honest opinion."

"In my brutally honest opinion," I say, "Dad is going to lose his mind when he sees you."

Weirdly enough, I can't wait to see this happen. I can't wait to see him happy again.

# CHAPTER FORTY-SIX

### Analee's Top 5 Reasons Why
### I Can Handle This Toast

1. Experience reading aloud to kids.
2. Fake dated Seb in front of the entire school.
3. Faced fear to meet Harris in person.
4. It would make Dad, Harlow, and Avery happy.
5. After what happened to Mom, I can do anything.

UNDER A CANOPY OF WHITE FLOWERS NEAR THE edge of the ocean, among yogis, WASPs, and Cubans, Dad and Harlow are making things official.

Predictably, Dad did lose it when Harlow made her way down the aisle. His eyes got big and watery, and while Dad hates crying in front of other people, he couldn't stop the tears from flowing. I was grateful to see him cry happy tears in this case.

Before Harlow's grand entrance, I successfully walked down the aisle in a pair of four-inch heels that I'll never wear again. I didn't trip on my dress or sprain my ankle, so as far as I'm concerned, I was a rousing success. I could even ignore the eyes that followed me along the way, thanks to all the practice I've had in East Bay's halls.

The best part about this wedding is that pretty much everyone is focused on Harlow, not me. She's the happiest I've ever seen her. No peaceful yogi smiles today—this one is beaming and bright.

The worst part of this wedding is that Seb isn't here. I officially haven't heard from him since last night. After walking down the aisle, I scanned the assortment of characters sitting in white folding chairs, and Seb wasn't one of them.

I try to focus on the vows being exchanged in front of me, but I have an unhealthy amount of anger coursing through my body. Am I being stood up? Last night Seb said he was excited to go to the wedding with me. How could that change over the course of eighteen hours? And if it did, why the hell didn't he text me?

Unless . . . did something awful happen in those eighteen hours? Something truly awful, that would render Seb incapable of making it to the wedding or even texting me?

When one of the worst things in life has happened to you, you have a tendency to assume worst-case scenarios. This is how my brain operates, tossing out all positive outcomes and moving straight to the most horrible what-ifs. If it happened once, it can happen again. The question is, what exactly happened? A car accident, maybe. I could call his house, ask the scary stepmom if he's okay. Or maybe he was taking a shower to get ready for the ceremony and he slipped. Oh God. What if something's really wrong?

My thoughts are interrupted by the thunderous applause of the crowd as Dad and Harlow take their first kiss as husband and wife.

I'm standing right here, and I'm missing my own father's wedding. I have to stop thinking about Seb. Harlow would remind me to breathe, to stay focused on the present and what's happening around me. So I try. I try really, really hard to see Avery wiggling around in excitement. To see the way Harlow won't let go of Dad's hand. Even to see Liz flirting with Dad's cousin, Adrian. I see all of it, but without focus, like when you have the TV on in the background.

"Congratulations!" I say before they make their way back down the aisle as husband and wife. I will not think about Seb. I will instead think about what a beautiful day this is, and how the sunset is turning the water pink, and look at how well I'm doing, not thinking about Seb. Dad gives me a giant kiss on the cheek, and Harlow lets go of his hand long enough to give me a hug.

There is a giant white tent a few feet away from the ceremony, where the reception will take place. Glowing lanterns hang from the beams, and the tables are decorated with delicate bouquets of baby's breath. It looks flawless. The living incarnation of a Pinterest board. And Harlow pulled it off almost completely by herself.

The fare is vegetarian but delicious. I eat an apple walnut salad, and unlike most salads, it doesn't make me want to gag. People are dancing to everything from merengue to Motown. Dad and Harlow sway and slow dance, even during the fast songs. My grandparents hold hands and dance with Avery, who is a jumping bean of energy. In spite of the screaming matches, the cursing, the prayers, my grandparents showed up. Because, ultimately, that's what family does. They show up, even when a member of the family marries a heathen. Everyone is smiling. I feel like the wedding Grinch, my heart growing three sizes.

But I'm separate from the crowd, just sitting here, crunching on my salad. Wondering how Seb could be missing this. Thinking that I rejected Harris, only to be left with no one. Stressing that in a few minutes I'll have to stand in front of all these people and read my words to them. The toast is folded into a tiny paper square tucked inside my cleavage. Every time I take a deep breath, the corners pinch my skin.

I send out another text. It feels like every message has been sucked into a black hole. Where are you??

When the music fades out and the lanterns dim, I know it's coming.

The people who were dancing return to their seats. The DJ lifts the microphone to his lips and announces my name in his big booming voice. I can barely hear how he pronounces it. My heart is beating too loudly.

There's clapping and smiles in my direction, and still I would rather do anything else in this moment.

No Mom, no Seb, no Harris by my side. The DJ strides over to me, grinning, completely unaware that he's leading me into my own personal hell. I slide my speech out from the top of my dress, glad that no one can tell how damp the paper is from my sweat.

I take the microphone from him. My hand is so clammy, it feels like the mic will spurt out of my fist and knock someone unconscious.

*Just breathe. Deep, meditative yogi breaths. In and out through the nose.* Harlow gives me an encouraging smile, and for a millisecond

I'm horribly bitter. This is all her fault, making me stand up in front of everyone like this.

I try to put it into perspective. All I'm doing is reading. I do it every Sunday with the kids. There will be no improvising, or off-the-cuff jokes. All I need to do is get through the next minute without dying.

"Hello, everyone," I start. "My name is Analee."

My voice comes out louder than I've ever heard it, filling up every tented inch of space. "First I want to thank you for attending this beautiful wedding today."

Shaky hands, flushed cheeks. Turns out yogi breathing doesn't work when you're hyperventilating.

*I can do this. I can, I can, I can. I am Analee, and I am strong, and this tiny moment is nothing compared to what I've been through.*

"Before Harlow and Avery came into our lives," I say, "I didn't realize how lonely our house had become. Dad and I were lucky to have each other, of course. We tried to ignore the fact that something was lacking. It's like we were drowning in separate pools, without a way to help each other breathe.

"Then he met Harlow. My dad had a reason to live again, to become the person he wanted to be. Someone calmer, happier . . . someone infinitely better dressed."

This gets a few encouraging laughs from the audience. I loosen my grip on the microphone.

"I was skeptical when I first met Harlow. This woman was obviously too beautiful, too centered, too . . . *everything* for me and Dad. I thought, *There's no way she'll settle for a couple of messes like us.* But here's the thing about Harlow. When you give her a chance, you start to see yourself through her eyes. You realize what you have to offer. Harlow is an amazing person, but not at the expense of others. With her help you recognize how amazing you've been all along. It takes someone really special to bring that out in people."

I let myself look up at this part, straight across the room at Harlow, who's dabbing at her eyes with a tissue.

"But Harlow didn't enter our lives alone," I continue. "She brought Avery with her, this little ball of energy barely contained in human form. Avery enjoys saying exactly what's on her mind, no matter how much you might not want to hear it. And believe me, a lot of the time I don't want to hear it. But sometimes I need to. Avery truly believes in love, in the purest, most optimistic way. Through knowing her, I've had to confront all my cynicism and open myself up to new possibilities . . . because, the thing is, I've seen Avery's belief in love pay off. Harlow and my dad have found a love that lives up to Avery's idealism. A love that makes them the best possible versions of themselves. A love that understands, encourages, communicates. A love that is exactly what we didn't know we needed.

"So. Please join me in a toast." I awkwardly switch my toast to the hand already holding the mic and raise my glass of soda. "To the many different forms that love can take, and the way they fit into our lives."

"Hear! Hear!" Liz shouts as the crowd raises their champagne glasses. I look out at a sea of smiling faces and liquid bubbles, and I'm filled with this strange ecstasy. It's absurd. I just stood up and read a minute-long speech, but it feels better than being Kiri and slaying monsters. I'm done. I did it. The scary, looming thing is over.

In the midst of the applause, I see him in the back corner of the tent.

Seb Matias has shown up as promised. He's alive. He's here. And he looks really freaking handsome in a suit. I think it's safe to say that this is the happiest I've felt in years. It's nice to know I'm able to feel like this, when I thought the possibility of being happy died a long time ago.

Before I can overthink it, I squeeze past tables and chairs to make my way over to him. I'm running on pure adrenaline. My brain has decided to stop calling the shots. I throw my arms around him and bury my face against his neck, inhaling the scent of soap and after-shave. If my life were a movie, this would be the climax—I give a triumphant toast and win the cute boy at the end.

But in my arms I feel Seb stiffen. That's not supposed to happen. He has his arms around me, but they're not holding me. They're not moving much at all.

I pull away. "Seb . . . what's wrong? Where have you been?"

He won't even make eye contact. A new sense of fear jolts through me. Yes, Seb is here, but he's not Seb right now. He's acting like a robot, devoid of any emotion or expression.

"Seb," I say sharply. Around us people have gotten up to dance. The DJ is playing horrible cheesy music decidedly not on Harlow's approved wedding playlist.

"I was at Chloe's," he says.

My entire body goes cold, the slight ocean breeze sending chills down my arms. He doesn't keep going, which allows my imagination to run rampant, painting elaborate pictures of all the things they could have done together today. A lot of naked things.

"And?" I say.

"We talked. A lot."

Seb is about to break up with me. How can I get dumped by someone I was never with? I knew I wouldn't be enough for him in real life. I was never anything more than a game.

"What did you talk about?" I ask.

"About . . . what had gone wrong in our relationship, and . . ."

Is he drawing this out to kill me?

"Just say it," I urge.

"She wants me back."

"She wants you back," I repeat.

"Yes."

"And what do *you* want?" It's going to be bad. I just know it's going to be bad. Even though this was the initial goal, Chleb restored, I've never felt a larger sense of failure. What I hate even more than this feeling is the part of me still hoping, despite all reasonable logic, that Seb will declare me the chosen one. That someone will finally choose me.

Seb looks down at his sneakers. Somehow the loud shoes and suit combo works on him. It kills me how good he looks, like the universe wanted this final blow delivered as painfully as possible.

"I wasn't sure," he says. "I didn't know what I wanted in that moment. So we . . ."

Another pause.

"You kissed?" I guess.

He looks at me with a wide-eyed expression, and it's clear that they did more than just kiss.

"Oh," I say, realizing. "You . . ."

My head is spinning. I'm going to throw up. I'm going to ruin Dad's wedding by puking right in the middle of the dance floor. "Celebration" by Kool & the Gang will forever be ruined for me.

Bathroom. I have to get to the bathroom.

But then Seb holds me by the shoulders before I can escape, and all my energy drains out of me.

"I have to go," I say weakly.

"Please." He looks at me earnestly. "Let me explain."

The DJ has the bass turned up, and it's thump-thump-thumping through my stomach.

"We—"

"I get it," I interrupt. "You don't have to spell it out for me."

"The whole time I felt guilty," he says. "Like I was doing something wrong."

"But not guilty enough to stop, right?"

"I'm not proud of it," he says. "But I think I needed to be with Chloe, one more time, to know."

"To know what?" I snap.

"To know that I don't want to be with her. I want to be with you."

I freeze.

There it is. Everything I thought I wanted to hear come out of his mouth.

So why doesn't it feel good to hear it? Why do I feel so unsatisfied? I picture Seb and Chloe, talking, kissing, having sex, while my texts go to his phone unread. If Seb and I did this, for real, that image would hang over me throughout our relationship. Because while I truly believe Seb when he says he wants to be with me, it doesn't change the fact that it took sleeping with Chloe one more time to convince him. It doesn't change that he's addicted to the adoration of others.

"Analee, talk to me."

I shake my head. "I can't stop picturing it."

My voice is wobbly, shaken. It's harder to speak now, just me and Seb, than it was in front of fifty wedding guests. It's not just him. It's me, too. I was unsure about my feelings for Harris, and something was holding me back from pursuing things with him, too.

"Chloe and I have a lot of history together," he says. "It's . . . complicated. But I made my decision. I know what I want." He reaches out to touch my arm, and I recoil.

"Stop," I say. "Just . . . stop for a second."

It's so loud in here, I can't think. Why am I so angry? Seb and I never actually committed to each other. I feel like I've been cheated on, but on top of it all I feel anxious about whether I have the right to feel this way. Our relationship was a sham, after all. He didn't owe me any degree of fidelity. My brain knows this fact, but my heart will not be convinced.

"Please, Analee," he says, his eyes pleading with me. It would be easier to give in to him like everyone else does, try to put this Chloe thing behind me.

"Why didn't you just talk to me?" I ask instead.

"What?"

"You could have told me you didn't know what you wanted. You could have texted me that you were going to be late tonight."

Seb starts to speak, then pauses. "I should have."

"It bothers me that you didn't. It also bothers me that you were out having sex with Chloe when you were supposed to be here, with me."

"I *am* here, with you."

"You are now. But what happens if Chloe calls you again? What happens if I agree to date you, for real, and all I can do is worry that you'll leave me for her, or for someone else?"

"Look at me," Seb says. I do. It's not easy to look him straight in the face because it makes my head feel fuzzy. All I want to do is turn away. "Chloe and I are finished. For good."

"There will always be other Chloes," I say softly.

"I don't understand."

I see things clearly now. I finally do. Seb isn't ready. And neither am I.

"Seb," I say. "I'm a mess."

"I don't care—"

"I know you don't. Or at least not now you don't. But I have a lot of crap I have to work through. I mean layers and layers of issues. I'm like a diseased onion."

"I don't care," he says again. He leans forward, kissing me right in front of the entire wedding, and my body wants to melt into his like it has done before. Then I think, *How long ago was it when his lips were on Chloe's instead of mine?* I step away.

"I'm sorry," I say to him. "I can't do this."

"Why not? Why are you so scared of being with me?" he asks.

"The thing is . . ." An unnatural laugh escapes me, even though none of this is particularly funny. "I'm not scared of being with you. I used to be."

"Then what is it?"

"I'm scared of *not* being with you."

"Too much talking, not enough dancing!" Liz stumbles over to us, her martini splashing out of its glass and narrowly missing my dress.

"Maybe later," Seb mutters, but she doesn't hear us. She whips her hair around and grinds against a chair. The visual would be funny if it weren't taking place at such an awful moment.

"Come on, Analee. Let's see your moves!" she slurs.

"Later," I lie. I motion for Seb to follow me outside the tent. As we walk out, Liz calls behind me, "Your makeup still looks fab! I knew you could be pretty!"

Outside, I feel like I can breathe a little better. I slip my heels off and scrunch my toes into the sand, concentrating on the grainy feeling between my toes instead of the terror running through my body.

"Liz is in fine form tonight," Seb comments. He keeps his sneakers on, because why wouldn't he? It's such a Seb trademark that it breaks my heart a little.

"Are we really going to do the small talk thing right now?" I ask.

"It seemed like you were going to say something bad, so yeah. I'm sticking to safer topics."

He looks ahead, out to where the ocean meets the sky. Out here the sky swirls deep purple and gold hues at twilight. Sometimes East Bay can be strikingly beautiful, when you remember to take a look around.

"If you're scared to not be with me, it seems like there's an easy solution," Seb finally says.

"I can't," I reply. "That's not a good enough reason."

"So you don't have feelings for me?"

"Of course I have feelings for you."

"Then I don't get it, Analee."

"I don't think I'm ready to be with you," I say. "Or anybody else. I'm barely comfortable with just me."

He links his hand with mine, presses his lips against my knuckles, and I am this close to saying, *Screw it. Let's do this.* Instead I squeeze his hand tight, and let go.

"I'm going to change your mind," he says. He has his determined soccer-player face on, the one he wears right before he shoots the ball above the goalie's head.

"Maybe," I say. "Just not right now."

I hope he's still around by the time I have my shit together, but I'm not counting on it.

If I keep looking at the sky, at the stars appearing little by little, twinkling against streaks of color . . . being scared is small in comparison. My whole life has been lived in fear. I was scared of Mom dying, but she did. I was scared of losing Lily, but I did. I was scared to try this thing with Seb and throw myself into the spotlight, but I did. And I'm still here.

I summon all my inner warrior strength, whatever I save up for Kiri. "You should go. I think it'll be too hard for me, the longer you stay."

I expect him to fight me on this. Maybe I kind of want him to.

He doesn't fight me, though. He nods slowly. "This is it, then?"

"Just for now."

He asks me how much time I need, and I say I'm not sure. I don't even know where to begin. Therapy? Extensive use of Harlow's meditation room?

"I'm going to miss you," he says. His voice catches, and I swear I feel a piece of myself break off at the sound of it.

"I'll miss you too."

He gives me one more kiss, this one on the cheek. And just like that, we're back to level one.

"Tell your dad and Harlow I said congratulations."

"I will."

He hesitates. I want to run back into his arms. I want to spend the rest of the night kissing him, pretending he'll be mine forever. I want, I want, I want.

"Bye, Anally," he says. I smile. I miss the days when the biggest problem in my life was a stupid nickname.

"Bye, Seb." He gives my hand one more squeeze before he walks away.

I wait until he's a safe distance away before I start crying. I'm alone again. Currently it feels pretty crappy. It always does when you have to say good-bye. But I know that at some point it'll feel okay. I've been here before. I sit down on the sand, in my ugly bridesmaid dress, and bring my knees to my chest. Inside the tent, I hear laughter and shouting and music, and I swear I can make out Liz's voice on top of it all.

I give myself ten more minutes. Ten more minutes to cry, and then I'll go back inside the tent and pretend to be happy.

*I am not Kiri. I am Analee, the strongest human in the world. And I fear nothing—not even fear itself.*

When I wipe my eyes, a glop of eyeliner, mascara, and whatever else Liz slathered on my face smears onto my hand.

*"Oye."* I turn and see Dad coming over to me, treading sand. "I've been looking for you."

I try to clean the makeup off my face, but I have a feeling I've only shifted it around.

"Sorry," I say, in my pitiful attempt at a lighthearted voice. "Just needed some air."

He sits down next to me. I feel him studying my face. Even as it gets dark out, there must be no hiding the fact that my face looks like a Jackson Pollock painting.

"*¿Qué carajo hizo él?*" he demands, which roughly translates to "What the fuck did he do?"

"It wasn't him."

"Don't protect him, Analee."

"I swear, Dad," I say. I can't keep the misery from seeping out of me now. "I broke up with him."

"Why? He pressured you?"

"No."

"Hurt you?"

"No."

There's some unintelligible muttering on his end.

"It just wasn't the time for us," I say.

God, I wish it were. I so wish I were at a place where I was ready to give myself away to someone.

"Raf? You ready to cut the cake?" I recognize Harlow's voice behind me, but I don't turn around. Oh God. What do I look like right now? I can't go back in there like this. I'll ruin all of Harlow's perfect wedding pictures. Liz will throw a drunken fit when she sees her makeover success story turned into a complete wreck.

There's a long pause. I can almost feel Dad and Harlow communicating with their eyes.

"What?" Avery's voice comes from out of nowhere. Again . . . oh God. It just gets worse. I didn't know she was here too. Like I need an audience right now. I hide my face between my knees. "What's wrong with Analee?"

Harlow lifts the skirt of her dress and sits on the sand next to me, her legs pressing against mine. I'm sandwiched between her and Dad.

"You're going to ruin your dress," I say to her from between my knees.

"It's okay. Your dad's stuck with me now, sandy butt and all."

She doesn't ask about Seb. Or what happened to me. She just rubs my back, left to right, in a slow, rhythmic motion. It's exactly what I need. I start to cry again, my head still buried in my legs.

"Why is everyone being weird and not talking?" Avery blurts out. "What's going on?"

"Analee is feeling sad," Harlow says to her in a hushed voice.

"Oh."

I feel Avery's tiny hand pat me on the head. Harlow scoots over so that Avery can squeeze in between us. She rests her head against my arm. I expect a comment about my makeup or a question about Seb, but even Avery manages to stay quiet. It's a miracle of miracles.

"You guys should get back to the wedding," I say. I take a breath and lift my head, which is an action suddenly requiring all of my physical strength.

"We *are* the wedding," Dad says. "Everyone else can wait."

"You take all the time you need," Harlow adds.

No one moves to get up. Not even Avery, who usually has the attention span of a fruit fly.

I wonder what I'll take away from tonight when I look back at this wedding years from now. Seb's revelation? Or the hours I spent trying to get ahold of him before the ceremony? Shaky hands and deep breaths as I made it through my toast? Dad's face when he saw Harlow in her perfect dress?

I think I'll remember all of it, in snippets and foggy details. The good and the bad, the uplifting and the soul-crushing. But this moment, right now . . . this will be the part that sticks out to me the most. The four of us, my new, ever-evolving family, sitting on the sand together and staring up at the stars.

# CHAPTER FORTY-SEVEN

"WELL. I, FOR ONE, AM NEVER WATCHING ONE OF his soccer games again," Elliott declares weeks later at lunch.

He, Jared, and I have claimed a table in the back of the cafeteria. Seb is sitting with Chloe and Matt near the front.

"Don't make promises you can't keep," I say. I take a bite of the lunch Harlow made me—butternut squash and quinoa salad. She's trying out a bunch of recipes in the hopes of writing a cookbook. I chew thoroughly, making a mental note to tell her it needs something sweet. Maybe some dried fruit or honey.

I've gotten to the point where I can look at Seb without wanting to burst into tears. I can even talk about him to Elliott and Jared. They don't know the details of our relationship, but they know enough.

"He's only saying that because soccer season's over," Jared says, rolling his eyes.

"You don't need to pretend to give up soccer for me, Elliott," I reply. "And anyway, we don't hate Seb, remember?"

"*You* don't hate Seb," Elliott corrects. Jared shoots him a wary glance, and Elliott raises his eyebrows in response. I suddenly feel like an outsider observing a private conversation.

"What was that?" I ask.

"What?" Elliott says innocently.

"That look you just gave each other." I put my fork down. "What's going on?"

"Nothing," they both answer in unison, much too quickly.

"Guys. The anti-Seb movement is out of control today."

Jared lets out a sigh. "There have been . . . rumors."

"About?"

"Seb. And . . . Chloe."

"They're back together?" I guess. The truth is, I was expecting this. Seb and I haven't spoken since the wedding. He and Chloe have been eating lunch together every day, and I've seen a nonfat vanilla latte in her hand every morning before class.

Still, it hurts to hear my suspicions confirmed. It hurts a lot.

Elliott reaches across the table for my hand. "I'm sorry, Analee. We wanted to tell you, but we didn't know when we should. You've been doing so well."

The resurgence of Chleb tells me everything I needed to know. I take a long look at Seb. He's talking animatedly, giving off his usual aura of charm and confidence. Basking in the adoration of his fans. And it's all monumentally fake. Underneath the facade I see a scared little boy who is afraid of losing his legions. Because the worst possible thing, in Seb's eyes, is to go through life by himself. It makes me feel a tad bit sorry for him. Of course, this is well underneath a lot of anger and rage I'm still working through with the help of my new therapist and Harlow's daily yoga routines.

"It's okay," I reply. "I'm okay. He needs to figure things out for himself."

"Just know most of the students are behind you," Elliott says. "Team Analee all the way."

"Oh God, no. Please shut that down."

"But I was going to make T-shirts," Elliott says with big puppy-dog eyes.

"Elliott. I will end you."

"Fine," he says grumpily. "But can I just make one for myself and wear it in private?"

"No."

"What if—" Then he turns quiet, his eyes lifting to somewhere above my head. Jared follows suit.

An instantly recognizable voice above me says, "Sorry to interrupt . . ."

I turn around, and holy crap.

It's Lily.

Hovering over me, looking every bit as uncomfortable as I now feel.

"Hi," I say dumbly.

"Hi. . . . Can we talk?"

Jared picks his food up from the table. "We were just leaving. Come on, Elliott."

They hurry out of the cafeteria, even though Elliott is only half-finished with his sandwich. The two of them shoot a last curious look behind them before slipping past the doors.

"May I?" Lily grips the chair next to mine. The question depresses me. The old Lily would never have to ask.

I nod, and she sits down, stiff and straight-backed. We look like proper ladies who lunch. We're just missing the white gloves and tea cozies.

"How are you?" she asks.

"Uh . . . fine. You?"

"Fine. . . . How was the wedding?"

"It was . . . also fine," I say. I'm so not good at this. Lily knows I'm not good at this. I can't pretend that it's normal for the two of us to sit here and make small talk, two people who used to share everything and have shared nothing for months.

"And how about your dad? And Harlow?" she asks. "Everyone good?"

"Lil . . ."

She slumps back in her chair and exhales like she's been holding her breath. "Sorry. I forgot how to do this with you."

"Why *are* you doing this with me?"

She bites down on her thumbnail. It's an old-school Lily move. She's nervous.

Then she looks at me. "Why didn't you ever tell me what Colton did on the night of Gabrielle's party?"

Of the top five things I would expect Lily to say to me, that one didn't make the cut. We had an unspoken agreement, Lily and me. Never discuss the Incident. Sweep it under the rug as we cut each other out of our lives.

I stir some quinoa with my fork, smashing down large chunks of squash. "You didn't ask."

"I didn't *know*, Analee."

My head snaps up. She's lying. There's no way she didn't know what Colton did. Or his version of it, at least—the version she chose to believe.

"What did Colton tell you about it?" I ask cautiously.

"Analee, I swear to you. He never, ever said anything. If I'd known, I would have broken up with him a lot sooner."

She stares at me fiercely, and I can almost convince myself she's telling me the truth. I *want* to believe her.

"So what changed?" I ask. "How did you figure it out?"

"Seb."

I look over at him and find that he's watching the two of us. He gives me a small smile that makes my heart flip-flop, like there's a goldfish in my chest. My body is a goddamn traitor. I think he'll always have this effect on me.

"He told me everything you said to him," Lily goes on. "And he said that I should stop being an idiot and just talk to you."

"He called you an idiot?" I ask in surprise.

"I know," Lily says. "It's so not Seb. And truthfully, it pissed me off a little."

I smile back at him. The optimistic part of me, as minuscule as it is, wonders if maybe Seb will prove me wrong one day.

Then I turn back to Lily. "So if you didn't know what Colton did, then why haven't you spoken to me for months?"

"You haven't spoken to me either," she replies.

I start to speak before I realize that I have no defense. I don't remember a time when Lily officially stopped speaking to me. It's not like kindergarten, when you can point to a definitive beginning of a fight, like when someone steals your Play-Doh. Our conversations had slowed to a trickle before they became a full-on drought. We were both to blame for it.

"You're right. I haven't," I say. "So, what was it, then? What happened to us?"

"Your mom," she says quietly. "And I feel awful admitting this, because you're her actual daughter, but . . . I was miserable when your mom got sick. And then when she died, I didn't know how to deal with it."

"How do you think I—"

"I know," Lily cuts me off. "I know you had it worse than I did. That's why I couldn't tell you. I thought I had no right to put the focus on me."

I don't try to speak again. I just listen.

"I felt so sad," Lily goes on. "Like, all the time. And I didn't want to be sad anymore."

"What about me?" I ask. I will not cry again. Enough is enough. I press my fingers against closed eyelids, compose myself for a second, and open my eyes. "Did you even care how I was feeling?"

"Of course, An. I felt like I was doing everything I could to make things better for you."

"I didn't need you to make things better for me," I spit out. "I just needed you to actually *be there*."

Lily nods. "I know that. I should have been, even if it was hard for me."

It doesn't make me feel better for her to admit it. I still don't have my friend back.

"Maybe I was just being selfish," she continues, "but I wanted to feel happy again. That's why I started dating Colton."

"Did he make you happy?" I ask.

Lily looks away. "Maybe. At first. Although, I don't know if I'd use the word 'happy.' It was more . . . exciting? And I so badly needed the excitement, because life had been so bleak for so long."

"I get it," I reply. I allow myself one more look at Seb, and the goldfish in my chest resumes its gymnastics. "How that can happen."

How easy was it for me to wrap myself up in him as if he could cloak me from the rest of the world? I think about kissing him in movie theaters and broom closets and forgetting that everyone else existed. I can't fault Lily for feeling that way with Colton. Not after going through it myself.

"The truth is," Lily says, "I think I was scared of letting you in when Colton and I started dating. I knew you would think less of me, and I just . . . I just wanted to enjoy having a boyfriend, as stupid as it sounds."

"You thought I would ruin it," I say. I'm not upset with her about this. I probably *would* have ruined it.

"Yes," she says.

"It was hard for me when you started dating Colton," I admit. "I felt like you were rejecting me. I didn't see how we could both fit into your life."

The cafeteria is emptying out. Students trickle through the doors on their way to class. I see Matt, Chloe, and Seb get up to throw their trash away.

"Things are different now," Lily says. "When you went out with Seb, I realized how you must have felt. I was so left out. I hated not knowing what was going on in your life."

Her eyes are filled with hurt, and again I realize that I haven't been the only one in pain over the past few months. Harris was right. I don't pay enough attention.

"If I started dating someone now, I would want you to know," Lily says. "I would want both of you in my life."

"And back then?" I ask.

"Back then . . . I don't know. I love you, Analee, but sometimes our friendship was suffocating. You were so angry all the time. It made me feel guilty for wanting to be happy."

"I'm sorry that I made you feel like that," I say, and I truly mean it. I'm sure I didn't make Lily's life easy, hating everyone who wasn't us.

"But that's just it. You weren't doing it on purpose. You were going through a lot, and I was too. I didn't want to burden you with my problems."

"You wouldn't have," I say. "You could have told me about them."

"I guess I wasn't dealing with it as well as I should have. And lately you seem so much happier. It reminded me of who I knew you were all along."

"I'm not always going to be happy, though," I say.

"I know."

"And as my friend, I'm going to need you to stick around when I get sad."

"I know that, too. And I will. I swear."

She looks like she's telling the truth. Or like she thinks she's telling the truth. But there are no guarantees. I can take the risk and count on her to be there for me, or I can reject her out of spite and make myself more miserable in the process.

"I missed you," I say to Lily. Even if she leaves again, this will hold true. And if she leaves again, I know that I'll be able to handle it. Again.

"I missed you too."

"Is it stupid if we hug?"

"Yes," she says. "You hate hugging."

"That was the old Analee. Plus, this is a hug-worthy moment."

"You sure you want to hug this idiot?" she asks, laughing, but I throw my arms around her before she can finish the question. Yes, I'm becoming grossly sentimental, but moments like these are rare. To lose people and get them back? I don't take it for granted.

"Can I come over tonight?" Lily asks into my shoulder.

"*Yes*. Stay for dinner."

She pulls away. "Wait. Harlow isn't still doing the raw-food thing, is she?"

"Occasionally," I reply. "But tonight is fried chicken night."

"You're kidding me."

"My idea. Once a month, but only if we eat super-healthy the rest of the time. Still, it's a big step for Harlow."

The late bell rings, signaling that we have two more minutes to get to class.

"Well," Lily says as we get up to throw away our garbage, "if it's fried chicken night, then obviously I'm there."

The two of us walk arm in arm down the hallway on our way to class, trying to catch each other up on the last seven months of our lives. It's surreal and yet completely normal. Lily and me. Talking. Friends again. Like nothing has changed but everything has, all at once.

We attract some stares from the other students. The hallways hum with speculation. I can just imagine the questions. What happened between me and Seb? Between Lily and Colton? How did Lily and I patch things up? I'm sure Elliott and Jared will grill me about what took place after they left.

I feel up to it. More than that, I'm excited. I'm excited to introduce them to Lily. I'm excited to go home tonight and eat fried chicken with my bonkers family. I'm excited for the future, to see if anything will happen between me and Seb, or me and Harris, or me and someone entirely new.

I'm not afraid of being alone. Not anymore. But it's nice to know that there are always people waiting in the wings—some of them new, some of them ready to be rediscovered. Just in case.

## Analee's Rules for Happiness

1. There are no rules for happiness. You'll be happy, then you'll be sad, then you'll be happy again. Enjoy the happiness when you have it. When you don't have it, remember: it'll come again. You just have to be open to it.

2. Chocolate also helps.

# ACKNOWLEDGMENTS

The idea of me publishing a book used to be pure fantasy. I'm still processing the fact that I've been lucky enough to do it twice in real life, and I owe much of it to an amazing group of people.

To my fierce agent, Jane Dystel, thanks for being a constant advocate of me and my writing. Jane, I am grateful for your tenacity and assuredness. Miriam Goderich, thank you for your openness and continued guidance as I navigate the world of publishing. I so appreciate both of you looking out for me.

Jen Ung, the greatest editor in existence, you deserve an entire book of thank-yous. I'm forever grateful for your encouragement and kindness. I'm not sure how you do it, but somehow even your edit letters always leave me smiling. Your feedback has made me a far, far better writer.

Massive thanks to the team at Simon & Schuster for the incredible work they do: Mara Anastas, Chriscynethia Floyd, Liesa Abrams, Caitlin Sweeny, Nicole Russo, Christina Pecorale, Rebecca Vitkus, Sara Berko, Michelle Leo, and Samantha Benson.

All the thanks in the world to my family—to Mom and Dad, for supporting me in every possible way, from book launch planning to educational marketing; to Alyssa, for being a fierce copy editor and "publicitor" and for teaching me the importance of using gifs; to Nick, for helping me figure out what I want to say and the best way to say it; and to Alex, for coming up with the perfect name for this book's main character.

Mima, me has enseñado tener pasión por todo lo que hago. Gracias por siempre creer en mi y por ayudarme a creer en mi misma. ¡Te quiero mucho mucho!

To the Mulhalls and Sanzos, a big thank-you for spreading the word about my books and being there for me. Massive thanks to my friends who help me survive the periods of stress and anxiety. I appreciate all of you so, so much. Thanks for always showing up to support me.

Thank you to all the book bloggers and librarians out there who champion diverse authors. I am so grateful to those of you who gave Victoria a chance and hope you love Analee just as much.

Finally, thank you to my husband, Dan. D-Train, you are the best partner, friend, and husband imaginable, and now you can add "father" to that list. Thank you for washing baby bottles while I finish copy edits, for scheduling writing days whenever we can squeeze them in, and for the countless other things you do.

# ABOUT THE AUTHOR

Janelle Milanes is the author of *The Victoria in My Head* and *Analee, in Real Life*. She's originally from Miami, Florida, and studied English literature at Davidson College. A lifelong YA addict, she moved to New York for her first job in children's publishing before leaving to pursue teaching and writing.

Janelle currently lives in Brooklyn with her husband, her daughter, and their two cats. Her favorite Disney princess is Belle, since she was also a big book nerd. You can find Janelle online at janellemilanes.com and on Instagram and Twitter @janellemilanes.

**Another funny, heartfelt romantic comedy from Janelle Milanes**

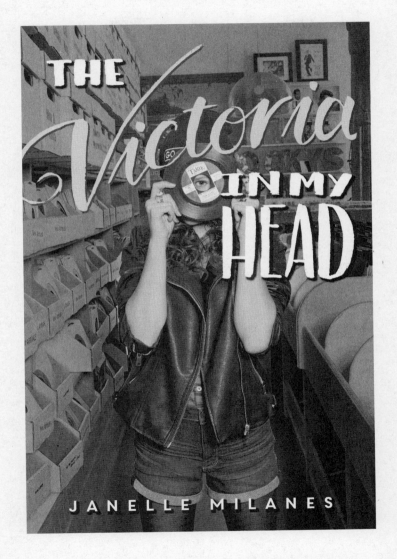

Turn the page for a sneak peek!

---
*Chapter One*
---

# "YOUR BEST
# AMERICAN GIRL"
## —MITSKI

I can predict my life with scary accuracy. I know my morning will
start with a piece of toast for breakfast, slathered in peanut butter
and topped with sliced banana. After breakfast I'll get on the downtown A train and put on a perfectly timed playlist for my twenty-
three minute commute to school. I'll meet my best friend, Annie
Lin, at my locker, and we'll go to first period with Mr. Davis and
stare at his mustard-yellow pit stains for forty-five minutes. I'll have
cross-country practice after school, where Coach B will make us run
six miles along the murky Hudson River. At home, Mom will make
spaghetti for dinner, and my bratty little brother, Matty, will complain that the tomato sauce is too chunky.

I'm not psychic. My life is just *that* boring. Every day moves like a treadmill, a straight line without fluctuation.

I shouldn't complain. I know it could be much worse. But when I really think about it, I realize that every day of my life is exactly the same, and it'll continue to be the same as it was yesterday, and the day before that, until the end of high school.

Until, suddenly, it isn't.

Across a sea of plaid uniforms on the opposite side of the sophomore hall, I see him, and the treadmill that is my life comes to a grinding halt.

"Hello?" Annie snaps her fingers at me. Her black hair is swept off her forehead by a satin headband that perfectly matches her pleated skirt. "What's with the face?"

"What face?" I reply. I have no awareness of what my face is doing. You know how in movies, when a girl sees a halfway-decent-looking guy and all of time stops and this wah wah indie song plays and it's so dumb because she doesn't even know the guy and that never happens in real life?

"You're blushing," Annie says with a frown, following my gaze.

It happens to me when I see this boy. Cue the soft, strumming guitar, the thumping drums, an airy falsetto in the background.

He's stapling a flyer onto the bulletin board, and when he lifts his arms to push into the stapler, I catch a glimpse of what I imagine to be soft cotton boxer-briefs peeking out from his pants. With his slouchy posture and tangled hair, he looks nothing like the preppy breed usually found at this school. He's . . . messier. Different. And yes, indisputably gorgeous, but that's not the point.

Annie thrusts her watch into my field of vision, effectively blocking my view of the pretty boy. "Helloooo. We're going to be late."

This is Annie's mantra. She's punctual to a fault, while I'm in no rush to snag a front row seat for Mr. Davis's underarm sweat.

"I'll meet you there," I say, blinking myself awake. "I forgot something in my locker."

"What did you forget?"

"My, um . . . snargenblag," I mumble.

"Your what?"

The warning bell shrieks overhead, which sends Annie into a panic. "Come on, Vi!"

"Go ahead. I'll meet you there," I assure her, and she gives me a final disapproving scowl before hurrying to math.

All at once the hallway drains as students swarm to their first period classes, but the boy doesn't rush. As he steps back to admire his handiwork, I inch toward him. I'm not entirely sure what my master plan is, but I have to know what's on this flyer. I have to know more about him.

He turns his head and looks right at me as soon as I reach him, like I tripped a sensor.

Holy sweet Jesus, his eyes. Those were unexpected. His eyes are the stuff of those Harlequin romances Mom reads, the kind of eyes that are always compared to something cheesy, like a midwinter sky. Annie and I used to sneak the books into my room and pore over passages about tight breeches and ripping bodices.

The thing about this boy's eyes, though? They *are* the color of a midwinter sky, which I didn't think was possible in reality.

"Do you sing?" His voice echoes through the empty hallway.

I stare at him, my brain officially a useless lump. "Huh?"

*Ugh. Get a freaking grip, Victoria.* I'm not one to turn into a puddle of idiocy when I see a cute guy. I'm better than that. Usually.

He nods toward the flyer he's posted. It's simple—black Sharpie against stark white computer paper. In large block print it says:

LEAD VOCALIST WANTED.
MUST HAVE A DECENT VOICE AND
GENERALLY NOT SUCK AS A HUMAN
BEING. BAND WILL PERFORM AT THE
BATTLE OF THE BOROUGHS IN THE
SPRING. MUSIC TASTE SHOULD
BE ECLECTIC.
PLEASE E—MAIL LEVI.SCHUSTER@EA.ORG
FOR AUDITION INFORMATION.

"Oh," I manage, brilliantly. I can't process the fact that a school like Evanston has other people like him, people who do things besides study and play lacrosse and run for student council. "Um . . . no."

"Maybe you should try." He twirls his stapler around and snaps it shut with one hand like some pistol-packing cowboy. It's weirdly hot.

The final bell rings. He and I are officially late for class, but neither one of us moves.

I should fess up at this point. I should let him know that I am way too boring to be a lead singer. I should let him know that I can barely speak, let alone sing, in front of people. I should also let him know that there is no way, under any circumstances, my overprotective Cuban parents would let me join a band.

"Okay," I blurt out instead of these important things he should know. Then, without another word, I bolt.

Mom studies me as we sit around the dinner table that night. "You okay? You look pale."

"I'm fine." I twirl some overcooked spaghetti noodles around my fork and silently refuse to go into any more detail. It's helpful to remember my Miranda rights when it comes to dinner with my family. Anything I say can and will be used against me.

"Are you sick?" Matty asks me, his eyes lighting up with interest. "Are you gonna puke?"

"Eat your food," Dad tells him.

Matty pokes at his pile of noodles. "I think I'm sick too."

We all ignore him. Matty will do anything to get out of eating dinner, unless it's one of the three meals that he tolerates: mac and cheese, pizza, or peanut butter sandwiches (no crust, hold the jelly). Sameness doesn't seem to affect him yet. Actually, he thrives on it.

"Maybe I'll make you a doctor's appointment," Mom says to me.

"I'm fine, Mom. Really."

"You don't look fine."

"I just have a lot on my mind."

"Are you depressed?" Mom asks, her voice rising. She eyes me with intensity. Ever since I bought a vintage Nirvana T-shirt last week, Mom has been on teen suicide watch. It's ridiculous.

"Of course she's not depressed," Dad says, speaking right through me. "What does she have to be depressed about?"

"Can I have a sandwich?" Matty asks. He pushes his plate away in disgust.

"You can eat spaghetti like the rest of us," Mom informs him.

"But I don't like spaghetti."

Dad points his fork at me. "Did you eat any dairy today?"

"Dairy?" I echo. I'm not fully here at the dinner table. I've been replaying the scene with the blue-eyed boy all day, wishing I had said something smarter, or funnier, or *anything at all*. I should have at least asked him his name.

"Yes. Dairy," Dad says. "Maybe at breakfast?"

Since he found out he was lactose intolerant, Dad believes dairy to be the root of all evil. In his opinion, it's the underlying cause of every malady known to man. He can't even look at a cow without a vein popping out of his neck.

"I had toast for breakfast," I reply absentmindedly.

He scratches the stubble on his chin. "What about lunch? You're always eating pizza for lunch."

"I'm making an appointment with Dr. Ferber," Mom decides.

"Fine," I concede, hoping it will shut them both up.

Of course it doesn't. Nothing does.

"I know you all insist on eating dairy," Dad continues, "but it's been linked to heart disease, diabetes—"

"Mrs. Soldera told us that milk is good for your bones," Matty pipes up.

"Mrs. Soldera is an idiot."

"Jorge . . . ," Mom cautions, pouring herself a glass of wine.

"Whatever." Matty's ten-year-old body heaves a weary sigh. "Can I have dessert now?"

We go through this every night. Practically word for word.

Mom closes her eyes and massages her forehead. "Matty, you didn't even *touch* your dinner. Jorge?"

"Eat your dinner, Matty," Dad says automatically. He's already wolfed down his entire plate of spaghetti, sopping up every drop of sauce with a bread roll.

"At least ten more bites," Mom adds.

"But the sauce is too chunky!" Matty slams his fist against the table, and my parents go bug-eyed.

"*Ten cuidado,*" Dad warns. "Listen to your mother or you'll go to bed hungry."

They continue to argue back and forth, Matty trying to haggle his way out of dinner and Mom and Dad crushing each attempt. In about ten minutes one of them will cave and fix him a sandwich. This is the Cruz family dinner experience, every night at seven.

I stare down at my fork and contemplate sticking it through my eye.

# Chapter Two

# "AMERIGO"
## —PATTI SMITH

I arrive at school five minutes later than usual, and the sophomore hallway buzzes with activity—lockers slamming shut, shoes squeaking against the tile floor. Life is back to moving at normal speed. Annie, I know, is already waiting for me at my locker, checking her watch and muttering to herself about my tardiness.

At the end of the hall a cluster of admirers surround the two best-looking girls in the grade, Sophia Lowell and Olivia Bennett. Together, they're a shampoo commercial, with silky curtains of hair spilling down their backs. Hair that grows vertically, not horizontally like mine. Both bask in the attention, wearing their usual shiny smiles.

They have plenty to smile about. They're tall, they have boobs, and they're perfectly groomed from head to toe. Because they're rich, they can afford to have our boxy Evanston uniforms tailored. Their collared shirts are taken in at the waist to accentuate their hourglass figures, and their hemlines graze the tops of their thighs for maximum leggy effect.

Mom scoffed when I asked if I could have my uniform tailored, and Dad flat-out refused, saying my school was costing him enough as it is. I'm forced to roll up my skirt so I don't look like a Puritan.

When I first interviewed at Evanston, I expected to become a member of the elite. I thought going to a school like this would finally help me become someone. Someone who had a life, a purpose. I could go to Harvard like my parents always dreamed, because Evanston placed that goal within reach.

I got my acceptance letter to Evanston on Friday the thirteenth. I should have taken it as a sign.

My parents hovered over my shoulders as I opened the letter, and before I could finish reading out "Congratulations," they enveloped me in a suffocating hug. In their arms I remember thinking that I should feel excited, or nervous. Scared, even. Something other than empty. I stretched my lips into a straight line, the best I could do at a smile, before pulling away from their grip.

As one of the top twenty-five high schools in the country, Evanston oozes exclusivity. It's a gated oasis amidst the mass of dour buildings comprising Manhattan's Upper West Side. The campus's ivy-laden buildings are arranged in a square with a manicured lawn in its center—Evanston's own mini Central Park. Inside Evanston, everything seems serious and scholarly. Students walk around in crisp buttoned uniforms, and teachers have essays published in renowned academic journals.

From the beginning it was clear that I wasn't one of them. My family doesn't own a summer home in the Hamptons, and we don't take luxurious trips to Turks and Caicos over winter break. We're not destitute, but we're strictly middle class. My parents came to the US from Cuba when they were young, and they act like they're playing a game of catch-up with the rest of the country. They don't just work to make money; they work like they have something to prove. Mom teaches Spanish at St. Mary's, the middle school where Annie and I went. Dad dropped out of high school to work at a company involved in refrigerators. I'm not sure what exactly he does with refrigerators, because I've never cared enough to find out. I think he either manufactures, repairs, or sells them. Maybe all of the above.

The only reason I'm here is because of my scholarship. Evanston pays half of my tuition (already enough to drown my parents in debt), as long as I keep my GPA above a 3.0. Being a scholarship kid adds one more layer of stress to the load I already carry. Most Evanston students can coast through their classes, knowing Mommy and Daddy will buy their admission to a top college, but I'll lose my scholarship, and my entire future, with the slightest dip of my GPA.

Sometimes I wonder whether getting kicked out of Evanston would really be so bad. What would happen if I just stopped?

Life would be easier. I could breathe again. But then I picture the disappointment on my parents' faces as I shatter their American Dream, as all their sacrifices are flushed down the drain, so I continue playing the dutiful daughter.

Students in tucked collared shirts swirl around me, and my mind flits back to the blue-eyed boy yesterday. To the midwinter sky and the small patch of skin exposed by his loose shirttail. There's no sign of him in the hall today. I doubt he's a sophomore, because I've never had a class with him. Is he the Levi Schuster from the flyer? Or is he a bandmate of Levi's? Maybe he's not even in the band. Maybe he just really enjoys stapling flyers.

If he appeared here and now, I could have a do-over. Force myself to speak like a normal human being. I envision him approaching me, and my brain flips through a slide show of our day off, Ferris Bueller–style.

*You wanna get out of here?* he might say, and I'd toss my stick-straight hair around (if I'm fantasizing, I might as well give myself manageable hair). I'd take his hand, and we'd skip school to spend the day holding hands and walking the Bow Bridge in Central Park.

He would save me from another day of my treadmill life.

My eye catches on the giant bulletin board where we met yesterday. It's plastered with flyers advertising everything from school clubs to student gov elections to puppies for adoption. Today I'm pulled to his flyer, tacked onto the board's top right corner.

*Maybe you should try,* he said, in a tone like it was no big deal.

I can't decipher any of my actions that follow. Momentary

demonic possession maybe, or a blip in my brain chemistry. The idea of me joining a band is laughable. There are glaring reasons why I shouldn't, like keeping my scholarship, the fact that I've never sung in front of anyone but Annie, and the teeny issue of my all-consuming stage fright, the kind that paralyzes me when I'm called on in class.

Yet inexplicably, despite all these reasons, I tear the flyer off the board and stick it in my blazer pocket.

## BELIEVE IN YOUR SHELF

Visit RivetedLit.com &
connect with us on social to:

**DISCOVER** NEW YA READS

**READ** BOOKS FOR FREE

**DISCUSS** YOUR FAVORITES

**SHARE** YOUR IDEAS

**ENTER SWEEPSTAKES** FOR THE CHANCE TO WIN BOOKS

Follow @SimonTeen on

to stay up to date with all things Riveted!

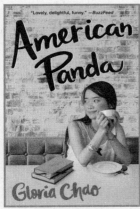

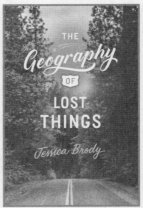

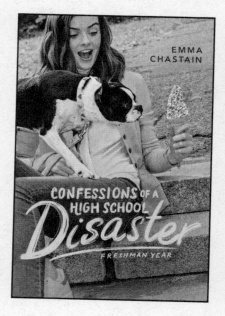